The Unlikely Heroes

St. Brendan Series, Book Three

By Carla Kelly

CAMEL PRESS

Kenmore, WA

CAMEL PRESS

A Camel Press book published by Epicenter Press

Epicenter Press
6524 NE 181st St. Suite 2
Kenmore, WA 98028.
www.Epicenterpress.com
www.Coffeetownpress.com
www.Camelpress.com

For more information go to: www.camelpress.com
www.carlakellyauthor.com

The Unlikely Heroes
Copyright © 2020 by Carla Kelly

ISBN: 9781603817080 (trade paper)
ISBN: 9781603817127 (ebook)

Printed in the United States of America

Dedicated to the memory of Commander Harry Ferrier, U.S. Navy, 1925-2016, who, at age seventeen, earned a Distinguished Flying Cross at the battle of Midway.

Mr. Ferrier was a lifelong family friend of my parents, also World War II veterans.

And Euclid, of course, that sly mathematician.

Books by Carla Kelly

FICTION

Daughter of Fortune
Summer Campaign
Miss Chartley's Guided Tour
Marian's Christmas Wish
Mrs. McVinnie's London Season
Libby's London Merchant
Miss Grimsley's Oxford Career
Miss Billings Treads the Boards
Miss Milton Speaks Her Mind
Miss Wittier Makes a List
Mrs. Drew Plays Her Hand
Reforming Lord Ragsdale
The Lady's Companion
With This Ring
One Good Turn
The Wedding Journey
Here's to the Ladies: Stories of the Frontier Army
Beau Crusoe
Marrying the Captain
The Surgeon's Lady
Marrying the Royal Marine
The Admiral's Penniless Bride
Borrowed Light
Enduring Light
Coming Home for Christmas: The Holiday Stories
Regency Christmas Gifts
Season's Regency Greetings
Marriage of Mercy
My Loving Vigil Keeping
Double Cross
Marco and the Devil's Bargain
Paloma and the Horse Traders
Star in the Meadow
Unlikely Master Genius
Unlikely Spy Catchers
Safe Passage
Softly Falling
One Step Enough
Courting Carrie in Wonderland
A Regency Royal Navy Christmas

But Love is a durable fire
In the mind ever burning
Never sick, never old, never dead
From itself, never turning.

Sir Walter Raleigh, "Walsinghame"

Chapter One

November, 1804

Captain Angus Ogilvie - widower, notorious and generally feared thug, and Trinity House Elder Brother - spoke horribly accented French and worse Spanish. Despite that, here he was in the port of Cádiz, where his relentless tracking of Claude Pascal had finally landed the two of them.

What a wretched man was Claude Pascal. The spy had insinuated himself aboard one of the prison hulks in Portsmouth's harbor, ruining far too many lives in his attempt to foul the Royal Navy's valuable factories producing war materiel. Captain Rose, warden of Trinity House, had allowed Pascal to escape, then assigned Ogilvie to track the man and see what he planned next.

The Baltic States seemed to be full of intriguers. Ogilvie blended in perfectly well and knew enough German to get by. Thank God the Danes and Swedes spoke enough English to make life endurable.

Following an agile fellow like Claude Pascal had shaken a good stone and more off Ogilvie's stoutish frame. In the Baltics, Ogilvie managed to quietly murder a handful of French agents – amazing what silent damage a wire could do, especially if the man wielding it had no particular problem with death.

The damage continued into the German states, where two more spies met their maker after Claude Pascal, still blithely unaware, left messages – some encrypted, some not – that went into Ogilvie's pocket, once their brief ownership in German hands was contested by a Scot of no mean ability. Pursued and pursuer continued down the coast of western Europe.

Ogilvie had no problem understanding the idioms of France and Spain. The difficulty lay in convincing his less-agile tongue to speak the words and not have them sound like they were native to Fort William, Scotland, where he was born and reared until he went to sea.

He managed well enough. A discreet card in French or Spanish, stating that the bearer was unable to speak due to an unfortunate injury had convinced enough innkeepers, especially when he displayed the coins in his purse. If anyone appeared skeptical, all he had to do was loosen his neckcloth and exhibit an impressive scar. That it was the result of a youthful fall from a tree and looked gruesome even now, was no one's business but his. Long practice at skulking had trained him to never stay more than one night in one place. He got by.

Past Belgium, Ogilvie headed for the coast of France, ordered there by Captain Rose to pop into northern France at Dunkerque, Calais, Ambleteuse and Boulogne to see with his own eyes if there was truth to rumors of smaller vessels under construction, the sort used to ferry soldiers across a short stretch of water like the Dover Strait. Angus Ogilvie followed orders because Claude Pascal seemed to be headed that way, too.

What he saw at Ambleteuse suggested to Angus that the French had miles to go before attacking England from the water. True, ships with masts but no rigging do look predictably disconsolate in a rainstorm.

An evening's amble down to the dock provided more information. He never had trouble blending in with the local *citoyennes,* as long as he wore a cockade in his hat and didn't shave or bathe often. "You, sir, are a nondescript sort of fellow," the Prime Minister himself had told him once, intending it as a compliment. "The perfect spy."

Perfect spy was no title to be proud of. There was no acclaim involved, only silence and dirty deeds. Besides, Angus suspected he was growing soft, or perhaps merely tired. Why else would he find himself, during lonely evenings, thinking so often of Portsmouth and people there who mattered to him?

Invariably his thoughts circled around to Captain Sir Belvedere St. Anthony, elegant fellow done in at the Battle of the Nile by the loss of a leg. How Sir B still managed to attract and win the heart and hand of Grace Croker, gentlewoman and spinster, baffled someone as realistic as Angus Ogilvie, especially since he had his eye on Grace, too.

In one dingy inn or another as he tracked Claude Pascal, Angus had too much time to reflect upon the workings of fate, never in his favor or so it seemed. Usually his rigorous Presbyterian upbringing still managed to poke through and remind Angus that he should feel more pity for Sir B, who was not healthy and who knew he was dwindling. How much pain can a man take, after all?

Sailing Master Able Six, unspeakably brilliant teacher at St. Brendan the Navigator School, had confided to Angus before this journey began that Lady Grace St. Anthony was with child. "I wonder if Sir B will live long enough to see his son or daughter," Able had commented on Angus Ogilvie's last night in Portsmouth before he began his European skulk. "I hope he does." Angus was not so certain he felt the same way.

That small-minded consideration generally ended the rattles in his head, at least for the evening, because Angus Ogilvie did have a conscience – not a huge one, but a conscience nonetheless. He reminded himself then of the business at hand, following Clause Pascal.

At Ambleteuse, Angus saw twenty *bateux cannoniers*, low-sided and fitted out with sweeps for rowing across the English Channel. What folly. He stopped long enough to estimate that each *bateux* might seat some one hundred soldiers, all of them likely to puke when they hit that channel chop. *I fear you will not prosper*, he thought, as he strolled past. Ogilvie knew better than to look back and keep counting, the mark of an amateur spy, which he was not.

He changed his mind at Boulogne, another coastal village which he had always known as an indifferent harbor. France could boast of few good harbors, and Boulogne was no exception, except that Ogilvie knew dredging scoops and shovels when he saw them.

The rumors were true. Napoleon was dredging a deeper harbor at Boulogne, and look, it was being widened, as well. He probably stared longer than he should have. Maybe it was the sight of all those workers that startled him. They swarmed like ants against the slopes, hauling dirt. At the harbor's mouth, he saw capable masons slapping mortar on trowels to build a fortress guarding the entrance.

He faced seaward, noting the lengthy sandbank which kept frigates of the Royal Navy at bay. Yes, Boulogne was becoming a good port from which to launch an invasion fleet. He could imagine it filled with small craft by 1805.

The idea irritated him, so Captain Angus Ogilvie set fire to two drydocks before he left the city, giving himself great satisfaction. So did a wire necklace for Claude Pascal's Boulogne connection, who thought he might withhold information about Pascal's next port of call and still live. "Cádiz, is it? *Merci, citoyen*," he told the corpse. "I like Cádiz."

And here was Cádiz, a place the captain had enjoyed in years past, when active duty took his ships into the excellent harbor, not then under Napoleon Bonaparte's greedy thumb. Cádiz, home of superior sea food and sultry women.

Either times had changed or he had changed. He settled for a humble bowl of fish soup in a *taberna* overlooking the harbor, and ignored a woman making eyes at him. She looked unclean, and Captain Ogilvie did have standards. What was this? A harbor full of Spanish ships, to be sure, but French ones, too, ships large and small, all bottled there by the Royal Navy blockade. Ogilvie had expected this, of course, but the proximity to so much fighting sail, all bent on England's destruction, fair took away his breath.

Looking up now and then from his newspaper, he counted them, from the biggest – the *Santísima Trinidad*, largest ship in both fleets – to the smallest pinnace. As he admired the lovely lines of the *Trinidad*, he mourned the men who would die aboard her when the Combined Fleet came out and Admiral Horatio Nelson waited, ready to pounce.

He didn't mourn long. He leaned back in his chair and thought about Able Six, that curly-haired, complicated fellow with the lovely wife, who had said they were in for another ten years of war, at least. He marveled at the ambition of Napoleon Bonaparte, a petty enough fellow to begin with, but enhanced by the revolution and allowed to strut upon a larger stage.

Ogilvie grudgingly admitted to himself that the Corsican upstart had some talent. Enough was enough, however. "You won't take your war onto English soil," he said under his breath. "Not while I can skulk and murder."

Speaking of which, he looked across the taberna to a table in the even more dimly lit corner, where sat Claude Pascal with another of his informants. The two men leaned close together, then the informant leaned back in surprise and looked around, almost as if he wanted to be anywhere than with Claude Pascal. Ogilvie could appreciate that.

As he looked closer, Ogilvie squinted to make sure he was right. *Well blow me down*, he thought, startled to see a familiar English face. He turned toward the wall, nearly certain he hadn't been noticed, as all manner of ideas ran through his tired brain. One idea connected with another until he forgot his fear and his surroundings. He knew that man.

Sir Clive Mortimer played a small role in the workings of the Admiralty. What was it? Something about first secretary over victualling and procurement, where his task was to review the ledgers and logs sent over from the Navy Board and give them his official stamp of approval.

By the time the papers reached Sir Clive's desk, the kegs of beef and pork, eggs nestled in salt, cheese, and hardtack were long on their way, voyaging the world. Never mind all that; bureaucracy, that mistress of the unimaginative, still required an official stamp before the papers were filed God knows where. Sir Clive's servant, a foxy-faced fellow name of Hébert, always seemed to be hanging about. And here Hébert, decidedly uncomfortable, sat with Claude Pascal. Sir Clive had casually mentioned once to Angus that Patrice Hébert came from an old Huguenot family long in England. Maybe not so long, eh?

Ogilvie watched them, thinking of Sir Clive's easy access to all the offices in the Admiralty. If memory served him, Clive's office was on the same floor as the Lords of the Admiralty. Imagine what an inquisitive fellow could learn, just hanging about.

Why would you do this, Sir Clive? Ogilvie asked himself, as he felt cold reason settle over him. *Too many debts? One too many expensive horses? A greedy mistress? It's time your career ended at Admiralty House. How low of you to make a servant do your work, because he must be retired, too.*

He nursed his flagon of rum and watched as a scrap of paper changed hands and ended in a pouch around Hébert's neck. Ogilvie made note of that repository, knowing the pouch had to go before the steel cord could do its best work.

He left the taberna ahead of the two spies, content to wait in the shadows outside where the air was better. He didn't have to wait long. The conspirators left the taberna, chatted quietly, heads together, then walked away in opposite directions. Ogilvie followed Hébert, keeping well back, until he started up one of the many labyrinthian streets that twisted and wound up from the harbor.

When Hébert paused in front of a door and took out a key, Ogilvie sidled up behind him. "Paddy Hébert, fancy seeing you in Cádiz. Did Sir Clive send you on holiday?"

Hébert whirled around, his eyes wide. He clutched the pouch around his neck and managed a weak smile. "Captain Ogilvie, is it?" An even weaker laugh followed the smile. "Why, yes, I have many friends in Cádiz."

"And my mother is a donkey," Ogilvie said.

Giving Hébert no time to react, Angus slit the pouch from the spy's neck, shoving it down his own shirt front. He banged Hébert's head against the door and clamped his hand over the terrified man's mouth.

"Here you are, trading secrets to a nasty man from a nasty man," he hissed. "Shame on you, and more shame on Sir Clive. Have you anything to say to me that would prevent me from ending your life this minute? I'll wait." He lifted his hand from Hébert's mouth, but not far.

"He said if I didn't help, he would kill my whole family," Hébert managed to gasp.

"My stars and garters, that's the wrong answer!" Ogilvie said cheerfully. "I know you're an orphan."

By then Ogilvie had his hand around the wire silencer he carried in his waistcoat. Moving faster now, he yanked on the servant's hair until he reached the precise angle to slip the wire around his neck and tighten it. Two jerks, then a third for good measure and Patrice Hébert collapsed at his feet.

Oops. Too much zeal this time. The wire had cut nearly through the unfortunate man's neck. Blood pounded out, then pulsated more slowly as the life drained away. Ogilvie wiped his useful wire on the dead man's jacket then slipped it back into his waistcoat, ready for a new adventure.

What adventure? He thought he could convince Captain Rose and the Admiralty, through Prime Minister William Pitt, to let Sir Clive continue his free roaming, but to watch him closely and see who else might be a traitor in high places. It shouldn't be too hard to insert an honest man – for the sake of argument, call him a spy – onto Clive's staff, once Hébert was presumed dead. This spy could report Sir Clive's business and do England no harm.

Ogilvie made his way casually, slowly, back to the harbor, the trail of blood following him. Someone would raise an alarm eventually, but that was the beauty of Spain. People were reserved and disinclined to intrude, even during such questionable times as these, or maybe because of such times.

Still, one couldn't overlook a stream of blood, even as night settled on Cádiz. Angus Ogilvie squeezed through an alley barely wide enough for skinny cats and came out into a different street.

Tired, so tired of following Pascal, Ogilvie walked to the dock and stared at the *Santísima Trinidad* riding on her anchors in the harbor. He admired the fine lines, convinced that while the French made the best fighting ships – the Royal Navy had copied them shamelessly for years – the Spanish created the most beautiful ones.

As he stood in the shadows – Christ, how much of his life had been spent in shadow lately – he noticed two men walking together, one of them in uniform and the other well-dressed and with a flair that some tried to duplicate, but only the Spanish managed to carry off.

Ogilvie was too tired to listen to their conversation, so that wasn't what made him pay closer attention. It was the Spaniard in the handsome frilled uniform that made Captain Ogilvie's mouth open in surprise, that same jaded and world-weary Captain Ogilvie who was never surprised by anything.

He could have sworn Sailing Master Able Six, that dratted genius, stood there.

Chapter Two

Six Months Later, 1805, Portsmouth

That night in Sir B's sickroom, Master Able Six thought the end would come during the Middle Watch, when wounded and dying men laid down their defenses and surrendered to death. On several occasions when he was forced to act in lieu of a ship's surgeon, he had sat beside men as they let out that last pre-dawn breath.

Even Davey Ten, now serving his apprenticeship as assistant pharmacist mate, had commented on the propensity of men to die in the wee hours. "Why, sir?" he had asked Able only last week over Sunday roast beef at the Sixes' home when he was granted leave from Portsmouth's Haslar Hospital.

"I don't know," Able had told him, a statement that hardly ever crossed his lips because he usually did know. Apparently even Euclid and Able's other unseen cranial friends were not privy to some secrets. People died when God dictated. Even a man of science understood that.

Able knew the end was close when he said goodnight to Sir B, and left the St. Anthonys' bedchamber arm in arm with his wife. He had watched his wife Meridee droop and wilt through the evening, partly from sorrow, and partly from her slow recovery after last month's miscarriage. She had offered no objection when Lady St. Anthony – better known still as Grace Croker – had quietly summoned the family carriage for the ride back to their house across from St. Brendan's School.

In the carriage, Meridee had gone right into his arms, or perhaps he had gone into hers, because the loss of someone so dear couldn't be borne alone. Thank God, yet again, that he was married. At the moment, Able couldn't fathom enduring such a death by himself. The loss of their much-wanted baby had been difficult enough, but Sir B had winkled out

Able's great mystery, and set him on a true course that had taken him to Portsmouth, St. Brendan's, and this life.

"This is hard," he whispered to Meri, realizing how inadequate that puny phrase sounded.

She held him closer. "I wanted our baby, oh my word, I did, but as much as that, I…I know we will have more children. There is only one Sir B."

It was a brave admission from the best woman he knew, and the best mother to both their little boy Ben, and to the Gunwharf Rats of St. Brendan the Navigator School she also mothered. The workhouse lads had earned their title of Gunwharf Rats, the result of finding the sorry carcass of a *rattus norvegicus* and prevailing upon squeamish Meri to help them boil the bones and then see them mounted on a plaque. Who knew how things like that took on a life of their own, and a meaning that went beyond a rat on a plaque? Because the rat belonged at St. Brendan's now, so did they, who had never belonged anywhere before. Simple.

There was never any question that Meri Six had enough mother in her heart to add the Rats to her special stewardship. She had told him once, as if he might think her a low-achieving failure, that all she wanted was to be a good wife and mother, and there was no way she could match or even fathom his brain. He had been happy to assure her that her practical, grounded nature, plus her bounteous love and fine looks, were precisely what a man with a too-busy brain craved. He thought she believed him, but he was never precisely certain. After one domestic disaster, she had wisely but firmly forbidden him from ever handling the simple arithmetic from butchers or tradesmen. Theirs was a fortunate marriage, because the easy stuff eluded him.

She was right; there was only one Sir B, Captain Sir Belvedere St. Anthony, who, along with Captain Benjamin Hallowell, had grasped the enormity of Durable Six's amazing brain and put it to good use. Sir B had commanded him in two oceans and on two seas, had seen to his mentorship as a sailing master, and landed him at St. Brendan School for Navigators to teach boys much like himself, bastard workhouse children with untapped promise.

Now Sir B lay dying, the result of seven years of pain from wounds earned the hard way at the Battle of the Nile in 1798. The loss of his leg had led to additional complications, over which physicians had no power. No physician knew enough.

When his wife Grace, a fellow St. Brendan instructor, had walked the Sixes to the door, her arms around both of them, she had told them her dear man had survived long enough for the birth of his son George Belvedere Routledge St. Anthony.

"Georgie kept him alive," Grace said, as they stood together, waiting for the St. Anthony carriage. "I could wish for more, but Able, he is so weary of pain."

"We know that," Able said. "Grace, should we…"

"No," she said softly. "Get Meridee home. She's drooping but she'll never admit it. Get her to bed. If something happens tonight, I believe you will know."

"I believe I will."

After getting Meri home and into her nightgown, she insisted on their nightly ritual of another look at Ben before she agreed to crawl into bed. They stood a moment, arm in arm, looking down at a sleeping boy, arms and legs stretched out so confidently: Benjamin Belvedere Six, seventeen months old, and ruler of all he surveyed.

"I hope he and George St. Anthony will be great friends," Meri whispered. She tucked his blanket a little higher.

"They will be," he agreed. "C'mon, Meri. You're about to drop."

"Am not," she insisted as her eyes closed. He picked her up and carried her to their bed, scene of much General Merrymaking, as his lover liked to call it. She was asleep before she even stretched out.

He watched her a moment, deeply satisfied and still a little amazed at so wonderful a creature in his bed, he who had come into this world with less than nothing, except for a prodigious brain often more curse than blessing. Now, in descending order of importance, he was a husband, father, respected instructor, Younger Brother at Trinity House, friend of Billy Pitt, England's First Minister, and almost-father to Nick Bonfort who slept down the corridor, a Gunwharf Rat at St. Brendan's. Last and often least, Able was a reluctant member of a group of genius dead men who gave him good advice upon occasion and ignored him if they felt like it.

Meri was always first, and their son a close second, Ben who would grow up knowing who his father was. Alas, poor Ben. Only last week, Able had sat Meri down in the dining room for the bad news. The conversation – remembered in its entirety, of course – made Able smile even now, when he was at his lowest.

"Meri, I have made a most unfortunate discovery."

"How bad can it be? You're holding our son and reading dear Euclid to him." She gave him her brightest smile. *"Ben looks so happy. You two are such a pair."*

"Brace yourself, Meri-deelicious. I have been reading with my finger under each word. Bless me if our little scamp didn't push my finger aside because I wasn't reading fast enough. Meri? Meri? Are we still friends?"

"Dear sir, I am digesting this news. He's reading? Tell me the worst: Is it the English translation or the original Greek?"

"I hate to admit it." He kissed his son's head. *"The Greek."*

"Lord help us."

He laughed softly at the memory. When he told Sir B last week, his mentor and friend Sir B had laughed, too. Grace told him later it was the final time he laughed.

Able took off his shoes and unbuttoned his trousers, but crawled into bed otherwise as-is, knowing the night had more sorrow ahead. Meri moved into his warmth and he pulled her close.

He woke three hours and ten minutes later in the Middle Watch. No one knocked on the door, but in his mind he heard the St. Anthony carriage coming down Saints Way.

He got up quietly, buttoned his trousers and pulled on his shoes. He was almost to the door when he noticed Meri beside him, knotting her robe, her slippers already on.

"You weren't trying to sneak out without me?" she asked in her sweet way. It was no accusation, but very near. As a dutiful husband, he knew he had lost.

He hurried down the stairs and knocked on Mrs. Perry's door to tell her that Ben was asleep and they didn't know when they would return. The carriage pulled up when Meri joined him at the front door, buttoning the last button and smoothing down her dress.

Lamps glowed in the St. Anthony rowhouse, sandwiched between other equally elegant homes belonging to successful captains and admirals who preferred to distance themselves from the bubbling broth of commerce and sin that was Portsmouth.

They hurried up the stairs and into the bedroom, lit with one lamp. Head bowed, Grace looked up. Her relief could have lit the old lighthouse of Alexandria. Able came to her first and rested his hands on her shoulders.

He looked down at his dear captain, pleased to see his month-old son nestled in the crook of his arm, asleep.

"He wanted George to be here," Grace whispered when Able bent down. Her voice went even softer. "I do believe George kept him alive."

"Aye, Grace," Able said. His mind went to Euclid, always hovering nearby. *You, sir, could you and your strange friends not allow this good man more years?* he asked the nosy Greek that Meridee had banished from their bedroom. Euclid chose not to reply, as he seemed to do more and more lately.

Sir B's eyes fluttered open. He tried to raise his free hand to Able, but the effort eluded him. Able knelt beside the bed and took his hand, holding it close to his chest.

"Captain…" What could he say? Able rested his head against his captain's arm instead.

"And you, Meridee?" Sir B asked. His voice was clear enough, but it had a dreamy quality. "You should be resting."

"I'll keep," Meri said. "Look here. I brought you a rout cake, one with the sugary sides that you always accused me of eating to excess, along with the lemony ones."

Sir B shook his head. "Can't swallow," he managed.

Meri knelt beside Able. "Doesn't matter. Let me touch it to your lips. I know you like the sugar."

She touched his lips gently with the little delicacy. Sir B licked it and smiled. "Capitol, my dear. Able, what did you ever do to deserve her?"

"I have no idea, sir," he said, nearly overcome.

Meri pressed close to him, then put her hand on Sir B's arm, too. "I'll take good care of him, Sir B," she said. "I promise. You told me I was his keeper."

"That's all I ask." He turned his head an inch or two toward them. "Able, you can do one thing for me."

"Anything, sir."

Able felt twelve years old again, when he had first come to Sir B's – Captain St. Anthony's – attention. It was in the southern Pacific near Otaiheite. The captain had caught him correcting the numbers on the blackboard on deck where Sailing Master Ferrier and midshipmen had been wrangling over an algebraic equation then left it, lesson over.

He had turned around to see the captain regarding him with

something close to awe. Certain he was about to be flogged for some infraction or other, Able had stood there with his head bowed. "I'm sorry, sir," he said.

"For what? For getting the equation right?" Captain St. Anthony had asked. "Master Ferrier told me about you." Right there on the deck by the main mast the captain erased the board and wrote a whole string of equations. He left out salient details, then ordered Able to fill them in. It had been the work of mere minutes for Ordinary Seaman Six. His life was never the same after that.

All the memories crashed down on him as he rested his now-wet cheek against his captain's hand. "Anything for you," he repeated.

"Good," Sir B said, sounding almost like himself. "I am nearly certain you will be recalled to the fleet this year."

Meri gasped. Sir B patted her cheek. "Meridee, we all knew it might happen," Sir B said. "That was the stipulation of your man's employment at St. Brendan's as our resident genius."

"I know, but…"

"My dear, we have reached that time of national emergency." With an effort, Sir B turned his attention to Able. "You must obey, of course, but do this: Speak to the Elder Brothers at Trinity House, specifically Warden Captain Rose."

"What do you have in mind, sir?"

"My *Jolly Roger* is a dandy yacht to use as a smallish sloop of war," he said. His voice began to fade. "Carry messages from the fleet to… Admiralty…House. Train the Rats in speed … evasion."

He was right. Able saw it instantly. He could fit his Gunwharf Rats for fleet actions and relay messages, because the *Jolly Roger* was fast. "Aye, aye, sir," Able said, twelve years old again for a millisecond. He kissed his mentor's hand. "Thank you for everything."

"You're welcome. Thank *you*." Sir B turned his attention to Meri one last time. Able knew it was one last time. "Keep doing what you do…Mrs. Heart of Oak…your Ben… Able…Gunwharf Rats."

She kissed his hand, tugged Able to his feet and stood back, her face calm and lovely in its serenity. "We'll leave you alone with Grace, Sir B."

Meri took him into the hall, then held him close in a fierce embrace. Only minutes passed. Grace opened the door and motioned to them. They joined her at her husband's bedside.

Sir B had drifted to sleep, his arm still firm around his infant son. Grace stood between Able and Meri. "He told me he loved me – had for years, wretched man – and not to wait too long to remarry, because George needs a father. What a man I married."

Meri kissed her and stepped back. Grace lay down beside her dying husband with a sigh.

Able took out his pocket watch. Grace's arms went around Sir B and Meri covered them with a light blanket. He put his arms around his wife and she leaned against him. He knew how tired she was, his Mrs. Heart of Oak.

The door opened and Junius Bolt came in, Grace's old retainer and Sir B's valet of sorts. To Able's surprise, Smitty sidled in, too. "I heard you leave, master," he said to Able. "I ran all the way."

"I'm glad you're here, Smitty," Able said, and he was, if puzzled to see him. His face giving away nothing, this most enigmatic of Gunwharf Rats stood beside Junius Bolt.

They waited in silence. Two or three rapid breaths and exhalations, a long one, and the final longer one that went on and on until the room was silent. Able heard an early bird, and then another, announcing a new day. George stirred and stretched in his dead father's arms.

Able looked at his watch. His dear friend, captain, mentor and almost-father had lived through the Middle Watch and into the Morning Watch. Able heard the imaginary two bells in his head. Five a.m., when the bosun roused the men for another day at sea, another day to protect England and her possessions from harm and folly. Sir B had told Able once that the Morning Watch was his favorite time of day. "I always think of the possibilities, at five o'clock," he said. "Anything is possible at five in the morning."

"Two Bells. Five in the morning. Good night, dear captain," Able said. "We will now stand the watch for you from this moment forward."

Chapter Three

"I don't like to wear black, Able," Meridee said, as she tucked a white crocheted collar into her dress, unworn since Mama's funeral some years ago. Grace's seamstress had kindly altered it to fit the fashion of 1805, but it was still so relentlessly black.

"You look nice in black," was the best her husband could come up with. She knew he was suffering, and felt some regret at her shallow remark.

"Thank you, my love," she said quietly. "I think the larger issue is that I do not care for this occasion of burying a dear, dear man."

He held out his arms to her and she found herself at home there, as she had through the last few days between death and this moment. No, it was longer, going back a month to her miscarriage. She knew she should stop dwelling on that sad event. After all, weren't well-meaning women telling her to cheer up because there would be other babies? To say, "I wanted this one," would disappoint well-wishers. "So hard," she whispered, uncertain whether she meant Sir B alone.

"I will always see little George crooked in his arm, never to know his remarkable father," Able said. "He won't know Sir B any more than I knew my father."

She never faulted Able's logic – how could anyone? – but in this he was not entirely correct, or so she reasoned. She held herself off enough to look into his eyes. "He will know who his mother is, and he will have stories a-plenty from all of us about his father."

"Aye, he will." He spoke into her hair, then kissed her head. "C'mon, Mrs. Six. Straighten my neck cloth."

She did, always happy to perform those mundane tasks that he had difficulty with, because his brain was too large for small things.

Finally satisfied with her man's appearance – never difficult because he was handsome with or without a neck cloth – she looked around for Ben. She reminded herself that Mrs. Perry had taken him across the street to St. Brendan's to stay with George's nurse. She would have left him with Mrs. Perry, except that her African housekeeper had stared down Able Six and insisted she was going to the funeral, too. He never argued with Mrs. Perry. *Nor do I*, Meridee thought.

She saw Able looking around for Ben too, and they smiled at each other; such a small thing. She hoped small things would usher them more gently into a world without Captain Sir Belvedere St. Anthony, Knight of the Bath, wealthy man, excellent seafarer, wounded warrior, more-than friend.

They came downstairs to a hall and sitting room filled with boys in the black uniform of St. Brendan the Navigator School her husband wore, with the patch of the saint himself over the left breast, close to the heart. The sight of well-scrubbed, earnest faces – some white as hers, others tan, some with almond-shaped eyes, others with curly hair and olive skin like her own dear man – never failed to move her. They came from everywhere and nowhere, the workhouse their one feature in common.

Here also were John and Pierre Goodrich, tidy and dressed as civilians, because they were the adopted sons of Simon Goodrich, who ran the block pulley factory, and his wife, who never could carry a child to term. Meridee felt Able start, and then move forward to bow to famed engineers Henry Maudsley and Marc Brunel, whose idea the factory was. Too bad it took a funeral to gather so many people with whom Meridee knew Able wanted to simply visit.

At her side again, Able knew what to do. "Very well, lads, I'll have no fidgeting in church," he said. "You're – we're – Gunwharf Rats and Sir B specifically wanted us to escort his coffin. You pall bearers walk alongside the hearse with me. Ladies: in the carriage with Gra…Lady St. Anthony. Remember: Handsomely now and eyes to the front."

Able opened the door onto Saints Way, which was full of the ordinary and extraordinary people of Portsmouth, waiting for the procession. "So many people," Meridee murmured.

"I daresay Sir B is taking a few secrets to the grave," he whispered to her. "His acquaintance far exceeded a baronet's usual sphere. He was an unusual man, wasn't he?"

She nodded, then smiled at Ezekiel Bartleby – baker, consoler of Gunwharf Rats with sweets left at St. Brendan's, and man who knew everything of interest on the street. Her smile faded, thinking that she would no longer need to take sugar-sided rout cakes to an invalid now past all pain and sorrow. Mr. Bartleby must have read her thoughts, because he patted his chest, then looked away.

Followed by Mrs. Perry, Meridee and Able took the few steps down to the street and waited as six Royal Marines gentled the plain coffin into the waiting wagon, no fancy feather-decked hearse. It was a common navy vehicle, such as a victualer might use to move his kegs and boxes to the docks, ready to be stowed aboard a ship bound for a distant shore. Meridee felt her ready tears rise. *Dear, dear Sir B, if you could lend a hand to my little one. She is also on a distant shore.*

"Why is it, Able, we knew he could not last, and yet we wish him with us still," she said as he headed her toward the carriage. "Are we so selfish?"

"I believe we are," he said. She heard all his chagrin. "Oh, and what is this? It appears to me that our equally singular Grace St. Anthony is not going to go meekly to church in a carriage."

"Good," Meridee said. "I'll keep her company."

He took her arm. "If you're up to it, Meri."

"I am. It's not so far to St. Thomas." *I owe the great man*, she thought, her heart full of sorrow and love. *Sir B, you found the perfect place for Able Six and me.*

Grace took her hand when she crossed the street. They touched foreheads and Grace murmured, "Meri, join me, but only if you feel you can."

"It's not so far," she said, nodding to her man, who stood with his young crew beside the victualling wagon. "And you?"

"We'll hold each other up," the new widow said, "much as we have held each other up on different occasions." She looked at the sky. "It's a fair day for my dear man. The wind is right, too, isn't it?" She squeezed Meridee's hand. "Tell me it is."

"It is, dear friend."

The short walk to Portsmouth's cathedral only taxed her toward the end, but Grace was there to put a supporting arm around her waist. Grace leaned closer.

"Meridee, how did you and I ever get entangled with navy men, of all specimens?" she asked. "They're ribald and frank and have a certain reputation, and we're ladies."

"Just lucky, perhaps," Meridee said, looking at her husband ahead of them, doing the slow funeral walk with his Rats. He looked back at her now and then, always appraising. "I would change nothing."

"Nor I. More time would have been nice, but he was in such pain." Grace spoke quietly, almost to herself.

Two rows of dignitaries lined the steps outside St. Thomas. Meridee was not surprised to see the Elder and Younger Brothers of Trinity House, but there stood Billy Pitt, England's Prime Minister, looking too old for his years and shaky on his feet.

She sighed with relief when Able moved closer to Smitty and whispered to him, which sent the stalwart Rat to stand beside William Pitt, and hesitate not a moment to support him, even as some mourners gasped. There was no mistaking Mr. Pitt's nod of gratitude, either.

She didn't know the officers – Royal Navy men, Royal Marines and a smattering of British Army – but many of them also wore the distinctive star designating them Knights of the Bath. There they stood, bareheaded as a mist fell, honoring one among their number who had left them too soon.

She breathed deep of the incense inside the old church, wondering how many navy men had been laid to rest in this vicinity, and how many women mourned them. *Please let me not be numbered among them*, she thought, watching as the Gunwharf Rats stood their watch around the plain coffin.

When William Pitt was seated, Smitty joined his fellow Rats. He did a strange thing first, walking behind the coffin and placing both hands on it. He touched his forehead to the flag draping the highly polished wood in a tender gesture she had not though to see from that formidable Rat who kept his secrets and confided in no one. He stood beside Able finally, their shoulders touching. She wondered who consoled whom.

Meridee bowed her head, exhausted. She heard a murmur, a brief rustle of skirts, then the blessed relief of Able beside her, his arm around her.

He only left her side when the service ended and the Rats listened for their note. Singing "Heart of Oak" was the perfect touch, the song Sir B wanted, the anthem of St. Brendan the Navigator School. She heard chuckles from the navy men around her. Some sang along.

Not for Sir B a pampered spot among his ancestral dead on his little-used estate in the Hampshire countryside. He had insisted upon a plot outside St. Thomas, Portsmouth's cathedral, a place with a view of the water. She and Grace followed the coffin carried now by the Gunwharf Rats into God's Acre, with its collection of wells and ne'er do wells, lowlife and high livers of a navy town.

"I have often thought that there was a shadier side to Sir B that he never shared with anyone, his wife included," Grace said as she and Meridee followed the coffin out of the church. "He was no particular angel." She gestured at the grave markers large and mostly small around them, then turned her gaze to the docks and tall-masted ships. "I loved him."

They held hands as the Archbishop of Canterbury, Charles Manners-Sutton, he who had conducted a most impeccable funeral service inside, continued with majestic words, the last resource of finite humans contemplating the great unknown. He stood before the coffin, looking down for a long time. He raised his eyes to heaven.

"'Man, that is born of woman, hath but a short time to live, and is full of misery. He cometh up, and is cut down, like a flower...'"

The hard words smote Meridee's heart. She thought of her man, and the Rats, and the danger only miles across the Channel, where a dictator of no mean skill strutted and postured, threatening all manner of harm to her darlings, usurping the Lord God Almighty in his desire to ordain death. *Cut down like a flower, indeed, sir,* she thought. *It will be a fight to the death, as it has been for decades.*

But this was no time to tell the Lord His business, she decided. *We do have a short time, sir,* she acknowledged. *Pardon me if I whine. You are right, of course. We are puny creatures.*

The graveside service ended, following one final prayer, spoken louder than the first, because the wind had picked up. Meridee watched her husband raise his face to the wind. She looked around, amused to see the other seafarers do the same. Trust Sir B to request a perfect wind for ships to sally forth from Portsmouth, bent on destruction of the French. Trust God to humor him.

She knew it was time for her and Grace to depart, to leave the lowering of the coffin into the ground to shipmates and brother officers. She released Grace's hand, as the widow moved to the coffin one last time for the touch of her lips to smooth wood.

As Grace took her final farewell on earth from the man she loved best,

Meridee observed the Gunwharf Rats, each almost as dear to her as her own son. She knew their stories and their sorrow. She loved them all.

She couldn't have explained to anyone the emotion she felt when her glance settled on Smitty. He still stood beside her husband, his face a study in contemplation. She had always thought him a handsome fellow, if formidable in the extreme. He had showed up on St. Brendan's doorstep one chilly morning, declaring to Headmaster Thaddeus Croker that he was Smitty, he wanted admission, and he had nothing else to say. For some reason, the headmaster never questioned him. None of them did. Smitty didn't invite interrogation.

She regarded the boy in silence, startled as she recognized the profile, the way he pursed his lips, and that certain tilt of his head. *It can't be*, she thought. *Or can it?* Then, *Why, before this moment, did I never notice?*

Confused, she looked at her husband, surprised to see him watching her so carefully. He touched his hand to his heart and nodded ever so slightly.

There was so much she wanted to ask, but it was time for the ladies to leave while the men buried Captain Sir Belvedere St. Anthony. She knew they would do it themselves, despite gravediggers standing by. She also remembered her own father's burial, and her mother's hysteria when she heard clods of earth thumping onto Papa's casket.

Meridee took Grace's hand. "Let us leave them to their work," she whispered.

Grace nodded, offering no objection. "I need Georgie," she said, then started to sag.

Of all people, Captain Angus Ogilvie scooped her up and carried her to the waiting carriage. Meridee hadn't seen him arrive, yet here he was. Didn't Able say the man had a real facility for materializing when least expected? He was needed now; here he was.

He set Grace in the seat. "Should I stay?" he asked her, brusque and to-the-point as usual.

"No, but thank you," Grace told him.

Captain Ogilvie handed Meridee into the carriage. "You look like crow bait yourself, Mrs. Six."

"It's been a long and trying month, captain," she told him, half exasperated, half amused by this strange fellow. What *wouldn't* he say?

He nodded in sympathy. "I fear we have many of those ahead, Mrs. Six." He looked toward the Solent and the Isle of Wight beyond. The wind had picked up and whitecaps danced on the water. "We're all sailing into troubled seas." He tipped his hat to them. "I'll see you both again, and soon." He closed the carriage door and nodded to the coachman.

Grace leaned back, her eyes closed. "All I want now is my baby at my breast and my feet on a hassock." Her eyes filled with tears. "The house will seem so empty. How is it that one frail man could suck out all the air? How will I manage?"

"One day at a time, possibly subdivided into hours and quarter hours," Meridee told her.

Grace opened her eyes at that. "Sometimes, dear friend, you sound remarkably like our master genius."

"That's what he told me after we lost our baby," Meridee said. "Of course, he was holding me close and his eyes looked like mine."

Grace nodded and took her hand. "Quarter hours right now for you?"

"I'm up to half hours," Meridee said simply. "Let's go find our little ones."

Chapter Four

The gravediggers stood respectfully by as the men from Trinity House, other officers of renown, and the Gunwharf Rats, lads of no renown, shoveled silently until the job was done.

As he shoveled, Able turned his mind over to the scenes, dialog, and thoughts swirling around in his brain, remembering the first time he came to Sir B's attention, all the way to their final conversation – just the two of them – a week ago.

Sir B's conversation began coherently enough, as the captain remembered those days at sea when he winkled out Able's astounding gifts, then set him on a path that let to sailing master, and now this, a Younger Brother of Trinity House. Even better, to Able's mind, Sir B had smoothed his way to St. Brendan's as an instructor of lads like him, bastards with nothing to recommend them but brains and courage.

"Of course, you owe your lovely wife for St. Brendan's more than I," Sir B said. "She refused to take no for an answer when poor Captain Hallowell tried to discourage her. She blacked his eye, so I heard, or was that a rumor?"

They laughed together over that only days ago, and then Sir B sighed. "I hate to leave you Sixes and my wife and son. Seems damned unfair. I had hopes…"

He made Able carry him to the window. Sir B weighed less than nothing, so Able held him easily, pointing out the warships at anchor. The prison hulks still brooded close by, less noisome, but no place for anyone yearning for liberté and egálite.

"Jean Hubert just walked away last week, you say?" he asked. "Did that surprise you?"

"No," Able replied. "He was homesick for France. I admit I envy a fellow who has a home to miss. I've never longed for the workhouse."

There was more, certainly, because POW Jean Hubert was no gentleman. St. Brendan's art and French instructor had broken his parole, but he had left Meridee a note with a cryptic comment: "We will meet again."

Back in bed, Sir B dozed and murmured about his younger brother, dead these several years, and something about "…nothing but heartache and worry," then, "… I tried to do right, once I learned. Did I?"

Did you what? Able thought, as he collected Nick Bonfort and Smitty. They stood together, looking down at the covered mound, the resting place of landsmen. He wondered if Captain Sir Belvedere St. Anthony would have preferred burial at sea.

He put a hand on each boy's shoulder. Nick moved closer, because that was Nick. At least Smitty didn't shy away.

"Care for company?"

Captain Ogilvie came toward them. *I already have company*, he wanted to say, but he knew better. Angus Ogilvie was still someone to be cautious around: a spy catcher, Trinity House's dogsbody and all-purpose killer. He was a man with blood on his hands. Able regarded the shorter man for the split second his brain required. *And a man with something to tell me*, he thought. *P'raps I should listen and not judge.*

Better be open with this man Able knew he should trust. "Aye, Captain," he said. "Is it private conversation?"

"It is, Master Six," Angus said most formally.

Able handed Smitty some coins. "I wager Ezekiel Bartleby has some petit fours or those treacle biscuits Mrs. Six is so fond of," he said. "See if you can get her some. I'll join you there."

Smitty pocketed the coins. "Master, you know Mr. Bartleby won't take payment if he knows it's for Mrs. Six."

"You can try. If he cuts up stiff as usual, there is generally a one-legged tar hanging about with a begging cup."

"Aye, Master. C'mon, Nick."

He watched the boys as they walked away. Smitty needed new trousers; Meri had let these out all she could. If the darling of his heart had a shilling for each pair of trousers she had altered, or all the socks she had darned belonging to her lads, she would be independently wealthy.

Nick looked back once, and Able smiled at him, content to call this lad son when no one else was around. Nick had already wrapped himself around Meridee's heart, since she had kindly loaned him her maiden name, because, as Nick put it, she wasn't using it.

"You love them, don't you?" Angus Ogilvie asked as they walked slowly away from God's Acre.

"Aye, one and all," Able replied. "It pains me when they leave us for the fleet."

"That's what they're supposed to do," the captain said, in that spare way of his that suggested he was a humorless fellow.

"Not all of them," he said quietly. He watched the Goodriches trundle themselves into a carriage with John Mark, another of his lads, and little Pierre, a former French POW. *Some leave us for real homes*, he knew, *and blooming careers in our modern mechanical age*. He thought of Davey Ten, already an assistant pharmacist mate, and Stephen Hoyt, clerking in the penal colony in New South Wales. There were others, some quick, some dead, because war was no respecter of age or ability.

"You're a soft touch, Master," Ogilvie said. He spoke with some hesitancy then, he who Able knew was not a sentimental man. "Mrs. Six looks somewhat down pin. Is she well?"

"She miscarried a daughter a month ago," Able said. "We're both a little down pin, I suppose, but her, most certainly." Should he say more? "Her pain is more than physical."

"Yours too, I think," Ogilvie said, surprising Able with sympathy.

"We love children." A glance at Captain Ogilvie told Able something more. Maybe he didn't know this man, not really. "Sir, did you and your late wife have children?" he asked.

"Yes and no, I suppose," the captain said, after a pause that took them half a block, walking slowly. "They were buried together, our son in her arms."

"I'm sorry," Able said, and meant it with all his heart.

"It was years ago. We carry on, Master Six. What else can we do?"

What was there to say to that? They walked in silence, but it was not an uncomfortable silence now.

"I have two matters of interest for you, Master Six," Ogilvie said finally.

"Call me Able, please," he said impulsively. Something had changed in their brief walk. "If you wish," Able added. After all, the man did outrank him.

"I do wish it," Ogilvie said promptly. "Able, then, if I will be Angus to you."

"Most certainly, when we are informal like this."

"It's this, Able. Make of it what you will," Angus said. "I was in Cádiz six months ago, following that damned Clause Pascal."

"I've heard of your trail of blood from the Baltic," Able said. "And your encrypted notes gleaned from less-than-eager Frenchmen."

"A day's work," Angus said, but the flippant comment seemed too glib. "You'll be pleased to know that our friend Claude met a fitting end in Cádiz."

"I *am* pleased."

"The strangest thing: He got in fight in a taberna down on the dock and ended up with a dagger in his eye. Imagine that."

"Yes. Imagine that."

The captain rubbed his hands together, either in glee or in an unconscious imitation of the also-late Pontius Pilate. Able didn't care to know which.

"He served his purpose. No, the matter I have for your consideration is more intriguing than the death of a scoundrel. Six months ago, I stood on the dock and saw the combined fleets of Spain and France."

"We know they are bottled up there."

"Bear with me, Able," Angus said, with a touch of that frosty impatience Able knew well. "What a sight! There before me, bobbing at anchor, was *Santísima Trinidad*, the biggest ship of the line I have ever seen."

"I remember her from the battle off Cape St. Vincent," Able said. "Fair took my breath away. And?"

"On the dock stood a sight to behold, a real Spanish grandee. He had gold epaulets and sparkly stuff everywhere else except possibly his crotch. Spaniards do have a certain elán."

He paused for what Able could only assume was dramatic effect. *Good Lord*, he thought. *Tell your tale.*

"Bless my soul if he didn't look exactly like you, with twenty-plus more years on'm."

Able stopped, his brain utterly silent. As he waited out the unusual silence inside his head, he began to hear, faintly at first, the rapid beat of two hearts. With a conviction that made him suck in his breath, he knew it was his father and mother in the act of creating him. He had heard it before, but now he knew who it meant.

"Francisco Jesus Domingo y Guzman, el Conde de Quintanar," he said with conviction.

Angus gaped at him. "You *know*?"

It was Able's turn to feel frosty impatience. This news was something to share with Meridee, not a man whom he was beginning to like a little more, but nothing else. He tamped down his own irritation.

"Last year, Captain Rose took me upstairs to Trinity House's storage rooms and showed me a small portrait of the Count of Quintanar. That's who you saw."

"Well, blow me," Angus said, making his vulgarity sound almost reverent. "I think he must be your father."

"I believe you are right," Able replied. "Awkward, isn't it?"

Angus recovered himself and shrugged. "I suppose there are stranger things, although at the moment I can't think of any. How in the world..."

Able shrugged this time. "Who knows? Captain Rose told me that years ago, Spain sent a delegation to England to consult with shipwrights. You know, back when our two countries were not at odds."

"You're from Dumfries?"

"Aye."

"How did the count get to Dumfries?"

"How would I know?"

Angus laughed, cutting through the odd tension. "I thought you knew everything."

"Apparently not."

They started walking again. "I shouldn't think the world needs to know this little tidbit," Angus said finally.

"I would agree." *Aye, let me mull this around and see how little I like it,* Able thought, with some curdling of his usual good temper.

Angus opened his mouth, closed it, and opened it again. "There is one other matter probably of more importance than your somewhat unusual origins."

So now you think you know what is more important for a bastard who has wondered all his life about his origins? Able asked himself. "Hmmm?" was the best he could do.

Ogilvie took his arm. "I was privy to a conversation at Admiralty only yesterday." He looked away. "I hardly know how to tell you, because I know it will not be welcome news to Meridee, at the very least."

"You have my full attention," Able said quietly. He could feel his odd and spectral mentors gathering close, listening in, breathing on his neck. What a nuisance they were.

"We have reached that time of national emergency," Angus said, with none of his usual posturing or superiority. "I believe you will be recalled to the fleet in a matter of days."

Chapter Five

This was not the moment for the government to rip him from Meridee and St. Brendan. "This is the wrong time," he blurted out, startled, even angry, because usually his cranial visitors had a way of alerting him to bad news. They had failed him.

"When is war ever convenient?" Angus retorted.

"Never," he said, sick at heart. "And here we are. I educate and send some young men to their deaths. You follow spies into dangerous places."

"…and my hands are bloody," was Ogilvie's equally quiet comment. "I'm weary of that and I fear we have only begun this war."

"I see at least ten years ahead," Able said, continuing their slow amble. "Napoleon will move on Spain and we must counter him there on land and sea. I see tedious blockade duty and many ship-to-ship encounters."

"I doubt our armies can match Napoleon's," Angus said.

"Perhaps not yet. We haven't found the right commander. We will."

Angus stopped again. "Your brain should be studied, perhaps after you are dead," he joked, at least Able thought it was a joke. "Do you think the Conde de Quintanar is as wickedly smart as you?"

"Let's ask him, shall we, Captain Ogilvie?" *Stop, Angus,* Able thought. *This is my life to ponder.*

They continued in silence to Bartleby Bakery. Angus turned to Able and held out his hand. "Let me wish you well." They shook hands. Ogilvie looked toward St. Brendan's down the street and across from Able's house. "D'ye think Lady St. Anthony will continue to instruct there?"

"I would be amazed if she didn't," Able replied. "She's a born teacher and she abhors idleness and aimless little boys."

Ogilvie nodded. "I like a determined woman."

"So do I."

With a nod, the shorter man built like a tree stump continued toward St. Brendan the Navigator School. Able watched him, still unable to make him out. Perhaps Meridee had some clues. He glanced into the bakery window.

Ezekiel Bartleby had already boxed up the dessert in question, plus treacle biscuits. From the look on Smitty's face, the redoubtable lad had tried and failed to force the baker to take the coins. Able knew Smitty never cared much for failure.

He put his hand on the boy's shoulder, pleased that he did not flinch. "Smitty, down the street, I see a one-legged tar propped against the building. He can use the coins, since our baker is a hard man to convince."

"Aye, master."

"When you're done, Mrs. Perry probably has hot bread with butter waiting in the kitchen."

"Could we take some to the beggar?" Nick asked. "I never cared much for hunger."

"Nor I," Smitty said. "We can convince Mrs. Perry."

"I daresay you can," Able said.

Smitty nodded and gestured to Nick, who followed with a grin. Able watched them go, pleased as always how good Smitty was at commanding others. Nick followed him without question.

"Thank you, Ezekiel," Able said as he took the parcel. "Every little bit helps." Able gave the baker a small salute and hurried home to Meridee, his heart lighter.

He saw the boys down the block, squatting beside the beggar, handing him the coins and then talking. He hurried up the steps, sniffing warm bread when he opened the door. This meant a stop in the kitchen, where Mrs. Perry handed him the well-buttered heel, his favorite slice, and gave him the next piece for Meridee.

"Two lads will be in here soon to petition some bread for a beggar," he told her.

"He might like a sandwich," Mrs. Perry said, and turned to the pantry. "Maybe two."

"You're a wonder," he said. "Thank you for helping us, of late."

"Where would we be, if left to our own devices?" She pointed to the door. "She's holding Ben in the sitting room. He's asleep." Able watched her expressive face. "Master Six, she looks content."

"Good."

He ate the heel, then eyed Meri's piece. Mrs. Perry scowled at him, and suddenly, things felt right again. He gave her a wink and walked to the sitting room, opening the door quietly in case both mother and son were asleep.

Mrs. Perry was right. Meri was awake, but he saw her contentment. She pursed her lips at him, which told him worlds about her mood. He kissed those pursed lips, which opened into a far more satisfactory kiss, and sat beside her on the sofa.

"I can carry him upstairs for you," he whispered.

"In a minute. I like this," she said softly. "It's nice for his brain to be less busy."

Able handed her the buttered bread, removed his shoes and propped his feet on the ottoman, tickling her bare toes, which made her smile. She ate the bread. "Just what I needed."

"Mrs. Perry seems to know."

"So do you," she said. She licked her lips, then nodded. "You may take him upstairs."

Able carefully extracted their son from Meri's arms and bedded him down in his room next to theirs. He looked in the empty chamber that had belonged to Jean Hubert, their escapee from a prisoner of war hulk in the harbor, who had inexplicably decided to leave them, after many months of service to St. Brendan's. Jean had left behind a magnificent pen and ink drawing of the Loire River valley, and a note thanking them for their hospitality. Cheeky Frenchman.

The door to Nick and Smitty's room was open. He peered in, mainly to assure himself that it was shipshape, then returned to the sitting room. Meri's eyes were closed, the sock she was darning on the floor. He picked it up, smiling at her tiny stitches, and set the sock, one of his, back in the never-empty mending basket.

He sat down, and in the peace of their sitting room, admired her loveliness. He thought that's what he did. When he opened his eyes, shadows had lengthened across the room and she was eyeing *him*.

Silent, he watched her face, pleased to see a certain game quality now. He held out his hand to her and she came to him, curling up in his lap and resting her head against his chest.

"I want to be happy again."

He held her closer, kissing her hair. "We will be."

She smelled of lilac talcum and little boy, a combination that made him smile and then chuckle. "What's so funny?" she asked in that gruff voice of hers she used when she felt playful. He could have gone down on his knees in gratitude to hear it again.

"You are." He sniffed around her ear then bit her ear lobe most tenderly. "You smell of lilacs and Ben."

She laughed and settled herself closer. "Headmaster Croker dropped by to say that you and I have been invited to the reading of Sir B's will tomorrow. It will be held in his chambers."

"Us? I'll wager you that our friend is leaving a tidy sum to St. Brendan's."

Meri nodded. "I doubt I am essential to any such reading, but Thaddeus Croker insisted." She sat up. "This is strange. He specifically requested that Smitty come with us."

"Is it so strange?"

"I wonder," she said, making herself comfortable again. "I watched him during the funeral, dour Smitty who looks older than his years. He…he.. you'll think this absurd…"

"Try me."

"There are times he reminds me of Sir B," she said in a rush, as if aware how silly that sounded, and wanted to get rid of the idea in a hurry.

"He reminds me, too."

"Is this even possible?" she asked, after looking around to assure herself that Smitty and Nick were nowhere near.

"Of all people, you and I know that anything is possible."

He kept the thought through dinner, which was subdued, until Meri started speaking of more memorable moments with Sir B, some of them humorous. This led to Able's stories of life at sea with Captain St. Anthony, when Able was a mere sprout and learning his craft, granted, faster than most.

Ben ate a good meal, then settled on his father's lap as Able read from Euclid in the original Greek, which made Meri roll her eyes and return to her darning. The long, painful day of sending a grand navy man off to his eternal watch had mellowed into a typical evening at the Sixes, almost as if they had permission to return to normal. Nick and Smitty commandeered the dining room table to spread out their next day's assignments, complain about too much extra work, and demolish the rest of that loaf of bread, well-buttered.

The boys went to bed in good spirits. Meri read to them as she always did – she reasoned they were never too old for that and no one complained – while Able did the same with Ben in his little room. "My boy, let me start you off with Xenophon," he said, hunkering down with his son. "Do you want the English or the Greek?"

"Greek, Papa," Ben said. "I should sound out some of the words, shouldn't I?"

You're seventeen months old, Able thought. *I wonder what your grandfather would think of you, that man near the Santísima Trinidad.* "Yes, you should. You try and I'll help if needed."

A page or two sufficed for the night. Ben tugged at his eyelids and his respirations slowed. "Goodnight, sweet boy," Able whispered. He thought of his own harsh days in the Dumfries workhouse, grateful with every fiber of his being that his son would never know that life. No one would ever chastise Ben for reading early, for knowing too much.

Able heard Meri in their room, but he went downstairs as usual, checking all the doors, doing the slow walk that remained a cherished holdover of his sailing master duties at sea. From quarterdeck to gundeck to fo'c'sle and back, he used to walk. Now the slow walk reminded him how much he missed the sea.

And yet, if Angus Ogilvie was correct, his time at St. Brendan's was coming to an end, at least until the current national emergency passed. He would be recalled to the fleet because Napoleon Bonaparte felt himself ready to conquer England. How on earth could he tell Meri?

Chapter Six

Meridee knew what her man was doing, because Mrs. Perry had told her a year ago how he walked through their house, perhaps even wishing himself at sea again. She smiled to herself as she sat in bed, wondering if he had any idea that she knew how much he wanted to return to sea. Some sixth sense of her own, not as stunning as her husband's mental equipment but yet there, nevertheless, had alerted her.

It might have been all the hours he and the St. Brendan boys spent on Sir B's yacht, the *Jolly Roger*, sailing around the Isle of Wight, and even taking messages to Plymouth. He always came home so happy, smelling of brine and tar. What else could she believe? The sea was a mistress she could live with.

She heard his footsteps on the stairs, listening as he took another look at Ben, then turned their doorknob.

She shouldn't feel shy, but she did, because she was Meridee and modest. He smiled at her, stretched and took off his shoes first. When he started on his trouser buttons, she thought this might be the moment to stand up and let her nightgown fall to the floor.

He watched her, his eyes appreciative. His smile grew, but he came no closer.

She stepped out of the silky pile around her feet. There were always going to be stretch marks, thanks to Ben. Her breasts had suffered some loss of firmness and her waist certainly couldn't be spanned by her husband's hands yet or even again, but did it matter? The light in Able's eyes suggested that the answer was an emphatic no.

"My love, we need some solace, you and I," she said and held out her arms.

"How did I ever manage without you?" she asked later, when the room stopped twirling about. "Granted, life was simpler as a spinster. Also deadly dull."

He laughed his nighttime laugh, the one she only heard in bed, two parts edgy and one part sleepy. "I've wondered how I ever managed without *you*."

"Come now, Able, I am no fool," she said, settling in, preparing for sleep. "I know you were a man of experience before we married."

"It's not the same," he assured her. "Those were for need and lust, after far too long at sea. You're different."

"Oh, you don't need me and lust a little bit?" she teased. "Have I been misinterpreting those looks of yours?"

"Not at all," he assured her. "My word, woman. There are times I have lusted so intensely in the... the kitchen, that I am surprised I didn't back you into the pantry and have my way with you next to the flour bin."

"Oh." She couldn't think of anything profound to say to that artless statement.

"'Oh?' That's the best you can do?" he teased in turn, this man of hers.

"Oh my," she teased back.

This was probably her best opportunity, before they both relaxed further into slumber. "If you know me so well, Master Six, then you must know that I am well aware you are holding something back from me."

He was silent a while, and she almost second-guessed herself. But no, she knew that look of uncertainty, that look of wondering how to tell her bad news. "I hope this is not something I will hear soon enough from someone else," she said, then rubbed his chest.

He put his hand over hers. "You know me. I cannot hide anything from you."

"Tell me straight up with no bark," she said. There was enough light in their room to see that he smiled at her slang.

"Blame Captain Ogilvie and his sources!" he began. "Very well: he has word that I will be recalled to the fleet at any moment, because we have reached that moment of grave national crisis."

"There is never a right time, is there?" she asked. "I need you here." Too bad that armies and navies care not a whit about men who fight and women who wait.

"I have been wondering when this would happen," she said. "Haven't you?"

He pulled her on top of his body as he would a coverlet. This bore an odd similarity to their recent lovemaking, but she could tell he was deadly serious in a different way. "I have no choice, my love."

"I know."

She rested her head on his chest. *I must savor every moment with this dear genius of mine*, she thought, as she drifted to sleep.

When she slept – God, how he loved it when she blew bubbles on his chest – Able moved her off him carefully, unwilling to wake her. He watched her face, noting the fine lines around her eyes. He saw all the strength in her, as well as her vulnerability. If something happened to him, where would she go? What would she do?

Euclid, if you have any suggestions, don't hang back please, he thought.

He waited for a response, and it came, sounding reluctant, even surly. *She banished me from your bedchamber*, he heard, from that first voice inside his head, years ago. He smiled at the petulance.

The others began to stir inside, van Leuwenhoek with a sigh and shake of his head. Newton appeared detached, which was no surprise. He had never enjoyed the delight, pleasure and care of a wife. He didn't expect any advice from Antoine Lavoisier, the French chemist who had lost his head to the recent revolution, and whose wife had been his lab partner. Able wondered if Lavoisier was aware that his wife had remarried last year. He thought it prudent not to consider the matter too intensely, the French being so prickly.

None of his fellow scientists and geniuses had any good advice. Lately, they had seemed to think he should rely more on himself.

But wait. There was some sort of clamor at the door to that spectral antechamber where he sometimes found himself. Able settled back, content with the pleasant warmth of Meri's breasts against his chest, and wondered who it might be.

We can't let you in. You're not one of us, he heard from William Harvey, who should have known better, considering his usual sense of humor.

Just listen to me then, Able heard.

He recognized the voice, and felt a great weight lift from his heart. He put his hands behind his head and smiled at the ceiling.

He strained to hear the whispered conversation there at the door, but it was indistinct. The Italians gesticulated, the Germans folded their arms, and van Leuwenhoek grinned, a merry Dutchman.

Able knew how persuasive Captain Sir Belvedere St. Anthony could be, and no one strode a quarterdeck with more elán. His heart grew tender as he heard Sir B through the door, his voice intense. *I should have thought of this earlier, but I was in great pain.*

Euclid seemed to have the final say among the quarreling specters. Able listened and thought he heard, *We'll make it right, sir, now return to your quarterdeck.* Trust Euclid to look out for him, even though Meri had insisted that he stay in the hall at nights.

Before the sun rose, he woke Meri with a kiss and a cuddle, aware that Ben would wake soon, and the household would be up and ready for another day.

"Some men take their wives to sea with them," Meri whispered in his ear.

"Captains, Meri, which I am not, and never in time of war," he told her. He smoothed back her hair and looked down at her lovely face. "Something tells me this nasty bit of news will work out."

"Something or someone?" she asked, her fingers in his curls.

By God, this woman knew him. "Very well, then, someone."

She laughed softly and raised up to kiss him. "Considering that I banished him, Euclid is remarkably kind to me."

"No Greek can resist a pretty face."

She grew serious then, and pulled him closer. "Never forget that I am your keeper."

Chapter Seven

The reading of Sir B's last will and testament began promptly at two bells in the forenoon watch, in Headmaster Thaddeus Croker's office. Classes had been dismissed and the students were under the thumb of Mrs. Parmley, bosun's widow who ran as taut a ship as her husband ever had. Spiders lurked in vain at St Brendan's. There were no decks to holystone here, but she had her boys scrubbing and cleaning.

Composed, her hands in her lap, Grace sat next to Meridee. Only the dark circles under her eyes betrayed the sorrow and despair that had taken their toll during the last few weeks of her husband's life on earth.

It wasn't dignified, but Meridee nudged Grace, pleased to feel an answering nudge. "This isn't the first time it has been you and me in a roomful of navy men," she whispered.

Grace took her hand. "You are remembering Trinity House, are you not? We were formidable then."

Meridee recalled the two of them pleading St. Brendan's case last year with the conviction born of experience; the Trinity Brothers had listened. *We need each other, Grace and I,* she thought. *Do other navy wives feel that way?* "I remember," she said, her voice low. "Grace, we are still formidable." The glance they exchanged warmed Meridee's heart.

Smitty sat on Meridee's other side, impeccable in his St. Brendan's uniform. Meridee admired his calm air, wondering how he managed. None of the other St. Brendan's lads were there. He betrayed his youth only once when he leaned toward her and whispered, "Mam, what do I do if someone calls on me?"

She had no idea. "You stand and give a respectful nod and look at them straight on."

"I won't frighten them?"

She touched his hand, then rested it lightly on his. "No, Smitty. What you are is capable-looking and courageous."

"I think they frighten *me*," he muttered under his breath.

He gave her a rare smile, belying his words and reminding her again of the man whose will they were about to hear. Why *she* was there made even less sense to her than why Smitty was, except that she loved Sir B as much as everyone in the room, including her husband, who sat between Headmaster Croker and the barrister. He had a "why am I here?" look on his face, which probably mirrored hers.

Captain Hector Rose, Trinity House's warden, had joined them, as well as the ubiquitous Captain Ogilvie. How did that man insinuate himself into so much? she wondered. There were other distinguished-looking fellows, enough of them to make Meridee wish for a kettle full of petit fours from Ezekiel Bartleby as solace for nerves.

I marry a bona fide genius, end up in raffish Portsmouth, and my life changed, she thought, still marveling at the difference of a few years. She smiled at her husband, reading his thoughts almost perfectly. *And you wish I were sitting beside you. So do I.*

Meridee prepared to be bored but look interested through the reading of Sir B's will, and she succeeded, to a point. Who could know anything about St. Brendan's usually denigrated students and not feel a catch in the throat when the barrister, Sir Charles Park, announced a huge bequest?

"He wrote this in his own hand," Sir Charles said, with a kindly glance at Grace St. Anthony. "'I know not what the coming years of war will bring, but St. Brendan's must continue as a school for workhouse lads of promise.'" He removed his spectacles and addressed Grace. "My dear Lady St. Anthony, he was so adamant that he word the matter correctly."

"He knew how important St. Brendan's was. He always knew," Grace said softly.

Sir Charles cleared his throat and continued through other bequests, then came to one which brought a smile to his face. To Meridee's surprise, he looked at her. "You are Mrs. Able Six?" he asked.

"Yes, Sir Charles," she said, then glanced at Able, who shrugged his shoulders, as mystified as she was.

"Very well, then!" Sir Charles gave her a deferential nod. "'To Meridee Bonfort Six, wife of Sailing Master Durable Six, should her husband predecease her in his service in the Royal Navy and/or St. Brendan the Navigator School, one thousand pounds per annum, as long as she shall live.'"

Meridee gasped. She looked across the room to her husband, who had bowed his head. When she saw his shoulders shake, she longed to leap to her feet and hold him.

Sir Charles held up his hand. "A little more, so humor me." Another throat clearing. "'The house at 11 Saints Way has already been purchased by me and will be assigned to Mrs. Six now, with the addition of a few signatures. She need never fear eviction, provided she does not mind living in this devil-may-care port.'"

Meridee struggled between laughter and tears, and tears won. Without a word, Smitty took a handkerchief from an inside pocket and pressed it in her hand.

It wasn't enough. She knew she wanted her husband right then; fortunately, he knew it, too. With no apology he left the table and was at her side in remarkable time. She clung to him, and he to her. After a moment, they turned their attention to Headmaster Croker.

"Sir, accept our apologies for this interruption," Able said. "By his unparalleled bequest to my wife, Sir B has allayed my only fear. God bless the man."

He returned to his seat and Meridee sat again, certain that everyone in the room could hear the pounding of her heart. She whispered to Grace, "Friend, did you know this?"

Grace nodded, and blew her a kiss.

After several more mundane bequests, all of which indicated to Meridee that Sir B was far wealthier than she ever could have imagined, Sir Charles finally reached the final page of the will. He looked and then looked again, showing it to the solicitor seated behind him. They conferred. Meridee heard, "I don't recall this. Do you?" and "But Sir Charles, it has been initialed, has it not?" "Someone's initials. Can you make them out?" "No, Sir Charles. It's Greek to me."

Sir Charles Park read the final entry to himself, shaking his head. He looked at Master Croker apologetically. "I daresay our firm has been working too many long hours." He tapped the page. "This little entry I disremember, but all things considered, it is a wise one, I have no doubt." He looked at his audience.

"It is this: "I will my yacht the *Jolly Roger* to St. Brendan's, with the proviso that it be assigned to the Royal Navy for the length of our current national emergency. She is a sweet vessel and can easily handle ship-to-shore messages from the blockade off France and Spain to Admiralty and the Navy Board." He smiled at the words. "'Trust me, she is fast.'"

He looked at Smitty this time, and then Able. "This part concerns you two." Smitty leaned forward. Gone was his usual veiled expression, replaced by an unmatched intensity. "'What better way to train lads for the fleet than to serve such a duty? Able Six will command, if he is recalled to the fleet, and Smitty will serve as sailing master.'"

Everyone in the room seemed to exhale at the same time. Sir Charles held up a warning hand and looked closer. "Let me continue. 'Be persuasive, you Gunwharf Rats, in convincing the starched shirts at Admiralty that I have not lost my wits entirely. I suggest you take it up with Billy Pitt.'" Amid quiet laughter, Sir Charles set down the will and his expression grew serious. "He finished this way, Master Six: 'Would that I could sail with you both. Your friend, Sir B.'"

There was nothing more to say, beyond the usual legalese that no one remembers except scribes and sticklers. "In coming weeks, we will handle all the finalizing of property and assigning of monetary bequeaths. In due time, you will hear from my firm," Sir Charles said.

There was one more matter, one that Sir Charles remembered when he folded the documents into his briefcase and a letter floated down.

He picked up the letter and handed it to Smitty. "Bless me if I hadn't forgotten precisely why else you were supposed to be here, my lad. This is my reminder. If you have any questions, let me know." He put a hand on Smitty's shoulder. "He wanted to tell you in person, but possibly for the first time in his life, words failed Sir B. Good day, all." He and the solicitor left the room.

Meridee watched Smitty's face, noting uncertainty for nearly the first time since she had known him. A quiet lad, but one of capable, sometimes fierce, mien that complimented his impressive build, he was seldom jostled or bothered. She sat beside him again. He looked up at her and she wondered if he did not want her close by.

"Would you rather I did not intrude upon this moment?" she asked quietly.

"Stay here, mam, if you please," he said. "I've never received a letter. How do I open it?" He handed it to her.

Yes, who would ever write to Smitty, a workhouse boy? she thought with sympathy. Meridee took out a hairpin from the chignon at the nape of her neck and slid it along the crease. She smiled to see Sir B's handwriting, remembering little notes from him when he was too ill to leave his house, but still eager to encourage and tease a bit. "He wrote this when he was feeling good, I think," she told Smitty.

"He didn't know me, mam," Smitty said.

I believe he knew you better than you think, she told herself. "Perhaps he did," she said. "Read it and find out."

She looked away while he read, unwilling to intrude. She heard him gasp, then lean against her, something he never did, unlike her other St. Brendan boys. She saw devastation on his face, and put her arm around him.

He held out the letter to her. "You read it, mam," he told her.

She read it to herself, amazed, understanding Smitty's resemblance to Sir B.

She handed it back to Smitty, who started reading out loud, as if to make it real. "'My brother was a worthless vagabond and spendthrift,'" Smitty read. She heard all the amazement, and then a cold sort of anger, the kind that festered. "'On his deathbed three years ago, he admitted to me that he had fathered a child. He had taken you, his son, Edward St. Anthony, to a workhouse at the age of six, when your mother died.'"

"Do you remember this?" Meridee asked, hoping for a little amnesia. She didn't want to imagine a boy, his mother dead, taken to the workhouse by his father and left there alone. She glanced at Able and saw all the horror on his face.

"Aye, mam, I remember all of it," Smitty said, and he sounded grim. "I was there almost seven years." He dropped the letter.

Able picked it up and continued reading. "'God forgive me, but I didn't know what to do. Smitty, if you are reading this now, I confess I should have taken you into my household three years ago when I learned this. I was still so angry at my brother for wasting his life and causing our late mother such grief that I couldn't do it.'" Able looked at Smitty. "Lad, he was human."

"Sir B never suffered in a workhouse, did he?" Smitty asked quietly, all the bitterness in plain view.

"No, but have some charity." Able indicated the letter. "I believe he did the next best thing. Tell us exactly how you got here."

The words spilled from the usually taciturn boy. "One day a kitchen girl slipped me a folded-up note. It was unsigned." He looked at the letter. "Same handwriting. Sir B's handwriting."

"What did the note say?" Meridee asked, when Smitty remained silent.

"Told me to run away to St. Brendan's in Portsmouth on Saints Way," he replied promptly. "I ran away the next day." He looked from Meridee to Able. "You know the rest, Master Six."

"So do we all now, Smitty."

Grace St. Anthony came closer, her expression pensive. "Meridee, didn't I say my husband took some secrets to the grave? Smitty, I had no idea." She pressed a handkerchief to her eyes. "I knew there was something more than pain bothering him in his last weeks, but he never told me. Sir B sent that unsigned note to you three years ago, because he couldn't bear to deal with it any other way."

"He was a coward," Smitty said, his words a condemnation.

"He was human," Grace repeated, her voice kind. "I hope you understand that someday."

"Never." Smitty shook his head. "I know my father wasn't a good man, either. He never gave Mam enough money to live on and we starved."

He said it simply, but his eyes showed all the hunger, and the longing worse than hunger. "I had two meals a day in the workhouse and that was better." He shook his head, as if trying to dislodge a worse memory. "I couldn't do nothing about the tormentors, though. I was too small then and they..." His expression took on a more Smitty aspect, the look of someone with scores to settle even now, and no way to do it. "I grew, though, I did."

"What's done is done. I have scores to settle, too, and no way to do it."

Smitty started to say something, then stopped, as if recalling himself to the moment. "Does anyone understand us, Master Six?"

"As long as we understand each other, does it matter? Let's go home, Smitty," Able said. "We need to strategize on how to fulfill Sir B's wish that we turn the *Jolly Roger* into a warship, a messenger."

"Name her the *Mercury*."

Meridee watched Captain Ogilvie join them, after a bow to Grace St. Anthony. Where had he come from? She hadn't heard a door open.

"The winged messenger of the gods?" Able asked.

"The very one." Ogilvie bowed a second time to Grace and included himself in the conversation. "We will ask you, Lady St. Anthony, to christen the *Mercury*."

She waited for Grace to put the upstart Captain Ogilvie in his place, but she did not.

"I will do that gladly," she said simply. "There is a condition, Captain Ogilvie."

"Only name it," he replied.

"Able will have someone in mind to teach in his stead," she said. "Could you please locate Jean Hubert? We still need his draftsman skills and his language instruction."

"You think I can find a Frenchman who has obviously, ahem, jumped ship?"

"I am certain of it."

Meridee watched with real glee as the two of them stared each other down. To her further delight, Captain Ogilvie looked away first.

He bowed to the new widow. "Very well," Angus said. "Give me a few days."

Chapter Eight

Finding Jean Hubert took a mere three days. When Angus Ogilvie sent Able a cryptic note – "expect JH anytime"- even Able had to grudgingly admit that Angus Ogilvie was at the top of his game, however questionable it might be. Who knew? He also admitted to Meri that he liked seeing that spark of interest return to Grace's eyes when he showed her the note after class. "She likes the rascal, same as we do."

It was evening now, with Smitty and Nick Bonfort at their usual spot in the dining room, finishing homework. Able held Ben on his lap as his son sounded out words in Isaac Newton's masterpiece, *Principia Mathematica*, the English version. Unperturbed by all the genius around her – what a woman he had married – Meri knitted a sock.

"Who should show up in my trigonometry class this afternoon but Jean Hubert, looking none the worse for wear, the scoundrel," Able said. "He wouldn't admit where he had been – gave me that half-insolent, all-French smile. As we speak, he is dining with Headmaster Croker. He'll be here soon."

Oh, predictions. Able heard a knock. He listened for Mrs. Perry's heavy footfall, and smiled to himself. Ah, yes, here it came. It was low-voiced but intense. He leaned toward his wife.

"Meri, I believe Mrs. Perry is giving our returning prodigal what for," he whispered sotto voce.

"Good," Meri replied. She smiled at Ben. "What say you, Ben?"

"I missed him," the little one replied, almost with his father's intonation and inflection.

"You are both scoundrels," she said, her affection for them obvious.

"Ben, there is an excellent pile of blocks over there that needs stacking. Give Sir Isaac a rest, won't you?"

"Aye, Mum." Ben hopped off his father's lap and made for the corner. In a few minutes he was busy stacking and humming.

Able touched Meridee's hand. "You are the leaven in our odd loaf," he told her.

"I know," she replied, straight-faced, which made him laugh out loud. "Let us see if our son can be both a child and a genius, shall we?"

"Amen to that," he said, thinking of his own rough start. Ben was already miles ahead of him in joy and comfort, the kind that comes from a loving mother who nurtured and admonished and smoothed his way. *And who keeps me sane with her unbounded love*, he thought, grateful.

Maybe he could test her a bit. He knew he had a minute, because Mrs. Perry had lit into their French POW with more than her usual verve. With the deepest, most unshakeable knowledge, Able knew Meri's love would last. He also knew she enjoyed occasional glimpses into his odd cranial world. He touched her hand again, closing around the knitting needles. She rested the needles in her lap.

"Something tells me..."

"Aye, mum," he teased. "I had the strongest feeling yesterday that the barrister had no idea who had added that interesting codicil about willing the *Jolly Roger* to St. Brendan's."

"He did seem surprised," she said, and gave him her intense look that, depending on its venue, excited him, or sent him into introspection. Here in the sitting room, he knew her lively mind was hard at work. "If it weren't possible – don't even try to tell me it is – I would suspect that Euclid has a hand in this. What gives, my love?"

Her use of schoolboy cant made him smile. No wonder every lad at St. Brendan's adored her, too. "I believe my meddling mental mentors – now there is a phrase – somehow engineered that codicil Sir Charles claimed never to have seen before."

"You *know* such things are impossible, don't you?" his practical skeptic asked.

"I have given up trying to figure it out," he told her. "Obviously, there is more afoot during this national emergency that will involve our boys in the fleet."

There. He had admitted it. Their boys. All of his extraordinary senses might caution him to take a more detached view of the lads of St. Brendan's who would come and go, some to distinguished service and others to a weighted canvas shroud in mid-ocean, but his deeply human side refused to cooperate. "Our boys," he repeated. "We are all in this together for the long game, no matter where it leads us." *Take that, Euclid*, he thought, but with no rancor. *In your clever engineering, you mind-bending specters, please let me always return to this woman beside me.*

He had spoken aloud without realizing it. He watched sadness cross Meri's face, to be replaced by calm acceptance. He leaned closer. "I won't say the next few months will be safe, Meri. I would be lying."

"I know," she said softly, after a glance at Ben. "My strength is returning, and my heart is in trim. Go and fight your battles. I will love you always." She turned her head toward the door. "Mrs. Perry is giving our unfortunate Frenchman a regular bear garden jaw. Able, rescue him."

He could never admit that Mrs. Perry fair terrified him, too. Meri knew him well, though. With a laugh, she got up and left the room. He heard her low voice, then silence, followed by the kitchen door closing decisively. Able had known Mrs. Perry since the age of fourteen, and could not deny, even now, a healthy respect bordering on abject fear, when she was on a tear.

But here came Jean Hubert with Meri, looking bruised by Mrs. Perry's ill treatment in the foyer, but otherwise unscathed. He returned bow for bow, and kissed Meri's cheek.

"*Merci* for the rescue, Madame Six," he said.

"You owe me a king's ransom for my intervention, Jean," Meri said as she sat down and resumed her knitting. "Where have you been? Should we worry that the next knock will be Royal Marines ready to clap you in irons?"

"No, no, madame," the scoundrel said. He was silent, looking at them both expectantly.

"Jean, you are a reprobate and an escapee," Able said. He said it mildly enough because it was far too easy to like the casual Frenchman who had been caught up in Napoleon's machinations the same as he was, no more no less, even if on opposite sides, and sentenced to a Portsmouth prison hulk. "Do answer Meri's question, if you know what's good for you."

"I do, Able," Jean said cheerfully. "It might amaze you, but then again, knowing you…"

"Belay the stall," Able said in his sailing master voice this time.

"Captain Ogilvie himself escorted me undercover to Trinity House – what was it – six months ago," he said promptly.

"He told me only three days ago that he would try to find you," Able grumbled. "He knew all along!"

"I am not responsible for someone else's lies," Jean said, managing to sound almost virtuous. "There truly is considerable interest in cryptography."

"Of which you know little?" Able prompted.

Jean laughed. "Of which I know nothing!"

"You convinced our Captain Ogilvie that you knew cryptographs?" Meri asked.

"It wasn't that hard," he said modesty.

"Captain Ogilvie is as astute a man as I know," she said, then sighed. "Jean, charm only works so long."

"As long as it works at all, I will try," he said candidly, and laughed when Meri did. "Very well! If you must know, I ran away, returned to France, did not like what I saw, and came back to Trinity House," he said. He waggled his hand. "Well, perhaps I didn't exactly run away. Captain Ogilvie encouraged me — shall we say — to visit Boulogne and see what I could see."

"So it wasn't all charm," Meri said.

"Alas, no," Jean admitted. "I suppose I could not fool Monsieur Ogilvie."

"Angus Ogilvie knew precisely what you were thinking," Able said. "Belay the circumlocution, Jean."

Jean laughed. "Able, it is my duty as a French officer and a prisoner of war to confuse and confound the enemy."

"For heaven's sake," Meri said. "You're no enemy, friend. Tell us what you know."

Trust Meri to cut directly to the chase. "I echo Meri's sentiments," he said. "Enlighten us, Jean."

"I saw many small invasion craft. I counted some three hundred vessels." He walked to the window and looked out, hands in his pockets and rocking back and forth on his heels as he used to do.

"Did you happen to get to Cádiz?" Able asked, almost certain where this was going now. "Did you locate Claude Pascal?"

His question startled Jean, whose face grew grim. "Captain Ogilvie told me where to find him." He glanced at Meridee. "This isn't a subject for a lady."

"You underestimate my capacity for vengeance," Able's lady said. He watched her face grow grim, too, and knew she was thinking of her own ill usage by Claude Pascal's goons sent to disrupt Portsmouth's factories and war effort. "I had dealings with Pascal's men. They tried to work mischief on me and drown me."

Jean sat beside her and took her hand. "I was thinking of that and other miscellaneous bits of mayhem when I called him out, made certain he knew he was facing Jean Hubert in that dark alley, and ended his spying career."

Meridee patted her heart. "Thank you."

"My pleasure." He sat back and regarded Able for a moment, as if wondering how much to say.

"Get on with it," Able said. "You have news."

"I do. I returned first to Admiralty to deliver it. You will know more soon," he said.

"I will know more now," Able said firmly. "What is it?"

"Here is what I learned in Cádiz. The combined fleets of Spain and France sailed for the Caribbean two weeks ago," Jean told them. He looked around to make sure no one else listened. He saw Ben and lowered his voice. "It was the last bit of news I wrested from Claude Pascal. Napoleon's plan is for Admiral Nelson and his fleet to follow the combined fleets, which will evade him, then sail into the English Channel while the Royal Navy is chasing will-of-the-wisps in the Caribbean."

Able let out a long, slow whistle that caught Ben's interest. His little son left the blocks and climbed into Meri's lap. She cuddled him close, her eyes full of worry.

"I imagine Admiralty was astounded at your information," Able managed to say.

"I doubt they would have believed a word if Captain Rose of Trinity House hadn't been beside me," Jean said candidly. "They sent a fast corvette after Admiral Nelson. Lord Barham is making plans for the blockade on the French coastline to draw back closer to the Dover Straits, you Englishmen's most vulnerable spot."

"Lord Barham? I thought there was no First Lord right now," Able said. "You know more than I do."

"A rare occurrence, I have no doubt," Jean said dryly. "Lord Barham – I believe he was Sir Charles Middleton – has the unenviable task of rounding up all ships at sea, and forestalling an invasion."

Able glanced at Meri, and saw her hand at her throat. "No fears, my love. You're safe."

She didn't answer.

"We always knew it could happen," he reminded her. She nodded.

"Napoleon thinks to land troops, with Nelson far away in the Caribbean," Able said to Jean. "I have no doubt I will receive official papers soon," Able said, after a glance at his wife.

"Sooner than you know," Jean said softly. He clapped his hands on his thighs and stood up again, as if sitting was too tame after such revelations. "And here I am, but not to stay."

"Oh, but…" Meri began.

"I believe I will escape again to France."

"Of your own free will and choice?" Able asked, knowing the answer and already missing Jean Hubert's casual association.

"Who of us does not dance to Napoleon's tune?" the Frenchman asked. "It appears that Trinity House has turned me into a spy."

"Any regrets? I know you love La Belle France," Able said.

"My, er, recent spontaneous holiday in France showed me a nation I do not know," he said simply. "I will cast my lot with England, at least until sanity returns to my native land." He shook his head. "If it ever does."

"I thank you," Able said.

Jean kissed Meri's cheek. "Perhaps when this war is over, I will show up and ask to teach here again." He took an envelope from inside his coat. "Here it is. Headmaster gave me this for you. It was delivered to him this evening during dinner."

Able knew what it was. He didn't want to touch the thing, but Jean held it out and he had no choice. Able noted the letterhead, the simple but all-powerful word: Admiralty.

"It begins," he said to no one in particular. He looked at his wife who took it from his hand, slit it open using a knitting needle, and handed it back, her face so calm. What could he do but pull out the letter and read it?

"'You are hereby requested and required to return to the Fleet,'" he read, wondering if his half-hearted attempt at a neutral voice betrayed his utter dislike of leaving his wife and students. "That is succinct enough," he said, trying to joke.

"Read it all," Meri said.

He did in a blink and smiled, thinking that Sir B still attended to his career. "It seems that Captain Sir Belvedere St. Anthony continues to grease my skids, Meri," he said when he could speak. "This could be worse." She was standing beside him now, leaning against his shoulder, right where he wanted her. "Look here. They could have told me to report with all possible speed to a designated frigate or ship of the line." He pointed further down the page. "It looks like Smitty and I are to be given that assignment to the *Jolly Roger*, just as Sir B wanted in his will. We're off for Admiralty House ourselves, my love."

He read down the page slowly like normal folk, savoring his new duty, because somewhere in his heart, despite the pleasure of home and school, the sea still beckoned. "We are to report to Admiralty as soon as possible, accompanied by Captain Rose, warden of Trinity House, for our assignment."

Meridee leaned harder and he touched her hand on his shoulder. "This is far better than being sent to blockade duty, or on a prisoner convoy to New South Wales."

"It's even less safe," she said. Able knew her tears would come later.

"Time will tell."

"Adieu to you both," Jean said. "God knows when or how we will meet again, but I have faith in that, if in little else."

Chapter Nine

A ll possible speed was the next day after luncheon, spurred on by Headmaster Croker. Over their breakfast toast and poached eggs, Mrs. Perry handed Able a note from across the street. Even she seemed subdued, after a look around the breakfast table showed no Jean Hubert in evidence.

"I may have been a little rough on the man," Mrs. Perry admitted.

"He had to leave right away," Able said.

"He couldn't even stay for breakfast?"

"Mrs. Perry, he has duties we cannot discuss," Meri said, as kindly as she could.

Mrs. Perry's eyes filled with tears. Apparently everyone loves a rascal. The housekeeper and cook shook her head and left the room, muttering to herself.

"Meri, it appears that I have been summoned to Headmaster Croker's chambers immediately," he said, happy to change the subject.

"Gor, master, what did you *do*?" Nick teased.

Able smiled, even as he noticed how wide Smitty's eyes grew. He and Nick had arrived at a pleasant camaraderie outside of the walls of St. Brendan's, where students toed the line. *Maybe someday you will see us as the humans we are, Smitty*, he thought, as he folded the note and stood up. He kissed Meri, always a pleasure, even with her mouth full of jam. Or maybe especially with her mouth full of jam. He did like strawberries. He didn't think the boys noticed that he ran his tongue inside her mouth, although Meri pinked up considerably.

"Never fear, Smitty," he said as he licked jam off his lips. "The most frightening thing I ever did was run away from the Dumfries workhouse.

I believe we three have all been that desperate." He tapped the note. "I'd better hurry off how?"

"Roundly now!" both boys chimed in. Even Smitty smiled. "Come over at your usual time, my dears," he said. And why not call them his dears? They were infinitely valuable to him, these workhouse boys.

Bertram, the headmaster's evil butler, ushered him into Thaddeus Croker's inner sanctum with the admonition "not t'wear out t'master."

"Master Croker sent me a note requesting my presence," Able said, wishing that he didn't feel like a workhouse lad every time the butler addressed him. The man guarded Thaddeus Croker like the three-headed hound of the underworld. Still, Able felt a pang of his own. Thaddeus had never recovered fully from last year's bout with the mumps, or maybe it was something else. Perhaps the headmaster required an over-attentive butler.

Thaddeus looked well enough, standing there and warming his hands at the fireplace. He pointed to a comfortable chair.

Able sat. "Your butler never suffers fools gladly," he commented.

"Bertram is tenacious," Thaddeus said, sounding cheerful about the matter.

"I am to report to Admiralty House as soon as possible, accompanied by Smitty and Captain Rose of Trinity House," Able said, not waiting for Thaddeus to explain *his* reason for the early-morning summons. "There it is, plus the agreement to use a St. Brendan crew in a ship-to-shore messaging capacity, just as Sir B wanted."

"I can't think of a better use of your skills and your pupils' needs," Thaddeus said. "It's finally come to national emergency. We will continue to prove our worth here at St. Brendan's."

"Aye, sir."

Thaddeus looked at the flames. "I only wish Sir B could have lived a little longer, to know that his plans have been accepted."

"I think he knows somehow." Able had no trouble with that confidence, considering the cacophony in his head as his irritating cranial cohorts practically hooted with delight and commented in various languages that of course Sir B knew what was going on. Able was surprised Thaddeus couldn't hear them.

"For a skeptical man of science, you have an unusual fondness for the divine, Master Six," Thaddeus said, sounding at least half in jest.

If you only knew, Able thought, and forced himself not to smile. *My brilliant pests are hardly divine.* A little nod would do. "Now, sir, what would you ask of me?" He tapped the note again.

"A replacement, if you please," Thaddeus said. "I gather that you will be in and out of Portsmouth, as demands of the service require. We need a substitute willing to take up the slack, as you would say. D'ye have anyone in mind?"

"I do, actually." He did, oh, he did. "I know just the man."

"Do tell."

Able had thought the matter through earlier while he was shaving, a boring activity enlivened now because Ben liked to watch and smear shaving soap on his face, too. That led to tears the first time, but Ben quickly learned to keep soap from his eyes. Able prudently kept his razor in Meri's drawer, hidden beneath her underthings.

The difficulty lay in locating Sailing Master Harry Ferrier, a Yorkshireman who had taken to the sea after the death of his father many years ago. At the tender age of sixteen he had fought in the second Battle of Cape Finisterre aboard the *HMS Weazel.* When a French cruiser escaped into the Atlantic, the *Weazel* was directed to alert Jamaica Station of other French warships on their way.

There was no time for rational thought in that pounding voyage across the Atlantic to Jamaica. The sailing master assumed command when the captain of the sloop died, and Harry Ferrier became sailing master even younger than Able Six. Such was war. In Ferrier's case, a subsequent battle near Jamaica had meant the destruction of a French fleet and salvage money in everyone's pockets, even a poor lad's. Ferrier's career was distinguished, but he was not a man to noise it about. He had retired a few years ago, living comfortably, Able assumed, on his prize money. Able thought he could find him. Whether Ferrier would hear him out remained the question.

He told all this to Headmaster Croker, who nodded. "I'll keep your lads busy in the classroom for a week or so. Go find that man." He chuckled. "Tell him we can pay him the grand sum of thirty-five pounds to fill in for you between now and the end of this year."

"That'll tempt a retired master," Able said with a smile of his own. "May I promise him sumptuous quarters here at St. Brendan's? Dancing girls in skimpy garb?"

"Certainly."

They both laughed at that. "Start thinking of our Jolly Roger as the *HMS Mercury*," Thaddeus said. "Admiralty has informed me that we may rename her. We'll have a quiet ceremony at the *Jolly Roger's* slip by Gunwharf."

Able breathed a deep lungful of low-tide effluvia as he stood on the steps of St. Brendan's and looked up at his home across the street. Thaddeus had given him permission to take Smitty along on this quick trip to Trinity House, and then Admiralty, all in one week or less, because duty called in the classroom. He wanted to know this lad better, who was going to be his second-in-command aboard the *Mercury*.

Thaddeus had assured him that Captain Rose was already waiting for him at Trinity House, which meant leaving immediately. He told Meri all this in the pantry, where he had found her counting jars of this and that.

"My love, until this national emergency passes, I'll be in and out at all hours and doing strange duty," he began.

She stopped him with a kiss, and another one. "I know," she said. "I know. Just remember where you live and whose bed you're most comfortable in."

"No fears there," he assured her.

"You should know something else," she began, after looking to make sure the pantry door was shut.

"There is a sturdy cot in here someplace where I can have you now? A blanket at least?" he teased. "I have to leave right away."

"Oh, you! No, it is this: Nick is feeling downcast because he has no role in events taking Smitty and you away."

"No fears there either." He took a deep breath, not certain what her reaction would be to his additional news. "As we speak, Headmaster Croker is arranging for a post chaise tomorrow to whisk our Bonfort boy to Plymouth and the counting house of Carter and Brustein."

"Whatever for?" she asked.

"He'll have a signed directive from Admiralty for David Brustein to give us the direction of Sailing Master Harry Ferrier. All we know is that Master Ferrier banks there. Anything else is privileged information."

"Nick is so young. All by himself?"

Able knew Meri would question it. Nick *was* young.

"We are all subject to the requirements of the fleet," Able reminded her. "I know Nick will succeed. When he gets Master Ferrier's direction, he will have additional orders to take the information to the harbormaster and forward it to me via coastal semaphore."

"My goodness, the semaphore? We do live in a modern age, don't we?"

"We do." In mere seconds he reviewed a calculus class with Jamie MacGregor, now serving in the Pacific, and the late Jan Yarmouth, dead and buried at sea, where his two promising lads had speculated on interplanetary travel and something to do with atoms. Modern age, indeed.

"And?" she prompted.

"Smitty and I will locate Master Ferrier and convince him that he wants to get into harness again, earn a pittance, live in a drafty monastery and teach my classes when I cannot."

"How can he resist?" she teased, then, "Durable, someone can open this door at any moment. Leave my buttons alone."

"But there they are, and you know how I feel about your bosom," he protested, but did as she said and rebuttoned her bodice. "I'll be back in a week, when I will hopefully be Able again."

"You are always able," she said. "Oh! *That* Able."

And so he was smiling when two post chaises pulled up to his home. Ben was unhappy in the extreme when his father ushered Smitty inside the vehicle then went in after him. He demanded his mother put him down, was ignored, and pouted. When Nick Bonfort, serious of face and dressed in his best St. Brendan's uniform, climbed into the second post chaise, Ben couldn't help his tears. His two favorite champions were leaving him alone with the ladies and he took it hard.

That left a crying son and Able's beloved Meridee on the steps, a handkerchief to her eyes, too, but waving them away with kisses. Able blew her a kiss and cheered up considerably to see Ezekiel Bartleby, box in hand, heading toward his house. Amazing how the old tar-turned-baker always seemed to know when something was afoot. Able thought there might be rout cakes in the box to cheer Meri.

It was two boxes. The postilion obligingly stopped and instructed the post boy to commandeer one, which ended up inside with Able and Smitty, after several cakes were handed to post boy and postilion. Ezekiel's cheery, "I'll keep an eye on'um," reassured Able as little else could have. Never more than now did he appreciate the camaraderie of the fleet.

"Urgent business?" the postilion asked.

"Time matters," was all Able said. "Since we can't bend time yet, we have to obey the clock."

Chapter Ten

They ate the rout cakes, and whatever else they could grab during brief stops to change horses, and made the trip to London in six hours, long enough for Able to learn more about Smitty and to encourage the lad to acquire a last name.

Smitty refused to consider his real name of St. Anthony. "He did me mum a wicked turn," Smitty said and folded his arms, daring Able to change his mind.

"Aye, he did," Able said, understanding this young man, understanding wicked men and preyed-upon women. Maybe this was a good moment to sound out his feelings for Sir B. He proceeded cautiously. "The name of St. Anthony may be anathema to you, but to those of us who really know Sir Belvedere St. Anthony, it is not."

"He could have helped me years sooner than he did," Smitty said.

"I cannot argue that," Able agreed. "There are times when I know I do not measure up to what my own conduct should be. Let me give you one example."

With no preamble, he told Smitty exactly what had happened to his own mother, as far as he knew, done in by a wicked Spaniard named the Count of Quintanar. He saw the shock and surprise on Smitty's face, when he said, "I am quite prepared to hate that Spaniard until I die. I understand your feelings because I share them." He took a cautious step. "There is one difference, which you must own."

"Maybe," Smitty said. "Sir."

"Sir B didn't know of your existence until his brother finally blurted it out."

"He could have acted once he knew!"

"He could have. Let us acknowledge, as Lady St. Anthony said, that Sir B was human."

Smitty considered the matter. "I will if you will, sir," he said in a low voice. "Suppose if you actually meet your father?"

"The possibility is remote," Able hedged, then acknowledged the obvious. "You are asking why you should be forgiving and I should not?"

"Aye, sir."

"That's fair, Smitty," he said, even though he didn't want to. It didn't help that his cranial spectators seemed to be applauding Smitty. "You win. We can both agree that we had mothers who cared. Yours fed you when she had nothing for herself. Mine could have left me in the back alley to die with her."

Smitty understood. "Still, how could men treat women so?" He turned away, trying to isolate himself in the small space of a post chaise.

"As long as *we* never treat them ill, lad, we have victory of sorts." Able touched Smitty's shoulder and met with no resistance. Wordless, Able put his arm around Smitty. They sat close together as the horses ate up the miles toward London.

"I have never regretted my own odd name," Able said, continuing where he had left off, as if the two of them had not shown themselves to be human and vulnerable like the other Gunwharf Rats. "Choose another name besides St. Anthony. Something tells me you will go far in the fleet. You need two names. What'll it be, lad?"

"I've been Smitty a long while and I like it, master."

"It suits you," Able agreed. "How about this? Brendan for our school, and Smith for your surname? Smitty is a logical nickname."

Smitty considered the matter and nodded, serious as ever. "I like it."

"We'll enter that name with the Navy Board," Able said. "Remember to say Brendan to yourself now and then, you know, so you don't forget."

The boy grinned. "Or better yet, how about Gunwharf? Or would the Board prefer Rat?"

Delighted at finding quick wit where he had not expected it, Able laughed. Smitty joined in. It was the first time Able had ever heard the boy laugh with such ease and it warmed his heart. "Stick with Brendan, you Rat," he said when he could talk, which only set Smitty off again.

Able considered one thing more. "When we get to Trinity House, I have something to show you." He wondered briefly at his own trepidation, him, a grown man. "It's a portrait that has given me food for thought."

"I would think you have plenty of food for thought already," Smitty said, with a small, lurking smile that told Able something had happened between the two of them. He sensed their relationship changing from teacher and student, to colleagues.

"I have ample food for thought, and it's a burden at times. I'd rather be like everyone else, truth be told," he said.

"Thank'ee, sir," Smitty said. "We know you are a genius, all of us Gunwharf Rats, but we wouldn't be here without your particular burden. Thank'ee from all of us."

Able leaned back, at ease with Smitty, probably for the first time. "D'ye mind my putting you on the spot as my sailing master, when I am relegated to captain of the…the *Mercury*? I know it is what Sir B stipulated in his will, but if you'd rather not…"

"I can do it," was Smitty's quiet reply. "Could it be Sir B's way of making amends with me, now that I think of it?"

"I doubt it not."

The sun was moving deep across the afternoon sky when the post chaise pulled up in front of Trinity House. Sutton, the one-legged doorman, must have been alerted to watch for them. Able remembered earlier visits to Trinity House, when Sutton was of all men most suspicious.

There was no mistaking the disappointment on the doorman's face. Able thought he understood; he felt the same way. "Sutton, are you languishing because my better half – certainly the prettier one – did not make the journey?" Able asked, by way of greeting.

Sutton was made of stronger stuff. "Nay, Master Six, nay," he said, then reconsidered. "Well, a little. Even a one-legged tar gets the dismals seeing mostly wind-scoured faces and squinty eyes. Your lady is a welcome antidote."

Wind-scoured faces and squinty eyes, the Royal Navy badge of office. Trust a former deep-water seaman to notice. "Aye, she can cure most ills, but sometimes duty calls at home."

The doorman sighed as he held out his hands for boat cloaks and lids. "I'll take ye to Captain Rose."

Trinity's newest warden waited for them at the top of the elegant branching staircase. Able glanced at Smitty, amused to see the look of wonder on his face, as if he could not fathom why a workhouse boy stood in such a place. He leaned closer to Smitty. "Until quite recently, I had the same look on my face, lad. Let's go upstairs and see what the good man has for us."

The good man had advice. After introductions, he asked them into his office, even as he swung his boat cloak around his shoulders. "Let me explain. We Brothers" – he gave a deferential nod to Able – "are keeping our oar in the water, when it comes to St. Brendan's. The Sea Lords have an urgent request for you already, you and the soon-to-be-named *Mercury.*" He gave Able a longer glance. "You, Master Six, and your mentor Sir B – God rest him – are casting a long shadow. Since the Admiralty came calling, I thought you might like a little moral support. I'll walk you over. We'll sup here when you're done."

God bless the man, but he understood. Able heard faint clapping inside his skull. "Aye, sir, we do appreciate your interest," he said. "This is still a strange environment for Gunwharf Rats."

Funny how such a rarefied atmosphere at both Trinity House and Admiralty a few blocks away turned Smitty – Brendan Smith – into a boy again, and not the more hardened thug who had the capacity to frighten the younger class at St. Brendan's. Able could not deny his own trepidation at passing through the three-columned entrance with awe. *What am I doing here?* he asked himself, and received all kinds of answers from the assorted brilliant minds inside his skull that obviously had nothing better to do.

A nod to the porter sitting behind a tall desk sent an escort out to direct them to, as it turned out, the chamber of Admiral James Gambier, Admiralty Lord Commissioner.

"Give him a good bow," Able whispered to Smitty, as he managed his own bow to such a powerful man.

Smitty did not hesitate. Luckily, his head was still down, so he missed the lurking smile on Dismal Jimmy's face. A veteran of all seven seas and their attendant woes, Admiral Gambier had seen it all, including awkward youths, some of whom commanded warships now.

"Hector, how good to see you again. Master Able Six? I have heard much of you. Very well, you three, let us never stand on too much ceremony. Sit sit."

They sat sat promptly, Smitty obviously in awe of the room, Captain Rose at home there, and Able somewhere in between. The lord commissioner wasted not a moment. He leaned forward, giving them the eye that had terrified a generation of seafaring men. "I have need of your services right now, bearing messages to and from the blockade. Can ye do it in a yacht? I hear it's a fair specimen."

"Aye, sir," Able said promptly. "We've only sailed beyond the Isle of Wight a time or two, but she's seaworthy and raring for more."

"Have you other capable lads like this one, Master Six?"

"Aye, sir," he said again. "Brendan Smith here will be my sailing master. We at St. Brendan's have a group of Gunwharf Rats that acquitted themselves well in our dealings with the prison hulks. They're rough and ready."

Gambier nodded. He eyed Smitty for a moment. Smitty sat straighter in his chair and returned the gaze, never flinching. "Pain of death," Gambier said slowly, enunciating each word.

"Aye, sir," Smitty said with no pause and no fear. He understood what was about to happen.

"I, as well, Admiral," Able said, when the glance swung to him.

The lord commissioner leaned back. "We have it on good authority from Admiral Calder, Channel Fleet commanding, that the combined fleet of France and Spain are lurking about Ferrol and off Cape Finisterre."

He looked at the map of Europe and Smitty followed his gaze. Able knew the map inside his head and stared at the ceiling instead, plainly seeing Finisterre jutting out from Spain's far western reach. Finisterre. Lands' end, where currents were tricky and many a good ship had been driven to death on the rocky shore.

"Napoleon had counted on Villeneuve leading our Nelson on a merry dance in the Caribbean, and leaving him behind, but it didn't work," Captain Rose added. "Sources tell us that the enemy raced back just ahead of Nelson and is contemplating a bolt north from Finisterre. His orders seem to involve driving the Channel Fleet away and protecting those invasion boats at Boulogne. Boney wants to cross the Channel in the worst way and he is getting impatient."

Admiral Gambier directed his attention to Captain Rose. "So your agents have informed us."

Able nodded. It was what he had suspected, too. Gambier noticed and turned toward him. "What would you do, Master Six, were you in my shoes?"

"Gather in more blockaders and send them to reinforce Admiral Calder, sir," he said promptly. "A wall of ship and sail will thwart those designs for a crossing and bottle up the Combined Fleet in Cadiz yet again, if done right."

"Precisely. Our sources suggest that Villeneuve is unloading upwards of a thousand ailing sailors all along the Spanish coast, following his Caribbean adventure. Beautiful islands, terrible diseases. And, Master Six?"

"Villeneuve will be understrength, sir, "Able said promptly. "He is a prudent man, perhaps too prudent to make much of an effort at Finisterre, if Admiral Calder is bold enough."

"If and if again." Gambier took a canvas bag from the corner of his desk and handed it to Able. "You are to deliver this message to Admiral Calder blockading France off Rochefort, ordering him to move south quickly to Finisterre and battle."

Able's hands closed on the bag, already tarred and weighted, should it be necessary to throw it overboard. He had seen Sir B, Captain Hallowell and other captains hold such bags. Now it was his turn, as commander of the *Mercury*. He breathed deep of the tar and appreciated silence from his cranial cohorts. He didn't need them. This was his moment.

"How soon, you are wondering? Master Six, you have short leeway. If you sail in five days for Rochefort, will that be enough time to see the *Mercury* victualled and shipshape?"

The *Mercury* was ready now. So were the Rats. He still needed to locate Harry Ferrier, however, to cover his classes in seamanship. Five days, and he didn't even know where Master Ferrier lived. He also knew there was only one answer.

"Aye, Admiral. We sail in five days for Rochefort, sooner if we can. After that, sir?"

"Return to your classroom. You will be subject to the requirements of the service, as ordered," Gambier said. He parceled out a smile then, did Dismal Jimmy, enthusiastic Christian who bored many an unrepentant crew with sermons of hellfire and damnation. "I suspect you will be more out of port than in, so find a suitable substitute at St. Brendan's for yourself."

"I have one in mind, Admiral, provided I can locate him."

There was nothing more to say. The three of them made their bows – Smitty's second time was an improvement on the first – and hurried back to Trinity House for dinner with the available Brothers, and the offer of beds for the night.

Able overruled the offer of lodging, as much as he wanted to stay. The upstairs chambers were comfortable, but time was wasting. Five days, after all, and so much to do. He had asked the postilion earlier to be ready for a return journey. A visit to the kitchen saw the man and his post boy eating to the bursting point and flirting with the scullery maid and cook. "Thirty minutes," was all Able needed to say.

With Captain Rose's permission after a quick meal, Able took Smitty up another flight of stairs to a little-used storeroom. He opened the door and held the lamp high over the gilt-framed portrait. "Here he is, Smitty, my father the enemy. Just as I told you."

"Good God," Smitty said, startled. He glanced at Able, and back at the likeness that watched them both under heavy-lidded, familiar eyes.

"His name is Francisco Jesus Domingo y Guzman, Conde de Quintanar," Able said. "You remember Captain Ogilvie, do you not?"

"Aye, sir. He gives me the willies. 'E just pops up here and there."

Well put, Able thought, amused. "This is the chap he saw in Cádiz by the *Santísima Trinidad*."

"Take the portrait with you."

Captain Rose stood in the doorway, quiet and composed, the perfect Elder Brother to lead Trinity House through a war. "If you meet the man in the frame…well, you will know what to do. He is an enemy to England."

Would he know? Small portrait in hand, Able went downstairs to see the aforementioned Captain Ogilvie standing beside the branching stairwell.

As usual, Angus Ogilvie wasted not a moment. "Stay here, boy," he ordered Smitty, and took Able by the arm into a darker corner. Come to think of it, Ogilvie flourished in dark corners.

"I need to leave n…"

"I know, I know. Give me a moment."

Able waited. Ogilvie looked around and moved closer. "Lord Gambier gave me orders, too, the kind that don't come with documents. You are to inform me when you sail with dispatches for the Channel Fleet."

"Why, sir?"

Ogilvie made an impatient gesture. "Sometimes I might need to accompany you and slip ashore. Whether this is the right time or not…" He shrugged. "Circumstance will dictate."

Able nodded. He was not surprised. "Where will I send such a notice?"

Ogilvie grinned at him. "Send a message to Ezekiel Bartleby at the bakery. He has a spare room and I do love doughnuts."

Able couldn't help his laughter. *Serve you right if you get too fat to fit into a jolly boat*, he thought. "Aye, sir."

He turned to go, but Ogilvie stopped him. "And Lady St. Anthony? How is she faring?"

"As well as can be."

Ogilvie surprised him then. His voice turned surprisingly tender, considering that the man probably hadn't a sympathetic bone in his body. "She was dealt a poor hand, but she knew that going in." He released Able's arm. "She played it well."

"She did," Able agreed. "I must go. Are you coming with us to Portsmouth?"

"Not now. I have work to do here," Ogilvie said. He backed into the shadows, then came forward again. "How about it, laddie? Will *you* know what to do if you come face to face with the Spaniard in the frame?"

Chapter Eleven

"And that was my trip, Meri. Hector Rose told me I would know what to do, should I meet my father. Our beloved friend Captain Ogilvie didn't sound so certain."

"Oh, him," Meridee said. She knew her husband was precisely where she wanted *him*, and she snuggled close, thinking of the months ahead when he would likely not be so available. She could also tell that Able had no idea what he would do. Her decisive genius sometimes floundered, and she loved him all the more for it.

She listened for more conversation, but he was done for the night, worn out with travel and trying to sleep in a post chaise. She heard deep breathing beside her, his hand relaxed and heavy on her hip now.

She turned over to face him. They hadn't bothered to close the draperies, so she admired him, envying his long eyelashes. As she watched, his dear face grew slack, making him look older than his twenty-nine years. She wondered how Nick Bonfort was faring in Plymouth at Carter and Brustein, with his note asking the whereabouts of Harry Ferrier. Her heart told her Nick was too young for such an assignment, but her head overruled her heart. Nick's service was needed by his country. How was a lad to train for the fleet if he was coddled? And hadn't Able sent him off with a bit of advice? "Initiative, my boy, initiative."

Meridee woke up before Able stirred, and before Ben started talking to himself in the next chamber. Ben had begun that when he started speaking in full sentences at age seven months. At first he seemed to play with words, rhyming them and giggling to himself, trying out language and finding it to his liking. Now he had graduated to what sounded like answers to questions posed by…someone. She didn't want to know who that someone was, but she was heartily tired of Greek mathematicians.

She cinched her robe tight and went downstairs, happy to admire the neatness and comfort all around. She had made a good, calm home for her man, who had awakened her an hour or so ago by nuzzling her neck and refreshing her thoroughly, before returning to deeper slumber. Goodness what a lover.

She stood at the window, looking down at St. Brendan's, thinking of the students and teachers. Soon enough, Grace St. Anthony née Croker would arrive by coach to begin her day teaching lower grade mathematics, and whatever odd assortment of subjects her agile brain agreed to. Lately, Meridee's heart went out to her dear friend as she paused at the top step each morning and gave herself a little shake, before squaring her shoulders and entering.

Nothing was worse in Meridee's mind than a good man gone. St. Brendan's had already lost students to the war, first among them Jan Yarmouth, whose death had devastated her husband. She knew Able could have easily died in the takeover of the prisoner of war hulk last year. She yearned for him to stay safe at school and let others do the adventuring and fighting, but she had no voice in the decisions of men and war.

She also could not overlook Able's occasional restlessness that took him to the edge of the seawall to stand there and watch the harbor, as if wishing to join the increasing number of warships sailing to war. She had confided to him her inadequacy to do for him what such a man of blinding intelligence probably craved. He had turned serious and assured her she was precisely what a man like him required. "You make my world bearable by being here and building a home of order for us both," he told her once, and she believed him. So far, the sea was a reasonable mistress in her demands.

"This is the life I chose," Meridee said softly as she heard steps behind her and turned to see her two favorite men eyeing her. She kissed them both. "Ben, are you starving?"

"Gut foundered," he assured her.

She rolled her eyes at his cant, but what could a mother do, when her son listened to Gunwharf Rats? And like his father, never seemed to forget anything? "Put on your clothes, wash your face, and don't wake up Smitty. He's tired," she said. A small pat to his rump sent him back upstairs.

He paused halfway up. "Nick isn't back, too?" he asked.

She shook her head. "Soon, I am certain. Scat now."

Able received a more extensive cuddle in the sitting room then plopped down with her in his favorite chair, hairy legs and all, nightshirt thigh-high.

"You are a disgrace to the service," she said, after he rubbed her cheek with his whiskers.

"You didn't mention that an hour and eighteen minutes ago," he said.

"You were upstairs in my bed. Stop now. Anyone could wander in."

He smiled and did as she said, then grew serious. "No word from Nick?"

"None. Not even a message from the harbormaster or the signaling crew," she said. "We should have had an address for Master Ferrier by now, shouldn't we?"

"I would have hoped so." He leaned back and pulled her closer. "Mrs. Six, you are a bountiful bundle."

"Do be serious."

"Never more so." He tugged at the sash on her robe. "We'll give Nick another day before we start to worry. There is plenty to do, meantime. Mrs. Six, you're not wearing anything under this robe!"

"Able, what will I do with you?"

"You're the one who married a sailor, and we do have a reputation to maintain." He tried to retie the sash, but the intricacy eluded him. She tied it neatly. "Beyond Smitty, plan on four more lads for dinner tonight. You'll be feeding the *Jolly Roger*'s crew." He touched his head to hers and lowered his voice. "We sale in five days toward France. No frowns, please. We're delivering a message to Admiral Calder, cruising off Rochefort."

She couldn't frown. He looked so delighted. "Is it now where I forget you just told me an Admiralty secret?"

"Aye, miss. No comment to anyone. That's to be the *Mercury*'s assignment: delivering messages, subject to the requirements of the service and the exigencies of war."

She rested her head against his chest, and his arms went tight around her.

She did have news for him, forgotten in the general tumult of his return. "I forgot to tell you. We are to assemble at the *Jolly Roger*'s slip for a re-christening at four bells in the forenoon watch." She prodded his chest. "I never can remember…"

He stood up, taking her with him. "Ten of the clock, my love." He sniffed the air. "And do I smell profiteroles?"

"You do. Mrs. Perry loves your weather-worn carcass."

"She still terrifies me. We'll eat and go to St. Brendan for early class. Would you and Ben like to walk with us to the Gunwharf later?"

"And Mrs. Perry. This is her war, too."

"Our war," he said softly. "We all pay the price."

At four bells in the forenoon watch, Lady St. Anthony, dressed in black but with a defiant yellow and red bow at her throat, took hold of a champagne bottle on a rope. She declared in a firm voice, "Dear old *Jolly Roger*, I re-christen you *Mercury*, in the service of His Majesty King George. May you swiftly sail in courage and faith and never hesitate to lay yourself alongside the enemy. Bless your able crew."

Grace swung the bottle on the rope and it shattered against the *Mercury*. She stood in silence a moment, her head bowed, as they all did, thinking of Sir B. Meridee raised her head to watch Grace's shoulders begin to shake as she covered her face.

Able tensed beside her and whispered, "Go to her, Meri."

Meridee took a step closer then stopped, holding her breath to see Captain Ogilvie reach Grace St. Anthony when she started to sag. He picked her up as if she weighed nothing and held her close. Grace turned her face into his shoulder and cried.

"No," she whispered back to Able. "Angus has the matter well in hand."

"How can…he doesn't…"

"Yes, he can," Meridee said. "What do you know about his first wife?"

"Nothing. I never pry."

"Maybe you should. Let's let Captain Ogilvie deal with our kind friend."

Able gave her that questioning look she was familiar with, when some action of mere mortals baffled him. *See there, Euclid*, she thought. *You don't know everything*. To her stunned amazement, Meridee felt the distinct snap of forefinger and thumb against her temple. She thought it prudent to say nothing, especially since Able had moved away and was speaking to his students. She looked around, saw no one close to administer such a rebuke, and blamed Euclid. Ben smiled up at her.

Her heart full, she watched Captain Ogilvie speak softly to Grace, then set her down. Grace leaned against him a moment, then nodded at something he said, which made her smile. The two of them joined her brother, St. Brendan's headmaster, and the sadness seemed to smooth away. Meridee resolved not to question too many things.

Looking thoughtful and less argumentative than usual, Captain Ogilvie joined them for dinner, along with four boys from St. Brendan's and Smitty, who lived here. She knew three of them, Tots and Whitticombe, upper level boys who more often than not crewed the newly named *Mercury* with Smitty and her husband. But oh, that third boy.

She held out her arms for Davey Ten. He hesitated a moment – maybe he was considering if an apprentice pharmacist mate should maintain some dignity – then let her envelope him in a hug with the added indignity of a kiss on the head.

She glanced at Tots and Whitticombe, hoping they wouldn't say something rude to Davey Ten because she kissed him. What she saw made her let go of Davy, march over to them and kiss their heads, too.

"Gor, Mrs. Six, no one's ever done that before," Tots said, but he didn't seem unhappy.

"Become accustomed to it, if you show up here for dinner often," she said, as Able blew *her* a kiss.

He ushered the fourth lad closer, someone small with a gleam in his eye and good cheer all over his face. "This fellow is Avon March and he comes highly recommended by Lady St. Anthony. Give a little bow, Avon."

Avon bowed and she curtsied, which made Ben chortle and turn in circles. She grabbed her son and kissed him, too. "Avon, were you lucky enough to be named for a river?"

"Aye, miss," he replied. "They found me by the Avon in March, eleven years ago."

A year ago, such an artless comment would have sent Meridee to another room in tears. "At least they didn't name you Daffodil. I know daffodils bloom beside the Avon in March. Welcome to our home. Let's eat."

"Well done, Mrs. Six," Captain Ogilvie said as Able ushered the boys into the dining room.

She was used to his sarcasm, but he seemed to mean it. "I'm learning, too," she told him. "St. Brendan's teaches strange lessons, doesn't it?" She touched his arm. "Thank you for looking after Grace."

He nodded, and she thought she saw a blush rising up from his collar. She said something then, blurted it out, then almost immediately wanted to take it back. "You miss your wife," she said. *What did I just do?* she asked herself in horror.

"I do, Mrs. Six," he replied, with no anger in his voice, and none of the disdain she remembered from other visits. "Never more than when I am in your house, or …" He stopped. "Let us leave it at that. There is a war on and we are busy men."

They sat down to dinner. The boys waited, eyes on her, except for Avon, who didn't know the routine. She looked at Able, who gave her a nod. "How about you, my dear lady?"

She bowed her head, peeking up once to see that Avon March was by no means slow. He bowed his head, after a quick glance around at his mates. "Gracious Lord, bless this bounty for us," she prayed. "Keep us safe on our island and bless the men who protect us on ships at sea. In our Savior's name, amen."

Startled, she looked around at a hearty "Amen" from the dining room door. Two of them, in fact.

There stood Nick Bonfort. Standing next to him was a tall man with gray hair and a slightly lowered left shoulder.

She heard a chair scrape back and knew Able was on his feet. Her husband crossed the small space and held out his hand. "Master Ferrier, this is a pleasant surprise!"

They shook hands. Still holding Able's hand, Master Ferrier nodded toward Nick, who beamed as if he had unearthed the greatest treasure in all seven seas.

"Master Six, what do you know?" Nick said. I learned I have initiative and then some!"

Chapter Twelve

"You are a welcome sight, Master Ferrier," Able said. A nod to Tots and Whitticombe sent the boys pulling up two more of the chairs that lined the wall. Another nod with two raised fingers sent Smitty into the kitchen. "And somewhat unexpected, I must add."

"You have both mentioned initiative." Master Ferrier smiled at Nick. "He is a most persuasive fellow, this Bonfort."

"Comes with the name," Able said, with a glance at Meri. "Nick convinced my wife, Meridee Bonfort, that since she wasn't using Bonfort anymore, he wanted it, because he needed a surname."

The old sailing master included Meri in his glance, turning a little since he had only one working eye, from the cloudy state of one pupil. "I suppose, madam, that this curly haired rascal will tell me that you persuaded *him* to marry *you*."

"He can try," she said. "Do sit down, sir. Wait. Let me take your cloak."

Followed by Smitty, Mrs. Perry came from the kitchen with two more plates. She saw Master Ferrier, gasped, handed the plates to Meri and threw her arms around him, nearly knocking him over. Able didn't try to hide his smile, both at the dignified man's mauling, and the open mouths of the Gunwharf Rats, who knew Mrs. Perry as a terrifying enforcer not easily given to displays of affection. He watched them relax, knowing that Mrs. Perry had just assured Master Ferrier's acceptance.

"The three of us sailed together on the *Defence*," Able explained. "Mr. Perry was ship's carpenter." Mrs. Perry returned to the kitchen for cutlery and serviettes. "Nick, an explanation is in order. All I requested was that you locate Master Ferrier's direction."

After Mrs. Perry returned with knives and forks, the bowls of food went around again to the latest arrivals.

"Master, you told me to use initiative and I did," Nick declared, as he piled on potatoes.

"Elaborate, please."

Nick's inquiring look at Master Ferrier told Able everything about his former master's future success with the Gunwharf Rats. Nick already looked to the older man for additional permission.

"Your story, Mr. Bonfort," Harry Ferrier said. "All I did was open my door to you and listen."

"I went to Carter and Brustein as you requested," Nick said eyeing his cooling dinner with a sigh. "Mr. David Brustein told me I was in luck, because Mr. Ferrier lived in Torquay. So I walked there."

"That's thirty-three miles," Able exclaimed.

"A nice man picked me up after ten miles," Nick informed them, with all his usual good-natured cheer. Nick was a hard Rat to deflate. "You see, master, you had given me enough money for lodging, meals and a return on the mail coach. What if I had spent it on conveyances to Torquay and hadn't enough to get home? And suppose Master Ferrier told me no?"

Able heard sniffles nearby. He had married such a tender woman. He leaned toward her. "Meri, think how resourceful Nick is." Her answer was another sniffle; he could comfort her later. "Carry on, Mr. Bonfort."

"I can do that, Master Six," Harry Ferrier said. "Nick is gazing at your excellent beef roast like a starving man." He nodded to Meridee. "Mrs. Six, let me compliment you on a fine table."

"We always have more later, in case someone gets the urge to nibble," she said.

Able glanced around the table to see nods of agreement. He even remembered an earlier maid from a workhouse, Jamie MacGregor's twin, who had squirreled away food, too. Now she lived a few doors down, mistress of her own household and wife of a respected Portsmouth constable. The Sixes seemed to nurture more than Gunwharf Rats.

"Very well then, Master Ferrier," he said. "If you've taken the edge off your own hunger, do continue."

"I invited him in. Standing right there in the foyer – soaking wet, I might add – Mister Bonfort carefully explained the dilemma. With that cheerful demeanor I am certain you are familiar with, he told me I wouldn't be making much money. To sweeten the pot, he assured me I'd be living in a drafty monastery, but the food was good and my country needed me. All that in practically one breath. He was a man on a mission." Ferrier looked around at the others. "Who could say no to that? Retirement is a damned bore. Here I am. Now you can do *your* duty at sea, Able, as I fill in for you here."

That was quintessential Harry Ferrier, not a man to waste words. He had one more thing to say before he returned to his dinner. "Is this your *Mercury* crew?"

"Aye, master. Smitty here is my sailing master, Tots and Whitticombe are good with sheets and sail, Davey Ten is my acting surgeon and Avon March comes highly recommended by another instructor. We will see what he can do. You already know Captain Ogilvie."

Mr. Ferrier took a leisurely glance at each face, stopping at Meridee. She reached for Able's hand under the table. "You, Mrs. Six, must be the glue that holds this crew together."

"All I do is love them," she said softly.

They sailed three days later on the *Mercury*, bound for the blockade off Rochefort, three busy days of acquainting Harry Ferrier with his duties, and Able feeling his own awe at such an exalted sailing master taking on this gaggle of workhouse lads.

"I must be honest," Ferrier said late the last night ashore, after Meridee had gone to bed, and they were drinking rum with Headmaster Croker across the street. "How does a man go from constant activity to nothing? I should never have retired, except that my eyesight isn't what it once was." He chuckled and pointed to his milky orb. "Especially in this eye."

He pulled out a slim case and put on his spectacles. He grinned his famous gallows grin that had startled many a midshipman laboring over sightings and paperwork. "Thought I'd wait to put these on until after I signed that contract for thirty-five pounds annually, plus quarters and found. A man can't be too careful."

They all laughed, even Captain Ogilvie, who had been remarkably quiet during the past few days. In fact, Ogilvie accompanied Able back across the street, after the headmaster's diabolical butler stoppered the rum bottle and gave men used to power a fishy stare of his own.

Ogilvie turned back to look at St. Brendan's. "If Bertram were my butler, I would shoot him."

Able couldn't help laughing. Perhaps he had drunk more rum than the law required, but it *was* funny. He held out his hand to Angus Ogilvie. "Good night to you, sir."

"And to you." He didn't leave. "Able, may I accompany you to the blockade?"

"We'll be crowded. The *Mercury* only has six berths."

"No matter," Ogilvie said, brushing aside any obstacles. "You'll be on hot racks anyway, with your small crew."

"True enough. I'll be acquainting my seafaring pupils with the joys of watch and watch about, so there should always be empty berths. Why now, sir, if I may ask?"

"If the occasion arises, you can set me ashore in Spain. I suspect Admiral Calder will order you to join his squadron for a while."

"Dangerous work," Able said, wondering how Headmaster Croker would appreciate the students of St. Brendan's heading into deeper trouble than mere messaging. "I'll remind you that my oldest crewmember is fourteen."

"If you can believe him. Smitty looks older."

"You were at the reading of Sir B's will. His brother Edward's by-blow would be fourteen. Why were *you* there at the reading?"

It sounded presumptuous to a man whose ears buzzed a little from overmuch rum. Even Euclid was silent, perhaps already sleeping off the rum. Still, Ogilvie's answer surprised him.

"I like Grace St. Anthony. Good night to you. You sail on the tide?"

And that was that. Able hoped Meri wasn't asleep. She wasn't. When he came into their chamber, she rose from bed, took his hand and walked him toward Ben's room. "Our son has turned into a bit of a martinet. He thought to order me about in French. I told him what I thought about that and he sobered up considerably."

Able watched their sleeping son, admiring such a complex creation from two people who loved each other. He would never tell Meri in a million years, but he stored up in his heart those wonderful moments when he had tapped on his sleeping wife's swollen belly and felt answering taps. They had developed a little code that he tried out, once Ben was born – two taps, answered by three taps, then so on through a lengthy sequence. He had sired a mathematician.

Meri didn't need to know that. "He'll always keep you on your toes," Able said.

"We'll manage. Come now, Able. We're wasting time and I know you sail on the tide."

She loved him thoroughly, and then again before anyone was awake. He hated partings as well as the next navy man. At least she was kind enough to brush the tears from his eyes.

"I don't like to be wept on," she whispered. "I do want another baby, however. You know, just a normal child this time. It might be a novelty."

How did she do it? Make him chuckle, and tear up, and go through the ecstasy of mad, slow love in an ordinary bed? He looked closer and saw her tears this time. "I did not know you when I sailed to war before," he said. "At the dock, I had watched other partings of my mates from their wives, and resolved never to do that to a woman."

"Thank goodness you changed your mind," she said, settling in, comfortable. "I trust I am strong enough for these farewells."

It remained unspoken between them, the thought that any farewell could be the final one.

The household woke at first light to the fragrance of ham, eggs, applesauce, cinnamon toast and beans from Mrs. Perry's kitchen. Avon joined them from across the street and they all tucked into a monstrous breakfast. No Rat complained. They, their master included, never forgot workhouse lessons of eating when the food was there, against a time when it was not.

After breakfast, Meri made her Rats open their duffels. She advised all of them to take more socks and smallclothes and waited until they obeyed.

"I put in enough socks and smallclothes," Able whispered in her ear. He whispered something else and she gasped.

He had never seen her blush so much. She thought a moment, this wife of his. "I could sprinkle more lilac talcum on whichever shimmy you stole."

"Not this time," he said. "It's a short voyage. I'll use it for my pillowcase and go to sleep a happy man."

Funny how the whole school decided to walk with them by the Gunwharf where the *Mercury* bobbed on the receding tide. Sailing Master Durable Six felt the wind precisely right against his cheek. Ideal. Over shorter heads, he smiled at Headmaster Croker, who shrugged and came closer.

"It was rank insubordination, but my instructors said the Gunwharf Rats walked out of class, so here we are." Thaddeus Croker appeared not even slightly unhappy about this minor mutiny.

What did surprise him about Headmaster Croker was the cane he leaned upon. "Sir, is this an old injury?" he asked, as he slowed his pace to accommodate the man.

"Something that flares up now and then," Thaddeus said. He changed the subject beyond redemption, but Able wondered.

It touched Able's heart to see others. The entire St. Brendan's kitchen staff, and look, Portsmouth's constables, headed by Walter Cornwall and his wife Betsy, were there, too, along with Royal Marines. He didn't see Captain Ogilvie, but suspected the man was already below.

With an audience, the Gunwharf Rats raised the sail on Smitty's command.

"Kiss me quick, Mrs. Six," Able said. "Ben, mind your mother." As if to leave no doubt, he added, "Ben, obéissez à votre mère." To be extra sure he added, "Obedece a tu madre."

Ezekiel Barnaby stopped him next. "We will all watch over your loved ones," he said. "Would that I could come along, too." The baker handed him a pasteboard box. "In case someone gets peckish in the next few days."

It was heavy. The baker must have stuffed in all of yesterday's leftovers and then some. "Watch over my dear ones, too," Able said.

"I already do," the former deepwater man said, "plus I left some iced rout cakes at your front door for t'missus."

Meri gave Able the sort of kiss that made him want to throw her down on the dock and have his way with her, but not before an audience. She did know how to send off a sailor, however. He took a step onto the yacht and nodded to Tots, who stood closest.

Lady St. Anthony herself, aided by Mr. Ferrier, untied the knot that held them to the dock. Mr. Ferrier tossed the line to Tots, who coiled it like an expert.

They set sail from Portsmouth into war.

Chapter Thirteen

Midsummer was the best time to sail across the English Channel. The sun was warm, the winds abundant but not overpowering. July provided days of suitable length to practice life aboard a sweet-sailing vessel with clean lines, a deep keel and impressive qualities unknown before a regular voyage. Sir B had known exactly what he wanted in a yacht. True, they had regularly sailed around Portsmouth harbor and the Isle of Wight, but the Channel was different. Sir B had built a seagoing yacht, nimble and powerful.

Predictably, as soon as the channel chop came into play, Able spotted Davey Ten kneeling by the railing, tossing up Mrs. Perry's magnificent breakfast. No one teased him. They knew better, especially when Smitty spent his own quieter time on the opposite side, feeding unwary fish. No one was about to twit Smitty over seasickness.

His brain was often a burden, except in moments like this, when he helmed the *Mercury* in solitude and recalled every detail of last night's General Merrymaking. He tried to wipe the silly smile off his face before Ogilvie came on deck, but the dratted man was wise to him. Feet braced apart, he stood next to Able at the wheel. "Either you prodigiously entertained the missus last night, or you're damned happy to be at sea again," he commented frankly.

Lord, but the man was vulgar. "Bit o' both, sir," he said, which made Ogilvie chuckle and say, "Touché." Surprisingly, the captain also added, "From now on, belay the *sir*. You're commanding the *Mercury* at sea and I am crew. I call *you* captain. I thought we already discussed this."

"I suppose we did. Very well, Angus. Smitty and I have set a course for Rochefort. We anticipate four days."

Ogilvie nodded. "That should be true, with no surprises."

As it turned out, there were two surprises on the first day, both of them pleasant, and both Avon March's doing, the quiet little fellow recommended by Lady St. Anthony. She had urged him on Able at the last minute with no explanation, but with a smile in eyes that hadn't done much smiling lately. He took her at her word.

The sun beamed on the *Mercury* as she bowled along, her sails catching every bit of wind, which was the secret weapon and glory of a yacht. Ogilvie took the wheel as Able summoned his young crew for a lesson in signaling.

"We'll be flying our signals from the mainsail. That's where the line and pulleys are and so is the flag locker. Refer to your signal books, if you please."

For their seamanship class at St. Brendan's, Able had insisted that every boy have his own book. Thaddeus Croker balked a bit at what seemed unnecessary expense for mere students, but Able knew better. The already much-used books came out, along with pencils and tablets. They looked at him, ready, even little Avon, who had joined Able's course a few times when Lady St. Anthony cut him loose from plane geometry.

As it turned out, Avon startled them all. No signal threw him, even the more complicated, "'Lay alongside enemy,' followed by 'Fire on command.'"

Able noticed Tots and Whitticombe exchanging humorous glances. He fixed them with an inquiring eye, and Tots gestured to Avon, who sat there, all innocence, hand folded.

"Lord bless me," Able said. "Avon, are you even looking up the signals?"

"Nossir. I know them."

He did. Better test him at the mast. "Let's see how fast you can string'um in proper order. Ready? I'll give you random orders. Maybe throw in some names."

Well, that was a revelation. Up they went at Able's command, flying in a spanking breeze. Avon didn't even forget the query flag when specified, or the answer flag, a common error of new signalmen.

Able looked around at the others, including Angus Ogilvie at the wheel, each as surprised as he was. "Good work, Avon. The best, in fact. Let's try a few more just for fun."

They did, with the same results. When Able finished, Avon folded the flags and put them away in their individual cubbies in the newly installed flag locker. Able rested a hand on his shoulder. "Mr. March, you are now signal officer on the HMS *Mercury*."

The other Rats cheered, and Avon bowed most formally, somehow touching in a lad of eleven. "Captain Six," he said. "I can also cook."

"D'ye cook as well as you signal?" Able asked, delighted by this crew member.

"Aye, sir."

No false modesty there, either; he did. Working in the Mercury's miniscule galley at noon, Avon produced a pease porridge to accompany the figgy dowdy that Ezekiel Barnaby had stuffed in that pasteboard box. With the exception of Davey Ten, who still wasn't up to food, the crew pronounced it good and wanted more.

Able sent Angus Ogilvie below for his dinner and took the helm again, after telling Smitty to shoot the sun and give him some figures while the others watched. Able didn't need the reading, but Smitty did. The result was spot on or near as, which was all Able wanted.

What he wanted most of all was what he had, the Gunwharf Rats seated around him by the wheel. "What's the principal task of small ships in a fleet action?" he asked, happy to be in a seagoing classroom instead of cooped up in a building.

They all knew; he saw it on their faces, which grew suddenly serious. Whitticombe's hand went up first. "To repeat signals from the commanding vessel to other ships more distant where signals are obscured by smoke," he said promptly.

"It's dangerous work, Rats," Able said, "weaving in and out of the line of fire." He smiled, thinking of past actions, with all their heart-pounding, gut-wrenching moments. "Protect your signalman with your life."

"But what if we're afraid?"

Bravo. He had trained his Rats well to speak up and never fear censure. "Good question, Tots," he said, with a glance at Smitty. "Smitty, take the wheel and steer another point closer to the wind."

"But sir."

"Do it."

Smitty did, and the Mercury heeled starboard abruptly. Able laughed to hear Ogilvie curse from the galley below. "I think he spilled his pease porridge," Able said. "As you were, Smitty." The yacht righted itself. "Men, we will be doing more heeling and backing, serving the fleet as repeaters.

Get used to that fear. You can all swim. You know you have been through worse fright living in a workhouse." He saw nods all around and it broke his heart as he knew it would. "But you're here and you survived, didn't you?" More nods, this time with confidence.

"Are you ever afraid, Master?" Whitticombe asked.

"I'm captain now."

"Captain Six," the boy corrected.

"Aye. I have many fears." Able smiled when Van Leuvenhoek and William Harvey gasped in fake surprise inside his brain. "I want with all my heart to always return from sea to Mrs. Six and my son. I also want to prove to the Royal Navy that St. Brendan's turns out splendid mariners. How we do that will require all our courage and knowledge. We rely on each other, and we trust to Providence. We calm each other's fears as we do so. This is our work, as long as France and Spain threaten our shores."

Here endeth the lesson, he thought.

"Ben, we must accustom ourselves to finding Papa away at sea now, and not just across the street," Meridee told her boy as they folded clothes on her bed.

She smiled to watch him stare at the unmatched stockings, and then venture to roll two inside each other. The task eluded him, which made her wonder how it was that genius could occasionally run aground on simple chores that everyone else accomplished as a matter of course.

"Mama, this is hard!"

"I'll show you slowly. See? Like this. You try it."

Ben did, with better success. He matched and rolled two more, then plumped himself down on the bed, neatly tidied after a night of magnificent tumult with her man. "Is this why Papa always comes to you to fix his neck cloth?"

"Ah, yes, it is. He's not very good at that."

"He's good at other things."

"My love, we all have our strengths and weaknesses."

It had taken her months to accept as normal that conversation with her child of one and a half years was unlike anything she had anticipated. In some ways, Ben was precisely normal, if a little ahead of most tykes his age. For the most part, he did not mess his nappies anymore or wet himself, but at times he did. He wasn't a neat eater.

What he had was what his remarkable father possessed – a brain of enormous, unfathomable capacity. She wondered about one thing more. She sat beside him, which meant flopping back, grabbing him and growling into his neck until he laughed. What little Able told her about his early years in the Dumfries workhouse had included nothing like this. She knew their son, this flesh and bone of their bodies, knew love. How something as basic as love might influence him later in life, she had no idea. She hoped Ben would be of all things confident in people.

What about that one other matter, the one that worried her? Might as well ask. "Tell me something, Ben. Do you ever hear people talking in your head?"

Knowing how irritated she was with Euclid, she hoped Ben would give her a blank stare. He didn't, and she sighed inwardly.

"I hear people and look around, but there is no one there," he said.

"What do they tell you?"

He stared at the ceiling through wide-open hands and gave her a look Meridee could only call charitable. "That I will always be understood by my mama and papa, even if no one else understands."

She tucked him close. "It's true."

After luncheon, they walked hand in hand a few doors down to Number Twenty, Saints Way. Betsy Cornwall had a decided green thumb. In all their riotous yellow and orange glory, nasturtiums spilled out of the window boxes. A flowering pot of asters by the front door spread their own beauty. Ben leaned over for a sniff and announced, "Aster tripolium, from the Greek word for star, a perennial favored by butterflies, lepidoptirae."

Oh mercy, Meridee thought, not certain whether to laugh or cry. *This goes in a letter to Papa immediately.*

"Was Papa reading to you from Linnaeus recently?" she decided upon. She knocked on the door.

He nodded, and took another sniff. "I do love flowers and Papa."

Betsy Cornwall opened the door holding her own little one, a blond baby with blue eyes who looked remarkably like the best of Betsy and her husband Walter Cornwall. A finger to her lips, she ushered them inside. "Walter is on night duty this month, so he is sleeping. My stepdaughter is at school."

"We can come back later," Meridee whispered back.

"You can stay with me in the kitchen and have some tea," her former servant said. "You don't mind the kitchen, do you?"

"You know I don't, my dear."

For a glorious hour, they drank tea and ate biscuits while Ben and Sally regarded each other with curiosity. In a short time, Ben tutored his younger friend in the fine art of block-stacking while Meridee and Betsy discussed teething and constipation, and the latest exploits of Betsy's brother Jamie MacGregor, one of the early Gunwharf Rats now serving in the Pacific Ocean.

Meridee looked around with pleasure at the order and neatness of Betsy's domain, she who had walked miles and miles from a distant workhouse in Carlisle to find her twin. Betsy had also found the man who loved her, even though, as Portsmouth constable, Walter Cornwall had nearly arrested her for vagrancy. Here Betsy was now, mistress of her own home, beloved wife and mother.

"Our lives hinge upon the strangest bits of fortune, don't they," Meridee said as they watched the children at their feet. "How brave you were to run away and look for Jamie. You took a chance."

"You understand me," Betsy said. "You took a chance, too, think on. I imagine there are some in your family who thought you had taken leave of your senses to marry a workhouse bastard on half-pay."

They laughed together. "I suppose they did," Meridee said. "I didn't care then and I still don't."

Betsy picked up her knitting. She nodded in the direction of the scullery, where Meridee saw a small girl watching them. "I took Tilly Blank from the St. Pancras workhouse only last week," Betsy said quietly. "Because she had no last name and there was a blank in that space for a name, someone wrote Blank." Her eyes filled with tears. "Walter says I can get another girl, later on. I wish I could do more."

"I think Mrs. Perry and I should find someone like Tilly," Meridee said.

"It will be a kindness," Betsy told her. She held out her hand to Meridee and squeezed it gently. "My Walter is asleep and I know right where he is. Is it hard…" She shook her head, unable to ask her question. Maybe it didn't need asking.

Wordless, Meridee nodded. "When I write to my man, I number my letters," she said, when she could speak. "Too many go astray. The first thing I write is, "As of whatever date it is, we are alive and well. And …and I hope… I pray, he is alive to read it."

They looked at each other. "I do that with my letters to Jamie,"

Betsy whispered. "I know theirs is the hard lot, fighting Napoleon and watching out for storms." She held Meridee's hand close to her cheek. "But women wait."

"We do," Meridee agree. "Where would we be without friends who share the same burden? Jamie is on my mind, too." She smiled inside, wondering at wisdom and how a body acquired it. One thing she knew beyond a doubt: she had a deeper well of courage now than the bride who had cast her lot with a genius teaching workhouse boys in a town as vile as Portsmouth, a town she loved more each day. Time would determine the depth of that well.

Pensive and full of tea and Betsy's good biscuits, Meridee left after hugging her former maid, who had come to her with the same terror she saw in little Tilly Blank's eyes. She stood with Ben on the steps as he sniffed the asters again, thankful for his good nature, glad to be his mama.

They crossed the road and stood on their own higher front steps a long while, watching the warships in the Solent. She sighed over the prison hulks, and returned her gaze to the frigates and ships of the line, some getting ready to sail, while others – some battered by war or the elements - moved toward Portsmouth's massive dry docks. A crane close to the slip where *Mercury* usually tied up swung a cannon from the wharf to a frigate. Soon it would be settled in place to join its fellows, ready to deal in death across the Channel, where her husband, if it pleased God, still lived.

She stared at the ships. Was he safe? Was he dead? Would he return?

Ben tugged on her hand. "Mama, don't worry."

How did he know?

Chapter Fourteen

On July 18, the *Mercury* joined Admiral Calder's blockading fleet flanking the broad river that flowed past the inland harbor of Rochefort, on the coast of France. Four days later they sailed into battle with Calder at Cape Finisterre, land's end of Spain.

They went to the blockade with full and settled stomachs, courtesy of a Spanish fishing smack they hailed and boarded. Perhaps to say that they boarded the *San Pedro* would have been stretching the matter, and so Able informed Smitty, who, as sailing master, kept the official ship's log.

They discussed the matter when both of them were groaning from the delight of too much hake fried in olive oil, both acquisitions paid for by Angus Ogilvie. Avon March must have been sent from heaven to prepare meals. Able knew he would owe the prescient Grace St. Anthony forever, by suggesting that her little fellow in lower mathematics come aboard.

"As tempting as the matter might seem to you, Smitty, we didn't really board the *San Pedro* screaming foul oaths and wielding cutlasses," Able said as Smitty sat, poised, read to write. "They welcomed us and sold us fish and olive oil."

And information. "*Sí señores*, we saw a huge fleet only days ago, closer to Finistierra," the captain of the *San Pedro* said, as he happily clinked the coins Ogilvie gave him for one dozen of his freshest *merluzas*. He shook his head. "They looked as if they had been on the sea for many weeks."

Able stretched for more information. He knew his Spanish was far better than Ogilvie's. "Did you get the feeling they were waiting for something?"

The captain shrugged and waggled his hand, palm down. "*Asi asi.* By the way, sir, *your* Spanish is excellent." He glanced at Ogilvie, who glared back. Even Spanish fishermen were polite and diplomatic, to Able's amusement. "But you, sir, perhaps you should let this tall one do the talking?" He bowed to Ogilvie. "It is merely a suggestion."

"Spanish is a language I enjoy," Able replied with haste. "I have another favor to ask. Could you sell me *una capa y sombrero*?"

That request brought a frown, and Able wondered if he had overplayed his hand. He waited, unwilling to say too much. Experience, or maybe that suspicious fellow Copernicus, had taught him that too much explanation sounded like the lie it generally was.

"I have a cloak, *señor*." *El pescador* held up two fingers. "*Dos pesos*."

It was highway robbery for the ragged, smelly cloak the fisherman produced. "Thank you no, but I'll wait until I can get a better one back home." Able rubbed at nonexistent pain in his shoulder. "*Un dolor pequeño, nada más*."

The fisherman clucked his tongue in sympathy. "Rain and fog are enemies to shoulders, are they not?" He held up one finger, Able nodded, and the matter was concluded. The *San Pedro* went on its way.

"Very well, Captain Six, no boarding," Smitty said, recalling Able to the moment. "May I at least write that we hailed them and they complied quickly?"

"Aye. Mention the information we gathered, too."

Smitty bent to his task. He looked up. "What is… is…Villy…"

"Villeneuve planning?"

"It's a deep game." Angus Ogilvie joined them in the cramped sitting area below deck and looked at the others, laid out in varying degrees of stupefaction after that meal. Whitticombe helmed the *Mercury*. "Aye or nay, Captain Six?" he asked. "It's your crew."

"Aye, Angus," Able said immediately. "We're all sharing the danger. Might as well share the news." He put a finger to his lips. "Pain of death, of course."

The Gunwharf Rats nodded, faces serious, even in their comatose state.

He was still their teacher. Why not make a teaching moment? "Why would Villeneuve of the French fleet and Gravina of the Spanish fleet linger at Finisterre, if the Combined Fleet is as tired as we think it is, and probably still carrying men ill with fever from the Caribbean?"

Silence, then Davey Ten's hand went up. Slowly to be sure, but Able was not surprised. Davey played the long game, too. What's more, he probably listened to gossip among patients at Haslar Naval Hospital.

"Maybe Napoleon has greater plans in…" He gulped, realizing their destination. "…right here in coastal France?"

"And those plans might be…"

"A channel crossing of soldiers, protected by the Combined Fleet," Davey finished. He looked around, not sure whether he had succeeded or failed. "I hear comments like that from the men I tend," he said, half apologetically.

"I believe you are entirely correct, Davey," Able said. He looked in each lad's face. "We deliver messages. This message to Admiral Calder is of vital importance." He saw their nods; they understood. "I think we will be asked to join Calder's fleet and sail into battle against Villeneuve."

Tots, ever practical, voiced what he knew they were all thinking. "Master…I mean, Captain, we have no guns, not even a carronade."

More serious nods all around. "We have speed and maneuverability," Able said quietly. "Never forget that. And we all know how to sail."

"Was that too much?" he asked later of Angus, when it was just the two of them on deck and the others in their berths.

"It was perfect," Ogilvie said. "You were born to teach." He chuckled. "Well, among one or two other things."

Flying Avon's signal – Admiralty Dispatches – the *Mercury* sailed alongside *HMS Prince of Wales*, Admiral Calder's flagship, the morning of July nineteenth. Able's heart pounded as he handed the tarry bag to the admiral, Smitty standing beside him in the sumptuously furnished cabin. Captain Ogilvie had elected to remain aboard the *Mercury*. "It's not my moment," he said in explanation. "You're the captain commanding."

Admiral Calder kept them standing and offered no refreshment. Able hadn't expected any. Calder read the dispatch, read it again and sighed. "What new intelligence have you, concerning the whereabout of the Combined Fleet?" He tapped the dispatch. "This is dated six days ago."

"Admiral, yesterday the captain of a fishing boat from Santander told me he had seen both French and Spanish warships heading north on a course for Cape Finisterre, the day previous," Able said. "He counted twenty-seven ships."

"To my fifteen ships of the line and two frigates," Calder said. "Are you certain you understood his Spanish?"

"I speak proficient Spanish, sir."

"And I am to advance and engage the Combined Fleet."

This was not a question. Even had it been, Able would not have presumed to respond. He stood at respectful attention.

"And who might you be?"

"The *Mercury*. Captain Saint Anthony's old yacht."

"What uniform is this lad wearing?"

"He is one of my students from St. Brendan the Navigator School in Portsmouth, sir," Able said. "This is their uniform."

"Aye, the bastard workhouse boys," Admiral Calder said.

"Indeed, sir. I am one of those bastards, too," Able said, keeping his tone cordial. "Admiral Gambier has assigned us messenger duty on an intermittent basis."

He had to give the palm to Admiral Calder. The man could have been really rude. He could have turned his back on Able and Smitty. Instead, he tossed the orders on his desk and turned to the man beside him who was watching the whole business with a certain air of amused detachment.

"Captain Cuming, these…these…I know you have a nickname, Master Six. It's been all around the fleet."

"Gunwharf Rats, sir?"

"Aye, that was it. Captain Rose told me that himself, and with some admiration, I might add. We shall see how well your Gunwharf Rats acquit yourselves in battle. Will, assign them a position in our fleet and give such orders as you feel necessary."

"Aye, sir. Do you want to summon captains here?"

"See to it. Good day, Master Six."

Relieved to be on deck again, Able felt no reservations from Captain Cuming. To the captain's question about victuals, Able said they could use hard bread and cheese. Captain Cuming directed Smitty to follow a midshipman below deck again to the commissary, then turned his attention to Able.

"What'd'ye think, Captain Six. Did you ask the fishermen about the general condition of the Combined Fleet?"

"I did, sir," Able replied. "He said the ships had that tired look. You know what I mean."

"I do. Anything else?"

"He had the same surmise I did, that probably many of the crew were sick with one or another of those Caribbean fevers."

"Our chances?"

"Probably close to equal, sir, even with the larger numbers. These are weakened men."

Smitty returned with a gunny sack and chewing on a bit of dried sausage, from the look of it.

"Off you go, Captain Six," Captain Cuming said. "Sail close enough to us. We'll use you as a repeater. Are your lads up to a fleet action?"

"We'll find out," Able said. Smitty had already tossed the sack to the *Mercury*, bobbing far below the *Prince of Wales*. He climbed down the chains after it. "I think you'll be pleasantly surprised, sir."

Admiral Calder's blockaders sailed through a moon-filled night for Cape Finisterre, and spotted the Combined Fleet before noon on the twenty-second of July. The winds were good, but they jostled for position until the battle began in late afternoon. Fog became an unwelcome combatant, rolling in thick, but dispersing into maddening patches until entire crews were disoriented.

Twice the *Mercury* darted in close so Avon March could read the signals from the *Prince of Wales*, as taken down by Davey Ten this time. Losing not a moment, Avon raised the flags and signaled to Whitticombe at the wheel, his eyes burning chips of fire, to take her out to the farthest ship needing the signal. Who knew the little fellow had so much heart in him? Grace Saint Anthony knew. Able reckoned he owed his fellow instructor a rum toddy toast, when they made port.

Able stood behind Whitticome, a hand on the boy's shoulder, as he followed Smitty's directions, spoken with confidence. Whitticombe trembled with the noise of guns all around, but calmed under Able's steadying hand.

Ogilvie stood by Tots at the sheets, both of them braced against the railing as the *Mercury* bent to the wind, sailed through the fleet with signals flying, and retreated out of harm's way, until the next summons, and the next.

Even Able was hard put to maintain his steady composure when the *Malta*, close by and surrounded by five Spanish warships, blasted all cannon port and starboard at the same time. "What a show!" Whitticombe shouted. "Isn't this the best, Master?"

"Undoubtedly," Able replied, his ears ringing. "Glad you enjoyed it."

Not a minute too soon it was dark and done. The ships broke off, the Combined Fleet leaving behind the *San Rafael* and the *Firme* as British prizes, and trying to escape toward the Cape, as near as Calder's fleet could make out in the gathering murk.

The confusion in the smoke and fog was so great that the big guns kept firing for another hour. "Should we take a cease-fire signal through the fleet?" Avon asked.

"Not unless Admiral Calder insists," Able said. "I personally don't have a death wish."

He couldn't help smiling at Avon's obvious disappointment. *Was I ever that young, Euclid?* he asked his brain. The answer was an undignified guffaw.

It was quickly obvious that the *Malta* and *Windsor Castle* were among the badly damaged. The *Mercury* bobbed near *Prince of Wales*, watching for signals. One came as darkness neared: *Report now*.

"Affirm, Avon," he said. "Tots, take us close to *Prince of Wales*. Smitty, come with me."

Prince of Wales looked like all ships of the line after a battle. Able noted spars gone, the rigging torn. He looked closer, eyes wide. The rudder was sheared off. Carpenters were already busy jury-rigging some sort of replacement.

"All we got is a rip in the jibsail," Smitty said.

"We were moving fast," Able replied. "Doing what Calder wanted."

What Admiral Calder wanted now – and he minced no words – was someone who could speak Spanish. "They claim not to understand us. Take *Mercury* in close and for the Lord's sake, wear your hanger."

"Sir, I have an acting surgeon on board. Should I take him?" Able asked.

"How old is he?" Calder asked, enjoying the moment, despite his obvious cares.

"Fourteen, sir."

"Why not? Aye, take him." Calder's look softened. "Your Rats did well today."

"Will we engage tomorrow?"

"Of course," Calder said, but he spoke too quickly. "Why wouldn't we?"

"Message for the *Firme*, sir?"

"Tell the blinking captain to surrender his sword to you. Tell him a boarding party of Marines will be there soon. Tell him to…to do whatever they demand, whether he understands them or not."

That made perfectly no sense, but Able knew the feeling of utter exhaustion, the moment an action ended. He saluted and returned to the *Mercury* with Smitty. Grateful Meridee had insisted he take the blamed thing along, he buckled on his sword belt and hooked on the cutlass.

Smitty had alerted Davey, who waited on deck with his medical kit slung over his shoulder. "You'll see more than you want to, but they need our help," Able said. "Come with us, Smitty. Angus, take the wheel."

Davey nodded. "I'll make you proud, Captain Six."

"You already do."

No one aboard the *Firme* challenged the *Mercury* as the nimble yacht came alongside the battered Spanish ship of the line, riddled from stem to stern with shot, masts gone. Announcing himself, and perhaps more valuable, announcing he had medical help with him, Able called for the Spanish deckhand to throw out a rope ladder. From a yacht to a ship of the line was a long climb.

The deck was disaster. In the tangle of ropes, sailcloth, body parts and splintered wood, a Spaniard in a familiar-looking surgeon's apron knelt by a writhing man. His hand firm on Davey's shoulder, Able threaded their way between the ruins of men and ship. He spoke in rapid Spanish and the surgeon listened with relief. In no time at all, Davey knelt beside his own patient.

In the near darkness, Able turned to see an officer holding out his sword. "I am Rafael de Villavicencio, commanding the *Firme*, a *su servicio*," the Spanish captain said, his eyes lowered by the humiliation of surrender.

Able took the sword with a bow of his own, acknowledging this courtesy of war for the first time, wondering at the events in his life that had taken him to this point. He handed the sword to Smitty and stepped close to the defeated captain. They chatted in Spanish until the man relaxed and lost the humiliation in his eyes. "I did my best," he said finally, still unwilling to maintain eye contact.

"I know you did," Able replied. He looked over his shoulder to see Royal Marines clambering over what remained of the railing. "Let me interpret for you here until everyone understands what is going on."

"I would greatly appreciate it, *capitan*."

They had been standing in twilight that gradually faded to black. The lieutenant of Marines brought over a torch and changed Able's life.

"Lieutenant, may I introduce…"

He got no farther. Capitan de Villavicencio stepped back in surprise. "It cannot be," he said softly and crossed himself.

"What is the matter?" Able asked.

"It cannot be," the captain repeated. He shook his head to clear it, as though the events of the afternoon could somehow be dislodged. "Ha… have you relatives in Spain, sir?"

How to answer that? "You recognize me," he decided on. He felt the constant clamor in his brain go silent, everyone in there listening.

Villavicencio stared. Courteous Spaniard that he was, he apologized and calmed himself. "I do recognize you," he said finally. Able heard all degrees of amazement in the man's voice.

"How, sir, if you please?" It was Able's turn to shake his head. In his surprise he had spoken in French. "I mean, *Como, capitan, si por favor.*"

"Come with me."

Capitan Villavicencio walked him to the starboard side of the now-listing vessel, the lee side facing Cape Finisterre in the distance. "My confession, sir," he began, his voice low. "I was ordered to keep you talking on the port side so a certain Conde de Quintanar could escape in a pinnace back to the *Argonauta*, flagship of Federico Gravina. If I may be so bold, you resemble the count to a remarkable degree."

The chatter in Able's head began again as he saw the portrait that had so intrigued Captain Hector Rose at Trinity House, the portrait that now hung in Able's sitting room.

What could he say, except, "Damn me, sir. P'raps we'll meet again, this count and I."

Chapter Fifteen

Meridee Six discovered, to her chagrin, that Able at sea produced a different feeling in her that she hadn't experienced with Able across the street at work or Able in London doing Trinity House business. Now she woke in the middle of the night to pat the empty, cold space beside her, and wonder where he was and how he did.

She found herself in the kitchen in the pre-dawn hours, the first time quietly hunting for something to eat, anything to take her mind off the hole in her heart. She hadn't reckoned on Mrs. Perry possessing such sharp ears, not after her years sailing with her husband and hearing cannon booming. On Meridee's subsequent trips to the kitchen, Mrs. Perry had a pot of tea and hot bread or biscuits, and even better, companionship.

"I shouldn't be rummaging around in the pantry and waking you up," Meridee said the first time food appeared.

Mrs. Perry popped a biscuit in her mouth. "There's been a Rat or two down here to rummage, now and then."

"I thought they were beyond that."

"Some are." She tilted her head and observed Meridee, as if wondering if she should speak. "Your husband came down here, especially after Ben was born."

"I didn't know. P'raps I should have been more attentive."

"No. Belay that!" Mrs. Perry exclaimed with her usual spirit. "He told me he was quiet because you were exhausted, and your body must heal, and there you were, feeding a little'un. 'How does she do it?' he asked me once."

"What did you tell my curly haired genius?" Meridee asked, her own cares fleeing, as she considered his much bigger burden.

"I told him you wouldn't want it any other way." Mrs. Perry laughed, but quietly, because Pegeen, the new scullery maid, slept in her own room close by. "He gave me such a fishy look, and then do you know what he said?"

"I…no, not a clue."

"'I am the luckiest man who ever walked the earth,' he told me, and so seriously."

Meridee felt her heart ease and her whole body relax. "Mrs. Perry, after all we have been through, you could have told me sooner. What a dear thing to say."

Mrs. Perry kissed her forehead, the first time she had ever done anything so personal. "I thought I would save it for a time like now, when you truly need it."

Meridee rested her head against Mrs. Perry's shoulder, closing her eyes with relief and joy when the big African woman, who terrified the entire staff across the street at St. Brendan's, put her arms around her. She hummed a wonderful tune that had all the sound of the Caribbean, or maybe more distant African shores.

"Mam?"

Meridee turned to see Pegeen standing in the door of her room. "Were we too loud, my dear?" she asked. "Join us."

Pegeen was the newest addition to the Six household. Spurred on by Betsy's yearning to take more children from the workhouse, Meridee and Ben, protected by Mrs. Perry, had marched to Portsmouth's workhouse mere days ago. The beadle had been eager to parade several bewildered young girls past them, extolling their abilities until Meridee felt nothing but suspicion. She had a better idea.

She took a handful of jackstraws from her reticule and handed them to Ben. "Find a nice corner and play," she told her son. "We won't be too long." She turned back to the beadle. "Now, sir, you were saying?"

"These girls cook and clean and can lay a fire to perfection," he said. "Can't you?" he barked out suddenly, causing several to jump in fright.

"That's fine, sir," Meridee said hastily, when one of the girls started to weep. "I'll chat with them. You may leave us."

"I can't never do that," he protested. "No telling what they would do." He clapped his hands like an explosion and the terrified girls drew together.

All except one child. Out of the corner of her eye, Meridee had watched her separate from the others and sidle along the wall. She sat cross legged by Ben now, helping him with the jackstraws, unmindful of the fear around her. Her red hair was drawn up in two uneven pigtails held together by bits of colorful cloth and she was painfully thin.

More irritated than fearful, the scrap of a girl turned when the beadle shouted, "Pegeen! Get in line!" and stood up reluctantly.

"She's more trouble than she's worth," the housemaster grumbled.

"She is the girl I want," Meridee said decisively, positive as almost never before. Hadn't the Gunwharf Rats been chosen because they stood out from other beaten-down children? "Pegeen, did you say?"

He stared at her. "But she won't do nuffink she doesn't want to," he declared. "I'd get rid of her, if I could."

Meridee shuddered inside at that.

He leaned closer, giving Meridee the benefit of rotting teeth. "To compound it, she's Irish."

"She's coming home with me," Meridee said firmly. "Does she have a last name?"

"O'Malley," the beadle said, resigned now. "Her father died of the drink and her mother dumped her off in a rainstorm. Her? Why, in the good Lord's name do you want her?"

"She is too thin," Meridee said. "Shame on you." She lowered her voice, remembering that she was a lady. "More to the point, she likes my son."

Pegeen O'Malley did. A bath, a clean shift and dress, shoes, a brush and better pieces of yarn later, the ten-year-old Irish girl could already scrape carrots and peel potatoes for Mrs. Perry, then play with Ben. She ate more than Meridee and Mrs. Perry put together, and here she was now, rubbing her eyes and wondering what had happened.

And probably blaming herself. Long experience with workhouse lads had taught Meridee Six a great deal. She held out her hand. "We didn't mean to wake you, Pegeen," she said. "Please join us. Believe me, this is not your fault. We were noisy."

"You're not sending me back?" the child asked, the Irish lilt to her speech so lovely, even when she worried.

"Never!" Meridee said. "Mrs. Perry says no one peels potatoes as efficiently as you do, and Ben would be upset if you left." She held out a biscuit. "I was feeling lonely and came downstairs for tea and comfort from Mrs. Perry. Are you ever lonely?"

Pegeen nodded. She sat beside Meridee and took the biscuit. Mrs.

Perry poured her some tea. When the child leaned against Meridee with a sigh, the universe righted itself once more and peace reigned in a little kitchen on Saints Way.

When everyone was full and Pegeen started to droop, Meridee picked her up and returned her to her room, hardly more than an alcove off the pantry, but warm and with a soft bed. "In the morning, maybe you will help me with some darning, Pegeen."

"Aye, Mam." The child nodded and slept. *I want a daughter just like you*, Meridee thought. *Someone kind who likes jackstraws and little boys.* She returned to the kitchen, happier. "Mrs. Perry, I believe I will go back to sleep."

She did sleep a little better then, even if it wasn't the good sleep she enjoyed with Able right there, keeping her warm, breathing along with her. She reminded herself that she was being a complete ninny, and that wives all over the British Isles were missing their men in the fleet. She thought of Pegeen O'Malley and knew she had work to do right here. Able would return when he could. She had to remember that.

When she opened the door a few days later to see Grace St. Anthony standing there, her eyes so sad, Meridee reminded herself that Grace had no such guarantee. Her man was gone from her sight forever, not just until he sailed back to Portsmouth.

Meridee could have said something wise and comforting, but she knew there were no words sufficient to the occasion. Wordless, she pulled Grace inside, closed the door and wrapped her in a huge hug as her friend sobbed on her shoulder.

Mrs. Perry must have heard the whole thing. In minutes they were both in the kitchen, a pot of tea between them on the table. The hot bread and melted butter perked up Grace. She dabbed at her tears, then picked up a buttery wad. Practical Pegeen came close with a handkerchief.

"I needed this," she said. "And this," she added, after a few sips of the strong brew that Mrs. Perry favored. "Mrs. Perry. You can almost make things right." She saw Pegeen and the handkerchief. "And I need this, too. Thank you, dear."

"We've all known loss," the housekeeper said. "I miss my little Mr. Perry. Even Mrs. Six is all about the place pining for Master Six." She shrugged. "I tell her the first time's always the hardest..." Mrs. Perry looked away. "I cannot fool myself. Each time is always the hardest."

They all reached for hot bread and butter, including Pegeen. Finally, Grace gave that little shake of her shoulders that broke Meridee's heart every time she saw it.

"Better," Grace said, as the tears slid quietly down her face now, practiced tears, the kind a woman probably learns to cry when her man is ill unto death and doesn't need to hear anyone weeping. Meridee remembered the awful time when Able wavered between life and an odd sort of death, accompanied, as near as she could tell, by commotion from the racket inside his odd brain.

Think, Meridee, think, she ordered her own brain, a brain mostly normal. How could she help her friend?

She sipped her tea in silence, thinking of how empty her not-empty house felt with her man gone. Grace's big house, Sir B's mansion many streets away in the more genteel part of Portsmouth, must seem like a tomb.

She knew what to do, as sure as she had known what to do in the workhouse. She looked into her friend's eyes. "Grace, you and little Georgie need to move into my house. We have an empty chamber, since Jean Hubert has flown the coop. If I'm not being impertinent, please at least think about it."

Grace looked away, her face unreadable. Meridee wondered how badly she had fumbled. "Maybe I shouldn't have…" she began.

"I accept," Grace said quickly. "Oh, my, yes. When may Georgie and I move in?"

Meridee let out the breath she had been holding. "Today. Now!" She gathered Grace into a generous embrace. "I have an empty crib. You needn't bring anything, really."

Grace held her off. "You'll need both your cradle and crib, Meridee, and don't you forget that," she said. "I can bring along George's crib."

Logistics reared its ugly head. "I haven't room for George's nanny, and there is Junius Bolt to consider. I doubt your man-of-all-work will take kindly to abandonment."

Grace supplied a genuine smile. "Meridee, we have been in the middle of a fleet action at my house! Miss Norton gave her notice last week and today is her last day." She giggled. "She and Junius have been competing for George's care, and she threw in the towel, if you will excuse a dreadful bit of cant." She didn't try to hide her smile, accompanied by an eye roll.

"My rascal students across the street have been acquainting me with all manner of low language, but sometimes it fits, doesn't it?"

"*Junius* is your nanny?" Meridee wasn't certain she had followed that conversation correctly.

"As good as, and maybe better. He does not flinch at smelly nappies. He says he's smelled much worse in a frigate's bilge after a long voyage."

As they all laughed together, the kitchen suddenly felt right, the house not so empty. The three of them reached for the last piece of bread at the same time. Mrs. Perry divided it into three pieces and Meridee slapped on more butter than anyone required, except perhaps Grace, who was nursing her son and eating butter for two.

She noticed Pegeen and motioned her closer. "Pegeen, let me introduce you to Lady St. Anthony."

Pegeen's mouth was a perfect o. "A real lady?" she asked, as she dropped a deep and surprisingly elegant curtsey.

"Indeed she is," Meridee said with a smile. "She has a baby named George. I think, no, I am certain, you could help her." She turned to Grace again. "All you need are clothes, yours and Georgie's. Perhaps your crib is the better idea," she said with a blush. "I know I will need mine again, eventually."

"Certainly you will," Grace agreed, sounding more like Grace again, the former spinster who used to be in complete control of her own destiny. "My carriage is out front. Georgie and I will be back here before you even miss us, or bedtime, whichever comes first."

Meridee saw her off from the front door. She smiled to herself as Grace started to whistle before the coachman opened the door. While Meridee tidied the empty room across the hall from her own, Mrs. Perry banged around in the room off the kitchen, better known as the servants' dining hall in more grandiose days, even though it wasn't large. Meridee sent little Pegeen with a quick message to Mr. Ferrier who was teaching the lads how to properly load ballast on small platforms in the stone basin. In minutes there was a swarm of slightly damp boys ready to wrestle the now-extra bed downstairs for Junius Bolt, as the dining hall became his new quarters.

The man in question arrived a mere hour later, bearing his own modest gear, and Grace's clothing and Georgie's, telling Meridee as nothing else could how quickly her friend wanted to leave her too-empty house, no matter how grand it was. "More will come later, I do not doubt," Junius said as those same boys, drier now, carried Grace's boxes upstairs.

Junius stayed at the foot of the stairs with Meridee. "Mrs. Six, this is a kind gesture on your part," he told her. "I was beginning to despair." A sturdy, if aging, veteran of many a naval fleet action in the past century, Junius Bolt had never appeared to be a man easily given to despair. This whole, sad business had added wrinkles to his face and a slump to his shoulders.

She looked closer and thought – hoped? – she saw serenity returning. "Lady St. Anthony and I will help each other through this national emergency," she said, understanding more fully how hard it must be to remain in a house where a witty, talented, clever fellow had departed. "Nothing is as bleak as a house where one of the inhabitants no longer resides."

Junius took his leave, declaring he would return soon enough with the lady in question and her son. Meridee pointed the helpful young crew – Ben trailing behind now and up from his nap – toward the kitchen, where Mrs. Perry and Pegeen had biscuits for all.

She stayed where she was, reminding herself that her own missing man was only a channel away, and not on that more distant shore from which travelers, resigned or otherwise, never returned. She felt a chill wind on her heart – no other way to explain it – that sent her into the sitting room to look into the mending basket she had neglected since Able left. She could keep her hands busy, even as her mind raced.

The basket never entirely emptied out, not with little boys or bigger ones with stockings to darn and cuffs to let out. It had become a bit of a family joke. She looked in the basket. "My goodness," she said. "What mischief is this?"

A small box with a red thread around it nestled between the legs of a pair of Able's smallclothes, which ordinarily would never find their way into the downstairs sewing basket. *What are you up to, husband*, she thought, and picked up the box.

Who doesn't love a present? She opened the box to see a gold locket, heart-shaped, on a plain gold chain. She wondered what damage this must have done to their household expenses, as she opened a note. *Meri, if you yearn for me in interesting ways, this will make you laugh*, she read to herself, thinking how much she wanted to laugh precisely now. *I know it is genteel to leave a lock of one's hair to a beloved person. You also know I am a bastard with no gentility. Your own very able, Able.*

Her face already flaming, she looked around to make sure the boys were occupied in the kitchen and opened the locket. She gasped and smothered her laughter with both hands over her mouth; one wouldn't do.

"You, Master Six, are a rascal," she whispered, as she stared down at coarse, curly hair that certainly didn't come from his head.

The locket and chain tucked nicely down the front of her bodice. When Lady St. Anthony arrived in time for dinner, Meridee still smiled.

Chapter Sixteen

Perhaps it was a conspiracy hatched by Headmaster Croker. Perhaps Master Harry Ferrier had a sixth sense about lonely ladies. The addition of Grace and George St. Anthony to the Six household found itself augmented at dinnertime by Able's substitute instructor, located by Nick Bonfort, a boy of initiative who still felt sadly neglected.

Master Ferrier came over one night at the dinner hour. He knocked on the door, which little Pegeen answered. Meridee heard her from the dining room, calling out, "Miz Six, I don't know what to do!"

Meridee put her napkin on the table and rose immediately. Nick rose, too. "Nick, you can keep eating," she said.

"No, Mam," he said, in that voice she knew from her own husband, the one that indicated she had no real say in the matter because his mind was made up. "I'm coming, too. We don't know who is at the door."

They walked to the wide-open front door to see Master Ferrier, grinning from ear to ear. He took off his hat and held it out like an urchin petitioning coins.

"Please, Mum, I want to eat with ladies and avoid Thaddeus Croker's evil butler," he said, his eyes lively.

Meridee laughed and ushered him inside. "Grace and I understand your peculiar dilemma," she assured him. "I'll take care of him, Pegeen."

"Did I do t'wrong thing, Miz?" the little one asked, her eyes anxious.

"Not at all," Meridee replied. "I've already told you never to trust a navy man, haven't I?" That earned a laugh from the quiet instructor.

"Aye, Miz," the scullery maid said. She thought a moment. "But I see navy men all around here."

"You did right to call for me. We can trust this one." She patted the child's cheek. "Now please help Mrs. Perry bring in the beef roast."

"You have a way with children," Master Ferrier said, as they adjourned to the dining room. "And with the rest of us old tars, I suspect, eh, Nick?"

Nick smiled, obviously happy to be lumped with old tars. *Able was right to insist upon you,* Meridee thought. "The evil butler is preying upon you?" she teased, to lighten the mood.

"Aye, Miz Six," Master Ferrier teased back. "Bertram is a demon from hell."

"Come now, sir," she admonished.

He ushered Nick ahead, but the boy seemed inclined to remain, which touched Meridee's heart. She knew she had a stalwart defender in Nick Bonfort.

"Very well, Nick, you listen, too," the master said, drawing him into the conspiracy. "Your headmaster knows his sister Grace St. Anthony is lonely and needs cheerful company." He nodded to Meridee. "Nick, would I be wrong in thinking that Master Six left you a careful message about championing Mrs. Six?"

Nick's head went up. "Aye, Master Ferrier, he did. I will go where she goes, if I have any qualms."

Meridee couldn't help the sudden tears in her eyes. "I should have known he would do that, Nick," she said, and kissed the top of his head.

"Aw, Mam!" Nick said. She saw how pleased he was, and yet how dignified. "Very well. I will return to the dining room if you need some mature conversation."

Meridee had to hide her chuckle at such a statement from a young boy. "We won't be long, I promise you."

"Quite the lad," Master Ferrier said, when the dining room door closed. "I have been getting my own education here."

"We all have. Yes, Master Ferrier, we do need your steadfast leaven in our loaf." She considered the quiet man. "Perhaps you need us, too."

"P'raps I do."

There was room and food enough for Master Ferrier, and he quickly became a regular at meals. Meridee and Grace both began to suspect a deeper game, one that caused no pain. "He keeps us company, answers any questions we might have about the fleet, and is happy to read Euclid's *Elements* – in English, mind you – to Ben," Meridee said, following dinner one night when Nick labored over his homework and she and Grace adjourned to the sitting room, their now-regular dinner companion having returned to St. Brendan's. "I think Thaddeus is determined we will not feel quite so lonely."

"He would to that," Grace agreed. "We know it wasn't the evil butler's idea." They laughed together.

Meridee darned stockings while Grace calmly nursed Georgie. Grace's eyes were closed, so Meridee had leisure to assess her friend. In mere days, she had begun to relax, her shoulders lower, the pinched look gone. Any fear that their home was too lively for a new widow dribbled away. Solitude would have been a monumental unkindness to a sociable lady like Grace St. Anthony. If regular visits from Sailing Master Harry Ferrier, RN (retired) was a plot to console two ladies, Meridee had no objection.

It was more, which only made him especially dear to her. Master Ferrier sought her out one evening after Grace had retired with Georgie, Ben was asleep and Nick studying in the dining room. She thought his return had something to do with her quiet-voiced comment to Mr. Ferrier earlier before dinner about Nick's sadness not to be included in the voyage of the *HMS Mercury*.

"I need advice, Mrs. Six," he said, when seated on the sofa. "In fact, if we could include Nick, that would be advantageous."

Nick came quickly and sat close to Meridee. Only a woman made of stone would have been unmoved by his always keeping himself between her and anyone else. Nick was only thirteen now, but his protection was unmatched by men much older.

"Nick, I want to ask something of you, but I need Mrs. Six's approval," Master Ferrier began.

"Aye, sir, ask what you wish," the boy said.

"You know what our seamanship class is like," Mr. Ferrier began, with no preamble. "A little bit of this and that, probably as Master Six taught."

Nick grinned and leaned back, relaxing. "As much as he moved from subject to subject, he left no idea abandoned, did he?"

"That is part of his genius," Master Ferrier said. "He could cover a subject like no other."

I agree, Meridee thought, as she threaded the darning needle. *It has made him a wonderfully proficient lover, too, but that is my business alone.*

She felt her face grow hot, and turned her attention to putting the stocking on the darning egg.

"All that genius is locked in a most fertile brain, but us ordinary mortals need more structure. Would you agree with that, Mister Bonfort?"

"I think so, sir."

"Here is my proposal, Nick. I have observed that you are most thorough in your note taking. What say you share your notes with me? At the end of this course, you and I can turn this hodge podge into a distinct manual."

"Me, sir?" Nick asked, his eyes wide, becoming a boy again and not just a protector.

"You, Mister Bonfort. You have ability I see in no one else at St. Brendan's," Master Ferrier said firmly. "We will put our heads together and create a manual, which will have both of our names on it as collaborating authors."

Nick was rendered speechless by this news, which warmed Meridee's heart as nothing else could. Her cup ran over when Mr. Ferrier leaned forward and gave Nick his undivided attention. "There are many ways a lad like you can succeed in the Royal Navy, especially in perilous times as face us now. Don't ever forget that."

"Aye, sir," Nick said in a faint voice.

"Master Ferrier would some grog be in place? You know, to celebrate this collaboration?" Meridee asked.

"I would never object," the sailing master said.

"Well-watered for you, Nick," Meridee added.

The boy grinned, his first genuine smile in many days, to her recollection. "I know you, Mam. Well-watered."

A quick word to Mrs. Perry was sufficient unto the day. The housekeeper returned with cups for three. "Oh, I didn't mean me," Meridee said. Her objection ended with a meaningful look from her housekeeper. "Well, perhaps this time."

They settled back in comfort. Meridee took a sip, and another. Maybe it loosened her tongue. "Master Ferrier, tell me why my husband chose you, above all sailing masters, for this assignment. I know he holds you in vast esteem, but is there more?"

She knew he was a quiet man, not given to much conversation. Perhaps the rum was working on him, too. "I sailed with Sir B on the *Defence*," he began, as he settled in. "Your good man was a lad a little younger than

Nick here. Ordinary seaman, he was. Nothing set him apart at first. He was quiet, calm and did his duties with no complaint. One of many."

"I can see that," Meridee said. She couldn't help the hard edge that crept in. "No workhouse lad sets himself up to be noticed."

"He didn't, at least at first." Master Ferrier took another sip. "That is, until the day I noticed what he was doing. Let me explain. I conducted my class in navigation for the midshipmen on deck by the foremast. I asked Able to set up my smooth board. He did, then returned to his regular duty."

"Which was…" Meridee said.

"He was usually to be found holystoning the deck, along with others." He smiled at the memory. "It took me a few weeks to notice that he always seemed to be working that part of the deck during my lectures. I started watching him. You know, out of the corner of my eye."

"Master Six was listening, wasn't he, Master Ferrier?" Nick asked. "He can take in everything, and you're none the wiser."

Master Ferrier nodded. "I noticed that he would look up from the pumice stone and the deck – just a quick glance, mind you – then return to his duties. I mean, mere seconds."

Meridee set aside her darning. "Nick, I can elaborate." She couldn't help the warmth that rose to her face. "Let me be candid. I was watching him in my brother-in-law's study when he came to teach my nephews while he was on half pay."

"Ah yes, that plaguey Treaty of Amiens," Master Ferrier murmured. "It grounded many a good man."

"Precisely. I was watching his face because he, well, he is so handsome."

Nick and Master Ferrier grinned at each other. "Oh, you two!" she exclaimed. "It's true. I watched his eyes sort of swoop over the contents of the bookshelves. I've never seen anything like it."

"He never forgets, does he?" Master Ferrier asked.

"Never. In an idle moment recently, I asked him if he could name all the book titles from almost three years ago. He laughed and recited them."

"Impressive. He was doing that with the equations on the smooth board," Master Ferrier said. "One day I left an unfinished equation and the chalk behind. When I came back, the equation was done correctly, and that young seaman was holystoning farther aft on the deck. He looked back at me and grinned."

Meridee nodded. *So many have been kind to my man*, she thought. "I understand why he wanted you, Master Ferrier," she said, picking up her darning again. "He knows you are observant and watchful of young minds. You are an instructor, too."

"Beyond my sailing master duties, I believe you are correct," he said later when she walked him to the front door. "I am enjoying this singular duty." He nodded toward the dining room, where Nick had resumed his studies. "What I suggested was no idle request, no bone to toss a boy thinking he was overlooked. Nick and I can craft a seamanship manual specifically for St. Brendan's."

"I believe you."

He nodded walked down the few steps to the street. "Don't worry about Able, Mrs. Six. He'll be back as soon as the fleet hands him enough messages intended for London. It's his first command, and long overdue, in my estimation. G'night."

"I do worry," she said softly to Master Ferrier's back as he crossed the street. "I always will. His first command? Oh no, sir. He commanded my heart the first time we saw each other."

Chapter Seventeen

Meridee waited, if not patiently, then at least with as much dignity as she could muster, for her husband to return from the Channel. News of the fleet action off Cape Finisterre sent her and Nick flying to Able's classroom to locate the Cape on his globe.

"Perhaps the *Mercury* will return with dispatches of the battle," Nick said, as they returned home.

"How long would that take?"

"Five days?"

Five days came and went and others brought news of the action, including a casualty list, which contained no familiar names, to her relief. She burst into tears anyway, which meant that Ben's lips began to quiver. Grace St. Anthony found that her lap was strong enough to hold one woman and a toddler.

"Dry your eyes, Meridee Six," Grace told her eventually. She handed her a handkerchief and started to laugh. "I wish Sir B could see you two watering pots."

How could anyone maintain much dignity? Meridee blew her nose and laughed, too, which meant that Ben hopped off his mama's lap and returned to stacking blocks, shaking his head, either at the folly of females, or wondering what Papa would think.

"The thing is, when Able returns and asks Ben how we fared, my traitor son will tell him exactly what happened, down to my last tear," she confided. She rubbed her damp cheek against Grace's. "Silly you for thinking that moving into the Six household was solely for your serenity. Maybe it was for mine."

"Then we are both well-served, friend," was Grace's quiet reply.

It should not have surprised Meridee that Ezekiel Bartleby had the first news of the *Mercury*, which he dispensed one morning after breakfast. Nick and Grace had already crossed the street for classes, and Junius Bolt had returned little George to his crib, well-fed and drowsy.

At the baker's three distinct raps on the back door, Mrs. Perry dried her hands on the dishtowel. She returned with Ezekiel bearing rout cakes and a wide grin. He set down the cakes with a flourish and Meridee picked up one with the most icing.

He didn't bear completely good news, but it was news that told Meridee precisely where her own wants and needs conflicted with the Royal Navy's. "Some of the fleet's in port now," he announced, but followed up those tidings with less happy ones. "The *Mercury* made port, dropped off someone, took on water and vittles and left immediately for Spithead. Your man is off to Admiralty House, bearing dispatches."

The rout cake halfway to her mouth returned to her plate uneaten. She wanted to cry; she wanted to storm about the room railing against cavalier treatment of wives by the Royal Navy; she wanted to give the innocent message-bearer an undeserved piece of her mind. Instead, she took a deep breath and another, reminded herself that this was a time of national emergency and she was a mature adult. Generally.

Ezekiel Bartleby must have recognized mutiny barely suppressed. He took the unusual step of taking her hand in his floury one, then reached into the bib of his apron and gave her a note. "From our genius," he said. "It was handed to Walter Cornwall on the wharf and the constable gave it to me. Walt said he looked tired and a little thin, but otherwise in good trim."

He turned to go, but Meridee stopped him. "You were so kind to bring this to me. I know you want to know what he wrote," she said. "I'll glance through it first."

My lovely one, she read quickly, *we are all fine. What a crew I have.* She smiled at that, thinking of Smitty and Davey and the other Gunwharf Rats, then teared up immediately, as she read on and his meaning became clear. *You and Ben are my constant crew. Never forget it.*

She savored those words, then read the rest of the note to the baker and Mrs. Perry. And there was Junius, listening from the doorway. Pegeen peeked around the scullery door. Meridee read of a battle; Whitticombe's steady hands on the wheel to obey Smitty's every order as the *Mercury* darted about; repeating signals read flawlessly and hoisted by little Avon March; Tots and Ogilvie at the sheets; Davey's tending to Spanish wounded.

"'Not one Rat failed to do his duty,'" she read. "'Sir B would be proud of them, as I am.'"

There was more: Admiral Calder had not engaged the enemy a second day, but sent the *Mercury* further south, with news of the action to Admiral Nelson. "'We delivered that dispatch to the admiral's secretary, and couldn't return to the *Mercury* fast enough to avoid hearing Nelson's outrage that Calder gave up too easily. For a small man, Nelson has powerful lungs.'"

Junius nodded. "Once I served with t'admiral, a captain then. Aye, he does." He shook his head. "Mark ye, there'll be a court martial coming Calder's way."

The note was nearly done. Able had run out of paper so he had resorted to the margins. She turned the note sideways then upside down to read it. "'We had the satisfaction of harrying Admiral Villeneueve's fleet back to Spain. Invasion from France is averted for now. All my love. Burn this letter.'"

Meridee looked down at Able's first war letter to her. She wanted to put it under her pillow, so she could read it over and over. Instead, she balled it in her fist and tossed it in the Rumford. The note crackled and disappeared.

Silence reigned for long moments in the kitchen. She felt a chill, even in early August, and rubbed her arms. "We are in for a long war, are we not?" she finally asked the room in general. She saw slow nods from these friends who knew ships and men far better than she did.

After some conversation of a consoling nature – Did she look that sad? Probably – the others returned to their duties, leaving her alone in the kitchen. She thought through the letter again, smiling to herself at the little ribald drawings she had hidden from the others, then wondered about the postscript she had kept to herself. She had no eidetic memory like Able Six, but it was short and she remembered. *I learned something about my father.*

Able came home a week later when she least expected him. It was the middle of the day; class was in session and she and Mrs. Perry had left Ben with the increasingly capable Pegeen. Now and then there was no substitute for a ramble through the Portsmouth market. She and Nick had decided they were in the mood for cod that night.

She never feared the market with Mrs. Perry close at hand. Sailors who might have been inclined to attempt impropriety – this was Portsmouth, after all – gave her a wide berth after a snarl from Mrs. Perry. Meridee had protested this once to Able, preceded by a statement that she was matronly now. "My waist isn't what it used to be, and my breasts aren't so perky. I'll never see twenty-five again," she had said early one morning in the privacy of their bedchamber. "I do hate to take Mrs. Perry away from other duties. Couldn't I go by myself?"

Her husband grinned into his shaving mirror. "Meridee-luscious, have you actually taken a good look in the mirror lately? C'mere."

She obliged him, thinking him silly, and looked into his mirror. He wiped some of the soap off his face and spoke directly into her ear, which set her nerves humming. "You have only grown more beautiful, Mrs. Six. I barely trust *me* around you."

That conversation had landed them back in bed in jig time, considering that he only had a towel around his waist and her shift was remarkably portable. "You will go to the market with Mrs. Perry or not at all," he said afterward in most unloverlike tones, as he wiped the rest of his shaving soap off her neck. And so she did.

"We'll fry the cod the way we like it, add some potatoes and gorge ourselves," Meridee said as they walked home. They stopped at Ezekiel Bartleby's bakery because it was on the way, ready for petit fours that Nick liked too well. Smitty, as well, but he was at sea.

Ezekiel wore a broad smile as she selected the petit fours. "Better add some more, Mrs. Six," he said most cheerfully. "Ye've got two more men at home." He jerked a thumb over his shoulder to his back rooms. "Make it three. You know Captain Ogilvie likes'um, too. He's sleeping now but I predict he'll be dining with you tonight."

Meridee gasped and dashed to the door. She stopped. *You are too old to be so undignified*, she scolded herself. "Why, yes, Ezekiel, let him know he is welcome to dinner. We dine at six."

She wanted to pick up her skirts and run home, but Meridee and Mrs. Perry left the bakery at a sedate pace. She slowed down when Mrs. Perry told her, "Mrs. Six he'll be dirty and tired."

I don't care, she thought. *I want to at least see him.*

The house was quiet when she opened the door and tiptoed in. Pegeen must have heard them, because she came from the kitchen, eyes merry, finger to her lips, and pointed to the sitting room. Meridee set down the shopping basket and peeked in.

Smitty lay sprawled near the fireplace, arms widespread. Able lay curled with Ben on the sofa, both asleep. Davey Ten had dropped into her chair, head back, legs out. She assessed this Gunwharf Rat who lived at Haslar Hospital now, noting that his trousers should be lengthened.

The other crew members must have gone home to St. Brendan's, where classes were still in session. She watched her men sleeping so soundly, suddenly wanting to gather all of them close, these men of war. *How long will you lovelies be here?* she asked herself as she closed the door quietly.

She stood in the hall a long moment, filled with love so deep that she could only thank God over and over for their safe return. Able had told her that he thought that Napoleon wouldn't be subdued for at least ten years. Ten years! She would be middle-aged by then, when she could hope that her man might come home after a day of teaching, eat dinner, sit with her and their children – she knew there would be more – then toddle off to bed, just an ordinary man living an ordinary life.

It was a foolish thought and she knew it. Nothing about Able Six was ordinary. And these two Rats, growing into men almost before her eyes, were not ordinary, either. They were remarkable beings, part of an experiment to prove to the world how good they were, how worthy. They need prove nothing to her, a gentleman's daughter, carefully raised, who in normal times never would have met any of them on equal footing. She knew their worth, and the knowledge warmed her heart.

"Mrs. Perry, I wonder: Do you reckon it is easier to go to war, or to stay home and wait?" she asked her great good friend when she tiptoed into the kitchen.

"War is easier," Mrs. Perry said promptly. "That is why I insisted Mr. Perry let me come with him. I hated to remain behind." She clapped her hands, but softly. "Help Pegeen fill the bathtub in the washroom. You won't want to get near your man until he sits in hot water for a while."

You don't know me, Mrs. Perry, Meridee thought. *If the sitting room weren't full of other people, I would cuddle him right now, dirt, whiskers and all.*

Her mutiny must have showed on her face because Mrs. Perry chuckled and swatted the back of Meridee's dress as if she were two and remarkably recalcitrant.

Chastened and cheerful, she returned to the sitting room to wait. The boys slumbered on, but in no time, Able opened his eyes. She crooked her little finger toward herself. He carefully disentangled himself from his sleeping son, took her hand in his and walked to the door. He closed it quietly behind him, then took her in his arms.

Mrs. Perry was wrong about the dirt and smell. True his face was a little scratchy, but his lips were as ever they were, so expert at making her pull him close and wrap her arms around him. She would have wrapped her legs around him, too, but she knew Mrs. Perry and Pegeen could come through that kitchen door any time they chose. Better let them think she had some dignity.

"I've missed you," she said finally.

"I can tell," he said. "What are the odds of you and I slipping upstairs?"

"Slim to none, I think." She did back away a little. Maybe Mrs. Perry was right. She wrinkled her nose. "Did you change your shirt and smallclothes at all?"

"Once. I thought Admiral Nelson deserved to see me at my better, if not my best self."

"Once in four weeks? Lord Nelson?"

"Aye, miss. I have quite a story for you." He touched his forehead to hers. "And there is the matter of my father."

Chapter Eighteen

To Able's abiding relief, the washroom door had a lock. Once he was clean, Meri was willing. Amazing how a woman could shed so many clothes in such a short time. A towel laid down on the floor with Meri on top of it, and he was in heaven.

"I've never coupled in a washroom," he said, when he could speak in normal tones and breathe without gasping.

"Neither have I," she replied. "If the floorboards leave a mark on my back, you're in trouble."

They both laughed. "Eventually everyone will eat, then go home, and I'll have my way with you on a mattress," he promised. He stood up and held out his hand. "Up you get, my saucy wench."

While he dressed, Meri-deelightful looked at the used bathwater, then decided against a quick dip. She settled for a damp washrag and giggled like a bride when he buttoned her bodice, after taking a few husbandly liberties.

He smiled inside, touched by her odd sort of modesty, when she patted her hair in place and asked, "Will I pass muster?"

After that glorious bit of General Merrymaking, he knew he could tease her. "No. You look like you've been romping about in the washroom with a randy fellow."

Ooh. Such a glare. He gave it eight seconds. Nay. Four, and she was in his arms again. "I don't like separations from you," she whispered into his neck.

"What a relief that I usually work at St. Brendan's. Some of those ocean voyages can last two years and more," he said.

"My goodness." Meri unlocked the door. "Do wives ever just lie down there on the dock when they see the right ship making harbor?"

He shouldn't have laughed so loud, but Lord, his genteel wife could pop out with a zinger, when the mood was on her. "Meridee Bonfort Six, you are a rascal."

"Oh dear, three names. Am I in trouble?" she teased back.

"We'll make it right later on tonight," he assured her. "Now let us ask the kind Pegeen to swab out that horrid bathtub and fill it for a lad or two."

Soon, everyone smelled much better. Before dinner, Ben had escorted Able upstairs so he could shave and put on a clean uniform. Sitting on the end of their bed, his little son informed his Papa of the times Mama cried. His face grew solemn. "I cried, too. Papa, where were you?"

"Sailing against France and keeping Napoleon away from you," he said. He yanked up Ben's shirt, blew a big raspberry on his stomach, and flopped down beside his boy so they could laugh together.

"Someone must like Napoleon," his son said. "Does he have a little boy of his own?"

"Alas, no," Able told him, touched at how Ben settled so close. There was none of the shy child about his son. It was as if they had known each other since conception. Someday he might ask Ben what his earliest recollection was, but now was not the time. Better to circulate in his son's orbit while he could, taste of Meri's sweetness on every level of his life, and return to sea a whole man. He raised up on one elbow to regard Ben. "If he had a little boy, do you think Boney would be a better man?"

Able knew this was not an argument for a one so young to entertain, but he knew this was no ordinary child. Still, Ben surprised him. "Probably, if he had a good mama, too."

Touché, Ben, he thought. "You have a good mama."

Ben nodded. "She would be upset if I decided to conquer the world. She wouldn't think it proper."

Able laughed and grabbed up his son, setting him on his shoulders. He trotted him down the stairs, Ben hanging on tight to his hair, and into the kitchen where the delight of his life was taking a ham from the Rumford.

"Ben, you'll never want to go to sea. The food is so good here," he said as he lifted his son off his shoulders and set him gently on his feet. "Only last week, all we had to eat was ship's bread, elderly cheese and fish."

"Mama should be on board to feed you," Ben pointed out.

He smiled at Meri, who was listening to this exchange with her usual good cheer. He watched her eyes grow misty, and knew how close to the surface her emotions were. *Let this war end*, he thought. *Let it end now.* He grabbed her in an all-encompassing embrace that nearly included the ham on the table. "Mama feeds me all she can," he whispered into her ear.

Dinner became a moveable feast that took the ham and accessories across the street, where it was joined by a beef roast large enough for a school of hungry boys, another ham and chicken pie. The whole school ate and celebrated the return of five Gunwharf Rats, six if he counted himself, and he did.

Ezekiel Bartleby was equal to the occasion, with bread and a cake with lemon icing. Captain Ogilvie carried the cake, a smile on his face. In fact, he looked more cheerfully normal than Able had ever seen. The trajectory of the captain's gaze rested squarely on Grace St. Anthony, who was busy helping Meri slice the bread. *Blows the wind from that quarter?* Able asked himself. This might bear a comment or two to Meri later on tonight, provided he took the time to think about anyone else's love besides his own.

Ben on his lap – Ben had turned into an amazing trencherman – he ate, enjoyed the camaraderie all around him in this former refectory of silent monks and what used to be frightened, cowed workhouse scum. They had changed. He saw the pride, the intelligence, and *bon amie* and it thrilled his heart as almost nothing else could.

He saw something else, and pointed it out to Meri, when he snagged her by her apron and made her sit beside him, reminding her there was a whole staff of kitchen help. "Look at the faces of my crew," he said. "They've seen more and know more than the others."

She gazed where he gazed, her hand resting proprietarily on his thigh, under the protection of the table. He watched her face become contemplative, even a little wistful. "Dare I say they look like men?"

He nodded. "We'll give little Avon another year or so, but he is a marvel." He leaned across Meri to Grace, who was carrying on her own conversation with Captain Ogilvie. "Lady St. Anthony, you certainly set me up for a huge surprise with Avon March."

She turned to him with a genuine, happy smile, a smile he hadn't seen in months from her. "Able, I'd like to have seen your expression when you discovered he could signal with the best men in the fleet."

"I was predictably surprised," Able replied. "He is a wonder." He leaned back. "They all are."

Surrounded by good cheer and celebration, Davey Ten's serious face came as no surprise to Able. He had clambered aboard the captured Spanish man o' war with him to render aid, and had seen up close what British guns could do. After an initial gasp, Davey had neither flinched nor held back, but worked alongside the Spanish surgeon until one of Admiral Calder's undamaged frigates sent over a surgeon's mate to assist. Able knew he would never tell even Meri that Davey Ten had sobbed in his arms back aboard the *Mercury*, after the other Gunswharf Rats were below deck, except for Smitty, who had taken the helm. Smitty understood.

Davey must have sensed Able's eyes on him, as he sat beside Smitty and Whitticombe. Shyly, the boy who already possessed the heart and mind of a surgeon gave him a small salute, which Able returned with pleasure. A corner of his remarkable brain was already planning an assault on Trinity House to sponsor David Ten at the medical school in Edinburgh.

His eyes went to Tots now, who sat next to Avon March with the younger class. Tots, who never cared what people thought, still seemed to be protecting Avon, his signalman, who Captain Six had told to guard with his life. "Avon is in good hands," he said, more to himself than to Grace, who had returned her attention to Captain Ogilvie.

"Can't Grace find someone less prickly than Angus Ogilvie?" he whispered to his wife.

"Hush, my man," Meri said, soothing her mild rebuke by sliding her hand much higher up his thigh.

Able was no fool. He hushed. He eyed his crew again, pleased with their competence, then settled his gaze on Nick Bonfort, hoping to see him less disappointed that he had not been selected to crew the *Mercury*. Master Ferrier sat with him, both of them looking down at what appeared to be a handle of notes.

"Has Nick found more than a teacher in Master Ferrier?" he asked Meri. "I was hoping."

"Indeed. Master Ferrier is going to compile Nick's meticulous notes into something approaching a textbook for your seamanship course," she said. "Nick is less unhappy." She smiled. "You know how earnest is our Nick. He told me only yesterday that his life has real purpose again."

They laughed together quietly. God, how he missed moments like this when he was at sea. He knew Meridee was indulgent of his mistress, the sea, which beckoned him and flirted, as any good mistress would. He wondered if she would believe him if he told her now that he was at sea again, all he wanted to do was come home to her each day.

"I want this celebration to end because I want to bed you more thoroughly," he whispered to his wife, who blushed and moved her hand closer down to his knee.

He turned his attention to Thaddeus Croker, who must have intercepted his thoughts, well, hopefully the one about adjournment only. The headmaster rose, tapped on the side of his glass with his knife, and achieved instant silence in the noisy hall. He looked around and cleared his throat.

"I believe that our estimable Master Six would tell us that we have just begun to fight," he said. "We Rats – let me include myself – should be mindful of what lies ahead." He nodded to the crew of the *Mercury*. "These Rats have a sure picture of what war is. We will all come to know it intimately, I both expect and fear."

He let the slight murmur die down. "Hard times, lads. Good times. I trust we will weather both well. Good night to you all. Classes tomorrow as usual. Shall we?"

Able felt the lump grow in his throat as everyone stood. Headmaster Croker pointed to a small boy standing next to Avon March, who closed his eyes and gave a perfect pitch.

They sang four verses of "Heart of Oak," those who could sing. Others, like Able Six, Harry Ferrier and Davey Ten, could only stare ahead, eyes full of what they had already seen. Smitty mouthed the words. Able sighed with relief when Meri's arm went around his waist. They held Ben between them, not even slightly surprised when he sang along.

Quite a son you have there. He'll make you proud. Good lad. Able smiled at the voices in his head. Now and then they could be reasonable.

Able and Meri saw Davey off to Haslar in a hackney, with the promise to keep in close contact. "I will need you again, Davey, unless you choose otherwise," Able said before he closed the door. "You know how hard it is."

"I choose to continue aboard the *Mercury*," Davey said firmly, sounding much older than his years. He swallowed, and the years dropped away. "I...I only wish I knew more."

"Hold that thought, Davey," Able said. He patted the hackney and the driver started off at a smart trot. "Let's get through this current national emergency and see what develops," he said after the hackney pulled away from the curb on a silent, dark street.

Everyone bedded down quickly. Grace and Captain Ogilvie remained in the sitting room, talking and even arguing a little. In the front hall, Able raised his eyebrows at Meri, who put her hand over her mouth, laughed, and tugged him away. "My love, you of all people should never question what it is that sparks attention in a gentlewoman," she whispered. "Let them be."

He could tease, too. "You informed me once that my high good looks attracted *you*."

"I did, didn't I? Thank goodness the genius that came along with them didn't send me screaming into the night." She kissed him. "I'll get Ben to sleep. You tell Euclid he can eavesdrop in the sitting room, if he must."

Bedding his wife on a mattress instead of the floor of the washroom met and exceeded all expectations. He loved her thoroughly, competently, and fiercely in turn. She held nothing back, not that she ever did, but there was a raw edge to their lovemaking that he could only credit to fear and war. He knew this woman in his arms and heart understood the toll of battle, especially when she whispered, "I worry every day. All the time."

He could be flippant and tell her not to. That might have assuaged a less intelligent woman, but Meri, in her normal, logical, reasonable way was far beyond that.

"Don't tell me not to worry, Able. Your ship is small, the Channel is dangerous, and the enemy all around."

"I would never toy with your intelligence," he said, as he settled her for slumber close to him. "At this point, all we can do is our duty to king and country."

"I know. I will wait and worry."

Chapter Nineteen

Able slept deep and peacefully, holding his wife close, savoring her warmth, even though it was August. They made love again before dawn, then spent the next hour in pleasant conversation. Even he hadn't reckoned on the bliss of love and conversation. Marriage had many surprises.

As Meri half-drowsed, he told her of his visit to Admiralty House, and the grilling he received concerning Admiral Calder's one-day battle at Cape Finisterre. "I could only tell them what I saw. I think he did his best." He put his hand over Meri's gentle fingers on his chest. "The only problem with Calder is that the threat of Napoleon demands more than our best."

"Are we in danger here in Portsmouth?" she asked.

"Aye, we could be, without supreme watchfulness. It's been averted for now, frankly, thanks to Calder," he told her. "For your ears only: We dropped Ogilvie off north of the cape, and one other fellow I did not mention who was aboard Calder's flagship, waiting for us. Can you guess?"

"Jean Hubert," she whispered, as if spies lurked under their bed.

"The very same."

"The two of them made it to Boulogne, where the small craft to cross the Channel waited. When we picked up Ogilvie after our rendezvous with Nelson's fleet, he told us how he and Jean watched Napoleon's troops abandon Boulogne. They have bigger fish to fry on the continent right now, to my relief." He turned thoughtful. "I wonder where the Grande Armée will land next. I pity whichever of our allies lies in its path."

She was silent a long while this time. He wondered if she had returned to sleep. When she spoke, her voice sounded studied and careful, as if she did not want to hear what he might say. "Only Angus returned? Did…did Jean…Is he…" She couldn't finish.

"You like that rascal Frenchman, don't you?" he asked, touched.

"We all do."

"Rest easy, my love. He is on his way to Spain. Probably there by now, watching the harbor of Cádiz, where the combined fleet is anchored."

"How can he be safe from detection there?" He heard all the worry. Meri had turned into the mother of many, even rascally Frenchmen, it would seem.

"Cádiz is full of Frogs now," he reminded her. "I must say that Villeneuve is not a man I would put in charge of such a fleet, but there you have it. Calder wasn't the only leader who lost his nerve at Cape Finisterre."

She had not yet asked the question he feared the most. He waited for it.

"How much danger are you in when you drop off spies and pick them up?"

He kissed her, which probably gave her the answer she dreaded. She kissed him back with all the ferocity of her loving nature. She knew.

"Terrible danger," he admitted, when he could speak. "Thankfully, the *Mercury* is the ship precisely right for maneuvering close and leaving fast."

"Is Captain Ogilvie a spy?" she asked outright. "I think he must be, but no one tells ladies. Not that it is my business, Able, but it seems that he is complicating your life with his demands."

What to tell her? Why not the truth? He knew this wife of his would say nothing. "No word of this anywhere, Meri. Your pledge?"

"You have it, my love. Cross my heart."

"With pleasure." He took her at her word, which meant some highly charged moments of pleasant fondling.

"That wasn't precisely what I meant, Able," she said, which made him laugh.

"Where were we? Ah, yes. Angus and I spent a few nights at the helm on this crossing, which the Rats slept below. He told me of the first time he saw my father in Cádiz. It was also the night he encountered the secretary of a prominent member of Admiralty house conversing with that demon Claude Pascal."

Meri gasped. "A member of our government? With Claude Pascal?"

"For money? Out of fondness for the French? Who knows? Once the traitor secretary was dead, Ogilvie carried the news to a select few –Mr. Pitt included – who agreed to let that Admiralty fellow continue to roam free but under close scrutiny now, in the hopes that he might implicate others."

Meri was silent, mulling the matter around, he knew. "How does anyone know who to trust?" she asked finally.

"That's the spy business," he said. "Personally, I deplore it." He ran his fingers through her hair, enjoying the feeling. "We take Angus Ogilvie inshore to more danger than I care to contemplate." He kissed her. "I want to teach, and now I must fight aboard ship again. You've turned me soft, Meri-deelightful."

"You're blaming me?" she asked in her gruff voice that always made him smile. She settled in more comfortably, and by God, she was soft.

"I'd rather be here," he admitted. "Don't go to sleep yet. I have another matter of interest."

"Please, no more spies," she said.

"No, I promise!"

"Cross your heart?" she teased, which meant more pleasantry, of which he was the beneficiary this time.

"Meri, how can I concentrate," he said finally, which made her snort, and mutter something about concentrating better than the entire population of England. "Enough, you scamp! Remember what I told you about my father?"

"You *saw* him?" That one content woman could move so rapidly from languor to high alert startled him.

"No, alas." He told her the story of his near encounter. "The captain of the *Firme* deliberately kept me away from the lee side of the ship."

"Meaning...."

"He didn't want me to see what was happening on that side of the ship closest to shore," he explained. "The captain wouldn't even look at me, but I assumed that was the humiliation of surrendering his sword and ship to the Royal Navy." He fiddled with her hair. "The sergeant of Marines brought over a lantern when he boarded. Capitan Villavicencio took a really good look at me and went pale."

"Spanish father and English son," Meri said.

"He admitted with some satisfaction that his ruse in occupying me had allowed the Conde de Quitanar to slip over the side into a pinnace and return to the Spanish flagship."

"My goodness. So close," Meri said.

"I wish we had engaged the enemy on the morrow," Able said. "I'd have given the earth to capture Gravina's *Argonauta* and meet the man who ruined my life."

"Maybe another time," she said.

"Most certainly. As it is, Admiral Calder has been recalled to Admiralty House – another dispatch carrier is taking that unwelcome invitation to the fleet – where he will suffer a court martial. I doubt the admiral will serve in the fleet again."

"Harsh."

"War."

Able resumed his duties across the street in the morning after a breakfast so huge as to render him sleepy by eight bells in the forenoon watch. Or perhaps it was the loving. He had said that to Meri on his return from St. Brendan's that afternoon, and she laughed.

"It's my right and privilege to jolly you back to life," she said in his ear, so the boys wouldn't overhear.

And so she did, for the rest of the week. He knew nothing could ruffle her own well-being, not even the letter he brought home after school at the end of the week. He saved it for dinner, because he wanted Grace and Master Ferrier, if he dropped in, and the Rats to listen, especially Nick.

"Headmaster Croker received this letter," he announced, after the mutton ragout. "It appears St. Brendan's will host Admiral Horatio Lord Nelson tomorrow. There will be a dinner for all of us." He nodded to Meri and Grace. "Ladies included," then turned his attention to Nick Bonfort, who had been quietly listening all week to the exploits – oh, call them boasts – of the *Mercury* crew. "He is bringing along his secretary, the Reverend Alexander Scott, who complained in my hearing that he was too busy with paperwork. Drowning in it, he said."

"Paperwork?" Smitty asked with some scorn.

Able saw Nick wince. Time to change that. "How do you think you are fed aboard ship, Mister Smith?" he asked, probably with more vigor than the question required.

"Well, I…" Smitty stopped and considered the matter. A wry smile revealed a humbler Smitty. "Without those bills of lading, nothing happens, does it?"

"No, Mr. Smith, it does not," Able agreed. "Mind you, when you are a warranted sailing master, you will inspect a numbing quantity of kegged beef, salt, ink, dried vegetables, then apply your initials and stow it just so in the hold. Without clerks and secretaries, you wouldn't eat."

"Aye, sir," Smitty replied with a more sincere smile. "We need our secretaries."

"Indeed we do," Able replied, hoping Nick felt better. "I had the honor of speaking with Admiral Nelson only weeks ago, and also Reverend Scott." He thought a conspiratorial lean closer to the boys across the cutlery and plates wouldn't go amiss. "They often deal with spies and odd arrangements in alleys that also influence the national scene. Bear that in mind."

Grace St. Anthony approached him when the boys had cleared the table and spread out their studies. "Speaking of odd arrangements in alleys, have you seen Captain Ogilvie lately?"

"He returned with me," Able said, after he stopped laughing. "Is he gone again?"

She nodded. He saw disappointment in her eyes, and regretted his laughter. "It's these damnable times, Grace," he said. "He has a baffling ability to vanish and reappear."

She nodded, hugging her little son to her, and walked to the window in the sitting room that overlooked St. Brendan's and Portsmouth harbor. She swayed to some inner music until her son slept, then left the room quietly.

Meri had been turning the cuffs on some lad's shirt. "She's better here, Able, but she is lonely."

"Are you?" he asked.

"We're learning to cope," she replied. "The nights here are long."

"They're long aboard the *Mercury*, too," he said. "To think some people believe we like war in the Royal Navy."

"They don't live in Portsmouth, do they?"

Vice-Admiral Horatio Lord Nelson spent the next afternoon at St. Brendan's, shown around by Headmaster Croker. They caught up with Able and Harry Ferrier and the Gunwharf Rats in the stone pool beside and behind the monastery, most of them nearly naked and balancing on the floating platforms, taking sextant readings. Others arranged ballast on additional platforms, with advice from Master Ferrier standing beside the pool.

Able had joined the half-naked crew. He saluted the admiral, who laughed and saluted back. Able watched as the little man looked closer at the platform's name. "HMS *Floaty*?" he asked.

"Admiral, my son Ben named the platform and christened it with a pint of milk," Able said.

"Benjamin Belvedere Six, if I recall Sir B told me once?" His eyes, so lively, turned serious. "I miss that man."

"We all do, admiral," Able said, thinking how much Sir B would enjoy sharing the deck of HMS *Floaty*. "Care to join us, sir?"

"Must I strip down, too?"

"No, sir. We'll take you as you are."

Admiral Nelson removed his bicorn and hanger and took a leap, balancing himself with some agility on the deck of *Floaty*. "As you were, men," he said, and watched as the now-terrified Rats froze. "I mean it," Nelson said, enjoying himself hugely, if his smile was any indication. "Plot your courses."

"Catching the last of the August sun, Master Six?" Nelson asked as he stood beside Able on the slightly elevated box dubbed the quarterdeck.

"Aye, admiral," Able said. "Breathing in great lungsful of Portsmouth at low tide, too."

Nelson chuckled. He indicated the Rats with a nod. "How are their skills with the sextant?"

"Better and better, sir. No one in the last few weeks has plotted the *Floaty* upriver in the Amazon."

Nelson pointed to the other platform. "HMS *Platform*?" he asked.

"No, sir. Ben thought that should be the *HMS Floaty Boaty*," Able said, wondering what the exalted admiral standing beside a man wearing only his small clothes was thinking of all this nonsense.

Admiral Nelson was silent in that self-contained way of his, hand behind his back, minding his own thoughts. Only a few weeks ago south of Cape Finisterre, Able had seen him in much the same pose on the far more exalted deck of HMS *Victory*, as he looked over an entire fleet.

Am I looking at greatness? Able asked himself. *I do believe he regards my Rats with the same effort he expends on well-trained foretopmen, gunners, Marines, and able seamen.* He knew better than to interrupt.

One of the younger Rats on *Floaty Boaty* stepped too close to the edge as he rearranged the ballast and fell into the stone pool. Able felt no alarm. No one entered this pool without proficiency in swimming. Still… His heart swelled with pride as nearly everyone on *Floaty Boaty* went into the pool after their mate, handing him out to the lad who by designation remained topside, ready to receive him. In a moment they were back at work.

"They look out for each other," Admiral Nelson said. "Brilliant."

"It's what workhouse lads do," Able said. "None of us would have survived without the others, I among them."

"Master Six, you are to be commended," Nelson said. "You and your doughty crew are training a generation of navigators." He looked around. "And I imagine others, too."

"We have one lad – our surgeon on the *Mercury* – who is at Haslar and should be in medical school in a year or two, Admiral Nelson." He pointed to Smitty, who was helping one of the younger Rats with his sextant. "That tall one will be a fine sailing master soon. He gave impeccable commands at Finisterre." He thought about Nick, who was arranging ballast with his usual flair on the *Floaty Boaty*. "That one with the red scarf around his neck would be an excellent secretary. Not all will be navigators."

"A secretary, you say? Give me his name at the banquet tonight, if you would, Master Six."

"Aye, sir."

"Let's go ashore."

"Aye, sir."

While Nelson regained his hat and hanger, Able wrapped a towel around his middle. "Walk with me a moment, Master."

They walked along the sea wall, an incongruous pair: the small man so impeccable, the tall one wearing a towel and a bosun's whistle.

"I have sent a message to Captain Lapenotiere of the HMS *Pickle*, another of my dispatch ships, a schooner. You have seen the *Pickle*?"

"Aye, sir. We passed each other two weeks ago."

"Stop next time and make yourself known to him." Nelson started back to the stone pool, his eyes on the Gunwharf Rats. "We will be relying on the *Mercury* as another dispatch ship, and so I have told Captain Lapenotiere. Say farewell to your classroom duties for the foreseeable future, Master Six. I assume that is why the excellent Master Ferrier is here."

"Aye, sir. I wanted the best." Able glanced up the slope to his house, where he knew Meri would not care to hear this news. "My wife will worry about me, sir."

"They do that," Nelson commented. "They must love us." He sighed and the sentiment passed quickly. "Call your…your…"

"Gunwharf Rats, sir?"

"Aye, your Gunwharf Rats to the side here. There will be Portsmouth dignitaries making all kinds of speeches and pronouncements tonight, I suppose. I want to say something to your stout fellows right now, words with no bark on them. Something they might remember."

"Absolutely, sir. They will treasure it, I am certain."

Able picked up the bosun's whistle around his neck and blew the call to assemble. In mere moments the Rats floated their armada in front of Admiral Horatio Lord Nelson. Able looked at his boys, saw their youth, their skill, their determination to prove themselves. He told the listeners in his brain to be gentle with him, because he cared so much.

For a little man, Nelson had a captain's commanding voice, the kind heard over cannon fire. "England needs you Gunwharf Rats," he said most distinctly. "More than that, sirs, England confides that every man will do his duty. Every man!" Nelson looked around. He might have been addressing each officer and sailor in the fleet, and not a handful of workhouse bastards. Able swallowed the lump in his throat.

"As you were, men," Lord Nelson said, his voice softer. Able heard all the affection, no, all the love. "Remember England."

Chapter Twenty

Meridee didn't have her husband long. She could have fooled herself at the banquet, which was all celebration, hero worship and platitudes, but she was no fool. Besides, there was Able Six beside her, holding her hand under the table, running his thumb gently across her knuckles, putting her nerves on edge with his simple touch.

"All is not well, Able," she told him finally. "You will tell me more when we are home."

But war speeds up time. War couldn't wait until they were home. A significant nod from Lord Nelson in their direction was enough to keep her man standing there in the long hall at St. Brendan's as other guests chatted and finally said goodnight to the banquet's main attraction.

One group of admirers refused to leave, but Lord Nelson was done with them. He gave a courtly bow and waved them off in mid-sentence, practically loping down the hall toward them.

"My apologies." He bowed to Meridee and cut directly to the thought obviously uppermost on his mind. "Master Six, where is the nearest room of easement? I have consumed far too much wine."

Able laughed and pointed to his classroom. "I keep a pot in here for emergencies," he said. "You would be astounded how some Gunwharf Rats loosen up with the terror of trigonometry. I can't begin to tell you what the calculus does." He winked at Meridee. "Give us a moment, my love."

Irritating man, she thought as she waved them off. She nodded to Grace, who detached herself from her brother and came closer, an inquiring look on her face. Meridee whispered to her. "They are peeing in a pot in Able's classroom."

"Oh, the economy of men," Grace said, as she tried and failed to smother a laugh. "Do you ever wish…"

"Who doesn't?" Meridee said, wanting to laugh, too, but reminding herself that her mother had raised her to ignore such things.

She was happier to admire Grace's good cheer, and equally pleased to think it had improved in recent weeks in the Sixes' smaller, mildly chaotic house on Saints Way. Grace's eyes no longer held the look of bleak desolation that Sir B's death had fixed in them, a sort of living rictus. Was she happy? Meridee doubted it supremely, but settled on gently content. A widow could do worse.

The men returned to the hall, deep in conversation, Able inclining his head toward the smaller man with the arsenal of gold military decorations on his otherwise plain uniform, his eyepatch and empty pinned sleeve. *I shall have to ask my husband if he ever wonders how a workhouse lad could even dream of finding himself shoulder to shoulder with this hero,* she thought, proud of Able Six, even if he did keep a pee pot in his classroom. Horrors.

She prepared to blend into the wall as the conversation continued, this time with Captain Ogilvie joining it. "I didn't even see him in the dining hall," she whispered to Grace, when Ogilvie moved toward Able and Admiral Nelson.

"He does have a way of materializing like a phantom, does he not?" Grace said. She inclined toward Meridee. "I must admit, though, that I know when he is present."

"How?"

"He wears the most marvelous lemon-scented cologne."

"I hadn't noticed."

"I have," Grace said in a soft voice for Meridee's ears only. "I like it."

"Should we stay here?" Meridee asked.

"Yes, we should." Grace nudged Meridee. "I think our august admiral is gesturing to you. Go on."

Meridee took a step back instead of forward, unable to think why England's darling wanted to chat with her. She thought of her introduction to him three years ago, when she came to Portsmouth as a woman in love to plead the cause of one poverty-stricken sailing master to teach at this all-but-unknown school. Surely a man as busy as Horatio Nelson wouldn't remember that.

He did. Admiral Nelson bowed to her curtsey, then turned to Able. "Master Six, you should have seen this lady pleading your cause several years ago. Wise of you to marry her."

"It was the smartest thing I ever did," Able said, tucking her close. He laughed and squeezed her, which made Meridee blush. "I can't say with equal confidence that it was the smartest thing *she* ever did, marrying a penniless bastard."

"Oh, you," was the best she could manage.

"And now we take him away," Nelson said. He looked down the hall to another man coming toward them. "Mrs. Six, we need Nick Bonfort, too."

"No!" Even though she knew how badly Nick wanted to go to sea with the other Rats, the word came out so quickly. The quiet boy who was always sick at sea had easily won her heart after he borrowed her maiden name. "I mean..."

"You mean no," the admiral said gently. "Nick Bonfort is like one of your own, isn't he?"

"They all are, sir," she said, "Nick a little more. I'm certain Able... Master Six...has told you why."

"He has. He also knows, as you do, that Nick wants to serve in the fleet with the other Rats," Nelson said. "I am only grateful that my daughter Horatia is too young to serve, and of the female variety."

Meridee knew all the scandal around Lord Nelson and Emma Hamilton, and their child. She also knew she was staring into kind eyes that understood her own love for a dear one. And there was Able, who went to sea in defense of England without question, when she knew he wanted to be home.

"It's my war, too, my lord," she said. "I'll send Nick off with a great whacking kiss...where is he going?"

"With me," Nelson said. "This man bearing down on us is Reverend Alexander Scott, my secretary and *Victory*'s chaplain." He glanced at Able. "When your sailing master mentioned that Nick Bonfort was a lad fond of detail, with excellent penmanship and a good brain, I knew we needed him."

"Then he's yours," Meridee said promptly, knowing she could cry later. She could almost see the joy in Nick's face when he heard the good news. "My Gunwharf Rats are growing up." She willed herself to stand a little taller. "When do you want him?"

"I will return to Portsmouth in the middle of September," Nelson said. "Reverend Scott will send you a note."

She moved a little closer to the great man, not wanting to be overheard. "Admiral Nelson, Nick is prone to seasickness. I should warn you."

To her amazement, and then her endearment, Horatio Nelson threw back his head and laughed. "Dear lady, I am, too," he said when he could speak. "In point of fact, nothing but my enthusiastic love for the profession keeps me one hour at sea."

Who could not trust a man like this one? "Very well, Admiral Nelson, you may have Nick," she told him, even as her heart broke. "I know he will be pleased." She held her head up. "I am pleased a Bonfort will serve with the fleet."

The implication of what she said made Nelson put his hand to his heart. "He's just a guttersnipe borrowing your name," he said, as if reminding her.

"He's *my* guttersnipe, *my* Gunwharf Rat." She hadn't meant that to come out so vehemently, so full of possession. She reconsidered. Yes, she did.

Again, that kind eye. "Master Six, I would venture that St. Brendan's has been equally well served by this lady. Equally."

"I never argue with superior officers, Admiral Nelson," Able said.

"I rather hope you will, master, in matters concerning navigation," the admiral replied. He bowed. "I am returning to Merton. I have a family, too." He nodded to Able. "Where away, Master Six?"

"The blockade in two days," he said, after a glance at Meridee.

She knew it was coming. Everyone was leaving and the ladies would wait. For a brief moment, she thought of her spinster years living outside Plymouth with her sister's family, beloved of them, but always on the outside. Was it easier or harder than this? She had no answer, except a smile. "Let's go home."

Able crooked out his arm and she put her arm through his, determined to treasure every small touch. He gestured to Lady St. Anthony. "And you, Grace? I have another arm."

"So do I, Able," Captain Ogilvie said as he bowed to a surprised Lady St. Anthony. "I'll get her back before curfew."

"I will be home sooner than that," Grace assured them all, with some of her former crispness. "Meridee, do tell Junius I will be back in thirty minutes. Hopefully my little lad is still asleep."

"May I join you?" Reverend Scott asked Meridee. "Alexander Scott at your service."

Please don't, Meridee wanted to tell the tall, courtly gentleman who looked nothing like a seaman. She nodded instead, knowing there was no point in putting off bad news for her that would send Nick into the rafters with joy. "Certainly, sir. I know Nick will want to meet you."

The three of them crossed the street in silence. Meridee could tell Able didn't know what to say to her. She only hoped he hadn't been harboring up this information about Nick, as if trying to determine the best time to tell her, a time with people around so she wouldn't cry. *Stop it, Meridee*, she scolded herself. *Just stop it. He has no more control over war than you do.*

Nick sat by himself in the dining room. Since Master Ferrier had requested he keep detailed notes of each class, Nick had accumulated a tidy pile of paper, which he had tabbed and separated into folders. Meridee watched him from the door of the dining room, mindful that his earlier chaotic years in the Dartmouth workhouse compelled order in his brain.

She knew that some of the other Rats had needed bits of food to squirrel away in their bedchambers against the nightly fear of hunger. With Nick, the need had been a hunger for the order found in books, paper and pencil. She wondered if he could manage the chaos of the HMS *Victory* in battle.

"Nick, there is someone here who has news for you," she said. "Do make yourself known to Reverend Scott. Sir? This is Nick Bonfort." Her heart breaking, she smiled at them both and ushered Lord Nelson's secretary forward. "He has wonderful news for you."

She turned away, blinded already by tears, and bumped into Able behind her. He tried to hold her there but she wrenched herself out of his grasp and hurried up the stairs, desperate to shut her bedroom door on them all. She stood against the door and gulped back her tears, listening. Silence, silence, and then a whoop from Nick.

Meridee covered her face with her hands and sobbed. Oddly, her ordinary mind took her on a journey of its own back to an afternoon when she had committed some childhood infraction and been sentenced to read several improving chapters in the book of…which one was it?

She went to her side of the bed and sat down, reaching for the Bible. Impatient with herself, wishing she had a brain like her traitor husband's, she stared at blurry pages. She didn't hear the door open, but Able sat beside her next, his arm around her.

She was no fool. She could have leaned away. She could have pushed him away. Instead, she burrowed closer. "Where does it say… someone mourning for her children? I have to know."

"The Jeremiah version or the St. Matthew one?" he asked sharply.

"Don't, Able, please don't."

"I'm sorry."

She knew he didn't need the Bible; he had memorized it on one voyage or another, but she wanted more. "Tell me in your own words," she demanded.

"What?" he asked in mock astonishment, which lightened her heart. "You prefer me to the Lord?"

"At times," she replied. "I know you know all verses by heart because your brain has no choice. Tell your brain I want *you*, not some dusty prophet."

She watched his face, hoping she hadn't offended his weird genius. When he smiled, she knew better. "Rachel won't let herself be comforted, because her children are gone."

"I'm going to miss Nick," she managed. "I miss them all, but Nick… You understand."

"I do, lady of my heart. Imagine leading them into danger, as I do."

She took a deep breath, amazed that she hadn't considered his view. "Shame on me for whining," she said softly.

She let herself be gathered in his arms. He gently pulled her down beside him until she rested her cheek against his uniform buttons. He gave her his handkerchief and she tucked it under her cheek. This was his best uniform; he didn't need tearstains on it.

"No shame there, Meri. You love your Gunwharf Rats, too. Remember the next verse?" he asked. He put the damp handkerchief over her nose. "Blow."

She did as he demanded and felt slightly better. Maybe she should lighten this dark moment she had brought on them both. "I know it doesn't say 'blow.'"

He chuckled. "Meri, what a mother you are. This is what Jeremiah wrote in the next verse."

"Your words, please."

"They'll return from enemy lands. For the sake of argument, let us add seas. Most people never think of that verse, but I do. It keeps me going. Will it keep you going?"

Would it? She kissed his cheek. "I believe it will."

"I know it will, because you are Meridee Six, mother of many, wife of one, and my heart of oak."

Chapter Twenty-one

The *Mercury* sailed two days later in early September with the tide and the wind from the right quarter, blowing them toward Spain. Meri and Ben saw them off from the Gunwharf, Nick standing beside the woman he called Mum, looking not even slightly sad, because he had his own sea duty ahead in mere weeks.

Even Smitty had been properly impressed when informed that Nick's duty would see him aboard the HMS *Victory*, the flagship of Lord Nelson himself. "Good God, Nick!" he had exclaimed in his inimitable Smitty way, "Who do you *know*?" That made all the Gunwharf Rats laugh, Able included. They knew they didn't know anybody.

"Smitty, sometimes you just get lucky," Able told his *Mercury* sailing master later that evening. "It so happens that the admiral's secretary is drowning in paperwork and needs an organizer to stack, file and collate."

"That would be Nick," Smitty agreed. And still being Smitty, he had given Able a long look. "We Rats don't get lucky often, though. Master Six, did *you* get lucky?"

Oh, my word did he ever. How to tell someone like Smitty? He could have described Sir B's mentoring, or Captain Benjamin Hollowell's willingness to take a chance, but that wasn't the supreme stroke of luck. "I did, Smitty," he said finally, and found himself hard put not to struggle. "I got lucky the day this half-pay bastard caught the eye of Meridee Bonfort. Since then, I don't know a richer man than I."

"A woman makes that big a difference?" Smitty asked, sounding younger than usual, which made Able feel surprisingly paternal toward this young-old Rat.

"She understands me," Able said, unable to think of a better answer, and if truth be told, a little surprised that all the geniuses inhabiting his skull couldn't suggest anything better. Perhaps he was right. "She's pretty, too," he added a bit feebly, which made Smitty laugh.

He regarded the *Mercury*'s young sailing master, seeing Smitty as an equal as he saw Jamie MacGregor, an earlier St. Brendan alumnus now serving well in the fleet. "Smitty, the luckiest thing you have done so far is show up at St. Brendan unannounced and declare that you were meant to be here," he said, "no matter how poorly Sir B's rascal brother treated you and your mother. You took a chance. It's making all the difference."

Able watched a light come into Smitty's eyes. He wondered if the normally taciturn lad would say something more, hoping he would, in fact. Smitty merely nodded, said "Aye, I did, sir," and walked away. Smitty made a point before the *Mercury* sailed to help Nick decide what should go in his duffel bag, as the younger boy prepared to ship out on the *Victory*. Bravo, Smitty.

But oh, the tug of domestic life, before shipping out again, with Ben to enjoy, and Meridee to tease and love. It was enough to make a seafaring man question if life on shore *was* better. He had said as much to Meri one early morning. "You, my love, are a sailor," she had reminded him seriously, or as serious as Meri could look with her hair a mess, and naked. "I've watched you stand at the window and stare out at the sound. You know you miss the ocean."

"I miss you when I'm at sea," he pointed out. They had had this conversation before.

"Then you are a total no-hoper…" When she hesitated, Euclid pointed out inside Able's head that she was probably going to call him Durable about now. "Able," she finished, which made Able chuckle. Even Euclid was wrong upon occasion. Come to think of it, what was Euclid doing in their bedroom? Maybe it was time for another stern talk with the mathematician, once he was alone and had the deck to himself on the way to Spain. Euclid knew better.

Meri had saved her best goodbye after Nick said he would run ahead to the Gunwharf, after Mrs. Perry had glared at him and threatened him to return in good shape, and after Ezekiel Bartleby had brought by his favorite sugared biscuits.

What a woman. She set his duffel outside the front door, told Ben to watch it for Papa in case of Barbary Pirates, closed the door, and hauled him in close for a kiss that left his knees weak. "There's more when you return," she said. She fluffed her hair, put on her bonnet, then smiled and patted the scurrilous locket he had left for her before the first voyage. Her long, slow wink nearly undid him.

"Come, my dear. Let us make our way to Gunwharf," she said, her shoulders squared and her back straight. He knew she would cry later, but this magnificent lady awed him almost as much as Mrs. Perry, on occasion.

Davey Ten had nearly missed the *Mercury*'s departure. "The surgeon showed me how to suture a wound," he announced to the others as he threw himself aboard at the last moment. "He made me do one."

Tots wrinkled his nose. "Eww!"

It was hard to remain dignified in a pile on the deck, tossed there by the sudden catch of wind in sail, but Davey tried, with surprising dignity. "Tottenham, be happy that I know a little more on this voyage," he said, as he stood up, balanced himself and snatched a stray bandage roll rolling from his medical satchel.

"Belay that, both of you," Able said, amused. "Take your duffel below, Mr. Ten."

They sailed on a spanking breeze, with Smitty deliberately wheeling the *Mercury* nearly over on her starboard beam to catch every puff of wind, knowing how beautiful Sir B's yacht looked under all sail, dancing along. Able stood beside Smitty, feeling the wind on his face. Meri was right; these moments with the odor of tar, and the rumble underfoot that meant waves and water were of paramount importance to him.

The canvas-wrapped, tar-covered dispatches were stowed safely below, heading for Admiral Collinwood on the *Royal Sovereign*, somewhere in the Gut, the strait of Gibraltar that beckoned into the Mediterranean Sea. Royal Navy blockaders had planted themselves firmly south of Cádiz to deny access to any of the Combined Fleet from sailing into that wide-open sea, where they could be hard to find.

Before that rendezvous with the *Royal Sovereign*, the *Mercury* had additional orders from Trinity House to sail under cover under darkness to Tarifa and drop off Captain Ogilvie. After that mail drop to the *Royal Sovereign*, they were to pick him up in a week, this time with Jean Hubert, who had been observing the Combined Fleet in Cádiz harbor and who was hopefully still among the quick and not the dead.

Admiral Nelson also wanted him to effect a rendezvous with the HMS *Pickle*, another message-bearer. "You and Captain Lapenotiere need to meet," he had said after the banquet. "If you happen to be with the fleet when the Frogs and Dons in Cádiz come out to fight, you'll be a repeater, too, along with the *Pickle*."

With that in mind, Able set Whitticombe, Tots, Davey and Avon Marsh to scanning the horizon for a schooner as fleet as the *Mercury*. On the fourth day, sailing south by southeast, they found the *Pickle*.

"Gor, what is she?" Tots asked. He and Whitticombe watched and Davey prepared to toss a line, as the *Pickle* took the hint and slowed.

"She's a lovely schooner, with two masts to our one. Look how that one mast is raked," Able said. "Steady as she goes, Smitty."

"Aye, Captain. Does she sail as close to the wind as we can?"

"As near as, considering her size. Her crew numbers about thirty."

The others came closer, watching and listening. "Is she American-made?" Tots asked.

"The first schooners were," Able said, enjoying the sight of the graceful ship with the incongruous name as much as his crew. "The speaking trumpet, Whitticombe, please."

"Ahoy, *Pickle*," Able called through the trumpet. "A moment of your time?"

"Toss your line. Come aboard, number Seven Two Six," they heard.

Avon looked up from his code book and grinned at Able. "Master, we're seven two six, under new and unnamed vessels!"

The line Davey tossed was grabbed handily and snugged tight. Little Avon tried twice to toss the line from the *Mercury*'s stern, but the rope's size defeated him. He frowned when one of the *Pickle* crew chuckled, but Able thought the smiles were friendly. Weren't they all part of the same navy?

Captain Ogilvie leant a hand and in a thrice, the vessels were bound together, floating as near as could be, considering a difference in size that made the decks unequal. A plank ended that problem.

"I'll take the wheel, Able," Ogilvie said. "Your crew should see the *Pickle*."

"Come, crew, let's pay a visit," Able said. He ushered the Gunwharf Rats up and over the plank. To his inward delight, the *Pickle*'s bosun even twittered a welcome on his pipe. Able couldn't help smiling to see his St. Brendan boys stand a little taller.

He didn't know Captain Lapenotiere, but the serious-looking man with thinning hair appeared to be the only officer on board. He gave a slight bow, then held out his hand.

"Welcome aboard, Captain Six, is it?" he asked. "I've been told to expect a visit."

"Captain Six, indeed, Captain Lapenotiere," Able said. He decided quickly that he liked being called captain. He gestured to his crew, standing tall as they could. It touched his heart to see how proud his fellow rats and bastards looked, eyes ahead and serious. "We're from St. Brendan the Navigator School, serving in the fleet as requested and required."

Lapenotiere nodded. He relaxed and nodded to a crew member in nondescript uniform. "Master Johnson, my gunny, will show your lads around the *Pickle*. Let me invite you to my miniscule cabin for a drink."

Smitty whispered to Able. "Captain, we would like to know the Pickle's origin," Able said. "They've never seen a schooner."

"She's Bermuda-built, on American lines," Captain Lapenotiere said promptly, as if he heard that question often, and this one: "And no, I have no idea why she is called the *Pickle*." The boys chuckled, and Able followed the captain below deck.

"Sir, it's a regular palace, compared to *my* below deck accommodations," Able said as he seated himself in Lapenotiere's cramped space. "We share six berths and a galley in the *Mercury*. Luckily, only Captain Ogilvie snores."

"Just John, please," Lapenotiere. He poured something amber and looking highly contraband into a mostly clean glass. "Able Six, I believe?"

"Yes, indeed," Able said and took a sip. "I can't even remember my last madeira." (Well, he did. It was in Lisbon on April 22, 1795.) He definitely couldn't recall having been treated so well by Admiral Calder in *his* private cabin.

"Madeira is one of the perks along these shores," John said, tapping his own glass. "Do you have a message for me?"

"Admiral Nelson specifically requested that we look for the *Pickle*, as we sail with dispatches for Admiral Cuthbert," Able said. "He told me that if the *Mercury* happened to be in attendance during the fleet action which he thinks is imminent, I might consider the *Mercury* as operating at *your* behest."

John Lapenotiere continued to impress him. "Possibly. From the way your helmsman so efficiently heeled the yacht toward us, and from what

I know of your own abilities – word gets around the fleet – all I ask for is that you note my relative position, and be prepared to repeat any messages that you see, in the heat of battle. I trust you have a reliable signalman?"

Able smiled inside to think of Avon Marsh, eleven years old and brilliant with code. "The very best, I suspect."

"Keep him safe then. That's all the advice you need." He stood up. "Drink it down, Able. I am certain you already know the principal rule of dispatch vessels: We move fast."

"Aye, we do." Able downed his madeira. "That possible fleet action? Coming soon, in your opinion?"

"I doubt Admiral Nelson will wait a moment." He held out his hand again. "Talleyho and good hunting to the *Mercury*. We'll meet soon enough."

Chapter Twenty-two

They found the *Royal Sovereign* and its numerous minions at Gibraltar with no difficulty, after a breath-taking approach to Tarifa by nightfall to drop off Captain Ogilvie.

The night was dark, and the *Mercury* even darker. To Whitticombe's real dismay, Able helped the Rats drape rotten old fishing nets around the ship's sides. "Oh sir," he said softly, when Able had them toss long-brewed tea on the spanking white sails, anything to turn the *Mercury* drab and forgettable. Even Tots groaned out loud when Able said the stains would have to remain, as long as they sailed so close to Spain or France in dangerous waters. They would stow the fishing nets below, once they left the shore.

Near midnight with the moon a mere sliver, the *Mercury* heeled close into shore, helmed this time by Able with Captain Ogilvie by his side, ever watchful. Angus had changed from his uniform to the sloppy, nondescript cape and a battered hat that smelled as bad as they looked. His filthy trousers defied comment from the Rats, who studiously tried to stay upwind.

Ogilvie seemed in a good mood to Able, whistling "Lilliburlero" in slow march time. Maybe this was the moment to express a wish – not that anything would come of it. Able waited for some opinion from his spectral confidantes, but nothing. Lately, it had been more nothing than even idle chatter. It was as if even Euclid waited for him to act. Maybe the others were bothering someone else. He hoped it wasn't Ben.

"I know I mentioned my near-encounter at Cape Finisterre with the man I think is my father," Able said, unwilling to sound hesitant, but there you are – he *was* hesitant, especially around Captain Ogilvie, a man with a well-known sharp tongue.

"You did. You've been thinking about him a lot," Ogilvie said, and he didn't sound unkind. "Able, you think about a lot of things at once, don't you?"

"Aye. It's a burden," he said simply. "All I know I learned from the captain of the *Firme*, who said that the Count of Quintanar was safely back *al buque insignia del Admirante Gravina*."

Angus stared at him, then chuckled. "Able, in English, please."

Grateful for darkness, Able felt his face grow hot. *Good Lord, I am within striking distance of Spain and I speak Spanish? I had better pay attention,* he thought, embarrassed. "He returned to Admiral Gravina's flagship," he muttered. Since he had just made a fool of himself, why not finish the job? "I want to see him. I want to find my father. I cannot leave this ship because it is my command, or I would try."

Ogilvie nodded. "I wish you could. What say you if I snoop around among the Spanish fleet? You know, see what I can learn about the count."

"You would do that for me?" Able asked. It seemed to be an evening of surprises.

"I believe I would," was Ogilvie's quiet reply.

"Is Sir Clive still roaming about Admiralty, unaware that he is on a short leash?" Able asked in a whisper.

"Aye, he is, but not for much longer. Thanks to the secretary *we* planted, I have about all the useful information I need to indict him and one other."

"This is a dirty business," Able said, thinking of Grace St. Anthony and her interest in the man who stood beside him. "How can you do it?"

"Lately, I have been asking myself the same question," Ogilvie replied.

With Tots sounding the depths, Able angled the *Mercury* close to shore, then nodded to Smitty. The *Mercury* had a small craft half the size of a jolly boat. Silently, Whitticombe and Davey Ten lifted the little vessel into the water, followed by Smitty, who sat down and quietly set the oars in the oarlocks.

"Happy hunting, Angus," Able said. "I hope you find Jean Hubert."

"I will if I have to dig him up to do it," was Ogilvie's cheerful reply, as he lowered himself into the boat.

If only you didn't sound so eager to do that, Able thought. *No wonder you make Meri uneasy.* "See you in five days right here," he said. "Two flashes, pause, two quick in succession from us. Three longs from you."

He turned into the wind so the sails luffed and the *Mercury* slowed. He knew it was only a matter of minutes for Smitty to row one slightly overweight spy to shore, so why did it seem forever? When Smitty clambered back over the side, Able let out the breath he had been holding. The grin on Smitty's face was ample evidence of his pleasure in a bit of derring-do.

After they stowed the boat, a tack and a turn sent them back to open waters, a far safer place to be. "Sir, I smelled what must be oranges," Smitty said. "Have you ever eaten an orange?"

"Aye, lad. We should've asked Captain Ogilvie to procure some."

"Are they good?"

Why should such a question make him struggle? "The best," Able replied, which meant narrowing a mountain of emotions down to two words. When Able clambered aboard his first ship as a nine-year-old escapee from a Dumfries workhouse, the captain sailed to a Spain not under Napoleon's thumb yet. The Royal Navy's newest recruit ate oranges until he nearly foundered. Somehow, oranges turned into freedom. He probably shouldn't tell that to Smitty. He probably should maintain his dignity as captain at sea and master instructor on land. Oh, hell no.

"Smitty, let me tell you about my first oranges," he started. Those few words must have somehow beckoned the others to sit cross legged on the deck, with only the light of the moon for illumination. He watched their faces, saw the anticipation for an orange, and hoped there might be oranges for them someday. "There is a wonderful city called Valencia…"

Another day of sailing a prudent distance from shore along the southern coast of Spain led them through the Gut and past the Rock of Gibraltar, called anciently the Pillars of Hercules. They had passed and identified themselves to frigates and smaller craft blockading the Spanish coast and been ushered onward. Smitty helmed the *Mercury* as they sailed by the Rock and into the Mediterranean. For the only time so far, Smitty let go of the wheel, staring open-mouthed at the majesty of it all.

"Mind your helm, Mr. Smith," Able said, enjoying all the Rats' amazement at the famous sight.

His eyes wide, Tots probably expressed it best. "Gor, every cove and rascal in England would go to sea, if they knew what they were missing."

Even better, it was a warm day, with North African winds ruffling the water and setting the waves dancing. Avon March lay on the deck, shirt off, eyes closed, bliss on his face. Able watched him, remembering a moment like that in the South Pacific, then toed Avon with his shoe. "Better turn over, lad, so you can burn equally on the other side."

Avon sat up, took a look at himself and reached for his shirt, at the same time Whitticombe called out, "*Royal Sovereign!*"

"Very good, Mr. Whitticombe," Able said. "Mr. March, if you please, signal "Permission to come aboard with dispatches. Mercury."

"Aye, sir." Avon raced to the flag locker and yanked it open. In remarkably few minutes, the flags snapped from the signal line.

They all watched as other flags soon fluttered. "'Permission granted,' Captain Six," Avon sang out.

"Bring her close, Smitty," Able said. "I'll be right beside you, if you need help."

Smitty flashed him a grateful look, but took the *Mercury* in like the helmsman he was. Avon was young enough to watch the business with his mouth agape, as the relative sizes of the two two-decker and the yacht became obvious. Able smiled at the good-natured catcalls from the men on the *Sovereign's* deck as they watched the whole business from high above the *Mercury*.

Able knew Smitty wanted to climb the chains with him, but he made no objection – in fact, stood taller – when Able said, "Master Smith, you are captain of the *Mercury* when I leave this ship."

"Aye, sir."

Able took Tots and Avon with him, Tots with the dispatches slung over his shoulder. Up they went, with a hand up from crewmen on deck when they cleared the railing. Able was in no way awed by the lieutenant who greeted him as Captain Six, but the moment did make Euclid exclaim, "Praise all gods," in Greek, and Sir Isaac Newton chuckle.

"Follow me, sir," the lieutenant said.

Able kept his two crew members close, Avon sufficiently awed, Tots with his eyes straight ahead, bearing the precious dispatches. Since the exalted *Royal Sovereign* smelled worse below deck than their yacht, both boys relaxed a little.

When the Royal Marine sentries standing guard at the door to Admiral Cuthbert Collingwood's cabin snapped to attention with a raise of their muskets and click of their shoes, Avon's hand crept into Able's hand and he leaned closer.

His eyes on the Marines, Able bent down and whispered, "No fears, Mr.

March. They're not here for you. Not now, not ever." Grace St. Anthony had told Able and Meri one night of the boy's terror when similarly armed men had shot at three workhouse lads who thought to run away, killing one.

"Here, Avon," Tots said quietly and reached for the signalman's hand. "T'captain needs his hands free. I'm with you."

Admiral Collingwood, currently commanding the Mediterranean fleet, rose to greet them. Able saluted, wishing Captain Sir Belvedere St. Anthony were beside him to see this moment, as their Gunwharf Rats large and small did credit to St. Brendan the Navigator School with their own salutes. Bless Grace St. Anthony for making them practice.

"Captain Six of the *Mercury* reporting with Admiralty dispatches, Admiral," Able said.

He stepped back.

"And these two crewman, Captain Six?" Collingwood said.

"Avon March, signalman and cook, and Tottenham, able seaman," Able said with a gesture. "I left my sailing master in command on the *Mercury*, sir."

He had heard from others, Sir B certainly, of Admiral Collingwood's firmness and his vast ability. Able saw kindness in the tall man's eyes, too, but he didn't expect what followed, not even slightly.

"Do be seated, gentlemen," the admiral said. He gestured to a chair and two stools, then opened a door and leaned in, speaking to someone. "We'll have refreshments in a moment, if you please. Don't be in a hurry to rush off."

"Thank you, sir," Able said as he seated himself, feeling not much older than Avon and just as wide-eyed at this unexpected honor.

Collingwood's steward brought cakes on a silver platter for the boys and watered down rum in silver cups. He smiled broadly the whole time, which warmed Able's heart as nothing else could have. His own chilly reception by Admiral Calder off Cape Finisterre had been nothing like this. He couldn't help the impish thought that perhaps Admiral Calder's court martial was well-earned.

"Tots, hand over the dispatches before you get too deep in your cups," Able said, which made the admiral chuckle.

With considerable dignity, Tots, the Gunwharf Rat found shivering in the rain near Tottenham Court, placed the tarry satchel on Collingwood's desk and sat down. Collingwood patted the satchel. "Thank you, Tots, for getting these to me with no mishap."

"Yer welcome, sir," the boy said.

Admiral Collingwood leaned back in his chair. "Captain Six, let me first tell you how saddened we all were by the death of Sir B. Please convey my deepest sympathy to Lady St. Anthony. Tell her if I had been remotely nearby, I would have been there for his funeral."

"I will, sir. She is still teaching at St. Brendan's and currently sharing the house with my wife and child. Sir B's mansion was too empty after he died."

"I do understand that." He leaned forward. "Is Admiral Nelson making his way to us here in Gibraltar?"

"He will be, as of September 12, sir. Well, tomorrow."

"So it begins."

"Sir?"

Admiral Collingwood leaned across the wide expanse of his desk. "Horatio will force out the Combined Fleet in Cádiz, mark my word, Captain Six."

"Aye, sir, and high time," Able said. Something in the saying of it made Able feel suddenly charged, like the key on the kite string of Dr. Benjamin Franklin's experiment with lightning. He knew he wasn't breathing any louder or faster than he ever did, but he heard the sounds of his spectator geniuses, breathing and murmuring among themselves. "We will fight, Admiral Collingwood?"

"To the death, Captain Six. It will be a battle like no other, because we have a leader like no other."

The admiral raised his silver cup and nodded to the others. The Gunwharf Rats lifted their cups high, too.

"One word, gentleman," Collingwood said. "Victory."

Chapter Twenty-three

The *Mercury* coasted for five days through the blockaders, delivering messages and mail, and even luxuries from one captain to another – including one dozen chickens and a seasick goat – all the while trending north toward Tarifa and the rendezvous with Captain Ogilvie and Jean Hubert.

The interesting thing about voyages such as this, Able decided, was the inescapable mashing of people together, which seemed to point out certain flaws, if flaws they were. Whitticombe continued to be upset by the non-shipshape appearance of the altered *Mercury*. Even the calm assurance from Captain Six that the yacht's lovely white color and spanking clean sails would eventually be restored in Portsmouth still left him grouchy and shaking his head.

"It's for the good of the service," Able assured him, then went down to the galley for a quiet laugh.

The galley reminded him that Avon March might rule supreme as a signalman, but his culinary skills were not far behind. "What in the world smells so good?" he asked. "We have been at sea three weeks now, and I know our supplies are running low."

Avon turned from the pot he stirred, but only a small turn, with one eye on the pot and the other on his captain, because he was a polite child. "Sir, it is dried apples and plums, with a touch of New England maple syrup."

"Where did that come from?" Able asked, mystified. He had signed the lading bill, and such a delectable concoction was nowhere in sight. He knew quite well that some captains were wealthy enough to supply their officers' wardroom with luxuries unimaginable to the crew that lived before the mast, but he was not one of them.

"Captain Six," Able said most formally, "Lady St. Anthony slipped me a small package before we sailed. She made me promise not to cook it until late in the voyage." Avon couldn't help himself then and giggled, reminding Able that he was a mere eleven years old. "She said to wait until we were gut-foundered and heartily tired of porridge and weavily biscuits."

"Lady St. Anthony never said gut-foundered," Able said.

"Aye, sir, she did," Avon contradicted, then exhibited his next delightful trait, a sense of humor. "She says she is an impressionable lady and our low origins are rubbing off on her, and more's the pity."

The two of them had a laugh over that.

In his own way, Davey Ten was equally remarkable. He had always been a quiet lad and nothing had changed. When he had no deck duties – Able made certain to include him in all the workings of the *Mercury* – he could invariably be found in his berth below deck, poring over his medical books. He had an endearing habit of nodding at the pages every time something seemed to agree with him.

Able gave Davey permission to enlist Tots and Whitticombe when he had to practice a particular bandage wrap, or splint. "You should be in medical school next year," Able said, after watching an elaborate splint of Whitticombe's healthy ankle. "Are you sixteen then?"

"Fourteen, sir; you know that, but fifteen is coming soon," Davey reminded him, not a bit fooled. He knew that Able remembered his age precisely. "I *would* like that, above everything," he added. Able heard all the longing.

"So would I. Let's see what we can do," Able said, knowing he had no pull with Haslar Hospital, but a man can dream, eh?

Denying every enemy ship entrance or exit, the Royal Navy's blockading frigates moved back and forth about thirty miles west from Cádiz, where Spanish and French warships languished, trapped by the Royal Navy and not bold enough to venture out for the battle everyone knew was overdue.

One night on the dark of the moon, Able directed his crew to sail closer and tempt fate a little. He had no fears of surprise or shipboard error. By now he knew the *Mercury* as well as he knew Meri's body, how she handled, how frisky she was, and how capable of twists and turns with the precise touch.

By great Zeus, you bastard, Euclid mildly scolded him as they sailed closer, Able at the helm. *You've been at sea a mere three weeks and listen to you.*

But that was the best part of his solitary sailing, the bliss and quiet to think all thoughts or none, or revisit other moments in his life. He had listened to Smitty singing, when he took his turn at the helm. The others took their turn on deck, staring in silence across the water, in itself most pleasant, especially for workhouse lads who never enjoyed solitude unless it was as punishment. Jamie MacGregor had told him once that the lapping of water or the hiss of spindrift spray was soothing to the mind and heart. "I will always need it," Jamie said simply. "It fills an empty space."

Cádiz itself was on an inlet, with the Combined Fleet tucked in close to the mainland. Able sniffed the evening breeze, pleased with the odor of olive oil and fish frying in some *taberna* along the shore. He had lost his virginity in Cádiz at a precocious age – Meri refused to believe him – so the seaport had its own meaning.

An old crone told his fortune there, too, years ago now. His mates hadn't believed him when he said he understood Spanish, but he did, even the hag's half-Castilian, half-Roma dialect. She promised him sons and daughters and lovers in many ports. He smiled at the memory. Sons and daughters would do fine, *muchas gracias*. He needed no other lover than his own wife.

They were close enough to Cádiz; it was time to play off and return to the fold. A touch of the wheel, a swing of the boom, and the *Mercury* sailed for the blockade like a son coming home from a party a little merry from spirits, but sober-enough to pass parental sniffs and inspection. He thought he saw Ben years from now in just such a predicament, and smiled into the future. Not everyone could do that, but he could.

Soon the *Mercury* was tucked in amongst the far-larger frigates, safe and sound, swinging on her anchor, a child beside strong parents. Another hour and he would wake Smitty for his turn on deck to stand the watch.

Making visits to each frigate in the morning, Able had informed the captains that *Mercury* would sail inshore in two days to pick up two agents, and then heel with the wind immediately to Portsmouth, and then Admiralty in London.

The result of this news was two canvas bags filled with official correspondence and letters home. From tars who could read and write, to Royal Marines, to midshipmen and officers, letters poured in, destined for cities, villages and rural manors throughout England, Scotland, Wales and Ireland. Able knew the mind-numbing duty of the blockade, completely without glamor but essential to keep the enemy at bay on the continent. He welcomed the personal letters more than the official mail, thinking to himself that before Meridee, he had never received any mail.

When darkness settled on that final evening, the *Mercury* swung out of line and beat for the coastline south of Cádiz, nearer to Tarifa where they had dropped off foul-smelling Captain Ogilvie.

"It's so dark, Captain," Whitticombe said. Able heard a touch of fear. "How will you know when we reach the coast?"

"Use your nose, son," he said, unmindful of the endearment, until he heard Whitticombe draw in his breath. "Aye, son. You are all my boys," he amended, as he felt a tightening in his chest. They were. *Please, God, no tragedy in whatever battle comes our way*, he thought, even though he wasn't as religious as Meri would have liked. *These are my sons and I cannot spare them.* "You'll smell land. Let me know when you do."

Whitticombe went to the railing and sniffed. Able smiled in the darkness. Then, "Ew, the tide is out."

"See there? Take a sounding, if you please. Tots, are you ready with the lantern?"

"Aye, sir."

Able knew the fathoms precisely where they sailed so stealthily, because he had traveled this sea lane years ago. This was for the Rats' education. Tots poised the lantern on the railing for the signal, when Able gave the word. The answer from shore would be three long flashes.

He looked around. All the Rats were on deck, silent and watchful, without even being requested. He knew the spy business seemed more exciting to impressible lads than it really was.

They sailed south from Cádiz until that midway point between the seaport and Tarifa, approaching the Gut of Gibraltar. When they were precisely at the drop-off spot, Able cleared his throat. "Two flashes, pause, two more quick, Tots, if you please."

Tots did as commanded, and they watched. Nothing. After two minutes, Able gave the same command, his fingers crossed, worried. They all squinted toward the shore. There it was this time: Three long flashes. They all let out their breath at the same time, which made Whitticombe giggle.

Smitty climbed into the small craft and started for shore. To Able's consternation, he came rowing back. "Sir, sir," he said in an urgent whisper. "I see three men on the beach."

Able moved fast. After he stripped off his uniform, he turned to the Rats. "Can one of you shoot?"

"Aye, sir," Davey said. "I'm a good shot."

"I'm surprised," Able said, and he was. Quiet Davey?

"Get the two pistols by my berth. They are loaded. You are not to fire unless I give a command. Bring my dagger, too."

Davey ran below deck, returning quickly. He steadied himself against the railing, a pistol poised. "Ready?" Able asked Smitty. "I'm going to hang onto the side of the boat. Pull for the shore as you did last time, then hold off. I'll go in first."

"I should be with you, sir," Smitty said in his quiet but unmistakable way that frightened everyone in the lower classes except Avon March. It was a statement, no suggestion.

"Hold off long enough for me to see what is going on," Able said. "That is an order."

Angry, his lips tight together, Smitty rowed for the shore. Able hung onto the gunnel out of reach of the oars. When his feet touched sand he told Smitty to stop.

Dagger in front of him, Able walked through the surf. He sighed with relief to see Angus and Jean, and they appeared in no trouble. He stood there, indecisive, a rare experience. "Angus," he said, in a quiet voice that he hoped carried far enough. "All is well?"

Ogilvie came to the water's edge, wearing a broad smile. "You look like a naked pirate, Able," he said in that half-joking, half-cutting way of his. "All you lack is a vulgar tattoo. I found Jean Hubert on schedule – take a bow, Jean – and someone else you should meet."

"This better be good."

"Meet your father."

Chapter Twenty-four

Silent, more uncertain than ever in his entire life, Able motioned Smitty to beach the craft, and walked toward a tall man impeccably dressed in uniform and cape. As he came closer, the man removed his hat to reveal curly hair, mostly gray. *I will look like this some day*, Able thought, amazed.

To Able's continuing astonishment, the man dropped to his knees, bowed his head and exclaimed over and over in Spanish, "Forgive me, my son!"

Able stared, mouth open, as memories pinged around in his head, from the first two hearts beating at his conception to the final whipping that drove him, frightened and hungry, from the Dumfries workhouse into cold rain, more hunger, and the Royal Navy. *And my salvation*, Able thought grimly as he stared at the kneeling man. *No thanks to you, cabrón.*

He stepped back, unwilling to move toward this distraught man. Anger, cold anger, surged over him until he shuddered from it. "If you knew me then, why did you not help me?" He couldn't help that his voice was rising. He had never known such fury.

Angus Ogilvie broke the spell. "Shut up, Able," he snapped in a fierce whisper. "There are French soldiers all along this Spanish coast and not a partisan in sight. Silence!"

He obeyed. "Angus, get him in the boat, if he is of a mind to explain himself later, or leave him here. I'll swim back because the boat won't take more weight. Jean, strip and join me. Toss your clothes in the boat." He did manage a grin. "I know you can swim."

In moments, Smitty pulled for the *Mercury* and Able and Jean swam in its wake. "How in the world…" Able started.

"We found him on the *Argonauta*, just as you said, and abducted him," Jean said, as calmly as if this were something that happened every other

149

day or so. "I, uh, had acquired a French naval officer's uniform. Got most of the blood off it."

"And you just marched on board the *Argonauta* and snatched him," Able said.

"Practically." Jean floated on his back for a moment and Able slowed down. "I can look amazingly official in uniform. Angus pulled out a parchment written in Latin and flashed it at the captain, while I said el Conde was required elsewhere. In rapid French, of course. Off we went."

"Astounding."

"He resisted eventually, until we told him of a remarkable genius who looked just like him. He couldn't escape fast enough, after that." He chuckled. "The Count of Quintanar even gave us the money for the conveyance so we could spirit him to this inlet faster!" He sobered quickly. "Able, when you hear his story...." Jean being Jean, he could not help himself. "I am going to savor this moment. It is the only time I know more than you do."

He swam ahead, mercifully leaving Able to himself, his brain entirely silent. Then he heard Euclid, of course Euclid, but he sounded more tender than usual, that old scoundrel. "High time, Able, high time. We never knew how to tell you." And that was it. His mentors and tormenters had known more than he did all along. His great anger turned to anguish at the misery of his early years. Could all that have been prevented? What was missing in this story?

He might have stayed in the water longer, but he saw horsemen on the beach, dismounting, shouting in French, and taking aim. *Oh no*, he thought, before he took a great breath and dove deep. *I have a score to settle with my father, or possibly a story to hear. I can die later.*

Captain Ogilvie was already at the helm when Smitty helped him aboard. Everyone on deck braced for the turn as the *Mercury* put wings to her heels and left the beach to the *fusiliers*.

"Where is he?" Able asked, as he gathered up his uniform.

"Below," Angus said. "Go on. Everyone else can stay up here."

"I...no."

"Go below," Angus said, with something close to tenderness. "Would you like me to come, too?"

Feeling six years old and surprisingly bewildered, Able nodded.

"I have the wheel," Jean Hubert said. He couldn't resist. "Angus stinks so bad that you'll send him topside soon enough."

A lantern swung gently, now that the *Mercury* had righted herself on a course toward England. The Count of Quintanar lay in a bottom berth, his eyes closed. He opened his eyes but said nothing, only observing his son with what looked like an expression of unfathomable relief, mingled with greater sadness or regret. Able couldn't tell.

Ogilvie tossed him a towel. He dug around for dry smallclothes, then put on his trousers and black turtleneck sweater that Meridee had knitted for him. He wanted her beside him precisely now.

Jean was right: Angus Ogilvie smelled as bad as a ship's bilge after a one-year cruise. "Captain Ogilvie," Able said as he buttoned his trousers. "As captain of the *Mercury*, I currently outrank you. Find something else to wear."

Angus saluted and dug in his duffel. Able hesitated only a moment then tapped his father's legs. "Move a little," he said in Spanish. "I am not certain I want to sit with you, but I need your story."

His father shifted and Able sat beside him. "Captain Villavalencia of the *Firme* distracted me so you could escape at Cape Finisterre, or we would have had this conversation sooner, Conde. What you said..."

"Forgive me?"

"Yes! You knew I existed," Able said, and felt the anger return. "If you knew, why did you not rescue me from the living hell of a workhouse?"

His father began to cry. He held out his hand, petitioning for something. Acceptance? Absolution? Able looked at his hand, fine-veined like his own hand, with long fingers. He waited, wondering when his cranial guests would weigh in with opinions. Nothing. He knew what Meridee would have him do, so he took a deep breath and clasped his father's hand.

He wiped his father's face with the sheet. "What were you doing in Dumfries with a common whore?"

The Count stared at him and shook his head. "Your mother was no common whore and I was never in Dumfries," he said firmly. "Never."

Able stared in surprise. When the count winced, Able realized he had been squeezing the man's hand too hard. He loosened his grasp but did not release him. He sniffed and turned around to see Angus Ogilvie dousing himself with lemon cologne, strong and Spanish. The captain shrugged. "It's the best I can do right now. Do speak in English, if you would. He refused to tell us much until he could speak to you first."

"That shouldn't be a problem at all," Able said. "Count, how many languages do you speak?" he asked in Spanish. His voice rose; he couldn't help himself. "How's your Greek? Your Latin? French? I needed a few days to learn German, but I learned. What about you?"

The count's mystified expression changed to calm acceptance. He raised Able's hand to his lips and kissed it. "My dear boy," he said in halting English. "You have it wrong. I speak Spanish." He shrugged. "And my English? It will improve. On the other hand, your mother..."

"My *mother*?"

"*Sí, tu madre, mijo*. Your mother, my son," he corrected, with a nod to Captain Ogilvie, whose mouth hung open. "She would hear a language and know it. Forget anything? *Nunca*."

"My mother," Able said, his voice scarcely above a whisper. "My mother! All I knew was that her name was Mary."

"*Su nombr*...Her name was Mary Carmichael and she was *la persona más inteligente del mundo*... I meet? No. meeted?" the count said, speaking slowly, trying out unused English, shaking his head over his errors. "Her father was...was...I do not know how to say." He spoke in rapid Spanish.

"He was the harbormaster at Portsmouth?" Able said, for Ogilvie's benefit. He looked at Angus. "Carmichael?" he asked.

Angus shrugged. "Before my time." He pulled up a stool, thought, then tried. "Conde, in what year?" Ogilvie asked in Spanish.

Able winced. The man's Spanish accent was as poor as his French one.

"Mil setecientos setenta y cinco," the count said promptly, then sighed in frustration.

"Seventeen seventy-five," Able said, groaning inside, like his father, at the cumbersome conversation. *Like his father*. The thought warmed him, even as his complex mind reeled with betrayal and neglect. There seemed to be some part of him that yearned for this man who was obviously his father. Able turned to Angus, hoping he would understand, but not really caring. "Sir, I am going to speak to my...my father in Spanish. I will tell you what he says later, because you know I can repeat it word for word. Excuse us, please."

He hoped the prickly captain wouldn't take it amiss, but he had to know everything at once. To his relief but not entirely his surprise, Ogilvie nodded. "I will go topside. Tell me later." He touched Able's shoulder, which also warmed his heart. Was this turning into an evening he would remember forever? Hell, he remembered everything forever.

Soon it was just the two of them. "Would you like something to eat?" he asked, using the polite form of "you"- *usted* – in Spanish. He knew he wasn't ready for the intimate form. "*¿Quiere usted algo de comer?*"

The count shook his head. "No. Let us talk. You have to know I did not abandon your mother. You have to know."

He spoke slowly, his voice soft, his Spanish impeccable and courtly. Also obvious was the sadness, particularly in his expressive eyes, those same eyes that Meridee said beguiled her even more than Able's broad shoulders. He reached for Able's hand, and Able clasped his again.

"Why were you even in Portsmouth?" Able asked. "I know our nations were not at war in 1775 – quite the contrary – but why Portsmouth?"

"In recent years, I have served the Spanish fleet as principal royal quartermaster," the count said. He relaxed and managed a smile. "I was a glorified clerk with a title, at least when I was young."

"Still…"

"Your quartermasters use an efficient counting and recording system that the world would like to copy," the count said, with a touch of humor. "When that foul Napoleon called England a nation of shopkeepers, I believe he was envious."

"*Foul* Napoleon?"

"Make no mistake; many of us hate him, too," the count said simply. "But that is not my story. As a young man, I was charged by Carlos el Rey with studying this method. I was a mere *teniente*. To Portmouth I went." He sighed. "I met your mother on the night of my arrival, when the Spanish delegation was feted by the harbormaster, a man name of Thomas Carmichael." He smiled then for the first time. "*Dios*, but she was lovely."

"What did she look like?"

The count reached into his uniform pocket and took out a small frame, elaborately carved and locked with a simple hasp. "I never go anywhere without it. Here."

Able took the miniature. "I never thought to see my mother," he said.

"Open it."

He could not help his intake of breath. Red-haired and blue-eyed, his mother smiled up at him. He swallowed and swallowed again, but was helpless against his tears. Able bowed his head over the miniature and wept. His father sat up and embraced him. They clung to each other.

"As you can see, I am on the other side of the frame," his father said, when he could speak.

Able wiped his eyes and looked. He might have been gazing into a mirror. He looked at Mary Carmichael and remembered something Meri had remarked on. She had noticed that after he washed his hair, it seemed to have reddish highlights. Now he knew they came from Mary Carmichael, who fell in love with the Spanish navy's future royal quartermaster, then a mere lieutenant.

Able handed back the miniature. "How did you know she was brilliant?" he asked, hoping she was at least treated better than he was in the Dumfries workhouse. "Did you happen to find out? I doubt she told you."

Meri had told him about ladies being advised to hide their lights under bushels, so as not to embarrass gentlemen. "Mama said a lady mustn't ever show her feelings, especially to men, who are superior in every way," she had told him once, after a child's simple card game in which she thrashed him. "I am so bad at that."

"It happened in odd fashion," the count said. He sat beside Able his arm around his son. "I swear I was in love at once, but I was young. Who knew? Not I. I was invited to the harbormaster's office to get my first instruction in Royal Navy accounts and bookkeeping and was sent into the office library. When I opened the door, I saw Mary hunched over a book. She was completely engrossed and did not hear me. I watched in amazement as she turned the pages at what couldn't have been more than one-second intervals. Swish, swish!"

"I read like that," Able said. "My wife says it makes her dizzy to watch."

"You have a wife?" the count asked almost pathetically, like someone hoping against hope for good news and expecting none.

"I do, a wonderful woman, and a wee son." *And you will meet them*, he thought, humbled to the dust at the idea. "You sir, I assume you have a wife and children? It's been many years since my mother…"

The count shook his head. "Neither. I never met anyone else I liked even half so well."

You poor man, Able thought. *Poor man.* He shivered inside, thinking how cruel life would be without Meri and Ben, and realized that as harsh as his birth and childhood, his life was vastly richer than his wealthy, titled father's.

"I am sorry for you," he said, and meant it with all his heart. "What did my mother say? Did she know you had been watching her?"

"Quite a self-possessed young lady, your mother was. She gave me an arch look and declared that was how she read. She said she remembered everything. I could quiz her if I doubted it. She folded her hands in her lap and gave me a level look – ah, the one I see right now from you – as if to ask, 'What are you going to do about it, simpleton?'"

They laughed together, then touched foreheads. The count looked away. When he spoke, Able knew he could live to be ninety and never hear anything so wistful. "We couldn't stay away from each other. I sneaked into her house every night after midnight."

Able could imagine that. It had taken supreme will to keep out of Meri's bedchamber during that remarkable four weeks they were under the same roof in rural Devonshire, while he taught her nephews and they mooned about, thinking no one was noticing. For a genius, he sometimes wasn't so bright.

"It came as no surprise when Mary told me she was with child," the count said. He looked away again. "This is hard to tell!"

"You must."

"I went immediately to her father, told him, and begged permission to marry her. He refused." The count's voice hardened, and rose with anger, then changed into that exquisite anguish beyond anger. "I pleaded. I begged on my knees. He said his daughter would never marry a Papist and a Spaniard. He went to the embassy in London and I was gone within two weeks." He bowed his head.

What could Able say? There was only one small thing he could do, and he felt like doing it now, he who had been prepared to hate his father all his life, the genius who whored with and deserted his prostitute-mother and left her. How could he have been so completely wrong? "*Tu eres mi padre*," he said simply, using that intimate word. "*Tu.*"

His father looked into his eyes. "I never thought to see you, not ever. I have spent my life knowing I would never hear "tu" from my child – he or she – who surely must hate me forever. *O dios*, I wish I knew how my *querida* Mary Carmichael ended up in… in Scotland, you say?"

For all his brilliance, Able had no idea, either. Better get the worst of it over. He took a deep breath. "All I know is that she gave birth to me on a cold February night in Dumfries, Scotland," he said, trying to control a flood of emotion and failing. All the swallowing and smashing of two fingers against the bridge of his nose amounted to nothing as his tears came. "She left a trail of blood as she dragged me to the steps of the parish church and laid me there wrapped in her cloak. She left a Book of Common Prayer with the name Mary inside. She…she crawled back to the alley and died alone." He kissed the count's hand. "She has a name now and I have a father."

They wept together.

Chapter Twenty-five

Able's plans to snatch some time, upon his return to Portsmouth, to begin the search for his mother came to nothing when they encountered the *Pickle* the following morning.

No one had slept well except the count. Once his story was told, he fell asleep. After tucking him in the berth, much as he would tuck in Ben, Able came on deck. Seven serious people sat close together wrapped in blankets, because the night had turned cold. They looked at him, full of questions.

Smitty. Tots. Whitticombe. Davey Ten. Avon March. They were his loyal crew, his true Gunwharf Rats, nearly as dear to Able as his own child. There at the wheel stood Frenchman Jean Hubert, with his own conflicts and loyalties all askew. He nodded to Angus Ogilvie, a man most ruthless and secretive, but tonight, tenderly kind. Able sat with them by the binnacle as Jean helmed the *Mercury*, and told them everything, word for word.

He wondered at first if he should have said so much, but knew he could not leave the Rats out of this stark account. Of all people, they knew the bleakness and loss of hope found within the walls of England and Scotland's workhouses. He knew their fears and their anger, because he shared them. To dismiss the Rats without telling his story would have been the worst sort of leadership.

"I am fervently hoping that when we return to Portsmouth, the navy will not need us immediately," he said, into great silence when he finished. "If Mr. Ferrier continues to be willing to stuff heads with knowledge, I will try to find out how my mother ended up in Scotland. As you were, men. There are five vacant berths below. Take them, Rats."

No one moved. Was this mutiny? "Um, that's an order," he said gently, loving them. He looked at Smitty, who had evolved into the natural leader. "Mr. Smith?"

Smitty nodded to the other Rats. "We think you should go below again and stay with your father. We're fine here on deck, aren't we, men?"

This called for compromise. Even if they sometimes forgot, Able knew what the Rats were like when they were tired. They were mere lads, after all, lads with hearts of oak, but young ones, all the same. "Let us do this, and I won't have an argument. You five take your berths. I will make a pallet and sleep on the deck beside my father. That way if he wakes up and forgets where he is, I can hold his hand. Will that satisfy you?"

It did. The boys trooped below. Able turned to his older crew, who had been watching that last exchange with barely disguised mirth. "I am sorry to condemn you to watch and watch about this night, but it appears that the Gunwharf Rats have spoken."

"Go below, Able," Ogilvie said. "Jean and I will stay awake by telling outrageous lies about how brave we are." He laughed. "What a story you have for Trinity House brothers when we next meet."

"The story had no ending yet," Able reminded them. "Maybe it never will."

The morning brought the *Pickle* alongside with unwelcome news. Able and Captain Ogilvie crossed over to the *Pickle*, where Captain Lapenotiere handed Able a tarry bag. "I must get to Portsmouth, and this must go to Plymouth immediately. I'm glad to see you, Captain Six."

And I am sheltering an enemy aboard the Mercury, Able thought, knowing that no amount of rouge and powder could cover up *that* pig. He accepted the bag, deeply disappointed but well aware of his duty.

He hadn't reckoned on Angus Ogilvie who, as it turned out, had a far better idea. Ogilvie took Captain Lapenotiere aside for a few whispered words. The *Pickle*'s skipper listened, then nodded. "Hurry him over smartly now," he said. "We have no brig. Is your prisoner aggressive?"

"Nay. He's an older gent and still bewildered how quickly we nabbed him. I can control him," Angus said. He ushered Able to the shaky plank uniting the yacht and the schooner.

Mystified, Able walked the plank to his own deck, Angus right behind him. "What deal did you just make?" he asked.

"The sort of deal secret agents make," Angus said, with a disarming smile that belied his reputation as a dab hand with a strangler's wire. "I told the good captain that I and a French double agent are escorting Spain's royal quartermaster to interrogation and incarceration, and we must get to Portsmouth quickly. He agreed to three supernumeraries. Get your father on deck." He looked suspiciously virtuous and glanced at the *Pickle*. "Every word I said is true. I expect Meridee will have any number of questions for her father-in-law when we arrive on her doorstep; ergo, interrogation. As a recipient of her boundless hospitality, I can vouch that she will be happy to incarcerate him in a comfortable bedchamber."

Able smiled, getting into the meat of the matter, even though he wanted to be the one to introduce the Count of Quintanar to his daughter-in-law. "And woe betide *mi padre* if he thinks to run afoul of Mrs. Perry." He clapped Angus on the shoulder. "Thank you. Tell Meri I'll wind up in her bed one of these days. On second thought, don't."

Captain Ogilvie grinned.

* * *

Thank goodness Able wasn't home to see her puking into a flowerpot. Meri wiped her mouth and eyed the now-pathetic cluster of violets. She had thought she could make it to the washroom just beyond the pantry, but no. Poor violets. After she ate the handful of ship's crackers she kept at the ready in her apron now, she would try to salvage the violets.

Mrs. Perry beat her to it. "I'll tend to these, Mrs. Six," the housekeeper said, coming up behind her and speaking in her most commanding voice (it also didn't hurt that she was nearly as tall as Able). "You *could* lie down."

"I could," Meridee said, as her stomach settled. "I'm already feeling better, though, even if this next little Six is so far no more well-mannered than my small genius." She touched her belly, happy it was no longer empty. When Able returned, she would have to tease him about their obviously fertile washroom.

But where was he? Meridee thought she understood the vagaries of life at sea, where nothing was predictable. She had been patient; she also knew she could barely wait to tell him about this latest development.

The other development had been her astonishing sorrow when Nick Bonfort – admit it, her boy – had left for the fleet with Reverend Alexander

Scott, Lord Nelson's private secretary and chaplain. Even now, Meridee did better not to remember her sadness, especially when Nick was so proud to be sailing with the fleet like other Gunwharf Rats.

Reverend Scott, bless him, had taken the time to reassure her that Nick would be as safe as houses on *Victory*, Admiral Nelson's flagship. "I'll keep a close eye on the lad," he said, after Nick darted upstairs to bring down his seabag. "I can't deny that I need his services. One of my assignments is to read and translate all foreign correspondence that falls into our hands from whatever source. If Nick is good at dictation, that will save me time."

"Nick is excellent at dictation," she assured Nelson's chaplain, even as her heart broke. "There is this, as well: My husband's own work with Admiralty has meant times when the lads of St. Brendan's must be circumspect and silent about what they hear. Nick will never betray a confidence."

"Even better." Nelson's secretary looked toward the sitting room door when they heard Nick hurrying downstairs. "Are you ready?"

"Aye, sir," her dear boy said. "Will I do, Mam?"

"Aye, you will," she said. "Make us proud, son."

It slipped out; for two years, Meridee had danced around her deep affection for this child who adopted her name. With a nod to Reverend Scott, she took Nick by the hand into the front hall. "What would you think if I asked Master Six if he and I could adopt you?"

She had seldom seen a smile so wide and genuine. "Is that an aye?" she asked, when he remained silent.

"Aye," he breathed, and hugged her.

"Then I shall ask him. I know what his answer will be. Come home safe to me," she said.

It was time then to let him go with a smile, a kiss and a wave until he was out of sight, and so she did, only to collapse in tears in Mrs. Perry's commodious embrace. "They're all hard to say goodbye to," she blubbered as Mrs. Perry held her close, "but this is worse."

Meridee told Mrs. Perry what she had promised the boy. To her pleasure, the housekeeper nodded her approval, which meant more tears, because she valued her housekeeper's opinion as much as she would have valued her late mother's.

"Come home safe to me," she whispered, when Mrs. Perry returned to her work. "And you, Able, my love. All of you." It became her continual prayer. There was much to tell her husband when he returned.

But now the house was quiet, Ben having accompanied Pegeen and Mrs. Perry to the end of the street to Ezekiel Bartleby's for rolls. Junius Bolt had settled Georgie down for his morning nap, singing any number of ribald sea ditties to Sir B's child, to Meridee's amusement. She did have a moment to sit and mend whatever poked out of her sewing basket, secure in the knowledge that all was as well as it ever could be on Saints Way during wartime.

Or she could lean back and consider the blessing of another baby. So far, no one knew except Mrs. Perry, Grace and Junius. She hesitated to inform the world at large, not after the last time. Better wait and let this newest acquisition grow in peace, quiet, and anonymity for a while.

Meridee remembered something Able had told her when she was carrying Ben. They had been sitting right here, Able for once just relaxing (if his mind was ever still, which she doubted). She was darning eternal stockings and contemplating the movement within her.

"I envy you at times, my dear," he had said.

"How is that? You're the glamorous entity in our marriage. I merely cook and clean and keep you from dabbling in household finances."

Able laughed at that; he knew his limitations. "All you have to do right now is simply to be. You know, breathe, eat and sleep, whilst someone inside you benefits. In your present condition, to be is to do."

He was right; she knew it. The baby they had begun was diligently growing, no matter how its mama puked in the morning, or gagged on porridge, or already wondered why her waist was disappearing so soon. No one had suggested that might happen earlier, now that she had already borne one baby, an eight-pounder.

"To be is to do," she said and closed her eyes. "I will sit here and simply be."

She barely closed her eyes when someone banged on the door. *Please, please no bad news* was her first thought, as always, when Able was at sea. She hurried toward the door, wondering if she should even open it, then stepped back in surprise when Captain Ogilvie solved the matter for her and barged right in.

Sometimes she wondered why Grace even tolerated the man; this was one of those times. Her next thought was one of fear for Able, but the captain put that fear to bed immediately. "Able is fine, Meridee, if irritated with the navy. He wanted to be here instead of me, but duty calls."

She stepped back again as Angus Ogilvie was followed quickly by Jean Hubert and a man she stared at, doubted her eyes, and stared again, gaping like a half-wit. Her hands went to her mouth as she gasped, "You're... you're..."

The man removed his elegant bicorn and bowed as if she were a queen. "Francisco Domingo y Guzman, Conde de Quintanar, at your service." It was a lovely bow, one to remember. "You are Mrs. Six?"

"I am, sir, er, count, or..." She turned to Captain Ogilvie. "I need to sit down."

"You do look a bit fine-stitched," Angus said. "Let us close the do...."

You can try, Meridee thought, as she watched Mrs. Perry's sudden arrival in the open door from the street, wielding her umbrella like a cudgel, murder in her eyes. Meridee hurried forward to stand between the housekeeper and the count. "Mrs. Perry! Please! Take a good look at him."

The housekeeper did, breathing fire and walking around the Spanish count, spending enough time to make the count forget himself and glare back. They were the same height, but Mrs. Perry easily outweighed him. She finally stopped and stared, then shook her head in amazement.

"How in the world do things like this happen?" Meridee asked Jean Hubert, who looked on with a smile.

"Captain Ogilvie and I found the count in Cádiz," Jean said, as if that explained the matter.

"They abducted me when I left the ship," the count corrected. "Captain Ogilvie" – it came out O-eel-vay – "threw a disgusting cape over my head. The fumes alone - *ay de mi*." He took a deep breath and put his hand to his heart. "But consider this, *señora*, if it please you: They took me to my son."

He started to move toward Meridee, until Mrs. Perry made it plain with a single look more-than-suggesting that another step would result in carnage.

"Mrs. Perry, we want to keep this man here," Meridee said firmly, even as she hoped she sounded serene. "Could you bring us some tea?" She looked toward the still-open door, where Pegeen clutched the rolls to her chest, her eyes wide. Ben stared at strange people in his little world and Mama suddenly too far away.

Meridee scooped him up and held him close to her. "Shh, shh, son. This is a man I would like you to meet. Does he look like someone you already know? Pegeen, take the rolls to the kitchen if you please. Mrs. Perry? Some tea. Take a good look, Ben."

"Masterfully done, Mrs. Six," Angus Ogilvie said. "You've outmaneuvered us all."

"Just trying to restore some decorum to the Six household," she said. "Able will tell you it is what I do best." She kissed Ben's cheek. "What do you think, my love?"

"Papa," Ben said faintly, then turned his face into Meridee's neck, suddenly shy.

"This is your grandson, Count," Meridee said.

The count's eyes filled with tears. He looked away to that distant place Meridee knew was the domain of men at war. She saw it often enough in her husband's eyes. In fact, she felt as though those were her husband's eyes. She came closer and touched his sleeve, with all its gilt and glory, and felt him tremble. "It's peaceful here." She chuckled, past tears because she felt all the delight. "Generally! You are welcome to stay."

Chapter Twenty-six

By nuncheon, even Mrs. Perry was captivated by the story the Count of Quintanar told them. He told it again when school ended and Grace St. Anthony crossed the street, saw him, and whooped with delight. At some point, Captain Ogilvie and Jean Hubert slipped away. "We have business in London," he whispered to Meridee. "Able will be along in a matter of days."

She had heard enough of the count's story, augmented by Angus and Jean's account, to feel gratitude deep in her heart at their courage in brazenly snatching a man of some importance from the heavily guarded dock in Cádiz, all because they knew Able needed him. She clasped Angus's hand in hers and when he bent down, kissed his cheek, as dirty as he was. "I doubt Able will ever be out of your debt," she whispered, when his ear was so close. "Thank you, Captain Ogilvie." She pronounced it O-eel-vay, which made him chuckle.

She knew Angus was a hard man to flummox. Even master assassins have their weak spots, if the look he returned was any indication. "There is so little in the world that we can set right," he told her. "We all suffer and there is no recourse."

She opened her mouth to speak, knowing his own sorrow at the loss of wife and child, but he put a finger to her lips. "My dear lady, what a triumph it is when now and then, we win one." He kissed *her* cheek this time. "Find Mary Carmichael's mother, will you?"

"If it is humanly possible," Meridee said, touched at this side of Angus Ogilvie she had never imagined. No wonder Grace St. Anthony had only kind words about him.

"Can you not wait at least until Grace returns from school?" she asked impulsively, then wondered at her impertinence. *Scold me now*, she thought, contrite. *I really am not a meddler, and I dread your sharp tongue.*

"I wish I could, I truly do," he said, to her surprise, then added more softly. "Mrs. Six I wish I were a better man." With a slight bow, he left, taking Jean Hubert with him. The Frenchman had heard the entire exchange. The rascal gave Meridee a slow wink, as he followed Captain Ogilvie.

The captain was right; there was more to think about. Where could she put the count? Angus had stressed that their Spanish abductee must be kept secret from suspicious eyes that might think Able Six was in league with the enemy. Grace and Georgie occupied one chamber upstairs. Smitty used the other one, when he was not at sea. Hopefully a high-in-the-instep count with more gilt on his uniform than Meridee had ever seen on any mortal would not object to sharing quarters with a formidable-looking workhouse lad now and then.

She made the bed while the count dozed downstairs in the sitting room, obviously worn out with adventures, but too much of an officer and gentleman to admit it. When he had shut his eyes in mid-conversation, Meridee had seized the moment to tiptoe out with Ben.

Ben had been happy to help her, pulling pillowslips off pillows, and flopping back on the bare mattress a few times, once the sheets were removed. "He is really my grandpapa?" he asked her.

"I believe he is, son," she said, settling beside him.

"Do I have a grandmama? The count didn't seem to think so, and he should know, shouldn't he?"

Meridee wondered when she would get used to such reasoning from a child so young. She expected brilliance from Able Six, but why her son? Able had told her many times that genius was a burden. She took Ben's hand in hers, pleased when he snuggled close. "I think there is much to this story we do not know. We will have to learn more."

That seemed to satisfy Ben, at least for now. She kissed the top of his head, called it good, and let the two of them snuggle into a nap. *To simply be is to do, my love*, she thought, as she drifted off, holding her son close, and letting the baby inside her grow.

Refreshed after his sitting room nap, the count held forth at dinner with a surprising ally, his grandson. Meridee hid her smile when Grace asked a question slowly and more loudly than usual, thinking that might make English more accessible. When the count shook his head, Ben translated for Lady St. Anthony. He spoke slowly, too, and hesitated, but the count nodded.

"Ben, you're a wonder," Meridee said as she buttered more bread for him. "Have you and Papa been conversing in Spanish now and then?"

Her son eyed his favorite treat, took a bite, then said, "When Papa puts me to bed, we speak Spanish one night and French another. He says it will round me out and make me useful in the fleet someday."

Everyone laughed. With considerable aplomb, Ben took advantage of the distraction to eat the rest of the bread, savoring the butter like a gourmand. Meridee calmly wiped the butter off his cheek and the front of his shirt, reminded of Able, who had trouble with ordinary things.

"Son, would you kindly translate for your…your…."

"*Abuelo*?" Ben asked. "*Con placer*." He gave her a big-eyed look, the property of a toddler willing to bargain. She knew all the signs because he had practiced them on her before. "Maybe for a little more butter."

Grace put her hand to her mouth and turned away to laugh. Meridee took it in stride; she knew her men. "Your request is not outrageous," she told him as she buttered another slice. "This will have to last you until breakfast, however."

Ben knew when to yield. He gave his mama a gracious nod, accepted the bread, and translated when necessary. When Mr. Ferrier arrived later, Ben was given a break, because, as Mr. Ferrier explained, many captured sailors – the enterprising ones, anyway – learned at least some Spanish and French while incarcerated. Eventually Ben retired to his favorite corner of the sitting room to play jackstraws, since Mr. Ferrier had matters in hand. Meridee watched him go, wondering what went on inside his brain. At least she knew he loved his mama.

"No one knows how Mary Carmichael ended up in Dumfries?" Mr. Ferrier asked, when he was abreast of the whole, fantastic chain of events that had landed a Spanish count in Able Six's sitting room.

"No. Her father was…" The count cleared his throat and spoke to Ben in Spanish

"Harbormaster," the little fellow replied, as he concentrated on jackstraws.

"Oh, I see," Mr. Ferrier said. He leaned forward, "I know who you mean, Conde. His name was Thomas Carmichael. He has been dead for ten years at least."

The count nodded. "An unpleasant man. I pleaded and begged but he would not allow Mary to ... *casarle conmigo*."

Meridee put her hand on the count's sleeve, needing no translation. It may have been years, but all the pain was there still. She could see a young man of noble birth, begging to do the right and honorable thing, not just because it was honorable, but because he loved this odd, quirky, brilliant and lovely young woman. *I would have wilted into a prune of an old maid, if I had not been allowed to marry the brilliant, quirky man I adore*, she told herself.

She regarded her father-in-law with sympathy. "How unkind of him, Count," Meridee said.

"Thomas Carmichael was not a kind man," Mr. Ferrier told them. "I remember any number of my captains suffering ill-usage through the years. When he died, no one mourned." He thought a moment in that deliberate way Nick had once commented upon: *Mum, Mr. Ferrier keeps us hanging on his words.* He deliberated with himself another moment. "I think his widow is still alive."

"If we only knew where she lived," the count said.

"I have no idea," Mr. Ferrier admitted. "I do remember that she regained her maiden name after her husband died." He shrugged. "Perhaps she didn't care for him, either. Funny what a person remembers. Her first name was Amelia."

It was a dead end, and they all knew it. "Would the current harbormaster have such information?" Meridee asked.

"I doubt it. There have been at least three harbormasters since then. After the reign of King Carmichael, Admiralty has been wisely shuffling those bureaucrats of the harbor here for a three-year term only. I can inquire tomorrow, if you wish. Amelia Amelia. What name do you use now?" he asked, more to himself than to the company at large.

The conversation changed to less highly charged subjects of English weather (too rainy) and food (too bland, compared to Spanish cuisine). Meridee could see that her father-in-law was tiring. So was Ben, who had made himself comfortable in her lap, done with jackstraws for the evening. Meridee wondered what her boy would do when her lap began to disappear.

Mr. Ferrier rose to take his leave. "I live across the street," he explained to the count. He gave Meridee a casual nod, which warmed her heart.

"Thanks to Mrs. Six, I am at liberty to come and go here, much like the Gunwharf Rats." He laughed and held up his hand. "Count, I will explain *that* to you tomorrow!"

"I know Gunwharf," the Count said.

Grace followed him, carrying her sleeping baby. "Let me escort you to the foot of the stairs," Mr. Ferrier said gallantly.

"We're all tired," Meridee said to her guest.

From the hall, she heard Mr. Ferrier shout, "That's it!" Silence, a low murmur, then Grace gasped. Laughter followed. Meridee and the count looked at each other.

Mr. Ferrier ran into the sitting room, Grace beside him, wide-eyed. "Surely it can't be," she said at once.

"What?" Meridee asked. Ben sat up, rubbing his eyes.

"You go first," Grace said.

"I remembered the last name of Master Carmichael's widow. Munro. Amelia Munro." Mr. Ferrier wore a huge smile. "Your turn, Grace."

"I can barely believe this…"

"Grace. Mr. Ferrier. I am going to throttle you both in a moment if you do not…" Meridee threatened. Ben stared at her in amazement. "Mama! You?"

Barely able to contain herself, Grace handed Georgie to Mr. Ferrier, who juggled and floundered, then tucked the baby in safely. Grace sat on the arm of Meridee's chair. "My dear, Amelia Munro lives four doors down from Sir B's house."

"You're making sport of me," Meridee said.

"No! I have no idea how long she has lived there." She looked away for a moment collecting herself. "I was only there a little over a year." Meridee held her hand, and Grace took a deep breath. "She's a quiet lady. I do know she is from Scotland."

"*Dios mio,*" the count said. "Four doors from your house?" He looked at Ben. "Who is this Sir B?" Ben told him in Spanish.

Grace shook Meridee's shoulder. "*You* have seen her, my dear. More to the point, so has Able."

"Surely not," Meridee said.

"Oh, yes." Grace was in tears, so Meridee handed her an old sock past mending from the endless basket, clean but done for. "Remember when you were starting to droop at…at the funeral?"

"Yes. Able…" Meridee sucked in her breath, remembering. "He asked an older lady seated beside me if she would move over so he could sit with me."

"That is Amelia Munro," Grace said in watery triumph. She blew her nose on the stocking. "Amelia Munro ended up sitting next to her grandson, Able Six!"

They looked at each other in stunned silence. Meridee cleared her throat. "Count, I know where we are going first thing tomorrow morning."

Chapter Twenty-seven

Meridee's morning sickness kindly cooperated the next day, alleviated by tea and toast. Grace talked her brother, Headmaster Croker, into taking her morning class. "Thaddeus needs to exert himself a little more," she said as she nursed Georgie in Meridee's room, sitting so companionably on the bed, a far remove from the straight-laced spinster of earlier days. "He isn't quite himself, since that last round of measles or mumps that passed through St. Brendan's. My lads in lower math will do him good." She frowned. "I hope."

They decided to take along their own little lads. "I have seen Mrs. Munro out and about, but I do not know her," Grace said. "Maybe she will see us as harmless, if we have our children along. After all, we have quite a story for her."

Junius Bolt objected strenuously to staying home until Mrs. Perry fixed him with her squinty-eyed glare that even Able feared. "Leave it to the ladies," she told him, turning each word into a thunderbolt hurled by Zeus himself.

After a debate – and finally a good look at Mrs. Perry in high dudgeon – the Conde de Quintanar agreed to wait in the carriage when they talked to Mrs. Munro. "I will not have you wounded any further," Merridee assured him.

His eyes were as expressive as his son's. Meridee saw the hurt that had lasted so long for this constant, honorable man who wanted to do the right thing from the start, but had been denied the opportunity.

"Grace, isn't it strange," Meridee said as they waited for the count to fetch his cape and join them. "Here we thought one thing all along, Able included, and the matter is quite the opposite. Mary Carmichael was no prostitute and the Count has mourned her disappearance all these years."

"Maybe we should never judge a matter until we know the details," Grace said. "Even then, p'raps we should not judge at all."

"We only knew what the workhouse beadle told Able," Meridee reminded her. She shook her head in frustration. "And the beadle knew nothing! He assumed; we all did."

They were silent on the drive, the silence broken only by the call of sea gulls wheeling around the harbor on the air currents. Grace sighed when the coachman stopped in front of a rowhouse four doors down from the more elegant mansion where Sir B lived and died too soon.

"I don't miss that house," Grace said. "I hope you do not tire of me too soon. I would still rather be with you."

"Never," Meridee said firmly. "I'll consider you and Georgie as Gunwharf Rats who need a good home. Oh! That does not sound so proper, does it?"

"It's the kindest thing you could have said, my dear. I love being a Gunwharf Rat." Grace turned to the count, who seemed to have followed the gist of that conversation. "Count, we should probably let Able explain the Rats to you. It's complicated."

The count managed an elegant bow, sitting there in the carriage. "You forget, Lady San Antonio. I have already met five of the Rats."

"Why, yes, you have," Grace said. She took a deep breath as the coachman opened the door. "Let us find out what kind of a lady Amelia Munro is, shall we?"

"I am not certain how to begin."

"At the beginning, Meridee. I will introduce you."

A freckled maid with red hair opened the door and took their calling cards. She ushered them into the front hall but no farther, and hurried away. She came back quickly. "Let me show you to the sitting room."

Meridee prepared to take a firmer grip on Ben's hand, but he was in strange surroundings and happily stayed close to her.

The maid opened the door and ushered them inside. Amelia Munro looked up from the card table, where she appeared to be involved in a game of Patience. She rose and held out her hand to Grace. "Lady St. Anthony, you've come to rescue me from cheating at Patience. How kind of you to call."

Grace was up to every social nicety, from her curtsey of proper depth, to Meridee's introduction, to her acknowledgement of Mrs. Munro's attendance at her husband's funeral in May. "I should have stopped by sooner to thank you for honoring him, but I am an instructor at St. Brendan School. With that and our son, I am occupied."

Pleasantries, pleasantries, and then Grace gave Meridee the floor. *Whatever happens, Able my love, I do it for you*, she thought. "Mrs. Munro, thank you for letting my husband edge in beside me at the funeral."

"I was happy to," the woman replied. "I could tell you were struggling and needed a good man nearby." She sounded wistful, to Meridee's ears and heart.

"I did. Sir B was my husband's mentor and great friend. My husband's name is Able Six and he is a sailing master who also teaches at St. Brendan's."

"Such a singular name," Mrs. Munro said, as Meridee had hoped she would.

"It is. He was born in a back alley in Dumfries, Scotland, the sixth foundling of the year, hence the name. The workhouse beadle named him Durable because he had survived a wintry night on the parish church steps, wrapped in a woman's cloak."

"Durable. That's the name a man of Calvinist persuasion would wish on a baby," Mrs. Munro said, with a touch of humor.

"Yes, isn't it? There was one other item left with the infant," Meridee continued, as her heart tried to crawl up her throat. "A prayer book with the name Mary in it."

"A common name," Mrs. Munro said, but she said it cautiously.

"Yes, it is. Mrs. Munro, did you happen to get a look at my husband? A good look?"

Mrs. Munro leaned back, her face thoughtful. Her smile threw ten or twenty years off her. "I did notice curly hair and a handsome face, but he turned to you immediately. He obviously cares for you." Again Meridee heard that wistful tone.

"Did he look something like this man?"

From a pasteboard sleeve, Meridee took the little painting of the Count of Quintanar that Captain Rose had given to Able. She held it out to Mrs. Munro.

The widow of Portsmouth's harbormaster slowly put her hand to her mouth. Her eyes widened and she took a deep breath, and another. "Where did you get this?" she demanded, then softened her tone. "I must know." Softer still. "I *beg* to know."

"My husband was given this by a man named Captain Hector Rose of

Trinity House." Meridee put down all her cards. "The man in the painting is the Count of Quintanar, Francisco Domingo y Guzman. But you already know that, don't you?"

Stunning silence fell over the sitting room. Mrs. Munro bowed her head just as the maid opened the door, pushing in a tea cart with sweets. The lady of the house waved her away and the door closed, to Ben's disappointment. His shoulders drooped.

"The count is now the royal quartermaster of the Spanish navy," Meridee continued. She watched Mrs. Munro's color fade. She worried, but she pressed on. "He was sent to Portsmouth in 1775 to learn something about the Royal Navy's method of bookkeeping." Another deep breath of her own. "I believe that is where he met your daughter, Mary Carmichael."

Mrs. Munro put her hands to her face and sobbed. Meridee and Grace exchanged glances. Grace put her baby down on the settee, whispered to Ben to watch him, and sat beside the widow, with Meridee on her other side. Meridee had something better than a sock from the mending basket this time. She pressed a cotton handkerchief in Mrs. Munro's hand, and put her arm around her shoulder.

They gave her time to weep. *What is she thinking?* Meridee wondered. *What does she know? Will she throw us out?* She glanced at Ben, who was frowning. She gestured to him and he hurried to her side, resting his face in her lap. "It's all right, my dear," she whispered.

Now or never. When the widow's tears subsided, Meridee kissed Ben. "Mrs. Munro, I believe this charming fellow beside you is your great-grandson."

When not in tears, Amelia Munro was obviously a woman who knew how to keep her own council. Mr. Ferrier had said last night that Thomas Carmichael was a vain and boasting fellow, probably with a temper to match, the kind of flash temper, perhaps accompanied by harsh words, that could make someone, perhaps a wife, cautious.

Even then, Mrs. Munro surprised her. She dried her tears, straightened up, and held out her arms to Ben. "Young man, would you please sit on my lap?"

Ben looked at Meridee. She nodded, touched by Mrs. Munro's generosity. "Go, son. There you are. We named him Benjamin Belvedere Six, after two of Able's mentors and former captains."

"Good names," Mrs. Munro said. She peered around Ben to see his face. "Ben, until only a few minutes ago, I didn't have a great grandson." Her face clouded. "I didn't even have a grandson. That would be your father."

Ben considered the matter. Meridee knew he tugged at his right earlobe when he was in deeper thought than usual. He tugged a moment then leaned back against Mrs. Munro, whose arms circled him so naturally, as if she hugged great-grandchildren every day. "My father is a little large to sit on your lap," Ben said, which made the widow laugh and say, "I expect he is."

"Mrs. Six, please summon the tea cart for me again," Mrs. Munro said. "I believe Ben would like some cakes, and possibly milk."

"He would enjoy that, wouldn't you, son?"

Meridee opened the door to see the maid right outside, frightened and unsure. "Did I do something wrong?" she whispered to Meridee.

"Not in the least," Meridee replied. "We gave your mistress some surprising news, is all."

In a few minutes, Ben was sitting at the card table with a napkin around his neck, eating tea cakes with considerable gusto. Mrs. Munro gathered Meridee and Grace close, her eyes on the little boy.

"My great-grandson doesn't need to hear all this," she said, her voice just above a whisper. "I never forgave my husband for driving that good man away. I begged him to yield and let them marry, but he wouldn't hear of it." She began to pick at the cotton square she clutched. "If you could only have seen the two of them together! They were in love. Everyone knew it. Mr. Carmichael chose not to believe it."

Meridee leaned closer. "The count told us that Mary was unbelievably intelligent."

"Aye, she was," the widow said promptly, and sighed. "She never forgot any conversation, or anything she read."

"Able is that way, too," Meridee said.

Mrs. Munro managed a smile. "Difficult, isn't it? Did he have as much trouble finding tutors?"

"Remember, Mrs. Munro, he ended up in a workhouse in Dumfries."

Mrs. Munro's smile disappeared. "If only we could have found her in time!" She savagely ripped a strip off the handkerchief. "When Mr. Carmichael drove the count away, I thought Mary would do herself an injury." The tears came again. Grace gave her another handkerchief. "Mr.

Carmichael insisted we send Mary away to my brother, William Munro, who had a large manor between Glasgow and Edinburgh. My husband" – she nearly spit out the word – "shamed Mary and cursed her ruin." Mrs. Munro hugged herself, playing out the whole ugly scene again, if her restlessly moving eyes were any indication. With a shock of recognition, Meridee thought of all the times she had put her hands over Able's eyes to slow him down.

"Scotland," Grace murmured. She picked up Georgie, who was starting to squirm on the settee. "Do you mind?" she asked. Mrs. Munro shook her head, so Grace opened her bodice.

"What happened?" Meridee asked. "Dumfries is some distance from Edinburgh and Glasgow."

"I doubt we will ever know," Mrs. Munroe said, calm again after her outburst. "I knew when Mary was due to be confined, but I heard nothing. I waited and waited." She shook her head in dismissal. "Mr. Carmichael yammered on about no news being good news until I wanted to…" She rubbed her shoulders, even though the room was pleasantly warm. "Mr. Carmichael received a letter in mid-March from Will's solicitor, announcing his death in January from pneumonia. There…there was no mention of Mary, but William had pledged not to tell anyone about her." Her voice hardened. "Mr. Carmichael refused to make any inquiries." Her eyes went to Ben, just finishing his milk. "I had no idea what happened to my daughter, and here I have a great-grandson. Tell me, Mrs. Six, where is my grandson?"

"He and some of the students from St. Brendan's are delivering dispatches to the Channel Fleet and the Mediterranean Squadron," Meridee said. "We expect him home in a few days."

"You'll bring him over as soon as he makes port," Mrs. Munro said.

"I promise you, Mrs. Munro," Meridee said. She hesitated, and the widow noticed.

"Are you wondering why I call myself Munro?" she said. Thomas Carmichael's widow rose and walked to the window. Meridee followed her. The view held no sight of the busy harbor, with warships coming and going. She wondered how much Mrs. Munro hated any mention of the navy of any country.

"My husband was ill for a long time," she said, her voice calm, normal even. "I listened to all his rantings and complaints without a murmur, as I had always done, secure in the knowledge – relieved – that I was going to outlive him. What else can ladies do? As soon as he died, I took up my maiden name. I am Amelia Munro to the world, and so I shall remain." She bowed her head. "Where did my lovely Mary die? In an alley, you say? All alone?" She shuddered and began a low, relentless keening that made Ben leap up from the table, scattering crumbs, as he ran to Meridee in terror.

She picked up her son, holding him close, as the widow rocked back and forth and keened. "I want to go home, Mama," he whispered into her neck. "Now!"

"Soon, my love, soon," Meridee whispered back, chilled to her heart. Was now the time to say that the count waited outside her doorstep?

"Let me sit you beside Georgie's mama for a moment. Shh, shh, you will be fine." Ben wasn't happy, but Grace gathered him close, too.

Meridee went back to the window, unsure what to do, until she asked herself what *she* would want, were she a widow who had lost everything in the disappearance of her pregnant daughter and despised her husband. She put her arms around Mrs. Munro, who stiffened, then rested her head against Meridee's shoulder.

"Mrs. Munro, the count is waiting in that carriage outside your house," she said finally, not knowing if it was the right thing to do, unsure of herself, wishing Able were here.

"He's here?" Mrs. Munro asked, alert. She sniffed back her tears then held herself off from Meridee, the grip on her shoulders nearly painful. "My dear, I have wanted to apologize to him for years! I want to tell him that I never felt the way my husband did. I want him to know that had I the resources – oh why do women count for nothing? – I would have scoured all of Scotland until I learned something. *Anything!*"

"Tell me now, dear lady," they heard from the doorway. "I could not wait another moment in the carriage."

They turned around to see Francisco Domingo y Guzman. He opened his arms. With a cry, Mrs. Munro crossed the room and embraced him. They clung together, two comrades in sorrow so wrenching that Meridee knew she would be awake and pacing the floor tonight. She sat beside Grace, who was burping Georgie. Ben didn't waste a moment getting into his mama's lap. She held him close.

"Mama, what is happening?" he asked, his hands on her face, commanding her attention.

"We're watching a family come into being," she told him. "Our family."

Chapter Twenty-eight

The *Mercury* made port in four days. Each day, Meridee sat with Mrs. Munro and the count, answering questions. It touched her heart how they wanted to know every detail of her husband's life, no matter how minute. Ben was there to translate, but less as Francisco Domingo y Guzman's rusty English revived. Her boy was content to eat his great-grandmama's cream-filled buns.

Ben thought they should tell Mr. Bartleby about the buns, but Meridee thought not. "He will wonder where you have picked up such culinary decadence."

Ben turned philosophical. "He might think I am not a loyal customer. He will think I am a gut-foundered parvenu."

"That is it," Meridee said, hard put not to howl with laughter at the incongruity of dockside slang mixed with French, coming from a charming lad not even two years old, a well-fed, nurtured and loved little genius.

Mrs. Munro understood her laughter. Her eyes lively now, and not dead with the bleakness of too much life still to live, she told her visitors of Mary's quirks. "For all that she could do quadrilateral equations when she was three, even at age fourteen she got lost between our house and the church, a matter of three blocks." She turned wistful then. "Does my grandson do better? One should hope, if he is a sailing master."

"Actually, he never gets lost." Meridee laughed. "What he can't do is tie a neck cloth properly or manage the simple arithmetic of grocer's bills. Mrs. Munro, I think their minds are too large for the simple things that never baffle the rest of us."

In her own loneliness, Meridee discovered that she craved the chance to tell two people about the man she adored. She left the most private moments private, but found there was plenty to tell them, from her first view of him, wet from a downpour while walking to Pomfrey for a chance to work for her brother-in-law briefly as a tutor.

"That cursed Treaty of Amiens between France and England sent a lot of good men home from sea on half pay," she said. "Able was one of them." She wiped cream off her son's face. "Thank goodness for that, Ben, or you wouldn't be here."

In halting English, shepherded occasionally by Ben, the Count of Quintanar told them about his family estate, located north of Granada. He told of orange groves and fighting bulls, and beautiful women with flouncy skirts. Ben's eyes brightened when the discussion turned to *paella*, a dish of saffron rice and seafood, that his great-grandfather, his *bisabuelo,* enjoyed.

"Next to reading, I believe that eating is Ben's favorite occupation," Meridee said.

"What about his father?" Mrs. Munro wanted to know. "Is he a gourmand like his son?"

Meridee had to be honest, but she could be gentle about it. "Able is somewhat indifferent to good or bad food, Mrs. Munro. Sometimes I think it is all the same to him." Let them surmise that years of grey meals of workhouse porridge, followed by occasional times of starvation at sea and in a French prison made Able happy to eat nearly anything, no matter how unappealing. But how sad Mrs. Munro looked! "He does love lemon curd on toast," Meridee amended hastily. She rosied up, remembering the time he had dabbed lemon curd on her neck and licked it away. Able's grandmama didn't need to know that.

The *Mercury* pulled into Portsmouth harbor after dinner four days later, as full dark settled over the city. Mrs. Perry had brought out the trifle, with the last strawberries anyone could find in the market and the aforementioned lemon curd between the spongy layers. The occasion was the count's birthday, which meant the addition of Headmaster Thaddeus Croker, and Mr. Ferrier, of course.

Ben had his father's way of hearing things before anyone else did. "Someone is here," he said, alert because Meridee had been promising him his father. "Any moment they will knock, unless it's Papa."

No one knocked. The door opened and Ben leaped up from the table. Meridee followed him in time to see her husband grab up his boy, tuck him close and plant a kiss on what remained of potatoes and gravy on his cheek. "Ben boy, you're tasty," he said, then eyed Meridee. "I'll wager your mama is tastier."

"No, Papa. Her face is clean," Ben said, which made Able give her a slow wink.

He set Ben down and reached for Meridee. "I miss you more every day I am gone," he told her after a long kiss.

"Able, we found your grandmama," she said, when she could.

He hugged her even tighter. "I'm sure there is a good story with it," he said before he kissed her again. "How far away is she?"

"Four doors down from Sir B's house on Jasper Road."

He stared at her. "You're serious?"

"Entirely. My goodness, your Rats will think we have no manners."

Smitty and Davey Ten stood in the doorway, grinning at their sailing master and Mam tangled up in each other. They were grimy but Ben didn't care, holding up his arms for Tots, who had followed behind. Meridee let go of her husband and admired her boys. *Why are they growing up so fast?* she thought, with some chagrin. At least Avon March still seemed like the child he was, until she looked closer into his old-too-early-eyes, the eyes of war or of the workhouse.

"I'm so happy to see you back," she told them. "There is plenty of food, but I want you to bathe before you sit at my table. I suggest across the street, where the bathing accommodations can handle the lot of you. Hurry back when you are done."

The boys darted out the door. She smiled to hear them yelling, "Gunwharf Rats! Ho, the *Mercury*!" as they ran across the street to St. Brendan's. They had never exhibited such exuberance when they first arrived at St. Brendan's, cowed and defeated.

"I'm hoping you will let me dunk myself in the washroom here," Able asked. His arm went around her waist. "Care to join me? We know the door has a good lock."

"It does," she agreed. The hall was empty, Ben having returned to the trifle in the dining room. This was as good a time as any, considering the general chaos when the Rats were in residence. "Not this time." She put her arms around his neck. "Mrs. Petty is going to have to light the kitchen fire again so we can feed the mob."

"She doesn't need you for that. She has Pegeen now."

"No, she doesn't need me, but we have guests." She kissed him. "I have a small piece of news for you, dear man. Bend down a bit." She whispered in his ear. He held her closer.

"I've been throwing up, my bodices are too tight, and I can't stay awake long in the evenings."

"And you're happy about it."

"I am." She leaned her forehead against his chest. His uniform smelled of brine and tar, which didn't help her unruly stomach. "Dear me. I shouldn't sniff your uniform until I can tolerate strong odors."

He laughed. "I'll wash. I know you like what's underneath. First, how is my father?"

"Go see for yourself," she nudged him with her hip. "He loves trifle – we've had it twice this week, at his request. Ben has been translating for him."

"That's our boy." He took her hand and walked her into the dining room.

The count stood up and embraced him. They spoke in rapid Spanish, laughed, and the count returned to his trifle. Able nodded to the others and took his smelly self through the kitchen.

When everyone had finished and before the next onslaught returned, hopefully clean, Meridee went upstairs to find clean clothes for her man. It was an easy task; he was always tidy. She found an old sweater and comfortable trousers. If the Royal Navy didn't need the *Mercury* for a week or two, she could finish the sweater she was knitting. She knew the Channel would be cold soon, the waves high and boisterous. A man standing the watch needed a good sweater.

The others had adjourned to the sitting room. She let herself into the washroom, Ben tagging along behind, in time to scrub Able's back. Since she had Ben close by, Meridee scrubbed her son's face, removing a layer of gravy with trifle on top. "Son, you need to stand a little closer to your fork and spoon," she said. He nodded, unperturbed.

She looked at father and son, remarkably alike, curly-haired and dark of eyes. She patted her belly, wondering what the new little Six would look like. Maybe she was vain to want a daughter with some of her own features. Maybe it didn't matter.

Ben was a most unruffled child and inquisitive. He regarded his naked father as Able toweled off, then looked down at himself. "Mama, am I going to look like that someday?" he asked.

It was a serious question from Ben. *If you're extremely lucky*, she wanted to say. She settled on, "I expect you will in fourteen or fifteen years."

He eyed his father up and down again, who was hugely amused and trying not to show it. "Doesn't all that get in the way?" Ben asked.

"No, son. Trousers help, I will admit. Hand me my smalls, please."

Ben did as bidden, then wandered toward the door. "I smell more gravy," he said on the way to the kitchen.

Able threw back his head and laughed silently. Meridee laughed into her apron. When she could talk, she grabbed him around the waist. "Did you ever think fatherhood would bear any resemblance to what just happened?"

He looked down at her with great tenderness. "I never in my life imagined I could be so happy," he said quietly.

"Neither did I. Welcome home from sea, my love."

Chapter Twenty-nine

Meridee was in bed long before Able came upstairs with his father. She listened to them talking in the hall, but softly. She heard father and son go into Ben's room. She imagined them watching the sleeping boy and wondered what was going through the count's mind. As she closed her eyes, Meridee knew better than to imagine what pinged around inside her husband's brain.

She woke when Able sat down beside her. "My father cannot fathom what has happened," he said. "He tells me over and over that he never expected such an experience as this." He took her hand. "Personally, I had given up, until Captain Rose showed me that painting at Trinity House. Then I wanted to know everything about that Spaniard in the frame."

He kicked off his shoes and lay down beside her on top of the coverlets. "I am still amazed at how wrong we all were."

"You're not wrong often," she said as she rested her head on his chest.

He patted her bare back, then caressed it. "Mrs. Six, I do believe you are naked."

"Aye, sir. Reporting for duty."

"Duty, is it? How about, 'requesting and requiring immediate admission,'" he teased as he stood up and started stripping. "Move over, but not too much."

"And leave my warm spot?" she said.

"It'll be much warmer soon, wife."

It was. Rational thought deserted her then as she loved her man home from war and tumult, bad food and duty. She doubted any other woman in Hampshire was providing a better homecoming to a man back from Napoleon's war.

"You are about two months along?" he asked later, his voice drowsy now. He seemed to speak more slowly than usual. She nearly teased him about the efficacy of a thorough homecoming to dismiss rational conversation, even in a genius.

"Almost." Well, heavens, she had a hard time with words, too.

She thought he slept then, and prepared herself for slumber.

"You awake?" he asked, as her eyes started to close.

"Sort of."

"I've been thinking."

She laughed. That comment had become a family joke no one except the Sixes and their closest friends would ever understand. "What else is new?" she asked, the standard reply.

He put his hand over hers. "If this little one is another girl, please name her Mary Munro."

A shiver darted down her back. "You will be here, too, Able. *We* will name her Mary Munro."

"However we word it, that is what I would like," he replied, and kissed her shoulder. "I know there is going to be a battle soon. I can feel it in my bones."

"Not Mary Carmichael?" she asked, when he changed his grip to a caress, understanding her unspoken terror.

"From what you have told me of Carmichael, I think Munro would be best," he said. Mary Munro. It trips off the tongue so lightly." He patted her belly. "In a few more months I can call you Mrs. Six and a half. And eventually Mrs. Six point seven five."

It may have been midnight silliness, but she felt his tension. How did any woman welcome a man home from war? Did he want her to know what he had seen? Would he rather not discuss the matter? She decided she did want to know. "How was the voyage?" she asked. Surely that was innocuous enough.

"Fast and hectic," he said. "Sir B's *Mercury* continues to be everything he could have hoped for us. I wish he could see us skimming along with Smitty at the wheel, Witticombe taking turns and singing something outrageous, Tots fishing, and Davey usually below deck studying. Avon March created a fish stew that I would have sworn had real cream in it."

She could see this, and wished herself along on a voyage. She also knew he was telling her only what was pleasant. "Will you ever tell me what happens really?"

She felt his sigh. "I do not know if I could, Meri. Maybe someday." He sat up. "This will interest you. We met up with the *Pickle* mid-voyage as we often do, the *Pickle* going one way, and we the other. She was having some trouble with the rigging and we stopped to assist."

"I know the Channel is not the Atlantic Ocean, but is it hard to find each other like that?"

"Not generally. We messengers make a point to stay the course to the same degrees of latitude and longitude, on the chance that we do need to hail each other." He lay down and pulled her on top of him. "You have a pretty face, Mrs. Six and a fourth. I have such a weakness for a woman who treats me tenderly and only snores a little."

She thumped him. "You're a pleasant sight, too, Master Six. Did you fix the *Pickle*?"

"We gave lots of unnecessary advice and I sent Avon aloft to help them."

"He's so little!"

"He needs to know what it's like to climb. Make yourself comfortable, Meri."

She did. That was easy, even if she did snore a little.

"It was Captain Lapenotiere's idea, but once the *Pickle* was shipshape again, he challenged us to a race. The wind was right; no other vessels in sight. Perfect time to race. I wish you could have seen it: two beautiful ships and a whole channel to frolic in."

She relaxed her body on his, tucking her arms around his back. "I wish I could sail with you once. Able, you are so comfortable."

"We can arrange that some day when we're in port and it's summer. Why, thank you. We bested the *Pickle* decisively. I have no doubt the *Mercury* is the fasted ship in the fleet. We Gunwharf Rats could drop off dispatches at Admiralty House and stroll about London before the *Pickle* by a day or two." He kissed her cheek, and politely spilled her off his body. "You're going to sleep, Meri. See you topside in a few hours, my love."

"I hope Mrs. Munro does not want this. I can't surrender it to her."

Able thumbed through his mother's prayer book as they walked to Jasper Street, Meri's arm through his. He wanted to walk, and she knew the exercise was good for her. He had told her earlier in their marriage that confinement to a quarterdeck for long periods made walking more than twenty feet forward and back a true luxury and not to be wasted.

"Surely Mrs. Munro won't ask for it," Meridee said. "I believe your mother left it with you on purpose."

"That's what I have told myself through the years."

What else have you told yourself through the years? she asked herself, kind enough to let him keep his private thoughts private. She needn't know everything. But she wanted to know. She wanted to know everything. She tugged on the arm she already held and stopped him.

"Aye, miss?" he asked in his teasing way. She had never seen kinder eyes.

What could she say here on the street, with people around? "I don't know." She leaned her forehead against his arm, speaking softly in this public place. "I feel so much love for you. I…I wish I could know everything you know. Even more than that, I wish…I don't know what I wish, but it fills me."

He moved them closer to the noisy ropewalk they were passing, wanting a quiet place, too, but seeing none. He seemed to know what she wanted to say. "Dear Meri, you'll never know everything I know. You wouldn't want to, believe me. Here's what you do know: you know my heart. The rest is fluff."

He enveloped her in his arms, putting his cloak around her, too, turning her face into his uniform. "Woman of mine, how I love you," he said. "I don't mind telling you that these past weeks have been nearly overwhelming, meeting my father, and soon my grandmama." He loosened his grip. "Can you breathe? Am I holding you too tight?"

"I am finer than frog's hair, as I heard Nick say once," she said, which made him laugh and accuse her of adopting schoolboy cant. He kept her cocooned with him in his cape another minute, then gave her a little pat. "If we don't move along, a constable will come by and ask me my business. This is sinful Portsmouth, after all."

They held hands the rest of the way to Jasper Street. "I would like to dream that you and the *Mercury* will be in port now for a few weeks, but I am not that feeble-minded," she said as they stood in front of Mrs. Munro's house.

"This is for your ears only, but I doubt that will happen," he said, his arm around her now. "Captain Lapenotiere and I compared notes at that mid-Channel meeting. He transports agents in and out of Cádiz, too. His sources indicate a stiffly-worded ultimatum from Boney to Villeneuve, ordering him to lead out the Combined Fleet and go on the attack. It's coming, Meri, and soon."

"I don't mind telling you that war is a confounded nuisance and cuts up my peace," Meridee said, which made him laugh and assure her, "Mine, too." He looked up at the house. "I don't know what to say to her."

"You sound like me a week ago! 'Hello, I am pleased to meet you,' is always a good beginning," she said.

Her eyes lively, the maid let them in and gestured toward the sitting room, a place Meridee was familiar with, after spending so much time in it during the past week. Before they reached the door, Mrs. Munro hurried into the hall.

Meridee glanced at Able, enjoying the little smile that turned into a big one. He walked toward her, his arms out, and Mrs. Munro hurried into them with a sob. She wept, patted his back, tried to talk, then gave it up as a bad business. She clung to him, and he to her, until Meridee felt tears in her own eyes.

"Did she look like you?" was the first thing he said. "I've seen my father's miniature of her, but miniatures are sometimes misleading."

"Aye, Mary did look like me," Mrs. Munro managed, as she fumbled for a handkerchief up her sleeve. "She was taller, and her hair was more auburn than mine." She held him off for a better look. "You greatly resemble your father, but I see my darling daughter in your eyes. Mr. Six, this is a pleasure I never imagined."

"I can echo that," he said, and held out his hand for Meridee. "Please call me Able."

"If you will call me Grandmama." Her hand went to her mouth, as if to somehow stifle the grief Meridee saw in her face, "You are my only grandchild. Mary's older sister died in childbirth. My son died without issue, serving king and country in India."

"Then this must be more than doubly strange to you...Grandmama," Able said. "You didn't even know of my existence until last week."

"I call it providential," Mrs. Munro said quietly.

Arm in arm, the three of them went into the sitting room. Meridee looked back to the corridor, not surprised to see Mrs. Munro's household staff gathered there. From earlier conversations, Meridee knew they were longtime staff, and had witnessed Mr. Carmichael's cavalier treatment of his wife and unusual daughter. The servants drew together now, and she saw satisfaction writ large.

"Sit beside me," Mrs. Munro said and patted the settee. He did, after pulling the nearest wing chair closer for Meridee. Mrs. Munro took his hand and filled her eyes with Durable Six, sailing master, instructor, genius, who had been left naked and freezing on the steps of a parish church. "You're tall."

"It's a hazard aboard ship, at times. I still bump my forehead now and then, going below deck in a hurry," he said.

"I know the curly hair comes from your father," Mrs. Munro said. "Mary's was straight."

"I believe I have something else from her. Meri?"

Meridee pulled the battered little Book of Common Prayer from her reticule and handed it to Mrs. Munro, as they had planned. The widow held it to her breast and closed her eyes. "Your Great Grandmother Agnes Frazer gave this to your mother on her fourth birthday," she said, her voice barely above a whisper. "Mary insisted on writing her name in it." She smiled through tears. "By the next day, she had read it." Her face clouded. "She told her father, and he scolded her for being a wicked girl, to tell lies."

"I was never understood in the workhouse," Able said. "I was beaten more times than I can tell you, until I learned to not say anything. I pray to God that my mother was not beaten."

"Oh, no, but is it worse to treat someone you should love with cold indifference?"

Meridee took Able's hand and squeezed it. He raised her hand to his lips. "And then, Grandmama, I became the luckiest man alive by finding my keeper. I can never forget everything that happened to me, but it all seems less important now. I have a wife, a son – has my keeper mentioned that she is in an interesting state again?"

"She did, and I'm delighted."

Able looked at Meridee, as if to ask, *You or me?* She nodded. "If it is a daughter, Able and I want to name her Mary Munro."

Mrs. Munro dabbed at her eyes. "How did you know that was your mother's middle name?"

"I have my sources," Able said, and tightened his grip on Meridee's hand. He hesitated, then shrugged. "This might sound ridiculous, but did…did my mother ever mention Euclid?"

Mrs. Munro gave a little start. "Aye, she did." She shook her head. "Some of my friends told me that their little ones had imaginary playmates. I assumed Euclid was my daughter's."

"He seems to get around," Able said.

"He *tells* you things?" Mrs. Mjunro asked in amazement.

"Someone inside my head does." Meridee thought him wise not to mention all the other geniuses and polymaths crowded in there, too. "Did…did my mother ever tell you about voices?"

"No, but by then her father had told her never to speak of such nonsense," Mrs. Munro said. Meridee heard the hard edge, but something else that sounded like relief, because at last she could talk about her child to someone who understood. "I did watch her at her embroidery hoop one day. She was diligent enough, but she sometimes stopped and cocked her head, as if she were listening. Was that Euclid?"

"Perhaps. I entertain other cranial vistors now and then. I expect Mama did, too."

Mama is such a simple word. It rests lightly on your lips, Meridee thought.

Mrs. Munro turned her attention to the prayer book. After a long perusal, she handed it back. "She obviously wanted you to have this, since she left it with you." It was her turn to hesitate, handkerchief to her eyes again. "I need to know where she is buried. Does she even have a headstone? I doubt that paupers' cemeteries are generous with such niceties."

Meridee watched her face and saw all the anxiety and the mother's longing. She thought of her little Ben, secure in his admittedly strange world, being raised by parents who understood him. Here she sat with two people who had no such security. She smiled at her husband, who was watching his grandmother. She knew he would look her way, because he knew when people focused on him. Here it came. He turned in her direction. She put her finger to her lips and touched his cheek.

Able leaned back then, relaxing. "She *is* buried in the pauper's cemetery. When I earned my first prize money in the fleet, I returned to Dumfries and replaced the wooden grave marker with a right proper granite one. All it says is 'Mary, Number 134,' because that was all I knew."

Mrs. Munro made a masterful attempt to control her emotions and succeeded. "D'ye think there is room to add her full name, and the…the dates?"

"There is." Able took her hand. "When this current national crisis ends and I am released from the fleet, you and I can travel to Dumfries and do what you would like, be it removal to another place, or a different gravestone altogether."

"We will keep your headstone, no matter what we decide about location," Mrs. Munro said decisively. "You have tended her well."

Chapter Thirty

A ble returned to the house on Jasper Street three more times, once by
himself, once with Meri and Ben, and another time with his father.
During his solitary visit, he took his grandmother to the Gunwharf, where
the *Mercury* was snugged to the dock. He had left Smitty in charge to see
to the lading of victuals and naval stores. Smitty gave her a dignified smile
– not for him the overwhelming enthusiasm of Tots or Whitticombe – and
returned to his work.

"He's as fine a sailing master-in-training as I could hope for," Able told
her. "Care to go aboard?"

She did, so he handed her in to Smitty and followed. She wanted to see
the whole yacht, so he assigned Tots, who did the honors, while he chatted
with Smitty.

"Is she shipshape and ready to sail?"

"Aye, sir," Smitty replied. Able heard all his pride in two sparse words,
and it warmed his heart. To his surprise, Smitty said more. "Is she your
grandmother?"

"Aye, she is, and a fine lady," Able said. "She's been telling me about my
mother."

"Could you bring her to dinner, Master Six?"

"I can and I will," he said, pleased, and took a chance. "I believe I will
send you in Lady St. Anthony's carriage to fetch her. Would you like to
do that?"

Smitty's normally stoic expression changed. He swallowed and looked
away. Touched to his core, Able watch the muscles work in the lad's face,
and took another chance. "Did you know your grandmama on your
mother's side?"

Smitty nodded. "I did. I liked her," he said. "I'll take good care of Mrs. Munro, when I fetch her."

"I know you will." Able returned to business, knowing better than to prod Smitty. "Back to your onerous task, Mr. Smith," he said, when Tots returned Mrs. Munro to the deck. "I used to nearly fall down with boredom reading through bills of lading. Be grateful this is not a frigate with pages and pages of dried cod, beans and misallocated nails to account for. The *Mercury*'s allocation shouldn't turn you surly and mean."

Smitty laughed out loud, which caused Tots to gape, his mouth open. Able frowned at him, and Tots looked away. Mrs. Munro watched the whole business with a smile of her own. Able could tell she liked the Rats.

Able spent two afternoons observing Mr. Ferrier at work in his seamanship class. He had been in awe of the quiet sailing master's skills for years. No one knew the running of a warship better than Mr. Ferrier, and for a man with no children of his own, he had a sure touch with the young and vulnerable.

Mr. Ferrier returned the favor. They stood at the stone basin, watching the little scamps practice their sextant readings on the HMS *Floaty*, and the stacking and arranging of smaller kegs and crates aboard HMS *Floaty Boaty*. "You've trained them well, Able," he said, his hands behind his back, tapping his foot to some internal rhythm, never raising his voice, as Able remembered from his conduct at sea. "It's made my work here so simple. For that I thank you."

"They're happy to please, so my task was easier than you would suppose," Able said as calmly as he could, when he really wanted to wriggle like a pup at his old sailing master's compliment. Mr. Ferrier had that effect on seamen, be they ordinary, able-bodied, or genius. He angled to another subject that Grace St. Anthony had broached only the night before. "Grace tells me you have been of real help to her brother, Headmaster Croker. For that, I thank *you*."

"She tells me he has not been quite himself, after an earlier illness. He's even shaky with a cane, or so I have noticed. I have the time to help, and the ability to keep him in my sights, since I am living here at St. Brendan's." Mr. Ferrier shook his head. "But oh, that butler. Can we not sedate him with laudanum and toss him aboard a ship bound for the Orient?"

Able laughed, recalling rumors of such a remedy aboard a frigate involving a purser. Mr. Ferrier always denied the rumors, but Able knew he was capable of it. "I fear not. Thaddeus seems adamant about allowing Atilla the Butler to continue his reign of terror."

They walked along the stone basin after Mr. Ferrier had the Rats snub their little vessels to iron rings and restore order, before hurrying across the street for dinner. Able remembered such stone basin walks with James McGregor, at last report sailing somewhere in the Pacific. He relished the shared experiences that had changed their roles to master and almost-master, from master to student. He felt it now with Mr. Ferrier.

"Headmaster Croker has hinted that I stay on here at St. Brendan's even after you return to classroom duties," Mr. Ferrier said as they strolled. "He says there is much need for more instruction and you can't do it all."

"I hope you will consider it seriously, sir," Able said, pleased at the notion.

"Why not? Retirement has no particular allure for me. If I had a growing family like yours, that might be different, but I was never so blessed."

Blessed was the right word. After dinner, Able spent his evenings with Meridee and Ben in the sitting room, usually occupied by a Rat or two, especially the tender ones who gravitated to Meridee's kindness and felt the need for a mum of their own. Beyond Smitty, Thaddeus had never assigned any more St. Brendan lads to live there. The Six home had become a welcome refuge for the headmaster's sister Grace, and her infant, and the Six family was expanding. With Meridee's approval, Thaddeus gave all his students the nod to take turns crossing the street to an actual home, something unfamiliar to most boys. Even if it was merely doing their homework in the Six's dining room, it was more than everything to the Rats.

Able's favorite moments were spent with Ben close by, reading out loud to each other, as his father watched. Meridee was never more than a glance away, mending or knitting, but more and more sitting there, eyes closed, her hands on her belly, following some internal rhythm. She said it was too soon to feel the baby moving, so he marveled all the more at her rapport with their unseen child.

When everyone slept, he could devote himself to his wife, sometimes doing nothing more than rubbing her feet, or enjoying the way she massaged his head and told him what had happened today in her world of sunken souffles, calming Pegeen when the scullery maid had her first monthly, or going to market with the redoubtable Mrs. Perry. He suspected Meri had no idea how soothing her voice was.

192 · CARLA KELLY

He knew the sharpness of her intellect, her vigilance and defense of him in his moments of exasperation with a brain that worked overtime, and her own down-to-earth wisdom. Perhaps he was no different than the Gunwharf Rats who crossed the street just to sit in her kind orbit and feel better.

Making love soothed his restless spirit. And to make love with this wife, the joy of his heart, surpassed any other earthly pleasure he could imagine. He knew a major fleet action was all but guaranteed, and soon. He also knew he could push the danger and terror to the background by loving Meri. What's more, she knew it, too. Their love intensified as the days passed and everyone waited for the *Mercury* to put to sea again.

"Why must such a man as Napoleon trouble the world?" she asked, after a breathtaking bit of General Merrymaking. It was hardly a lover's banter, but Boney, damn him, had a way of weaseling into the most intimate of places.

"Why? I suppose Boney needs to prove himself." Able chuckled. "He's short."

"That's silly."

"I suppose it is," he agreed, making himself comfortable, and breathing deep of her ineffable Meridee fragrance, storing it against a fraught time when he could call her to mind and find serenity in the worst places.

The next day would have gone the same, except that Captain Ogilvie surprised them at breakfast, ate heartily and with good cheer, then pushed Able into a post chaise for a trip to London, all in the space of thirty-three minutes. "Billy Pitt wants to see us," was all the explanation Angus Ogilvie gave to Grace and Meridee, sitting at the breakfast table and watching all this unfold. The Count preferred sleeping later and missed the fun.

Smart women, they knew better than to inquire further. Meridee reminded Able to put a change of linen in his small duffel, and do his best with a neckcloth. She gave him a scorching kiss on the doorstep and sent him on his way.

That kiss startled the usually unflappable Angus Ogilvie. "If you need another twenty minutes upstairs, I'll wait here in the post chaise," he said as Able joined him.

My blushes, Able thought, as his face flamed. "I suppose I have no dignity in your eyes."

"What you have are my supreme compliments," Angus said. "I will now change the subject. I lied. Billy Pitt doesn't know we're coming.

What I am asking you to do is tell him that your father is staying with you right now."

"In God's name, why?" Able asked, when he could speak. "What are you doing to me?"

"Perhaps keeping you from the gallows." He patted a portfolio on his lap. "I have here an indictment against Sir Clive Mortimer and a man so high up in the army that I won't even mention his name."

"I am involved with neither," Able snapped. Only strength of will and, he had to admit, some curiosity, kept him from sticking out his head to demand that the postilion stop the chaise.

"I know you are not," Ogilvie said with some impatience. "Once these traitors are removed, I predict – no, I am certain – there will be a lot of scrutiny leveled at everyone with any involvement in the war. Tell Mr. Pitt about your father before that happens. Assure him that the count will be gone on the next tide, or as soon as."

"We have been so careful," Able said, even though he understood Ogilvie and his motives. In fact, he felt something very close to affection for this troublesome, taciturn, infuriating fellow who was possibly risking his own career for a workhouse bastard. Able raised his hand, as if to brush away comment, whether from Ogilvie or his spectral mentors, he was not certain. "I know, I know. Even a careless word could bring down wrath on St. Brendan's, me and my family."

"Aye, Able. That is it. You understand."

"Most emphatically."

To Able's irritation, and then his whole-hearted relief, because he was coming to appreciate this wily fellow, Ogilvie reverted to type. He rubbed his hands together with some glee. "Trust me, Able, and you won't swing from a gibbet!"

He could return the favor. He tried not to smile. "I had better not, Captain Ogilvie," Able said, "or someday you might find yourself facing a firing squad and I will give the order to shoot."

"Touché, you bastard."

They laughed, but Ogilvie sobered quickly. "I'm sorry, lad," he said. "I truly am, but your father must return to Spain. You will understand when we talk to Billy Boy."

They arrived at 10 Downing Street as darkness fell and lamplighters plied their vocation. Able regarded the unpretentious home of the prime minister. His father had described what his estate looked like near Granada. The Count of Quintanar would have laughed in disbelief at this seat of power far plainer than his own mansion.

I do not laugh, Able thought as he followed Angus to the entrance. *I hope I come out alive, and not bound in chains to the Tower.*

A few whispered words with the butler, and they were shown directly to a booklined, empty office. To relieve his stress, Able did his usual rapid perusal of book titles, which made Angus shake his head. "You really do that," he said. "Meridee told me. Like a fool I didn't believe her."

"If you trust the ladies more, think what you'll learn," Able said, when he finished his scan. "I wonder if Mr. Pitt would loan me his copy of *Gargantua et Pantagruel* on the second shelf down, second bookcase over, fourth book from the left. I've never read it. Perhaps I can read it in the Tower before I am drawn and quartered."

"Come, come, Able. It won't be as bad as you think! I dare you for a bad shilling…" was Ogilvie's pithy rejoinder.

"…to ask about the book? You're on."

Chapter Thirty-one

Angus was right. Able had never seen a man so worn down by the cares of government as the man who came on halting steps into his own office, leaning on a cane. Mr. Pitt's eyes brightened to see them, however. He made no objection when Ogilvie helped him to his chair behind his desk.

"Sit, you two," he said with a wave of his hand. "Pour me some port, Master Six, and take some for yourself."

Able did as asked, but took none for himself, fearing it would come right back up.

William Pitt drank deep, then looked at the two of them. "Captain Ogilvie, I am not used to be summoned this way, without a by your leave. This had better be good."

"It is of vital importance, Mr. Pitt," Ogilvie said. He opened his portfolio and took out a single sheet. "Please read this, sir. It is under the aegis of both Admiralty and Trinity House." He indicated the portfolio. "All of the supporting documents are here."

The prime minister took the sheet. His eyes opened wider as he read. "Damn," he uttered softly, then read it again. "Admiral Gambier warned me that something was afoot." He slapped the page with some vigor. "But this?"

"It is the result of nine months of observation, both here and in France and Spain," Ogilvie said.

"I don't doubt you. Please assure me that – my God, him! – this…this traitor at Horse Guards is no longer roaming free."

Ogilvie took out his timepiece and gave it a good appraisal. "I believe he has already met with an unforeseen accident, while in the custody of Royal Marines sworn on pain of death to secrecy."

"Good. And Sir Clive Mortimer? Admiral Gambier has told me about Sir Clive."

"Rumor has it that very soon, most likely this afternoon, Gambier will remove him from his position at Admiralty and send him home to Kent for a repairing lease." He sighed most theatrically. "I anticipate a brutal roadside accident."

Pitt leaned back in his chair. "That should end the matter most discreetly. Captain Ogilvie, join with me and the Privy Council soon. I think we should take a thorough look at *all* levels of government to see if there are others....so inclined. We must be merciless."

"Aye, sir, and that brings me to Master Six."

Able took a deep breath as the prime minister looked at him down the length of his long nose. "Sir, why are you here?"

Able didn't bother to make a rapid inquiry of his mental mentors. All he needed to do was tell the truth, as odd as it would sound. "Sir, my father is a grandee of Spain, Francisco Jesus Domingo y Guzman, Conde de Quintanar. He is the royal accountant – quartermaster if you will – of the Spanish fleet and he is currently a guest in my home in Portsmouth."

The silence was stunning. Mr. Pitt blinked a few times, tried to speak, blinked some more, then slammed his hand down on a desk that had probably suffered similar torment through many a prime minister.

"Able, why in God's name are you harboring the enemy in your home, in the vicinity of a sensitive naval base?" Mr. Pitt glared at Ogilvie. "Angus, is this the first traitor we are flushing out of the sewer? Is that why you brought him here?"

"No, most emphatically," Angus said. "We are here to acquaint you with his story. If the word gets out about the count – yes, yes, our enemy – I would not for the world want you to ever think Master Six is anything but a loyal servant of the Crown and a damned good one."

Mr. Pitt nodded, his expression enigmatic. "Angus, there had always been some suspicion that you did not have a heart. I am starting to think you do."

Able noted Angus's sour expression. "He does have a heart, Mr. Pitt. It is a generous one. May I tell you my story?"

"Please do, Master Six."

Able told him of the portrait Captain Rose had shown him at Trinity House. "I looked just like the portrait. I never thought to see him until Captain Ogilvie...I..."

"Will, let me assure you that Able did not expect to meet the count," Ogilvie said, interrupting. "On one of my, ahem, expeditions to Cádiz, I noticed a gentleman aboard the *Santísima Trinidad* who looked remarkably like our master genius here. Jean Hubert…"

"…a thorough-going scoundrel," Pitt inserted under his breath.

"Possibly, although we need him now and then to forge documents," Ogilvie said smoothly. "On impulse, I suppose, Jean and I snatched the count, trussed him good and carried him to the *Mercury*. Able wanted to know who his father was. What an opportunity! Back to you, my friend."

My friend. Able didn't try to rein in his emotions as he described his reunion with his father and grandmother, and the knowledge about his mother's actual origins and her own thwarted genius. "Everything I thought was wrong, sir," he concluded. "The count and my mother loved each other, and were cruelly kept apart by her father."

"How long have you been harboring an enemy of England?"

Well, that didn't sound too promising. "For a little over two weeks now, sir," Able continued. "We have been getting acquainted. I have come to know a good man who never intended to desert my mother, and who has suffered ever since."

He knew he had said enough, but there was one thing more. "I know we are at war with Spain and France, sir. I acknowledge that freely, but you will agree with me that we all dance to Napoleon's gavotte."

"Aye, we do, lad," Pitt said, his voice much kinder. "It has turned me into an old man at forty-seven."

"I saw this reunion as a small moment of grace," Able said softly, not wanting to disturb the camaraderie that had settled in the room between a prime minister, a spy and a bastard genius. "With your permission, I will return my father to a spot near Cádiz, alive and well."

"I have no objection to that. Do it immediately, Master Six. Let's have no suspicion ever fall upon you."

The tension in the room vanished. "Thank you, sir," Able replied. "Back to Spain he goes. I admit it will pain me, now that I know him. He is a good man who was cruelly used by Mrs. Munro's husband, a Portsmouth harbormaster."

"And because he was cruelly used, so were you," Ogilvie said simply.

"I was, but I know the truth now, which makes it easier to bear," Able said. "The war will not last forever. I will see my father again under better circumstances."

"I daresay you will," Mr. Pitt said.

"Aye, sir, the sooner the better. I don't really trust Bertram, Headmaster Croker's butler, not to give my father up to the authorities. I think he suspects something. I sometimes wonder why Thaddeus Croker does not give him the sack."

Pitt looked from Able to Ogilvie, who grinned broadly. "Master Six, how do you feel on those rare occasions when you are completely wrong?"

Mr. Pitt and Captain Ogilvie exchanged glances. Able sighed. "All right, gentlemen, what *else* don't I know? In the past few weeks the list has lengthened."

"I am well aware that you have wondered who actually started St. Brendan's," Ogilvie said. "Sir B told me as much, and we had a quiet chuckle about it."

"I have suspected Sir B. Are you going to tell me it was *Bertram*?"

"As near as," Mr. Pitt said. "You recall that I have known Thaddeus Croker for years, and our Gracie, his sister."

"That I do remember," Able said, with sarcasm spread so thick that both men laughed.

"Thaddeus was a man of business, devoted to it, dedicated to making money," Mr. Pitt said. "As you know, his family is gentry, with wealth in land. That was never enough for Thaddeus."

Able couldn't help his surprise. "That doesn't gibe with the kind fellow who is so patient with students. Sir, if you could see him managing the lads." He shook his head. "Hard to believe."

"He married a lady much like him from the gentry, who brought money to the marriage. She was not really healthy, sad to say," Ogilvie added. He stood, walked to the globe and spun it around. "Thaddeus had the opportunity to travel to St. Petersburg for fur. It was all he could talk about, how he was going to buy beautiful pelts, then sell them to the Mandarin rulers of China for a huge profit. He was ambitious." He smiled with no humor. "Bertram was his valet."

Ogilvie spun the globe again, faster this time. "He was determined to go to St. Petersburg, despite the fact that his wife begged him not to leave her. She was in ill-health, and I must admit, did use such a complaint to her advantage."

"She was never as sick as she claimed, so Thaddeus discounted it and went anyway," Mr. Pitt said. "She was dead three weeks later and he could not forgive himself."

Ogilvie gave the globe a vicious spin. "He came home to a gravestone and the enmity of her relatives. Only Bertram stood by him, even when he retreated into a bottle and stayed there for months."

Able thought of Headmaster Croker's dignified and elegant serenity, even when things were not going well at St. Brendan's. "Nothing seems to faze him now."

"You should have known him then," Ogilvie said. He gave the globe a last spin, gentler this time, and returned to his chair.

"You were his friend?" Able asked. "Thaddeus has never mentioned you to me."

"I was his brother-in-law."

Ogilvie said it calmly, even as Able watched his expression change from anger to sorrow. "For all her foibles, Matilda Ogilvie was a bonny lass. She deserved better." He left the room.

Able sat back, stunned. "That's still a raw wound," he managed to say. He thought through Ogilvie's dealings with Headmaster Croker, acutely aware how little the two men interacted. "Painful even today. What did Bertram do to change matters?"

Mr. Pitt poured himself another glass of port and held it up to the morning light. "Such a lovely color," he said, then recalled himself to the moment. "Bertram was workhouse bred, like yourself."

"He is so arrogant! He always looks at me as if I don't measure up," Able said.

"Sometimes that is how workhouse alumni behave. You should know that."

He did. Able thought of boys who left the workhouse because someone, generally a relative, wanted them. He felt the sting of their sudden superiority as they strutted about until the moment they left for a real home. Yes, he knew how some behaved, and believed it of Bertram.

"Bertram was also devoted to Thaddeus Croker, despite that yawning gap between their social spheres. He was from the Portsmouth docks and liked to wander there. One day he dragged a sodden and hungover Thaddeus Croker to St. Brendan's, an old ruin where squatters of all ages fought each other to stay alive. Perhaps you know the desperation of hungry children."

"I've seen that, too," Able said, unwilling to remember, but unable to stop the scroll that was his brain unroll. In that unerring eye of his mind, he saw children barely older than toddlers pummeling each other for food while older children, equally hungry, egged them on for sport.

Angus Ogilvie opened the door. "I apologize," he said. "This is still hard story, even though some years have passed. Have you come to Bertram yet, Will?"

"That's where I am."

Ogilvie picked up the story. "Bertram took my brother-in-law to St. Brendan's, hauled him upstairs and into what is a classroom today, possibly yours, where two children pawed through slimy cabbage for something edible. You should hear Bertram tell this story: 'Says I to me master, "git yerself out of t'dumps and make a school here. Fit these little wretches for sumpin'." Ogilvie was silent a long moment. "And so he did. It's no wonder Thaddeus keeps Bertram on. His debt is enormous."

"I need to think better of Bertram," Able said, filling the yawning silence with contrition.

"I would advise it," Mr. Pitt said. "Yes, Bertram is irritating, but he pointed Thaddeus toward a great work." He gestured to Captain Ogilvie. "Angus, take this genius home to his wife and family. Able, leave as soon as you can with the count. It matters."

Able stood and bowed. "Thank you both for not throwing me to the wolves without a chance to speak for myself. I found my father, and I am better for it."

"Then I am pleased. When the war ends, you will see him again, I have no doubt."

Angus Ogilvie made a visible effort to lighten his own load. He stared at the bookcase, then smiled. "Mr. Pitt, Able is too shy to ask, but he would like to borrow your copy of *Gargantua*. Our genius scanned your titles in ten seconds flat…"

Six seconds, Able thought, but said nothing.

"…and saw it – where?"

With a blush, Able pointed. "By all means, borrow it," Pitt said. "I'll warn you, it's in antique French."

"That won't make any difference," Ogilvie said with a laugh.

Able retrieved the volume in question. "I'll take good care of it." Perhaps he could tease Ogilvie in turn. "If the captain is not too voluble on the return to Portsmouth, I'll read it and have it back in your hands with the next courier north."

Oh, the mellowing sound of laughter. Pitt gestured grandly to the door. "Stay the night in London. Stop here in the morning. By then I will have a letter for your father. It won't be of any importance, I suppose. This personal letter won't wander into history, especially since I will write it and not involve my secretary."

When Pitt spread his hands out on his desk, Able noticed they were shaking. Pitt watched him. "Able, I have grown old too soon in the service of England, as you can plainly see. I want to express my sincere wish to your father that we here on this island would like nothing more than to be friends of Spain again."

"I look forward to it myself," Able said most formally. "I pledge my best efforts to you, and those of the Gunwharf Rats."

"Even when England has treated you all so poorly?" Mr. Pitt asked gently.

"Even then." Able looked at Captain Ogilvie, really looked at him. "We all have our sorrows, and now and then, our victories. My story is no harder than anyone else's. Good night, sir. God keep you."

Chapter Thirty-two

"If this letter conveys even a tiny portion of the admiration and respect I have always felt toward the Spanish people, I will be content," Mr. Pitt told Able the next morning as he handed him the promised letter. "I fear Spain is in for more years of continental misery from Napoleon, which grieves me."

And probably keeps you sleepless, Able thought as he accepted the letter. To say that William Pitt looked wretched so early in the morning was a gross understatement. *I am looking at a man too young to have aged so much.* "I'll give this to the count and he will treasure it, I am certain. Thank you for your kindness to my father."

"I wish he could stay, but we daren't keep him here, mainly for your safety," Mr. Pitt said. He produced a familiar bag from his desk. "These things reek to high heaven," he said. "The First Lord obliged me by issuing what he called folderol orders for you, giving you permission to do anything you want. It's a marvel of obfuscation." His eyes bored into Able's. "What you are to do is to take the Count of Quintanar to Spain as soon as possible, then get the hell out."

"I will do that, Mr. Pitt," Able said, as he took the bag.

"I know you will," the prime minister said. He held out his hand. "Good sailing. If there is a battle – all signs point that way – Admiral Nelson will want a swift ship to bring the news home. I hope, for the memory of our Sir B, that it is the *Mercury*."

Able shook hands with the prime minister of England, accompanies by a cranial chorus of "aahs" from his brainy residents. In a blinding rush, his birth, his entire life in the workhouse, his early years in the fleet, and his recent successes rushed through his head. As he shook the hand of

William Pitt, Prime Minister, he was hard put not to caper about with the sheer delight of the moment.

"I hope it is the *Mercury*, too," Able said. "You know we Rats will do our best."

"I know. I have great faith in you." He smiled and it threw off illness and premature age, if only for a moment. "My best to your sweet wife, as well. And if you would, give Gracie a nudge from me."

How easy it was to laugh and enjoy the small moment with a man of such power. "A nudge? She might slap me for my impertinence. I'll chance it, Mr. Pitt, for you."

What a pleasure to part in such a way, and so Able commented to Captain Ogilvie, when they were seated in the post chaise for the return to Portsmouth. "I must say, Angus, never in the midst of my bleak early years did I ever suppose I would be joshing someday with England's prime minister."

"Never in my life did I expect to be party to anything like this, either," Ogilvie said. "Able, you have a remarkable capacity to land on your feet." He shook his head and looked out the window at London waking up to a new day. "You're starting to astound me."

Where was the curt and sometimes dismissive Captain Ogilvie? Able wondered about making some comment. He listened to the interlopers hanging about in his brain, heard nothing, and decided to say nothing. He opened the borrowed copy of *Gargantua et Pantagruel*, accustomed his brain to earlier French than he spoke, and spent a delightful hour digging around in Rabelais's inventive brain.

He closed the volume with some satisfaction. Since Angus was snoring and therefore unavailable for conversation, Able tried something he hadn't done before, just for fun: he decided to see if he could summon Rabelais.

Are you in there, Monsieur Rabelais? he inquired in his best classical French, and listened. Nothing, nothing, and then a faint, "*Mas oui*, except these oafs and mountebanks will not allow me any closer."

Jealous, are we? he asked the usual possessors of his brain. *Dog in the manger? There is enough of me to go around. I like literature, too.*

Really, Monsieur Six, at times you are a trial to scientists, came the reply from Lavoisier, who Able had thought would champion a fellow Frenchman, rather than bar him admission.

I suppose I am, Able thought. *You see, gentlemen, everything interests me.*

The silence inside his head was overwhelming. Able grinned, thinking he had offended all the brainy folk who inhabited his mind. Maybe they would go away and leave him in peace. The path seemed clearer, so he quietly thanked Rabelais for writing such a charming work, assured him he would read the other volumes eventually, and said *adieu.*

He napped then, the pleasure of an imaginative book lulling him into slumber. The added bonus was dreaming about Meri, right down to how pretty her hair looked spread out on his pillow. *Good God, Able, someone would think you have been on a twelve-month voyage, and not a mere overnight away from your wife,* someone told him. It might have been Copernicus, a well-known prude.

When Able woke up, Angus Ogilvie regarded him with a frown. Hopefully, he hadn't called out for Meri in his sleep or committed some other indiscretion. "Your eyes have an odd way of twitching behind your eyelids when you sleep," Ogilvie said.

"Aye, they do," he said, refusing to assume any defensive mode. "Meri said it used to bother her."

"And it doesn't now?"

"If it does, she hasn't said," Able said firmly, hoping this sounded like a conclusion.

It must have, because Ogilvie turned his attention the view outside. He wasn't through, though. He faced Able again, his expression guarded, his words muted.

"D'ye think – tell me truly – if perhaps next year, I might ask Lady St. Anthony if I could visit her upon occasion? Discreetly, mind you."

"Able, my love, any woman with eyes can see that Captain Ogilvie would like to pursue something permanent with Grace St. Anthony."

Meri had him, as usual, and he admitted it. "I didn't see it." He stopped brushing her hair – excellent prelude for having his way with her after he returned from London – and kissed her shoulder. "Captain Ogilvie?"

At least he had the satisfaction of watching his rational, competent Meridee start to breathe more rapidly. He kissed her neck this time, and gleefully enjoyed seeing her respirations increase. "I have no skills in observation."

She took the hairbrush from his hand. "You have others," she informed him quite firmly. "We're going to bed." By the time she pulled back the coverlet, her robe was gone and her shift off one shoulder.

In the morning, Able regarded Grace St. Anthony seated across from him in the breakfast room, her eyes on her small son in her lap as she buttered a piece of toast. Oh, the competence of women! It pleased him to see how one thoroughly confirmed spinster could turn into a mother with four hands. She never spilled a drop of tea, never misplaced a toast crumb, and still kept up conversation with Meri as she patted a loose lock of hair back into place.

Pay attention, Able. They were both looking at him. "Yoo hoo, my love," Meri said. "When do you sail?"

"Tomorrow." Better lower the boom. Last night resting so comfortably in Meri's arms hadn't been the time to discuss war. "Between the three of us – and you, Georgie, of course – Mr. Pitt told me to return my father to Spain immediately."

"I wish he could stay longer," Meri said. "Have you told him yet?"

"I am going to do that after our breakfast." He looked away from the ladies. "I've become fond of taking breakfast to him and … and just sitting with him while he eats."

"Why must he leave so soon?" Grace asked.

"We here have overlooked something that a prime minister dare not do: The Count of Quintanar is the enemy. The fact that I am harboring him could land me in trouble. Some might question my loyalty."

He heard no argument. "We've kept the matter so quiet," was as close as she came to a protest.

"Mr. Pitt is concerned," Able replied. They didn't need to know about Angus Ogilvie's major role in silencing two traitors to England's cause only yesterday.

"I can understand, my love, but I don't have to like it," Meri said.

"Neither do I." Able gave Meri his attention. "Forgive the short notice, but could you and Mrs. Perry concoct something special for dinner tonight? We'll have Angus and Mr. Ferrier, Captain Ogilvie, and Headmaster Croker, if he feels well enough. And the *Mercury* crew, of course." He smiled, thinking of Smitty. "I have already commissioned Smitty to escort Mrs. Munro here in Grace's carriage, if Grace is agreeable to such a loan."

"Completely agreeable," Grace said. "I'm glad you invited Captain Ogilvie."

A sidelong glance at Meri earned a wink from his proper wife.

Taking breakfast to his father had quickly become a ritual both men enjoyed. The count was no early riser. He was also no aficionado of trooping downstairs for breakfast, when a servant could bring it upstairs. Such a custom told Able everything he wanted to know about his father's opulent life, when he wasn't at sea. Truth to tell, he enjoyed taking Mrs. Perry's good food upstairs after Smitty had crossed the street for lessons or work on the *Mercury*, and the room was theirs.

He let his father eat before he brought down the mallet on his visit. His father finished with a pleased sigh. "I shall have to teach Mrs. Perry how to make paella," he said, "provided we can keep Ben from counting the grains of rice and stacking them in bundles of thirty."

There was no other way to say it but blurt it out. "*Padre*, I spoke with England's prime minister yesterday. He is most adamant that you leave England immediately."

The count took it well. "I was wondering when I might come to his attention," he said, after a long silence.

"You hadn't, not really. I was, shall we say, encouraged to disclose your presence in my house. Mr. Pitt informed me that others might find out. You would hang as a war criminal, and I would hang for sheltering you. That is all I know." He didn't mean to sound so curt, but the matter was stark. "I am sorry, but this is war. We cannot escape it."

The count took a final sip of his chocolate and dabbed at his lips. "I see the necessity for my removal, *mi hijo*," he said. "*No te preocupes.*"

"*Gracias.* The *Mercury* is nearly read to sail," Able said. "We'll cast off tomorrow."

"I would like to have stayed longer," was the count's wistful reply. "I was just getting to know you."

It was too much. Able gathered the breakfast dishes, pausing in the door to say, "*Padre,* I love you."

"And I you, my son," his father replied. Able heard all the sorrow. "We are puppets in the hands of an ambitious man, damn him."

Able shook his head when Meri took the tray from him downstairs and asked if he wanted to play with Ben. He said something, tears in his eyes, and left her standing there.

He knew the walk to Haslar Hospital to alert Davey Ten would shake off the cobwebs. It gave him time to remind himself that there was a war raging too close to his loved ones here in England; that he had managed twenty-nine years without his father, so what were a few years more until the war ended; that his life of hard things was still a life of hard things and nothing could change that.

He derived no consolation from the words of commiseration circling around his head from his spectral mentors. What did they remember of love and loss? "Leave me alone," he told them out loud.

"Oh, no."

He felt Meri's arm through his. "Slow down, my love."

"I didn't mean you, Meri," he said. "I would never say that to you."

"Dearest, I *know* the competition vying for your attention in that outsized brain of yours," she said. "I also know how you feel about me." She smiled. "But do slow down, please. I had to run to catch you."

He did as she commanded, relieved she had not left him alone. "Mrs. Perry is consoling Ben because he wanted to come along. I told him you would take him aboard the *Mercury* this afternoon to make up for it." She nudged him. "Don't make me a liar, Able."

"I wouldn't dare," he said, and nudged her back. "I'll take you aboard, too, if you'd like."

"Not this time," she told him. "Maybe next year. If the *Mercury* were to bob about, I'll puke, sure as the world. Where away?" She peered around his arm to see him better. "Is that correct?"

"You're the perfect sailing master's wife," he assured her. "Where away? To Haslar to tell Davey's surgeon that we're sailing tomorrow."

"May I come along?"

"I'd be miserable if you didn't."

God bless his wife. Gradually he slowed down until they strolled along the Gunwharf, then past warehouses and up the incline to Haslar. Her quiet presence calmed his brain. The hard things were never so hard when Meri was close.

Davey took the news with his quiet smile. Able saw no fear in his face.

"Ask your surgeon if he can spare some capital knives for your kit," Able added. "No worries, Davey. Should you need to use them, I'll be right by your side."

He told him about dinner that evening. "You can bed down in the sitting room later and we'll all walk to the Gunwharf together in the morning. I want my crew around me."

Chapter Thirty-three

They sailed the next morning on a fair wind to Spain. Meri and Ben saw them off, along with Ezekiel Bartleby, and all the students and teachers from St. Brendan's. The count was already stashed below, amused at the whole business. Able knew his father was more at home on a splendid Spanish three-decker, but he bore with good grace this humble setting of a yacht captained by a bastard and manned by workhouse lads.

Last night's dinner had been a fitting send-off for the *Mercury*'s crew. Able compared this dinner with the one before that first voyage. He looked at the faces of his crew and saw a maturing in them, even in Avon March, youngest by several years. They had seen firsthand what war could do to ships and men in the battle off Cape Finisterre. It had sobered them, but he saw no fear.

Smitty surprised him by his attention to Mrs. Munro. The widow had been voluble in her praise of Smitty's lively conversation as he escorted her to the dinner in Grace's carriage. "He's a fine boy," she said, when the fine boy was out of earshot.

Perhaps Smitty wasn't out of earshot. At her praise, "Fine boy," Able watched his back straighten as he rejoined the crew. "That he is," Able answered, making sure Smitty could hear him.

Unlike this cheerful send-off, every trip to sea before now was a solitary entity for Able. He packed his duffel, then usually ate a meal in the best taproom he could afford. Able never considered himself lonely, not with all the interlopers in his brain, but there were times when he watched other officers playing cards or laughing over shared memories with their friends, that he knew he was missing something not even Sir Isaac Newton could supply.

He felt it acutely if he decided to walk through a neighborhood some blocks from the wharf of whatever naval port his ship lay at anchor. He knew it was rag manners to stare into people's houses, but if curtains were drawn back, and if he heard laughter, he justified a quick glance at fathers and mothers with children around. After a few such solitary walks – at the risk of argument let us call them lonely walks – he didn't go again.

Here he sat at their last dinner before sailing, Meri close by with Ben in his chair, his father seated at the other end of the table, Mrs. Munro next to the count, and all his other sons – beg pardon, the Rats – crowded together, and look, Grace and Captain Ogilvie close enough that their shoulders were probably touching. (Well, they *were* all crammed close together like whelks in a basket.)

He smiled to see improved table manners, and what passed as polite conversation, even though the subject always seemed to be the sea. He didn't mind; he loved the ocean, too. Be his ship large or small, there was no feeling like the joy of balancing on a deck as the rhythm of waves under the keel traveled from the soles of his shoes through his whole body.

He knew he would be even happier in a few hours when he enjoyed quiet time with Meri. He knew they would talk, laugh, maybe argue a little, tease each other, and make love. He knew he would never be lonely again.

When Meri turned her attention to Ben at the table, Able waited for his spectral busybodies to twit him about his emotions. They were not above amusing themselves at his expense, upon occasion. He waited, but nothing happened. He entertained the heretical notion that perhaps he did not need them as much, if at all. Had they been his champions and buffers when life was bleak? What was the meaning of all this? He took comfort in the knowledge that in this next crossing of the Channel, he might have time to think about the matter during the middle watch when the deck was his.

Dinner over, every subject discussed, Able felt a pang when his father gave his best bow to Mrs. Munro, the lady who would have been the count's mother-in-law if the world were even slightly fair, then folded her into a gentle embrace. "*Señora* Munro, only think what good times we will have when this stupid war ends and you can be my guest in Spain."

"I look forward to it…" She hesitated. "Son."

Completely undone, the count bowed over her hand this time, then made his dignified way upstairs. Able took his turn, his hand in hers, as he and Meri walked her outside where Smitty and the carriage waited.

"I'll see you in two weeks at the outside," he said, and kissed her cheek. "My only task is to get my father to Spain. I am certain Meri will take Ben to Jasper Street for visits and crème buns."

"We will visit," she said, "crème buns or not. Ben is a grubby little trencherman."

There it came, the inevitable scroll unwinding to remind Able of his bleak and desperate life at Ben's age. *No*, he said to his mind. *Stop. I don't want to see what I ate and how poorly I was treated. I want to see Ben's pleasure at food, and his delight in his Mama and Papa. Don't trouble me with all my memories. Not tonight. In fact, how about never again?*

To his astonishment, the scroll snapped shut and vanished. When he drew in his breath in surprise, Meri touched his hand, concerned. "No worries," he whispered. "I am fine." And he was.

He knew how late it was, and he had noticed Mrs. Munro yawning discreetly in the sitting room. Instead of joining Smitty by the carriage, Mrs. Munro took his hand and Meri's.

"Yes, you and Ben visit me," she said. "Grubby or not, Ben is most welcome." She leaned toward Meri. "I might be inclined to supply crème buns, but that is the prerogative of a great grandmama, something I thought never to be."

She squeezed their hands. "I do not command anything approaching a huge fortune. Let us say I am comfortable." She lowered her voice to a whisper. "I also have no one to leave it to. May I please fix it upon you and your children?"

Trust Meri to say the right thing. "You are a dear to think of us, but we already want for nothing." The smile she turned on Able could have guided ships at sea. "Able is an excellent provider."

Bless you, Meri, he thought. "Mrs. Munro, The estimable Sir B who was married to Grace St. Anthony has already deeded our house to Meri," Able said, after he raised Meri's hand to his lips and kissed it. "On the event of my death at sea, she is to receive one thousand pounds a year. We are well enough off."

He knew Mrs. Munro was a tenacious woman. Any lady with the courage to resume her maiden name after the death of her husband and not fret over the social consequences was not someone inclined to hang back. She did not surprise him.

"I should still like to fix five hundred pounds a year on your family," she said firmly. "You speak of money *after* your death. That is well and good, grandson, but I am thinking of the niceties which all of you can enjoy after I am gone, and while you live. Kindly do not argue with me."

He knew better; he was a Scot, too. "I won't argue. Yes, do consider us in your will, if you wish." He couldn't help a quiet laugh. "Why do I have the feeling that you already have a pen poised over just such a document with your solicitor?"

She joined in his laughter. "As soon as his office opens tomorrow! As one Scot to another, you are wise beyond your years!"

One Scot to another. In that humorous moment, Able knew in his bones that he belonged to this woman whom he should have met years ago, as well as to the wife beside him, their baby she carried, and their boy Ben. To his undying delight, Able Six knew he had become one of the families he used to envy on his lonely walks. The knowledge gave him the confidence to make a request.

"On the other hand, I know something you could do right now that would prove of great benefit to the recipient and this nation," he said. "Scotland, too."

"Say on, Able."

He glanced at Meri, who knew him so well. She mouthed "Davey?" and he returned the slightest nod. "Grandmama, there is a St. Brendan's lad who has a sure touch with medicine. You met him tonight, Davey Ten."

"I liked how the others stopped and listened when he spoke," Mrs. Munro said. "I believe you said he is apprenticed to a pharmacist's mate at Haslar Hospital."

"Aye. He's my surgeon aboard the *Mercury*. In a few years, he will be sixteen. He should attend a good medical school, which I know is found at the University of Edinburgh. He could be a surgeon, I have no doubt, or even a physician, should he choose."

"The university is certainly well-known for medicine," Mrs. Munro said. "Would you like me to sponsor him and pay his tuition?"

"I would, most emphatically," Able said, and tested his luck further. "There will be other lads like Davey. One of mi…ours is already learning the engineering of machinery from his adoptive father."

Meri tugged on his sleeve. "Able, I forgot to tell you. John Mark told me before you returned last from sea that he will soon be apprenticed to Henry Maudsley himself."

"That *is* good news," he said. "You see, Grandmama, we at St. Brendan's have discovered that our workhouse brats have talent enough for other ventures."

"I can help your Rats, too," his grandmama said quietly. "I will."

"And that is that," Meri said, after they waved goodbye to Mrs. Munro. "I hope Smitty will let himself in quietly when he returns, because I want to be in bed with you."

Smitty did; she was. When Meri finally slept beside him, content, Able lay awake a little longer, doing nothing more than breathing in and out and savoring the bliss of total relaxation. Nothing raced through his brain except his vast love for Meridee Bonfort Six.

On a whim, he placed his hand on her bare belly. He had noticed a thickening of her waist, and she had complained about never getting back to her original shape. He loved her this way, all mutterings aside. He knew it was too soon to feel movement, but as he kept his hand on her belly, he could have sworn… He pushed lightly with his index finger and waited.

There it was, the tiniest answering, finger to finger, his own Sistine Chapel. He knew the acknowledgement was between him and his daughter alone. A daughter was it? *Why yes, Able Six, a daughter*. He wasn't sure which of his mentors spoke, but he did not question. He knew he would never mention the matter to Meri before they sailed. She knew it was too early, and so did he. This was his secret.

Chapter Thirty-four

Wind and tide took them smartly away from Portsmouth. Able faced the shore as long as he could, enjoying the last glimpse of his wife and son as Smitty took them into the Channel with a sure hand on the wheel, plus Witticombe's able handling of the sail. Davey had gone aft to quietly vomit in peace, Avon was already below plotting the first meal at sea, and Tots was lifting the sextant from its velvet-lined case. It was business as usual aboard the *Mercury*. He hunched his neck down against October's chill.

The day before, he had spent a quiet hour by the stone basin with Mr. Ferrier, discussing his students and Grace's, too. Able's former sailing master had nothing but praise for Sir B's widow and her intensity in the classroom. "I dare any lad in her orbit to not excel. She takes such time with each pupil."

"Her brother has told me on more than one occasion that his sister would be a better headmaster than he," Able said. "I didn't argue with him. In a perfect world, she would be headmaster."

Mr. Ferrier stopped walking. He hesitated and Able waited, almost certain what was coming next. After another try, Able stepped in. "I think I know what you want to tell me, sir," was all it took.

"Able, Thaddeus has offered me the position of headmaster when he is gone," Mr. Ferrier said, his face troubled. "He says he does not have long to live and is hoping to survive this term. What can be wrong with him?"

"I have noticed a yellow cast to his skin," Able said. "Perhaps you have, as well, sir?"

Mr. Ferrier shook his head, then managed a quiet chuckle. "You always were the more observant among the crew on the *Defence*. Tell me now what you think."

Master Ferrier was never a man to dance around. "I believe our Thaddeus has cancer of the liver, sir. It is simply a matter of time. I know you will make an excellent headmaster."

"Sad news, indeed, but thank you for your endorsement," Master Ferrier said. "You relieve my mind. I was afraid you might think I was usurping a promotion that you would feel was yours by your own leadership abilities." He looked at St. Brendan's. "The Rats would follow you into the jaws of hell."

"I want nothing more than to return to my classroom, sir."

"And I have discovered that retirement is a galloping bore," Mr. Ferrier said.

But Mr. Ferrier was miles away now, teaching and ready to assume additional duties Thaddeus allotted to him. Able glanced at Smitty, steering a true course on the *Mercury*, and at Tots taking his morning reading with his sextant. Able knew he belonged in the classroom, as soon as this issue of Frogs and Spaniards playing too close to England was resolved. *Very well, Admiral Nelson, it's time to tease out the Combined Fleet from Cádiz. I have other work to do*, he thought, *and a wife who waits. You are keeping me from both of them, sir.*

The first night out he had gone below for the letter Meri had handed to him, after another of her incendiary kisses in the privacy of their bedroom. "Ben and I wrote you letters," she said as she slipped it in his uniform pocket. "Read them when you have a quiet moment."

He found that quiet moment in the middle watch as everyone else slept and he manned the helm. He read the one from Ben first. "Pretty good handwriting, lad," he said out loud. Ben had drawn him a picture of the *Mercury. Mama says you are to tack this in a convenient place*, he read. Able's eyes misted. *And more specifically, you are to be very careful because I need you at home. Your loving son, Benjamin.*

He saved Meri's letter for another hour, for that time when he knew he would be growing tired and getting ready for Smitty to relieve him. She had drawn herself in profile, with the smallest bump outlined under her dress. The bump had a question mark inside, which made him smile. *It's a girl, Meri*, he thought. *Trust me though: I will look wonderfully surprised.*

He read on as his wife professed her deep love for him, her anxiety when he was at sea, and her confidence that there wasn't anything that could possibly prevent his return to her in due time. He turned over the page and found himself reading reality, this time. *But you are only human, my love, and anything can happen,* he read. *Waiting at home is onerous. Putting on a smile every day is difficult. Patting your pillow at night makes me long for you. I miss your lap as much as Ben does. I feel better, safer, wiser, and happier when you are in my sight.*

"So do I Meri," he whispered.

He smiled through the mist when she told him she was wearing his scandalous locket, and that she had tucked one of his unlaundered shirts under her pillow. She finished, Meri-style, with a flourish. *I love you and long to see you soon. Damn Napoleon, anyway. Yours, completely yours through it all, Meridee Six and a third.*

Able read her letter every night. He wondered how he, a man skilled beyond normal facility in navigation, had ever managed to plot his earlier solitary course through life. *Here we are, Meri, trying to be man and wife at such a time when nations war against each other and I must do my duty, and no one cares about us except us,* he thought.

If the worst happened, there wouldn't even be a grave for her and Ben to visit and leave flowers. Meri knew that sailors were buried at sea. He would never tell her what it looked like in battle, when corpses were simply tossed into the water to clear the decks, without the comfort of a prayer.

He steered his course, watched the stars, longed for his wife, and did his duty in the silence of that middle watch, when prime ministers dreamed of better worlds, and women and little ones at home slept in safety, because captains sailed to war.

The more immediate blessing was one he and his whole crew shared. Like him, they had become fond of the Count of Quintanar, courtly, gregarious and generous with his affections. Able marveled at his father's sure touch with boys, even as he regretted that he had only come into this charming man's orbit a scant month ago. The Count had a way of leaning forward and drawing all closer as he told stories of his life in Spain. What a father he would have made.

As the *Mercury* cruised closer to Spain and their inevitable parting, Able found himself wanting to slow the yacht's passage. He knew his father felt it, too. As the count took turns helming the yacht with Able through the middle watch, he told other stories. The count spoke of his love for Mary Carmichael that had never left him. "Son, when I returned to Spain so devastated, your grandfather nagged at me to find a wife among our own," he said one night. "I tried, but no one came close to touching my heart as she did."

"You've told me you have two sisters and no brothers," Able said. "Who will inherit your land and title?"

"It should be you, but you see the impossibility of such a thing."

"*Por supuesto*," Able replied. "English law doesn't allow bastards to inherit titles. I doubt you Spaniards are of a different mind. And besides, we are enemies, are we not?"

They both laughed at that. The count sobered first. "I have a nephew, a supercilious *tonto*, who will inherit." He shrugged. "I am reconciled to the matter. I will be dead, after all."

"It is enough to know you, Father," Able said, and it was.

There was no slowing the *Mercury*. In fact, the wind grew stronger when they rounded Cabo de São Vicente, Portugal's furthermost point into the Atlantic, and turned more east by southeast toward the coast of Spain. The count secreted himself below when the *Mercury* hailed the frigate *Discovery*, one of a line of vessels that like a barbed necklace kept Spanish and French ships prudently hugging their coastlines.

"Where away?" the captain asked through his speaking tube.

"Dispatches for the Mediterranean Fleet," Able called back. "What news?"

"We're hearing rumors," the captain returned. "One of the fishing smacks from Rota near Cádiz said the tall ships are setting their yardarms."

Able felt that familiar tightening of his gut, the one that every man in the Royal Navy probably understood, with news like that. He hadn't felt it since the Treaty of Amiens turned to dust in 1803 and war came roaring back.

"We'll mind our manners," he shouted. "D'ye have dispatches for the fleet?"

The *Discovery*'s captain laughed. "Tell them to rescue us from boredom and let us join the fight!"

"Aye, sir."

When he set down the speaking trumpet, he turned around to see all the Rats on deck, and the count. "Sounds to me like the Combined Fleet is coming out to play," he said, trying to keep his tone conversational. "Count, we won't be landing you a moment too soon, from the sound of it."

The wind held that day as Able directed Smitty to edge closer to the Spanish coast. He kept Smitty with him through the middle watch that night, quietly instructing him what to do this time, when they arrived at the landing site. "I will row my father in, and you will hold a steady course."

"Aye, sir," Smitty said. He cleared his throat, and sounded surprisingly young when he continued. "Wi…will we be going into battle?"

"Hard to say. The Spaniards and Frogs constitute a huge fleet, and some have been bottled up in Cádiz for months. After we finish our business, we'll sail immediately to England, as Mr. Pitt intended. We're messengers, Smitty, that's all, with not a gun on deck."

Now was a good time to chivvy Smitty a bit, nothing major, but a reminder of his duty as sailing master. "When was the last time you wrote in the log? You know that's a sailing master's duty."

Smitty showed him a wry face. "Two days ago?"

"I know it's not your favorite task, lad, but duty is duty. Let's see. We've turned the hour and it is October twenty-first. Tonight after we discharge the count, you will bring the log up to date. That is an order."

"Aye, sir."

They sailed on toward morning. The wind had dropped and Able felt that greasy swell underfoot, the one signifying a storm in a day or two. Whitticombe had remarked on it at breakfast. Able was impressed how the lad took an interest in the wind. There was every possibility he would be a fine sailing master, too.

Everything changed when Avon came up from below deck an hour later and proclaimed that the best fish strew ever prepared by the hand of man was ready below, and was that thunder he heard? Something was reverberating below deck.

"Avon, you don't feel thunder in your feet," Whitticombe said. He frowned, then looked at Able, the confidence gone. "Sir? Sir?"

Able raised his hand for silence. He tried to move casually to the lee side of the *Mercury*, that side closest to land. He picked up his telescope from its hanger by the flag locker. Just a look. That was all.

"Bring us a point closer to the wind, Smitty," he said as he steadied himself and raised the glass. He couldn't be certain, because the *Mercury* was small and no three-decker, with masts reaching skyward that allowed a better view from the top. He clipped his telescope to his waist and climbed.

Just a look, he thought, *just a look*, and raised the telescope to his eye. His gut tightened more. He knew it was too late for him to eat the best fish stew ever prepared by the hand of man. He never cared to eat before sailing into a fleet action.

Crowning the distant horizon was the entire Combined Fleet, freed from the harbor and fighting. He saw the *Santísima Trinidad,* largest ship in any navy and the pride of Spain, in the middle of a line that appeared to be breaking up. He steadied his hand on the glass and watched as two columns of Nelson's Mediterranean Fleet sailed into the enemy line with majestic purpose, all flags flying, even more than usual. Sometimes that was the only way to tell friend from enemy, when the guns belched and the sky turned dark.

That was it: Nelson had decided to sail toward the enemy on the perpendicular in two columns and not the parallel, the better to divide the enemy line and fight ship to ship in a wild melee that was as brutal as it was effective. The Battle of the Nile had proved that point.

He was too late. He could not return his father to Spain yet, and he knew in his heart this was not a time to hang back, even if the *Mercury* was small. He was sailing his crew of school boys in an unarmed yacht toward danger of the worst sort. Able closed his eyes and saw the map of the coast, helpfully scrolled out for him by someone in his head. He knew there was a little outreach of land, nothing like Cabo São Vicente or even Finisterre far to the north. Trafalgar. That was it. Trafalgar.

Chapter Thirty-five

I believe the Rats would follow you into the jaws of hell. Master Ferrier had said it only days ago, and here they were. Thoughtful now, his fear in retreat, Able made his way down to the deck.

"Gather around, Rats," he said, motioning to them. "Avon, call down for Davey. My father, too. This is a council of war."

He waited, trying to keep his face expressionless, for those below to hurry topside. A glance at his father's face told him the count fully understood that rumbling under foot. He gave Able a slight nod.

"We're heading toward a fight, a big one," Able said. He squatted on the deck by the wheel where Smitty stood and motioned the others to join him. He smiled to see a pencil behind Davey's ear and plucked it out. He drew a series of dots on the deck, and then two perpendicular lines, moving them forward until they intersected the dots.

"Admiral Nelson has engaged the Combined Fleet and I believe they have smashed through the line. What follows now is ship-to-ship combat in a wild free-for-all."

"Gor," Tots whispered under his breath. "Sounds bad."

"It is." He looked toward his father. "Sir, we cannot return you to the coast tonight for obvious reasons. Perhaps in a few days." The count gave a courtly little bow. "For us to hang back, when we could serve as a repeater, would be cowardice."

He looked around and saw nothing but resolve. "Guns or not, we're going in." Still nothing but resolve.

"Avon, in your flag locker you should find several Union Jacks. Whitticombe, you will hang them from our mast and from the jib boom. We'll be sailing into dense, dark smoke. Those flags will identify us. Alas,

Father, you must go below. If anyone sees your Spanish uniform, and our flags, we would be a prime target for both navies. I won't have it."

"*Sí, capitán,*" his father said, "but there is this: would you allow me to remove my uniform jacket and put on that dark sweater that Meridee knitted for you? Possibly I can be of help on deck."

"Your loyalties, *señor*?" Able demanded in Spanish, hating himself for asking.

Again that little bow. "Ii is to you and the *Mercury*. You have my word."

"Then we thank you," Able said quietly. "I had to ask."

"Certainly you did. I would have thought less of you, if you hadn't."

Able sat back on his heels, aware that everyone's eyes were in him. "I will remind all of you that we have absolutely no firepower. All we have is speed, and there is little wind today. I propose that we sail toward the guns and see if we can use Avon's skills with signals to be a repeater, as we did at Finisterre. If that isn't necessary, we will look for British tars in the water and fetch them out. Anyone, for that matter. Are you with me so far?"

Every Gunwharf Rat nodded; he knew they would. He couldn't help his sigh, counting them as close to his dear sons as Ben. "You will see and hear the worst. I expect every man to do his duty. You will stay by your posts and obey every order I give, without exception. Smitty, if I am killed, you will find a way to take the *Mercury* out of the battle."

"Aye, sir," came Smitty's quiet reply. "I can do that. And we will get your father to Spain."

"To your posts," Able said. "Eat first, if you think you can keep it down. Avon, douse the galley fire, then stand by the signal locker. Tots, you will protect Avon with your life. Whitticombe, stand ready to work the sail and call on Tots if you need him. Davey, clear off the table and get out your instruments. *Padre*, watch over us all."

Able could have wished for more wind, but the god of wind was fickle that early afternoon. Soon the stench of black powder reached his nostrils. He stood beside the wheel, his hand on Smitty's shoulder. "Closer to the wind, such as it is, if you would, Mr. Smith," he said most formally.

The noise quickly overwhelmed them. The sound of cannon belching regularly soothed Able's soul, because he knew how well-trained Royal Navy gunners were. The more intermittent firing told him that the Spaniards and Frenchies, while brave, never would have practiced enough in the confines of the Cádiz harbor to achieve that same efficiency. That simple fact gave him confidence, despite the sight of wounded Royal Navy vessels, some with masts crashing down, as the little *Mercury* heeled and dodged into the center of the fight.

Able felt a hand on his own shoulder, and turned to smile at his father, wearing Meri's beautiful navy blue sweater she had knitted when there weren't stockings to darn and trousers to let out for growing Rats. He closed his eyes for a brief moment, rewarding himself with the sight of his wife darning in her chair beside his in the sitting room, and laughing at some bit of wisdom from Ben. *Meri, think of me now*, crossed his mind.

"Hot work," was all his father said.

Smitty gasped at the sight of the *Belleisle*, masts gone, as the *Mercury* edged by, its decks piled with the dead and dying. Ahead, the *Mars* fought off two French ships, crammed next to the *Santa Ana* which fired round after round into the wounded but still savage *Royal Sovereign*, Admiral Collingwood's flagship.

Admiral Nelson relished a good fight at close quarters. Able wondered where the *Victory* was, even as he knew the little admiral was probably standing, imperturbable, beside his flag captain Thomas Hardy, and commenting upon the action.

But here was the *Mars*, surrounded and brave. Able squeezed Smitty's shoulder. "Son, sail between the *Mars* and that Frenchie. Can you do it?"

In silence, Smitty heeled the *Mercury* precisely into the narrow space, which caused the French double decker to veer just enough to give the *Mars* room to play, like a wolfhound momentarily startled by a pup. Able knew Captain Duff from the Battle of the Nile. He knew George Duff would back off and go at the Frenchie from the vulnerable rear. When the *Mercury* sailed through, the *Mars* took the invitation and dropped back. Well-named, the *Mars* rained fire on the stern that roared through the quarterdeck and knocked down scores of Frenchmen like bowling pins on a peaceful greensward. Out of the corner of his eye, Able saw Captain Duff give the *Mercury* a wave.

Too soon, the *Fougeaux* dealt in kind from the *Mars's* other side, letting go with a barrage that left Able deaf for long seconds. Smitty's mouth opened in horror as Captain Duff's head and neck separated from his body and the parts collapsed on the *Mars's* bloody deck, a good man gone in a blink.

"He never knew what hit him, Mr. Smith. Take us out through that space dead ahead," Able said, his voice firm. He yawned to clear his ears and pressed down on Smitty's shoulder. Able looked toward the signal locker. "Mr. March," he hollered, surprised that he could barely hear himself. "Signal, Surgeon on Board."

As Smitty wheeled the *Mercury* to open space, Avon had the flags fluttering. Able looked back. They had woven their way through the center of the action. All around was carnage, with bodies and parts of bodies dipping and bobbing on the water.

"Watch the water, Rats," he ordered. "If you see life and movement, sing out."

Whitticombe called from starboard. "Over here, Smitty! Come in slow."

As Able watched, Whitticombe and the count hauled a man roughly over the side and onto the deck. Whitticombe called for Davey Ten, who, seconds later knelt beside the sailor, feeling for a pulse in his neck. "Too late," he shouted. He and Whitticombe unceremoniously pushed him back into the water as the count pulled another man aboard, and Tots one more.

Between them, they carried the two injured men below deck. The count remained where he was, then turned in surprise as a French ship bore down on them.

It was the *Pluton*, the other double-decker that had given such misery to the *Mars*, swinging around like a sightless fighter in the smoky haze, aware of motion but little else, angry and ready to fight….something. Able glanced up at the *Pluton*'s riggings, chilled to see sharpshooters there, aiming at Smitty.

With an oath, he shoved Smitty down to the deck and took his place, turning the wheel, knowing full well the sails would luff and swing about, ruining the aim, if the god of war felt like smiling upon them. No Frog was going to kill his Gunwharf Rat.

A rifle ball carved a path through the skin above his left ear. Wet warmth dripped down his neck and his ears rang. He glanced up, saw two more sharpshooters, and knew the next balls would take him. *So be it. I love you, Meri.*

Upon later reflection in the quiet of the return voyage, Able wondered if he should have expected what happened next. Perhaps he would have, had he felt the love of a father for a son when he was a baby like Ben. Over the noise and screech of falling masts and ripping sail and guns booming, he heard that rifle ball meant for him. In seconds divided by miniscule increments, his amazing brain told him that the ball was spiraling directly toward his frontal lobe, where it would explode in bloody, gray froth and he would be as dead as poor Captain Duff.

He heard a huge gasp and wondered why his cranial inhabitants hadn't already deserted him. He didn't think they were much for a fight, because he had heard nothing from them in several hours. Why would they exclaim so loud now, and in Spanish? *O dios mio!*

The gasp was followed by darkness and a heavy weight, two distinct thuds, and then a sigh. Able crashed to the deck, his father on top of him. Was this death? Able felt suddenly warm and peaceful. It must be death.

Maybe it wasn't death. Hands other than his own wrenched away the heavy weight, then reached for him.

"Sharpshooters," he managed to say. "Lie flat."

"No, Master Six. The *Mars* just gave the *Pluton* what for. Gor, what a fight!"

Tots held out his hand and pulled Able into a sitting position. Smitty was sitting beside him, blinking as if the grey gloom of battle was too bright for him. Then Davey was beside him with a cloth. "Hold this to your head, sir, and press hard. I'll look at your father."

His father. *O dios mio*. Able dropped the bandage and stared at the heavy weight across his legs. He saw where the rifle balls had spiraled their way into the Count of Quintanar, royal naval quartermaster of the Kingdom of Spain, ruining Meri's wonderful warm sweater. When Davey turned his father over so gently with his surgeon's delicate touch, Able knew he would see carnage and death, and extraordinary love. He swallowed and blinked.

Little Avon pressed the bandage back on Able's head, as Able stared down at his father, whose eyes were open and watching him. Davey expertly wound another bandage around to anchor the compression pad on Able's head and knotted it firmly. Able rested his hand on his father's ruined chest, his father who lay across his legs.

"*Padre mio,* you shouldn't have," Able murmured in Spanish.

"It was the crowning act of my life," the count said. "I would do it again."

Able looked up at Davey, a question in his eyes. His young surgeon's lips tightened as he shook his head slightly. Able looked down. Davey was right. He saw much ruin, disguised only because the dark blood blended with the dark wool. A person could almost be fooled into thinking that a bandage here and another one there, perhaps a drain, plus plenty of rest and a low diet would have the count on his feet in no time.

He took his father's hand in his, speechless with sorrow. The count smiled at him, but it was a wistful smile. "I would like to have stayed longer," he said, his words starting to run together, the words of a sleepy man ready to lay down his burdens for the night and wake up somewhere else. "I was just getting acquainted with you."

Able couldn't help the moan that escaped him. It seemed to pour out of his entire body. Those were the exact words his father had said mere days ago, when they chatted and laughed together on the night of the dinner with Mrs. Munro.

Able knew it was pointless to try to sniff back his tears in a manly way. He sobbed over his father, assuaged this time by Smitty's hand so firm on *his* shoulder. Duty took over briefly. He looked to the wheel, where Whitticombe steered so expertly, then back at his father, whose eyes had followed his.

"You have trained them well, my son," his father said. "Please give my best to Meri."

"I will," Able said, as his heart started beating again. That four-chambered miracle had no choice; he was alive, thanks to a final sacrifice. "Father, I wish it weren't ending this way."

"Never mind, dear son." Able had to lean closer to hear fading words. "I, who could never protect you before, protected you in the end." He closed his eyes and Able tensed. "It is a father's duty and privilege. *Adios*."

He was gone like that, quietly and with dignity. Able sat back, stunned and silent. All around him he could see the sound of battle. The *Pluton* had drifted away, mortally wounded by the *Tonnant*, which then turned as if to shepherd the little *Mercury* to safety out of the line. Able knew he *should* be hearing the sound of battle but all was silent, waiting. Next he saw in his amazing mind a cemetery in Dumfries, one with a granite grave marker with the single word Mary carved on it, and the number 134. He saw another grave, much smaller, in their parish cemetery in Portsmouth. All it read was Baby Six, and one sad date reflecting birth and death. He had bought a large plot; there was room for others. Mrs. Munro could bring her daughter closer, and what would be the harm in the count lying beside Mary Carmichael again, as he had wanted to all his life? His parents. It would truly become the family cemetery he never thought to see.

The sounds returned; so did his resolve. "Davey, fetch a blanket. I know we should toss the count over the side, but I will not do that. I cannot."

Smitty grinned at him. How had they all gotten so grimy with black powder, when they had no guns? "I was hoping you wouldn't, sir."

"It'll be a fearful stink below deck until we raise Portsmouth again," Able said. "We'll discover that dead Spaniards smell as bad as we do." *Where is this coming from?* he asked himself aghast at his ill-mannered reference to his father. *From your heart,* he heard inside his brain, and knew that Euclid, that old rip, hadn't deserted him. *This isn't funny,* he thought.

Someone else responded, who, he wasn't certain. *No, but it is war,* he heard. *Sometimes we laugh to hold the tears at bay.*

Indeed we do, whoever you are. Oh, you, Sir B?

Tots leaned closer. "Sir, you don't think Gunwharf Rats haven't smelled plenty of reek from the workhouse, do you? Was it all roses and marmalade in Dumfries, or summat like that?"

The Rats all laughed together, holding tears at bay.

Chapter Thirty-six

Working quickly, they rolled el Conde de Quintanar into a blanket, along with his uniform jacket, medals, gold frill and all, and his bicorn and sword. Able felt the miniature painting of his mother in the uniform jacket, tempted to remove it. No. His father had treasured Mary's tiny portrait all his life. He patted the miniature through the woolen fabric, content to leave it there.

As twilight approached, Smitty threaded the *Mercury* through one dying fleet, and another victorious but battered one. Tots sat on the deck and took turns with Whitticombe, sewing the count into his shroud.

After a long moment watching his father – his face so peaceful – disappear behind the fold of the blanket, Able went below deck with Davey, who sat him down, removed the compression pad and took a good look at the wound.

"Will I live?" Able asked. "Mrs. Six will be so disappointed if I come home addled."

"Oh, sir," Davey said in an affectionate tone that soothed Able as nothing else could have.

With a remarkable future ahead of him – William Harvey himself was even now showing Able Davey's eventual honors and accolades– the Gunwharf Rat who loved medicine examined the furrowed wound. "I won't need to suture anything. I will clip around the wound, clean it well (this'll sting a bit), bandage you neatly and call it good. You were lucky, sir."

Lucky, my great Aunt Lydia's fifth vertebrae! Good God, Hippocrates, that cranky fellow. "Yes, I was lucky," Able said, ignoring Hippocrates, who uttered another oath. "Now let us take a look at your patients, Davey. Could you use some help?"

They were below deck an hour, Davey suturing a foretopman from the *Thunderer*, then a powder monkey not much older than Avon from an unknown ship, while Able tried to convince the Frenchman that his leg must to be amputated. "I know you understand the situation," Able told the man in his best French. "We cannot fix your leg. Look down and see."

Still the man refused. Able turned away, ready to help two more sailors plucked from the water who looked hopeful and cooperative. He spoke over his shoulder. "It's your choice," he said. "When you die, Davey will record your cause of death as stubbornness."

Another sailor was less reluctant to part with his mangled arm below the elbow. Able guided Davey through his first use of capital knives. He took over when Davey started to sway. "Sit down, lad, head between your knees." Able tied off an artery and blood vessels. By the time he was suturing the flap of skin, Davey stood beside him again, watching intently.

The noise of battle gradually faded, punctuated as darkness neared by a spectacular explosion that brought Able and Davey on deck, as well as two patients more spry than the others.

"What should I do, sir?" Smitty asked at the wheel as the *Achille* burned from stem to stern and French sailors dropped into the water, some on fire.

"Stay well back," Able warned. "The *Achille*'s guns are cooking off in the heat and ready to explode."

They ducked by the railing as the French two-decker's guns blew apart with a roar, raining red-hot metal on men already in the water and swimming for their lives. Avon turned his face into Able's side and shuddered, reminding Able that his stalwart Rats were still boys. He patted Avon's shoulder. "No fears, my lad. We're safe here." He hugged his littlest Rat. "In fact, would you go below deck, light the galley fire and make us some beef broth?"

"Aye, sir." Able heard the quiet answer that touched him more than almost anything that had happened on this never-to-be-forgotten day. "I'm sorry, sir."

"No need to apologize, Avon. You're the bravest eleven-year-old I know."

The *Mercury* held back as the *Pickle* swooped in alongside a Royal Navy cutter to rescue the men in the water, then sailed closer cautiously.

"Good God, a woman!" Tots exclaimed and pointed.

It didn't take an anatomist to see that one of the survivors was a naked woman. *Trust the French*, Able thought, startled, then amused, as one of the cutter's officers whipped off his uniform jacket and handed it to the woman as others helped her aboard. Able chuckled when she blew a kiss to her rescuer and took a bow – a short one. Ooh la la, the French.

Able and Davey went below deck, where Avon worked miracles with a pot of beef broth containing little meat, but a superabundance of onions. Soon there were steaming tin cups to pass around. Davey assisted the injured men, and Able argued with the Frenchman again, to no avail.

The Frenchman, Jean Baptiste Soileau, changed his mind at three bells in the middle watch, after extracting a promise that Able would cut and splice and not *le gamin*.

"What did he call me, Master?" Davey asked in no good humor.

"A child," Able replied. "We will humor him and happily turn him over to a larger ship in the morning."

And they did, along with the other patients, all of them sleeping peacefully and perhaps destined to recover, when morning came and the *Revenge* loomed large on the starboard bow. Smitty angled them smartly alongside the *Pickle*, waiting their turn to unload their miniscule sickbay with its inmates all alive, even the Frenchman, who had fainted halfway through the midnight amputation and had no recollection that *le gamin*, under supervised direction, finished what Able began.

Since they were so close, Captain Lapenotiere jumped down onto the *Mercury*'s deck. "You didn't lose anyone in yesterday's dust-up?" he asked, the master of exaggeration.

Able thought of his father, sewn tight into a blanket and stashed under a lower berth. "No," he lied. "We were fortunate."

"You were also braver than most of us," the other captain said. "Were you planning to make explosion noises and fake cannon roars to frighten away the Frogs?" He said it kindly, which made Able only wince a little. "Snug your yacht tight to us. We've been ordered to join the other officers on the *Euryalus*. The cutter on my port side will ferry us. Bring along your acting sailing master. "

"Aye, aye, sir," Able said, amused by Captain Lapenotiere's tone of command, when he knew they were equals in command. One would have thought the *Pickle* was a four-decker to rival the *Santísima Trinidad*, dismasted, humiliated and wallowing under tow in the wake of *HMS Prince*.

"We'll join you, once our wounded men are safely aboard the *Revenge*," Able said, not willing to be ordered about.

The transfer was accomplished in a matter of minutes, with Able wondering why anyone needed him and Smitty on the *Euryalus*. "Why there?" he asked. "Where's the *Victory*?"

Lapenotiere gave Able a fishy look and then his expression softened. "You don't know, do you?"

"I suppose I do not," Able said, as dread flapped low across the greasy swell and settled on his shoulder like an albatross. "Adm… Admiral Nelson?"

Lapenotiere nodded, all officiousness gone. "Yesterday afternoon. A sharpshooter." He sighed. "He lived long enough to know of victory. At least there is that comfort. The *Royal Sovereign* took a beating, so Collingwood now commands the fleet on the *Euryalus*."

What was there to say? Able looked across the water at victorious Royal Navy ships as mauled and battered as those of the Combined Fleet. Bodies and pieces of men bobbed on the increasingly choppy water. Everywhere was the reek of burned wood and the shriek of metal pulleys noisy with nothing to hoist.

"He will be greatly missed," Able said quietly. "Greatly."

"Sir?"

Able turned to Smitty. "Aye, lad? This is sad news for all of us."

Smitty nodded. "I remember what Admiral Nelson told us, you know, at the stone basin."

"I remember, too," Able replied, as his recollection returned of that sunny, late summer day. "There I stood in my smalls, with a bosun's whistle around my neck."

"It was what Admiral Nelson said."

They were passing the *Victory*, forlorn with its little admiral dead, the mainmast leaning precariously while the foremast had given up entirely. Smitty turned and faced the ship with its chequerboard yellow and black sides. "'England confides that every man will do his duty.'" He sighed. "Then he fair shouted, 'Every man!'"

"He did," Able said. "And what else?"

Smitty bowed his head, struggling. Able's hand went to his shoulder. "'Remember England.'"

They were the last three to arrive in Admiral Collingwood's main cabin, from the looks of the glut of post captains, captains and lieutenants crowded together. *Officers' call*, Able thought, surprised. *This is one to tell Meri about.* For some odd reason, he and his acting sailing master had been included. His discomfort grew as he noticed every eye upon him and Smitty. "What did we do wrong?" Smitty whispered, barely moving his lips.

Smitty felt the scrutiny, too, which increased Able's unease. "I have no idea," he whispered just as quietly. Good God, did they know he had stowed the body of an enemy in the *Mercury*? "Let us lean against the bulkhead and breathe quietly." That brought a half smile to Smitty's lips. "Whatever it is, Smitty, I take full blame and you say nothing. Promise me."

Smitty nodded, but his eyes were mutinous.

"That is an order, Mr. Smith."

Admiral Collingwood cleared his throat. "Gentlemen, on your feet, you lazy lubbers."

Able relaxed. The officers chuckled. They knew their commander better than he did. Maybe he and Smitty could eventually slip out the door.

No, it was nothing like that, nothing at all. Able held his breath as Admiral Collinwood moved from behind his desk and made his deliberate way toward them. Other officers stepped aside, proud men Able remember from Camperdown and the Battle of the Nile and dozens of small skirmishes across oceans and seas. Some of these officers even sat with him in Trinity House, but they were Elder Brothers, and not the newest Younger Brother at the far end of the table.

"Master Six, front and center, and er, you lad, what is your name?"

This can't be, Able thought, alarmed, uncertain as never before. He listened for inward advice, but his cranial spectators were silent.

"Brendan Smith, Admiral Collingwood," came Smitty's quiet reply.

"Come, come, you two, I haven't all day," the admiral said with some impatience.

Again Able listened. Nothing. He had been abandoned by his interesting array of observers, even Euclid, apparently. He stepped forward, Smitty at his side.

The admiral came closer until he stood less than a foot away from Able, who braced himself for the tongue lashing of his life, without knowing why. Pray God they wouldn't take him back to Portsmouth in irons, and flog him around the fleet for whatever error he had committed at a battle he knew would never be forgotten, as long as Englishmen gathered. Please God that Meri wouldn't have to share his shame. He closed his eyes.

When he opened them, Admiral Collingwood was smiling. "Master Six, without exception, every commander in this room sailed into action yesterday with loaded cannon and powder and balls to spare. You and the *Mercury* sailed in with absolutely nothing except…" He paused. Able stared to see the great man's eyes misting. He swallowed. "Except raw courage such as none of us have ever seen. Why?"

"Admiral, we didn't *have* any cannon," Able managed to say. He was unprepared for the laughter that followed. At least it didn't sound malicious. Collingwood raised his eyebrows and the laugher stopped.

"We…we had nothing, but England needed us. All we workhouse bastards ever have is nothing. We're used to nothing." He didn't mean to raise his voice. "Sir."

The silence in the cabin was so complete that Able heard sea birds for the first time in two days. He heard pots banging several decks below as cooks prepared the noon meal. Two ships over he heard pumps clanging, homely sounds he had listened to all of his nautical life. And much farther away, was that Meri singing to Ben, his own dear wife and others like her, safe from Napoleon now? He felt himself relax, even as he wished he hadn't sounded so emphatic.

Collingwood cleared his throat again. He looked around the cabin. "You are right. England does need you. We will never forget your courage, you and your…Smitty, what are you called?"

God bless Smitty. "Gunwharf Rats, sir," he said, his voice firm.

"None of us will forget, will we, gentlemen?"

Someone started a hip-hip-hooray. Three times it rang out. Able looked down at his feet, wishing with all his heart, lungs and various other viscera that Sir B were there to hear this, and Thaddeus Croker, and even his butler Bertram, who saw St. Brendan the Navigator School as a tool for resuscitating a man in need of reformation. And the workhouse lads, eager to prove themselves, once they knew they mattered. *Meri, would to God you were here beside me, you and Ben and our tiny portable daughter.*

"We would do it again, and gladly, sir," he said quietly, his words meant for Admiral Collingwood's ears alone.

"I know you would, Master Six," the Mediterranean fleet's new commander said. He clapped his hands together, recalling them all to the moment. "We tricked you here, Master Six! I have already concluded my fleet business with these gentlemen, who may now return to their ships and prepare for what awaits us next. I doubt it will be pleasant, but that is war. No, you and Captain Lapenotiere remain, please, and you, Smitty."

In mere moments it was just the four of them. Collingwood returned to his desk, gestured them closer, and picked up a canvas bag. "The news of yesterday's work, and our extreme sorrow at the loss of my dear friend and ablest of men, must be carried swiftly to England." He looked from Able to Captain Lapenotiere. "Which of you commands the fastest vessel?"

I do, Able thought, but remained silent. He knew that the captain of that fast ship would be signaled out for promotion and other accolades, because the public loved heroes. He also knew Captain Lapenotiere was an ambitious commander – and a good one – who had not advanced far in the navy because for all his talents, he had no patronage or famous relative to help him along. He also outranked Able in all the ways known to the society they inhabited.

"In actual fact, sir, it is the *Mercury*," Captain Lapenotiere said, with no hesitation.

Was it possible to be so stupefied, so blindsided in the course of one morning? For his entire life, his cranial busybodies had invaded all aspects of his life, coaxing, prodding, letting him know what might come to pass, warning him. Where were they, now that something so kind had been thrown into his lap?

Maybe not so far away. He heard Euclid chuckle, and say, *You know what to do*. Able Six, master genius, took heart. "But not by much, Admiral," he said promptly, and took a deep, satisfying breath. "I yield to the *Pickle*. She is bigger, and we are looking at stormy seas."

Captain Lapenotiere flashed him a grateful look, which Admiral Collingwood took note of, but made no comment, addressing himself to Able. "You're an exceptional man, Master Six. Not one ambitious tar in ten thousand would have turned down this opportunity to sail into history, because that is what the *Pickle* will do."

"As she should," Able said. "Admiral, all I wish is to return to St. Brendan's and teach future sailing masters," he said, "or whatever else my workhouse bastards might become. I know my acting surgeon is destined for greatness. You should have seen him yesterday."

"You've convinced me," Collingwood said as he handed the tarry bag to Captain Lapenotiere, who stared at it like he held frankincense and myrrh, before he tucked it under his arm. "Leave immediately, Captain, and fair winds to the *Pickle*. Your promotion is assured."

The *Pickle*'s commander saluted and darted from the cabin. Able smiled to hear him pounding up the ladder, then laughed out loud. "There goes our ride, Smitty!"

"No matter. I will see you to a jolly boat," the admiral said. He clapped his hand on Smitty's shoulder. "It's going to be a long war, young man. Before you and Master Six came in here, I heard several of my captains wondering how soon they could spring you from St. Brendan's. You'll find a home in the fleet soon enough."

"I do have one request, admiral," Able said as Collingwood walked them to the door of his cabin.

"Say on."

"I would like to retrieve Nick Bonfort from the *Victory*. He has been serving as Reverend Scott's assistant. Correct me if I'm wrong, sir" – he heard Smitty snicker – "but I suspect that Napoleon will not attempt to invade our shores now."

"I think not." Admiral Collingwood waggled his finger at Able. "Would you also like me to suggest to Admiralty that the *Mercury* be relieved from further duties in the fleet?"

"If you would, sir, but do assure Admiralty that we will remain subject to the requirements of the service. I need to teach my Rats more, and Nick is one," Able said simply. "We can confine our practice sails to the Solent, or perhaps down to Plymouth. Our goal remains training workhouse lads for the Royal Navy, in whatever capacity suits their skills. They are valuable in wartime, as you have expressed."

"Consider it done." The admiral opened the door, and his Marine guard snapped to attention. "We owe you a great debt."

"We did our duty, sir."

Chapter Thirty-seven

Meridee Six had always thought of herself as a patient person. Even one of her sisters, in a less-then-diplomatic moment, had remarked that Meridee was a wise spinster to not let herself be caught in endless regret, but to wait patiently upon the hand of the Lord. Meridee had nothing in particular against the hand of the Lord, but this was Able Six she was dwelling upon, her lover, father of her son and the tiny baby making its presence known as Meridee puked regularly every morning. Maybe it was best not to think of *that*.

Her lot might have been easier, if Ben hadn't been a genius. He was not a child to be distracted by a toy, or even a rout cake, although he did relish his meals. All she knew to do was cuddle him and try to answer his questions.

"Mama, where is Papa?"

"Son, he and the Rats and your great grandpapa are sailing somewhere near Spain."

"Is Napoleon Bonaparte, that upstart, responsible for Papa's absence?"

"I fear he is, Ben. Papa is keeping us safe from him."

This brought a sigh from the boy on her lap. "I want Papa here."

"My love, so do I."

Able had told her that sailing to Spain was usually a nine-day journey. Dropping off the count would be accomplished in a dark evening, and then there would be nine days back to Portsmouth. The *Mercury* had left Portsmouth with good winds on October 12, which would put the little yacht inshore by October 21, off the coast of Spain.

"Durable Six, you should have been home by All Hallows Eve," Meridee growled at the calendar in the kitchen. "It is now November 6 and I won't stand for it."

All that declaration earned her this morning was raised eyebrows from Mrs. Perry, who had the effrontery to take her by the arm, sit her down at the kitchen table and hand her a mug of tea. When Meridee burst into noisy tears, Mrs. Perry had the further effrontery to hold her close and let her cry it out, all the while smoothing her hair, and humming low in her throat.

"I don't mean to be a child about this," Meridee said when the bout of tears ended. With a watery smile, she took the offered handkerchief. "You must be thoroughly tired of me, Mrs. Perry."

"Hardly! I am worried, too," her housekeeper said. "Don't ever forget that I knew Able years before you did. I watched him turn into someone unique and special, someone finally given the…the privilege of believing in himself." Mrs. Perry looked into that middle distance just beyond the walls of the kitchen. "Sailors come and go, but he was…is…the best of the lot."

"I want him home," Meridee said softly.

She kept herself busy all day, which was never hard. If only she didn't keep stopping to listen for…what? Mrs. Perry was busy in the kitchen now with dinner. If she wanted a moment to herself, now was the time. She looked into the sitting room.

Through empty days without the reassurance that Able was just across the street, Junius Bolt proved to be a singular ally. Grace's baby had become his grandchild, or as near as. Grace's old retainer also adopted Ben, moving in smoothly and swiftly when the Count of Quintanar embraced Ben, set him down, and followed his son to sea. Junius knew what a little boy needed and provided books and blocks, but mainly a lap.

After some high-level conferencing in the kitchen, Junius also acquired Pegeen O'Malley to help entertain Ben, even though Mrs. Perry extracted a promise nearly written in blood that Pegeen would be hers for all meal preparation. Junius knew when to pick his fights.

Like most little fellows, genius or normal, Ben calmly accepted their attention as his due. "Pegeen is a useful sort," he announced to his Mama one night, sounding as imperious as Prinny himself.

"I'm happy you feel that way," Meridee said, holding in her smiles. "I hope you are useful to Pegeen."

He nodded. "I let her stack blocks with me, even though her strong suit is not symmetry." That matter-of-fact comment – one of many from Ben – went into a letter to Able after bedtime. She never mailed the letter with all of their son's clever comments, only because she had no place to send it. He could read the pages when he returned.

Meridee peered in on the four of them, Pegeen holding Georgie, who watched Ben with the wide-eyed amazement of the very young, while Ben tied knots to Junius Bolt's exacting specifications.

"I'm going out for air," Meridee said softly. "Back soon."

"No hurries or worries, love," the old fellow said. "Pegeen and I are in command, aren't we, my dear?"

Pegeen nodded. Meridee watched another moment, tucking into her own tender heart the scullery maid's smile to hear someone call her "dear." Life was built on such kindness.

First stop was Ezekiel Bartleby's bakery. She used to think it was a coincidence that he always seemed to have her favorite sugar-sided rout cakes on hand whenever she dropped in. Mrs. Bartleby had set her straight. "He insists there must be rout cakes every day, and I do not argue."

That was as close to real affection that the prickly Mrs. Bartleby ever came. Almost. A week ago Meridee told Mrs. Bartleby that there was a baby coming. "Outside of my house, I haven't told anyone but you," she whispered, and discovered that an anticipating lady never had a better friend than Mrs. Bartleby, the baker of little cakes.

Two treats later, Meridee continued her stroll toward the Gunwharf, but only part way, because she had promised her husband that she wouldn't venture too far into the sinful cesspit that was Portsmouth. She pulled her cloak tighter against November's chill, and stared at the wharf in the distance.

Open water soothed her, especially on a day like this, with just enough breeze to set the waves dancing. She found her favorite stone bench and sat there, happy to be by herself, if one discounted the baby inside, which she never did. "Papa will be home soon," she told her littlest one with a pat.

She thought of her friend Grace, who always began each day's class asking her little Rats what they had learned the day before. She smiled to remember a recent answer that Grace had shared with her. "It was my Jacob," Grace said. "He told me he learned yesterday that if you eat many dried apricots and drink water, your belly will turn on you." She made a face. "And here I was expecting some wisdom about borrowing and carrying numbers!"

"What have I learned?" she asked softly. "I have learned that I am constant in love, courageous as I wait, and more patient today that I was yesterday. Generally, if I am honest." She thought of Grace. "I know that my widowed friend depends upon me, but that I depend on her equally. We need each other, because we are navy wives."

As she watched the water, the parish church bells of nearby St. Andrew begin to peal. Startled, she clutched her belly, always her reaction to a surprise because she was a protective mother to the unborn as well as to Ben. As she held her breath, she heard other bells, including bells from ships anchored in the Solent. The clamor grew into a chorus.

Big bells, little bells, and soon the resonating bong bong of St. Thomas, Portsmouth's cathedral. *Please, please, God,* was as far as her prayer extended, a plea that covered the good, the bad, and the horrifying.

What had happened? Meridee started for home, when someone gave her a squeeze. She gasped and turned to see Captain Ogilvie holding her firmly. "Mrs. Six, the news is good."

She stopped and took his hands. "What news? Tell me everything you know."

"Such a grip, Mrs. Six! It's short, because the message came by semaphore relay, but this we know: There was a massive battle. The Royal Navy was victorious over the combined fleets of France and Spain."

Angus planted a loud, smacking kiss on her cheek and she didn't mind a bit. He held her off and she saw something else on his usually impassive, reveal-nothing face.

"No, please no," she whispered.

"Not Able, no, not Able." He released her. "Admiral Nelson was killed by a sharpshooter dangling from some damned French rigging."

She absorbed that sad news, remembering the little admiral with the eyepatch, one arm and look of calm imperturbability. Yes, it was sad, but what about the man who mattered more to her? "Able should have been here a week ago, I think. Do you know *anything* more?"

He shook his head. He put his arm around her shoulder and guided her into motion toward her home. "From what I know of major fleet actions, there is a period of repair and resuscitation before anything more can happen. We don't even know if the *Mercury* was involved, do we? Hopefully, your man was able to return his father to Spain. That was his mission."

Meridee relaxed. "You are telling me I should be patient and not fret?"

"If you can."

She glanced at the captain's face, and saw something else that didn't frighten her. In fact, it was probably the reason he was in Portsmouth right now. "Did Grace write to you?" she asked.

"Aye, she did. Hasn't that fine lady had enough sorrow for one year? Why this, too?"

There were nearly home, but Meridee slowed her steps, telling her impromptu escort how Headmaster Croker had gradually faded in the last week. "He isn't eating, and drifts in and out of consciousness. When her classes have adjourned for the day, Grace sits by his bed, holding his hand." She faltered then, and felt familiar tears gather. "Just like with Sir B. Angus, why must life be so hard, at times?"

"The question for the ages, little lady," he said. He raised her hand to his lips and kissed it. "None of us are strangers to sorrow."

She knew of his own pain: the death of a wife and child at birth, not long after the loss of his sister, Gladys Croker. *Who held your hands*, she thought, and knew the answer was no one.

"Where is Grace now?" he asked.

"With her brother."

"I'll see you to your door, then go to her."

"She will be pleased to see you."

"Do you think so?" Captain Ogilvie asked, sounding nothing like a sea captain, an assassin, and a spy catcher. He sounded like a man in love.

"I am certain of it," she said firmly.

He surprised her. "This time, I have come to ask forgiveness from Thaddeus. I planned to hate him forever, after my sister's death, but I cannot. He must know my altered opinion before he dies. Here you are. Come to Grace when you have a moment, please."

"I've been spending evenings across the street, once Ben is asleep," she assured him.

"I should have known."

"It's a small thing," she said, shy around this man who exuded power and strength.

Meridee said goodbye and watched him cross the street, a confident, strong man, above all a healthy one. As she watched his swinging walk – sailors never seemed to entirely lose the swagger that bordered on oddly intimate – it occurred to Meridee Six that Grace St. Anthony had never known the love of a man in all his powers.

I wonder, she thought. The bells continued to ring throughout Portsmouth. Now she had to wait patiently upon the Lord, as her older sister had told her years ago. Her man was coming home; she knew it, he had to be. Perhaps Grace's was even closer.

Chapter Thirty-eight

The bells pealed throughout the supper hour and Meridee learned a little more, brought to her by Mr. Ferrier. This time he sat down to Mrs. Perry's good fish stew and muffins and wasted not a moment. "Here is what else we know, Meridee."

He planted his elbows on the table, which meant Ben gave her an inquiring look and opened his mouth. Meridee gave her son the grave look that Able had dubbed, "Mama's admiral squint," and he closed his mouth. She knew he would ask her later, when Mr. Ferrier left, why *that man* was allowed to rest his elbows on the table when a small and earnest child could not. "Small and earnest child." That had been Benjamin Six's latest ploy for avoidance of a well-deserved scold. She must remember to tell Able that one. *Please be safe, my love.*

"What?" she asked calmly, feeling like a small and earnest wife badly in need of her husband.

"The *Pickle* brought the news to Admiralty House," Mr. Ferrier said. He took his elbows off the table, which made Ben sigh and dish himself more potatoes.

The *Pickle*? Hadn't Able told her that the *Pickle* had challenged *Mercury* to a race mid-Channel, and *Mercury* had won handily? Her brain might not have raced at the speed of light like her husband's, but she quickly considered two surmises. The *Mercury* had been nowhere near that major battle, so could not carry the news to London. That encouraged her. Her next thought was less encouraging: The *Mercury* had been in the heat of the battle and sunk by enemy fire, all hands dead or missing.

"Meridee?"

"Oh! Yes, Mr. Ferrier, the *Pickle*. Does anyone know anything else?" Dear me, she had raised her voice. She glanced at Ben, saw his sudden distress, and kissed his potatoey cheek. "Forgive me, son. I'm a little on edge."

"Papa?"

"…is fine," she said firmly. "Remember to use your serviette."

She walked Mr. Ferrier to the door after supper. Dear, competent Mr. Ferrier. Able had been so right to ask him to teach in his stead. Mr. Ferrier had shouldered more and more burdens as Headmaster Croker weakened.

"Come over when you can, my dear," he said. "I fear that Thaddeus hasn't long." She heard endless meaning in his softly spoken words. "Grace might need to…to stay longer than usual tonight."

"She might. Thank you, sir, for your reassurance. I wish I didn't worry so much."

"You worry because you love," he said simply.

She did. For a while, placing Able's pillow next to her side had helped. Sniffing a shirt he left behind did, as well. If his only assignment had been to return his father to Spain, Able should be back by now. Able had teased her once, asking if she would follow him to a longhouse in the Iroquois nation, if things ever fell out poorly at St. Brendan's. *I would follow you anywhere*, she thought, *unless anywhere is a watery grave off the Spanish coast, where I cannot follow.*

She spent a lengthier time than usual cuddling Ben before bed. He wanted to read to her from Isaac Newton's *Principia Mathematica*, so she humored him, then followed up that august tome – the English translation – with nursery rhymes.

Before she crossed the street to St. Brendan's, Meridee gave herself the firm administration of her own admiral stare as she looked in the mirror, reminding her worried image to present a serene face to someone who had lost a husband only months ago, and was soon to lose a brother. Meridee stared at her face, looked around to make certain no one was within hearing distance, and whispered, "Euclid, watch over my man."

Why that made her feel immediately better, she couldn't have told anyone, but she did. Even entering Thaddeus Croker's sickroom couldn't dispel her sudden buoyancy. Her heart went out to Grace St. Anthony, who sat so calmly beside her brother. What made the moment both poignant and sweet was Captain Ogilvie standing behind her, his hands on her shoulders. *You're not alone, Grace*, she thought, as she sat quietly on Headmaster Croker's other side.

"He isn't conscious, Meridee," Grace said. "I fear this is his last night."

Meridee nodded and glanced at Angus Ogilvie. "Captain, were you in time?"

"Aye, Meridee," he replied. She heard all the relief in a man who seldom showed any feelings at all, much less personal ones. "He accepted my apology." He smiled shyly, looking suddenly like a schoolboy. "I also took care of another matter."

"He won't tell me what that other matter is," Grace said.

I know what it is, Meridee thought. *Give her time, Angus. She'll be yours.*

When Grace leaned closer to her brother and gave him all her attention, Meridee put her hand to her heart and smiled in the captain's direction. He nodded, his eyes kind.

She sat in silence with the others until Thaddeus Croker opened his eyes and looked around. "I am tired," he said. "God bless St. Brendan's." He closed his eyes and died.

Rest in peace, good man, good headmaster, good soul who took a chance on my genius, Meridee told herself as she covered her face with her hands for a moment of privacy. She breathed in and out the fragrance of buttery potatoes and knew she should have washed her hands better after cleaning up after Ben. Still, it was a pleasant aroma, and reminded her where she needed to be.

Beyond a quick kiss, Grace didn't need her at the moment, not with Captain Ogilvie kneeling beside her, his arm around her waist. Meridee quietly let herself out of the room.

Serene, at peace, she knew what to do for the man sobbing in the corridor. "Bertram, thank you for your splendid care of this man," she said, her hand on the valet's arm.

She thought he might shake her off, because he was Bertram, after all. Instead, he let her gather him close for a gentle embrace. "Thank you even more for your wisdom in putting Headmaster Croker in this old ruin and demanding that he do something for workhouse boys."

"Who told you that?" Bertram spoke quickly, but she heard no accusation.

Captain Ogilvie."

After the prickly valet dried his tears, blew his nose and became again the Man To Be Feared, Meridee walked slowly down the corridor. She knew which classrooms belonged to which instructor. The pupils were all abed at this late hour, so she took her time, breathing in the familiar odor of chalk dust.

She opened the door to Able's room and felt a momentary pang. She walked to the plaque on the wall, the one with *Rattus norvegicus* stretched out in all his skeletal splendor. She remembered the hours she and her new little boarders had boiled those nasty bones, and then rescued them in the rain with Davey Ten and Nick Bonfort, but only Nick then because he didn't have a last name. Now Davey was acting surgeon on the *Mercury* and Nick assistant secretary on *HMS Victory*. *Be safe, my lovelies*, she thought.

In permanent metal letters, she read *Gunwharf Rats*. There were more little metal plaques with the names of Rats from two years ago to the present. She kissed her finger then ran it lightly across her husband's name. "Plighting my troth to you was the smartest thing I ever did," she told her man.

She went downstairs thoughtfully, hopeful that the grand experiment of St. Brendan the Navigator School would continue. She glanced back up the stairs, putting all her trust in Mr. Ferrier to step into the vacant spot. Able wanted nothing more than to teach here. She put her hope in that, too.

She drew her cloak tighter, unwilling to think of Christmas arriving next month, except that her morning sickness should have ended, and she should be feeling their baby move.

On the sidewalk, she turned around to gaze at St. Brendan's, pleased with what she saw. She thought she heard boys singing "Heart of Oak," which made her smile. When they were joined by a wonderful baritone, her heart stopped, reconsidered, then started again.

She saw a little knot of six figures passing Bartleby's Bakery, one considerably taller than the rest, moving at that rollicking pace of men freed from the pitch and yaw of the seafaring life, with legs trying to figure out land again.

"Able? Able!" She picked up her skirts and ran, not caring who saw her legs, only determined to grab that man as soon as she could.

The last few steps were easier because he grabbed her first. She knew it was scandalous, but she wrapped her legs around his hips as he hoisted her up and kissed her soundly. He reeked, he positively reeked, but she didn't care. His beard scratched her face, but never mind. He was home and he seemed to have all his parts, as well as all his Gunwharf Rats.

"My goodness, better set me down," she whispered in his filthy ear. "Any constable in Portsmouth would lock me up as a menace to public morals."

Able hugged her tighter. "If I must," he said, patting her rump. "You can do this later and no constable will know."

Decorous again, her skirts where they belonged, she faced her Rats, who were grinning. "You are such a welcome sight." She noticed Nick for the first time. "Nick! Did the secretary let you leave the *Victory*?"

"Master Six is persuasive," he said in that solemn manner she had missed.

She looked them over. Tots had a plaster on his cheek, but only a small one. When Able removed his bicorn, she saw the bandage on his head, low by his right ear. The light was dim, but she saw no blood seeping through. "This is your work, isn't it?" she asked Davey Ten.

Davey nodded, his pride unmistakable. "We did some fast surgery in a hot place, Mam, but no one's the worse off." He grinned. "Not even that nasty-faced Frenchman."

Able nudged him and he laughed. "We saved his wretched life in spite of him, didn't we, Davey?" When the others added their laughter, Meridee knew they belonged to a fraternity that she could never join. She knew they would tell her their war stories eventually, but their shared experiences would never be hers. She knew that was right and proper, even though she dreaded every moment they were away, which was its own purgatory. Because they went to war, she could stay home in peace and raise little ones without fear.

She somehow managed to hug all the Rats at least once, standing there in front of the bakery. Their noisy high spirits finally meant the baker himself came out, clad in a nightshirt, ready to complain until he saw who lounged outside his shop at midnight. "Lord bless you all," he exclaimed, beaming. "I'll bring over cinnamon buns in a few hours. Good night!"

Held close by her grimy husband, Meridee look around. "Despite everything, you managed to drop off your father, my love?"

His face changed. He slowly shook his head. "Meri, we fought at Trafalgar with the fleet. My father gave his life for mine." He pulled her close. "I'll tell you more later."

In an hour, they were cleaner, but packed back into dirty clothes, except for Able. Mrs. Perry woke up and worked some kitchen miracle that saw them all fed, while Meridee pulled out sheets and blankets and spread them in the sitting room, except for Smitty and Nick, who shared a room upstairs.

Meridee sent Able into the washroom by himself, while she hurried around with Mrs. Perry. He came out in a clean nightshirt, minus the bandage. She stared at him, not minding that his curly hair had been clipped away from around his ear – it would grow back – but startled to see a generous peppering of white hairs among the black ones.

He shrugged. "It was that kind of warfare, my love."

The Rats' stories tumbled out, treating Meridee to a hodge podge of two-deckers here and there, the frightening size of *Santísima Trinidad*, cannon blasting, dark smoke, the crack of falling masts and spars, the groan of ships under duress that sounded nearly human, the awful sight of men on fire, men sliced in half or clutching their entrails, overheated guns cooking and exploding. She listened, horrified, holding tight to Able's hand.

"It's so confusing," she said into his much cleaner ear as the boys chattered on, needing to talk. She understood that.

"That was Trafalgar," he told her. "It was ship to ship and devil take the hindmost. Our little admiral would have called it a grand business, had he lived. What loss!"

Gradually the talk petered out and the boys lay down to sleep. Smitty and Nick went upstairs to their room. Meridee helped Able to his feet and took his hand as they walked to their room. She pulled back the coverlets, plumped up his pillow and kissed him after he lay down.

He got up quickly and went next door to look at Ben. She joined him by their son's crib, watching as he touched their son's head, almost as a benediction.

Arms around each other's waists, they walked back to their room. Able lay down with a sigh that went right to Meridee's heart. She cuddled close, relishing the briny fragrance of him, now that the smoke, tar and fear-sweat were gone. She touched the wound by his ear. "What happened?"

"Another half inch…" He stopped took several deep breaths and did what she knew he had to do, what he had probably held in for days. He tried to turn away but she didn't allow that.

"My darling, why am I here if not to hold you and mourn, too?" she asked.

He cried into her breast as quietly as he could,. She rubbed his back, making soothing sounds she knew he liked. He sobbed until her nightgown was damp across the front.

When he could speak, he told her what happened, how his father had leaped between him and sharpshooters on the *Pluton*, drifting close. "I took the first ball, and he took the next two from others in the rigging," Able said. "Before he died, he told me it was a father's duty to protect his child, something he had yearned to do."

"I would think he died peacefully then."

"Oddly enough, I believe he did," Able replied.

"How can that be odd? I know you would gladly die for Ben."

"I would, and for you, as well." He seemed to consider her words. "You're right."

"Where is he? Did you bury him at sea?"

"He's in the *Mercury*."

"*What?*"

"That's one reason we were longer returning to Portsmouth. Admiral Collingwood ordered us to deliver dispatches to the blockade off the northern Spanish coast, acquainting them with the sad news of Lord Nelson's death." He spoke calmly. "There was a carpenter's mate I knew aboard one of the frigates. He made a coffin, and we put my father in." His arm went around her shoulder and he tugged her closer. "It's a rough coffin, but what is that to anything? He was a sailor. We will have him interred in our family plot."

"A thousand times yes," she said. "I wonder…could you and Mrs. Munro go to Dumfries and bring Mary Number 134 home?"

"Let us visit my grandmama tomorrow," Able said. "I have not time to make the journey with her – too much to do here – but Mrs. Munro is a woman of some persuasion. She can bring her daughter south to lie beside the count." He kissed her shoulder. "That was all my parents ever wanted. Good Lord, but I am tired."

Silence. Meridee heard his even, deep breathing. *My love, you are home*, she thought. The news of Headmaster Croker's death would keep. Before anyone else was up, he might like to hear her predictions about Captain Ogilvie and Grace St. Anthony. Ben would be delighted to see his Papa when he bounded into their bedroom, although Meridee suspected he would complain of poor treatment dished out to a small, earnest child. A visit to Mrs. Munro would take away some of Ben's sense of ill-usage, because his great grandmama knew how he felt about crème buns.

Meridee composed herself for sleep, content to lie beside her sleeping man, home from war. She rested her hand on his chest, enjoying the steady beat of his heart. He slept so soundly that she moved closer and rested her head against his heart. *You are my heart of oak*, she thought, *my summum bonum, my nonpareil, my lover, my husband.*

She yawned and heartily wished Napoleon to the devil. She thanked all the heroes of the Royal Navy still at sea, those iron men in wooden ships, guarding their homes and families. *You are my hero, Master Six*, she thought, and closed her eyes. *Never forget it.*

"I won't. *Sumum bonum*, eh?"

Epilog

June, 1806

Jamie MacGregor, acting sailing master, raised port after a lucrative Pacific voyage which had added his first prize money to his pocket. He fretted because he had missed the monstrous fleet action simply called Trafalgar. He and Able took their usual walk by the stone basin in late afternoon.

"It chafes me, sir, that I missed the fight," Jamie exclaimed. As an earlier Gunwharf Rat, he knew enough of humility to follow that outburst with a shake of his head. "Like a fool, I complained about the matter to Captain Pettibone."

"Whereupon he told you..." Able knew David Pettibone. He could almost hear the man's pithy reply.

"... don't be an ass, Mr. MacGregor,'" Jamie said with a smile. The smile faded. "Still...I know you had a hard time of it, sir. My sister told me about your father and also your mother."

Able heard the longing of a workhouse boy who felt a pang that he and his twin sister had been abandoned by their parents. "Jamie, my parents now lie at peace next to each other in the Six family plot," Able told him. "That was more than I ever expected." He broke the solemn moment, because it was still tender. "And our Ben has a great-grandmama who spoils him outrageously. We have been blessed, Jamie."

They were in no hurry. Able told Jamie about the state funeral for Admiral Lord Nelson, whose body had been preserved in a vat of brandy and returned to England eventually. "What a funeral! I've never seen such pomp and circumstance," Able said, "or so much gold lace and epaulets. He was interred in the crypt at St. Paul's, a fitting place."

Able also told him of William Pitt's death this year in January. "He lies buried in Westminster Abbey. What a man," he said quietly, remembering his first and only visit to 10 Downing Street, where the prime minister took such care to see that he was kept safe from any consequences of the Conde de Quintanar's surreptitious visit to Portsmouth.

"What a career he had," Jamie noted as they strolled slowly. "Will there ever be another prime minister like him?"

"Not in our lifetimes. I miss him," Able said. "At his funeral, his physician told me Mr. Pitt died of old age at forty-six, as much as if he had been ninety. War and governing are both hard businesses. Taken simultaneously…" He shrugged. "Who can say?"

"Forty-six?" Jamie questioned. "Lord Nelson was forty-seven, wasn't he?"

"Aye, he was. A coincidence?"

Jamie shook his head. "No. War and responsibility wear on a man. I feel it, myself."

"I thought you might, Jamie."

"You, sir, have a definite sprinkle of gray in your hair," Jamie said.

"*My* Trafalgar medal," Able said, and they laughed. It was, though, and hard earned.

They walked in silence for a few moments, matching each other's stride. Jamie had likely reached his full height, since he was eighteen. "Were you nervous when your sailing master died on your return voyage and the job fell to you?" Able asked, curious.

Jamie considered the question in that deliberate way Able had always admired about him. "Would you think me prideful if I said no?"

"Not at all. I know you."

"I suspect you know all of us Rats is ways we can't comprehend." Jamie's statement was as candid as he was. "You trained me well, sir. I knew I would not disappoint St. Brendan's. Or you."

Able nodded, his hands behind his back as they walked on. He told Jamie of the recent birth of a daughter, curly-haired like him, but bonny of face like Meri Six. "Ben is smitten, Meri is delighted, and I am over the moon. I love my family," he concluded, mainly because he knew all his workhouse lads still needed reminders that family life was well within their grasp. *I am ever the teacher*, he thought.

"My twin is remarkably content with her little one, her step-daughter, and that constable who tried to nab us both once," Jamie said. They laughed together, workhouse lads still and pleased to outwit the law now and then.

Jamie saw the bigger picture, though. "We've changed, haven't we?" he asked, showing by the question that their master and student relationship continued to grow into a collegial friendship.

"Aye, we have changed. I believe that was what our late headmaster wanted, in addition to sufficient training to serve in the fleet in the best capacity."

"I cannot argue that." Jamie smiled. "Perhaps someday I will find someone as good for me as Mrs. Six is for you."

"I have no doubt you will. But now it is back to sea for you, where women are scarce. Tell me truly, Jamie, are you reconciled to serving as an apprentice sailing master again, after a taste as master?"

Jamie responded as Able hoped he would, with the wide-eyed wonder of it all. "Aye, sir! Aboard Admiral Collingwood's flagship!" The wonder changed to calm introspection, a superior quality in a sailing master. "I know I still have much to learn."

"Aye, lad, but you're on your way to a distinguished career. That is all I ever wanted for you."

Jamie stopped. "I know I owe you that assignment," he said quietly. "I know I do."

"Captain Pettibone recommended you, too," Able assured him. "Credit me if you wish – I'll take some of it – but consider more that St. Brendan the Navigator School has a growing and well-deserved reputation for excellence."

As they continued their stroll, Able told Jamie of Davey Ten's exemplary service as acting surgeon of the *Mercury,* and how it had recently led to early admission to the school of medicine at the University of Edinburgh. "My grandmother Mrs. Munro is a persuasive woman who knows the chancellor. Davey will shine there; I have no doubt."

"He's so young."

"Trafalgar changed that."

After requesting and requiring secrecy, Able spoke of Captain Ogilvie and Grace St. Anthony, who had begun a tentative courtship, whenever Trinity House's dogsbody and all-around thug was in port. "What will happen, who can tell, but Grace has a spring in her step and Captain Ogilvie doesn't scowl nearly as much. I agree that it is hard to fathom such an odd partnership, but I would never have believed Meri would give *me* a second glance. Love is strange. Trust me, Jamie."

"I have a question for you, sir, one that has been batted about in a wardroom or two," Jamie said, sounding tentative, as if he wondered at the wisdom of plain speaking.

"Carry on."

"I know *Pickle* took the news of Trafalgar and Nelson's death to London. I know he received a full captaincy for his effort, as well as money and certainly fame."

"Aye, this is so," Able said, smiling inside. He knew the question coming.

"I, uh, have heard from reliable sources that in a contest, *Mercury* sailed faster than the *Pickle*. Tell me what really happened, sir. Were you offered the chance to carry the news?"

"I was," Able said. "I turned it down in favor of Captain Lapenotiere, who was richly deserving."

"Why, sir? Think of the fame and fortune."

For all Jamie's growing maturity, it was a young man's question. "I have no need of either, Jamie. I am a teacher. Admiral Collingwood and Captain Rose of Trinity House convinced Admiralty that the Royal Navy benefits when I train others for the fleet, rather than serve at sea, myself. At least for now. I can still be recalled to the fleet if necessary, but it is less likely."

They had arrived back home, where Ben's calm brilliance became more apparent every day; where nearly brand-new Mary Munro Six sucked contentedly at her mama's breast; where Meri Six loved him without reservation; where Smitty still learned and observed so quietly; where Nick Bonfort-Six – ah, yes – was returning soon to the fleet as secretary's assistant to Admiral Collingwood, now that Nick and Headmaster Ferrier had completed their manual of seamanship for not only St. Brendan's, but also the Navy Board.

There was no need to tell Jamie that his own brain had quieted. The genius remained, but his spectral mentors had become observers. They did not clamor for attention, because he did not need them as he once had. Trafalgar had been his own proving ground, putting all his hard-won skills to work. Euclid was available for consultation, as always, but even his great Greek mentor wisely let him go about his business with a modest amount of commentary.

He had a new crop of boys to teach, among then veteran Avon March, who had moved into the upper level with his same good cheer. He hadn't told Smitty yet, but there were two frigate captains competing as politely as determined men could, for his apprenticeship as sailing master on their vessels. The enigmatic man, for man Smitty was, would be leaving soon for the Channel Fleet. The new workhouse lads would turn into Gunwharf Rats, because it had become a title of excellence, and not of derision.

And I remain here, Euclid, no fame or fortune for me, he thought. *I will teach and train and live with my wife and children. I doubt Mary Munro Carmichael and the Count of Quintanar would have wanted more for me than that I am happy. Do let them know, please, if you can, any of you. I am happy.*

"Come inside, Jamie. Meri wants to see you. And please answer any questions the Rats might have for you tomorrow in our seamanship class at the stone basin."

"With pleasure, Master Six, with pleasure."

"It's chaotic here," Able warned, as he opened the door.

"As it should be."

As it should be.

Historical Note

Lieutenant John Richards Lapenotiere of the schooner HMS *Pickle* was handed the dispatches for Admiralty in which Admiral Collingwood described the fleet action off Cape Trafalgar, the decisive battle which confirmed for more than a century the Royal Navy's maritime superiority on all oceans.

Bearing only ten guns, and small ones at that, the *Pickle* played no belligerent role at Trafalgar, serving mainly as a rescue vessel, the same as my fictitious *Mercury*. Having suffered no battle damage, the nimble and swift *Pickle* was the ideal choice to carry the news of victory to England. Lapenotiere was a skilled navigator and not lacking in courage. He was the ideal commander for the *Pickle*, both at Trafalgar, and in carrying the message home.

Incidentally, Lapenotiere was descended from French Huguenots, Protestant exiles who had fled to England in 1688. In an era of imaginative spelling, his last name appears in Royal Navy records and logs using a variety of letter combinations. Hardly any scribe ever got it right.

The *Pickle*'s historic voyage to Great Britain was not an easy one. Following the battle of Trafalgar, a series of storms beset victors and vanquished, sinking several captured warships of the Combined Fleet, which had been severely mauled in the fight on October 21, 1805. Many Royal Navy vessels suffered greatly, too. The *Pickle*, in company (for a while at least) with the sloop of war *Nautilus*, clawed her way through a week of storms toward England.

This was the age of sail, with ships totally dependent upon the winds. The storms were of such magnitude and direction that *Pickle* was forced put in at Falmouth, located not far from Land's End in Cornwall, rather than at Plymouth, the naval base farther east by northeast in Devonshire.

Docked in Falmouth on November 4, Lapenotiere wasted not a moment in engaging a post-chaise for the 271-mile journey to London on the route which is now called The Trafalgar Way. The journey took 37 hours, with 21 changes of horses at posting houses along the route.

At one a.m. on the morning of November 6, 1805, Lapenotiere delivered his dispatches to William Marsden, First Secretary of the Board of the Admiralty. Marsden had been working late in the board room and was on his way to bed when Lt. Lapenotiere hurried into the room with Collingwood's dispatches, declaring, "Sir, we have gained a great victory, but we have lost Lord Nelson."

Marsden immediately took the news to Lord Barham, First Lord of the Admiralty, where the dispatch was copied and promptly sent to Prime Minister William Pitt, King George, and the press. Bells tolled as England rejoiced in the victory, but also mourned the loss of Vice-Admiral Horatio Lord Nelson.

True to Collingwood's prediction, for his service Lt. Lapenotiere was immediately promoted to commander, the intermediate rank before captain. He was awarded a sword by Lloyd's Patriotic Fund, and £500, as well. Other senior and junior officers at Trafalgar also received promotions, swords, and similar monetary rewards.

With that, the HMS *Pickle* faded into history. Commander Lapenotiere was given command of a larger vessel. He served the Royal Navy dependably and well throughout the Napoleonic Wars, but with none of the flash and dash that caught the eye of the public. Wounded badly in the bombardment of Copenhagen in 1807, Lapenotiere continued his sea service until 1811. Although he was finally promoted to Post Captain, he was never given another ship to command after 1811. He retired to Cornwall and died in 1834.

The fact that Capt. Lapenotiere did not receive another ship had nothing to do with his ability. One of the odd facts of Trafalgar was that when all the participating officers were moved up a grade in rank, this meant there were more line officers than available ships to command. Only those men with familial connections or other "interest," as it was termed, were able to captain coveted warships.

As Sailing Master Able Six pointed out to Smitty, Lapenotiere had the ability but lacked the connections. Able knew that although the *Mercury* could easily have bested the *Pickle* in a race to London, his own total lack

255 • THE UNLIKELY HEROES

of connections or worthy social sphere would amount to nothing in the world he inhabited. Able had no qualms about passing on the great honor of carrying the news to London. He wanted to return to St. Brendan's, the Gunwharf Rats, and his growing family. Simply put, he was a teacher.

This is the fun of historical fiction. Chances are, many of my readers have never heard of the *Pickle* and its fifteen minutes of fame after Trafalgar. The little schooner played a historical role in a major world battle, but fame is fleeting. It was easy for me to slide the HMS *Mercury*, Sir B's yacht, into the scenario alongside the *Pickle*, and just as easily slide her out. Could it have happened? Certainly. Did it? No, and that is the pleasure and challenge of writing accurate historical fiction; all the relevant facts are true, which means the fiction must be equallly plausible and seamless.

But what of the HMS *Pickle*? The Bermuda-built schooner continued to serve in the Channel Fleet, carrying dispatches, and whatever else the fleet needed. On occasion, she also captured enemy vessels of war. The end came on July 26, 1808. While carrying dispatches from Admiral Collinwood, she ran aground in the middle of the night at Cape Santa Maria near Cádiz. Her skipper compounded a previous navigational error, and the *Pickle* came to her untimely end. The bottom caved in, and there was barely time for the crew to escape. After three days, Maltese divers were able to locate the dispatches and return them to the surface. The *Pickle* was declared unsalvageable.

As in all cases involving the sinking of a Royal Navy vessel, a court martial promptly convened. The facts were presented, which declared the cause of Pickle's wreck to be "an unaccountable error in reckoning." The skipper and sailing master were reprimanded, but otherwise suffered no punishment – at the time, anyway. Lieutenant Moses Cannady was given another small ship called *Black Joke,* but he never advanced in rank beyond lieutenant.

Through the years, there have been other Royal Navy ships named *Pickle*. This is done to honor historic warships. The names of the *Royal Sovereign, Mars, Euryalus, Thunderer* and other Trafalgar veterans were used on a later series of battleships, some of which saw service during World War II. The most recent *Pickle* was a minesweeper launched in 1943. Her service continued after World War II, until she was sold to the Royal Ceylon Navy in 1959, and broken up in 1964.

The exception to this re-use of famous names on subsequent ships is HMS *Victory*, Lord Nelson's flagship. There was and ever will be only one

Victory, and she remains drydocked in Portsmouth, a museum dedicated to the Napoleonic Wars and Lord Nelson. The *Victory* has also never been decommissioned and is the oldest naval ship still on the books. As of 2020, she was launched 256 years ago.

As a bit of trivia, the USS *Constitution* ("Old Ironsides") is the oldest, still-commissioned ship that remains afloat and is capable of movement under sail, something the *Victory* is not. Launched in 1797, fourteen years after the Treaty of Paris that ended the American Revolution, the U.S. Navy's Old Ironsides was 223 years old in 2020.

Acknowledgment

May I add this about the dedication of this book to Commander Harry Ferrier? After I learned of Mr. Ferrier's death at age 91 in 2016, I wanted to remember him in some pertinent way. I knew Commander Ferrier as Mr. Ferrier, because my sisters and I were polite little girls. Mr. Ferrier and my father, also in naval aviation, crossed paths during World War II in the South Pacific and became lifelong friends. Whenever one or the other was on a nearby navy base, we always visited. In fact, my parents and the Ferriers both retired on Whidbey Island, off the coast of Washington State.

As a kid, all I knew about Mr. Ferrier's role in the South Pacific was that he had a metal plate in his head, courtesy of battle. I learned that from Harry, Jr., who is my age. (Children do like the macabre, don't they?) I learned eventually that Mr. Ferrier fought in the Battle of Midway (June 4-7, 1942), which is considered by naval historians as the turning point in the South Pacific in World War II.

Not until I read his obituary, did I find out that Mr. Ferrier received the Distinguished Flying Cross and a Purple Heart at age seventeen for his heroic actions as radioman/tail gunner for Ensign Albert Earnest in their Grumman TBF Avenger, Torpedo Squadron Eight.

With his Avenger shot to pieces and turret gunner Jay Manning dead, Bert Earnest managed to land that battered aircraft on Midway Island. Not certain he had been able to release his torpedo over a Japanese target, Ensign Earnest asked Mr. Ferrier to look out his small window to see, before he attempted to land. Mr. Ferrier couldn't tell, because the window was covered in his blood. Over their target during the battle, he had been hit by shrapnel and knocked unconscious for a while. The Avenger was the only surviving plane of the squadron.

With no way of knowing if he still carried a live torpedo, Ensign Earnest managed to land the Avenger on Midway Island, after two wave-aways. For his role during three days of battle, Earnest received two Navy Crosses. Before the war ended, he received another one. Bert Earnest went on to a notable career in the Navy and died, age 92, in 2009.

Mr. Ferrier, the seventeen-year-old radioman and tail gunner, received a Purple Heart and the Distinguished Flying Cross for Midway, and also had a notable Navy career. I never knew about his impressive war record until I read his obituary, because he never spoke of it in my hearing.

I recall Mr. Ferrier as a quiet man who never boasted or bragged about anything. Why should he? He had nothing to prove. When I knew I needed a substitute teacher at St. Brendan's for Sailing Master Able Six, I knew "my" Mr. Ferrier would find a home in *The Unlikely Heroes*.

Because the real Mr. Ferrier ended up as the last of only three survivors of his squadron, in later years he found himself in demand as a talking head on Midway/War in the Pacific documentaries. Check him out on YouTube: Harry Ferrier Midway. In one segment, he shows the ballcap he wore in the air over the battle, with a big hole in it.

Mr. Ferrier had another side, the Smitty side. He grew up in Massachusetts during the Great Depression. His father died when Harry was thirteen, and life became even harder. In and out of trouble and restless, Harry persuaded his mother to alter his birth record and let him join the U.S. Navy. Harry Ferrier enlisted in January, 1941, three days after his sixteenth birthday. I could see Smitty doing something like that, if he had lived in another place and time. Like Mr. Ferrier, I wrote Smitty as equally quiet, but also capable and courageous.

I like to think Mr. Ferrier is pleased that I wrote him as two characters in *The Unlikely Heroes*. Probably he would just be embarrassed. Like most of that Greatest Generation, he commented on one documentary that he never saw himself as a hero.

Fair winds and following seas, Commander Ferrier.

About the Author

A well-known veteran of the romance writing field, Carla Kelly is the author of forty-three novels and three non-fiction works, as well as numerous short stories and articles for various publications. She is the recipient of two RITA Awards from Romance Writers of America for Best Regency of the Year; two Spur Awards from Western Writers of America; three Whitney Awards, 2011, 2012, and 2014; and a Lifetime Achievement Award from *Romantic Times*.

Carla's interest in historical fiction is a byproduct of her lifelong study of history. She's held a variety of jobs, including medical public relations work, feature writer and columnist for a North Dakota daily newspaper, and ranger in the National Park Service (her favorite job) at Fort Laramie National Historic Site and Fort Union Trading Post National Historic Site. She has worked for the North Dakota Historical Society as a contract researcher.

Interest in the Napoleonic Wars at sea led to numerous novels about the British Channel Fleet during that conflict. Carla has also written novels set in Wyoming during the Indian wars, and in the early twentieth century that focus on her interest in Rocky Mountain ranching.

Readers might also enjoy her Spanish Brand Series, set against the background of 18th century New Mexico, where ranchers struggle to thrive in a dangerous place as Spanish power declines.

CPSIA information can be obtained
at www.ICGtesting.com
Printed in the USA
LVHW051101291020
670168LV00002B/441